DEDI

This book is dedicated to three outstanding women in my life.

My mother taught me to read at an early age and encouraged me to read any chance I got.

Mary Prentice pushed me to do my best, against my will.

My wife, Marcia McDowell Garner, has put up with more than any human should and has encouraged me every step of the way.

ACKNOWLEDGEMENTS

First and foremost, I'd like to thank Mona Syring, of MJS Publishing Group, LLC, for invaluable help with the editing and formatting of this book.

I'd like to thank all the various representatives of the Huntsville, Alabama, and Fayetteville, Tennessee, police departments for their cooperation in answering my numerous questions about their cities.

I'd also like to thank all the crazy bastards I know who inspired this book.

D-E-D DEAD

A Novel by
Larry "Animal" Garner

Thanks for your support & encouragement!

Larry "Animal" Garner

Two Fingers and a Thumb Enterprises

Hooper, Colorado

Printed in the United States of America

Published by: Two Fingers and a Thumb Enterprises
PO Box 535
Hooper, Colorado 81136

ISBN: 978-144646597-8

ATTENTION!   You are not in this book. Neither am I. All of the characters in this work of fiction (that means it's not real) are made up. Any similarities to real people are strictly coincidental (that means I didn't mean it). It's okay to relate to the characters, but none of them is based on you (or me) . . . really. Places and incidents are generally made up, as well, except for places that are real.

ONE

Damn, it's cold out here! I've been working on the pit in the barn for about five hours and it was pretty warm inside while I was digging. My back is screaming at me and the smell of horseshit was getting pretty thick, so I came outside to get some fresh air and stand up straight for awhile under the lean-to attached to the barn wall.

It's been raining for nearly three days, which is both good and bad. There hasn't been anyone driving around this little hollow for a few days; that's good. It's Friday night. No, it's Saturday morning, and I haven't been willing to sneak out and do any exploring for fear that my tracks will give me away; that's bad. My old buddy, Kenneth Dutton, the owner of this property, is in Memphis for a few days and all the locals know he's gone. It wouldn't do to have fresh tire tracks showing up in the mud on the two-track he calls a driveway. Someone would surely come snooping around. Neighborhood watch isn't a concept confined to cities. Country folk have refined the idea for decades; in an area where you can hear a car door shut from better than a mile away, those up to no good had better be damned sneaky. I am. At least I have been so far. Kenneth is the only one who knows I'm here, and my health and welfare depend on keeping it that way.

The rain is starting to let up a little now, and the wind has settled down some, as well. I'm all for that because the gusts make it seem even colder, whipping the torrent sideways in sheets. Good thing the barn has a sound roof, because I've been hiding and sleeping in there for the last four days, up in the loft, hoping that those looking for me will have lost my trail. I started the pit yesterday and have been working at it pretty steadily as my sore back allows. The dirt floor is fairly easy to dig in, thank God. I really should get back in there and try to get it finished, filled, and covered so I'll be ready to split when Kenneth gets back tomorrow— er . . . later today.

I hear a vehicle out on the paved road on the other side of the bramble patch about a hundred yards behind Kenneth's house, and whoever is driving it is in a hell of a hurry. I can clearly hear him shifting up and down, taking the turns and dips at full song. It sounds like he's having fun, and Molino road is a good place to do it. There isn't ever much traffic, and almost none on a weeknight after dark.

But this ol' boy is out there in a downpour, with no moon, and driving like the devil himself is on his ass. "Haul ass, Bubba," I wish the unknown driver, and turn to go back into the barn.

I hear Bubba's exhaust note change, then the unmistakable sound of someone dynamiting the brakes. Even on wet pavement, the sound is hair-raising, signaling impending doom for some unlucky bastard.

The next noise that reaches my straining ears is even more unnerving. Whump! It's obvious that Bubba has struck something solid. No more engine noise. Silence. I keep hoping to hear Bubba cussing and hollering so I can go back to work with a clear conscience.

I really can't afford to appear out of the brambles in the middle of the night to help some drunk who drove past the limit of his skill. "Come on, dammit!" I whisper. Let's hear a car door, maybe some good old fender-kicking. Minutes pass, and I get more and more agitated. Shit, shit, shit! I really don't need this, but I just can't ignore the fact that someone might be out there broken up and in need of help.

I go into the barn to retrieve my slicker and my old boonie hat. While I'm at it, I grab my big-ass Maglite, my nine-millimeter S&W auto, and my Buck knife for good measure. You never know what (or whom) you might run into in the woods at night. I've spent quite a bit of time learning different routes from the barn to a few different hidey-holes in the woods, using the terrain to hide my tracks as well as possible. Before he left, Kenneth showed me a way through the brambles, just in case I ever have to get to or from the paved road in an emergency.

I head that way now, constantly listening for any sign of life from Bubba. It is black as sin out here, and I tear my slicker and my skin in a few places as I make my way through the tangled mess. As I get closer, I slow to a crawl, hoping to hear something that will let me go back to my hiding and digging. No such luck. All I can hear is the rain in the trees and on the pavement.

I peer out of the brambles, trying to find the vehicle. Maybe he drove off, and I just didn't hear it. Yeah, right, like anyone could drive by here without me hearing it, even on a night like this. Damn, why couldn't I have been inside digging my little ass off, instead of loitering around outside when Bubba Andretti decided to haul ass down a twisty, dark, wet road in the middle of the night?

I hear an almost imperceptible pinging sound from a ways down the road to my right. I still don't want to use the Maglite unless it's necessary, so I walk down the middle of the road, hoping my night vision is sufficient to keep me from busting my ass.

There's a dark shadow in the road about twenty yards away, and it isn't moving. At least I don't think it is. I keep looking for the car as I approach the shadow, and finally see it off the road on the left, another hundred feet away. It is in the embrace of a huge tree, and the pinging I hear is the engine and exhaust system slowly cooling down. There are a few creaks and groans, either from the tree or the car, but no human sounds at all. As I stand there, the rain picks up again. "Well, let's get on with it, dumb-ass," I tell myself, hoping to get this over with and return to my dry and relatively warm barn.

As I approach the shadow, it slowly takes shape. It's a full-grown boar, big as a fucking calf, and it is right in the middle of the road. I lean down to see if maybe I can salvage any of the meat, when the son of a bitch bolts upright and snorts at me like a berserk freight train. If I'd had much of anything to eat in the last few hours, I'd have shit my pants. As it is, the boar is still woozy and I am freaked right the fuck out. My flight-or-fight mechanism must've gotten shorted out, because I levitate backwards about ten feet or so while pulling the nine mil from by belt.

I jack a round into the chamber and fire three times as soon as my feet return to earth. The boar goes down and stays there. I feel bad for killing the damned thing after he'd just survived getting knocked on his ass, but he scared the shit out of me and I get pissed off when something or someone scares the shit out of me. Especially in the dark.

"Now you've done it," I say to myself. I figure a whole passel of Bubbas will come around the corner any second, drawn by the gunfire. I haul ass back to my little trail and hunker down, waiting for company. Maybe the rain masked the sound, or maybe it is impossible for people to tell where it came from. Or maybe they figure someone is out poaching and decide to mind their own business. Which is what I should've done . . . minded my own damned business. It's hell having a conscience. I've tried unsuccessfully to make mine inoperable for years. I guess my folks just did too good a job.

Anyway, there's no posse, so I decide to get on

with it. I walk back up the road, taking a path well clear of the boar. I even turn on the light, verifying the fact that he is indeed dead. D-E-D, DEAD, as Kenneth would say. He's gonna shit himself laughing when I tell him about it. I notice the car is wrapped tightly around the trunk of the tree, and my hopes for Bubba's good health fade.

I call out, and my voice is almost lost in the wind and rain. "Yo! Are you okay?"

Jesus, what a stupid question. Silence. I walk up to the driver's window, not really wanting to look inside. The driver is . . . what the fuck? It's a kid, a little kid. But something's not right here. This kid has a pretty damned nice beard and tattoos covering both arms. It's a midget, or dwarf, or little person, or whatever the fuck the p.c. thing to call midgets is. The airbag has just knocked the crap out of him. He was sitting about six inches from the steering wheel, and the force broke him up like a bag of light bulbs. His head is at an impossible angle, and there is blood coming from his mouth, nose, and ears. There is absolutely no sign of life, and I'm not a bit surprised. Holy shit, what a way to go. "Sorry, Bubba," I tell him, and shift the light to the passenger seat.

The poor dude sitting on the passenger side was even unluckier than Bubba. A branch from the tree has come through the windshield and skewered his right eye. This poor son of a bitch hadn't croaked right away, though. I can tell that he'd been squirming around for a while. There is blood everywhere, and his hands are wrapped around the offending projectile. He'd lived long enough to try to get it out of his eye. No signs of life from him, either. Once again, I'm not surprised.

Nobody is in the back seat, and I am relieved. I've seen dead people before, but it isn't at the top of my list of things I want to repeat. Now that there isn't anything that requires my immediate attention, I step back to take stock of the situation. The rain has decided to slow down again, making things a little more tolerable.

The car is a new Ford Crown Victoria, blacker than a coal miner's lungs with tinted windows, fat tires, and stock-looking wheels. From what I remember of the way the exhaust sounded, this baby has some serious grunt under the hood. A real sleeper, built for hauling ass without looking the part.

I've let my conscience have its say, and now it is my curiosity's turn. I look back in on Bubba and Mister Branch. They are (or, more correctly, were) hard boys. I know the signs, seeing as how that is the kind of people I've been hanging out with for the last ten years or so; mullets, tattoos everywhere, Harley Davidson shirts, and skull belt buckles.

They look like trouble, and I'm pretty sure they'd been up to no good hauling ass down this back road in the middle of such a god-awful night. I look a little closer while trying to stay out of the gore. There are a lot of fast-food wrappers, empty beer bottles, and assorted trash on the car's floor. That and the fact that

Bubba just kind of oozes around when I happen to bump or jostle him makes for a slow search.

Amid the debris is a sawed-off twelve-gauge shotgun on the floor at Mister Branch's feet—normal hardware for the likes of these two. After doing some careful rearranging of Bubba, I find a .45 caliber auto in the pocket on his door panel. I figure they won't have any use for the guns, so I wipe them off on a jacket I discover on the back floor. I set them on top of the car, along with a six-pack of Miller I find under the jacket. I figure it will settle down enough to open by the time I get back to the barn, and I'm pretty sure I'll need a drink by then.

Seeing as how there aren't any witnesses and I am basically a criminal at heart, I reach in and get the keys out of the ignition. Bubba needs a little persuading to get him out of the way, but I'm pretty sure I won't hurt him.

The trunk is jammed up a little from the hit the car took, but I finally get it open. On the floor of the trunk are five cases of beer. Smiling, I think, "my kind of guys."

On top of the beer are a couple duffle bags. Parachute bags, we called them in the Navy. They're filled with a few days' supply of black t-shirts, socks, tightywhiteys, and jeans. Rolled up in the bottom of each bag is a denim vest, or more correctly, a "cut-off." Denim jackets with the sleeves hacked off are pretty much the official bike club uniform. They're used mainly to display a club's "colors." Colors are a club's insignia, their trademark, and they're serious shit. The members of most outlaw bike clubs will defend to the death their club's colors. I'm not surprised to find out that Bubba and Mr. Branch are part of an outlaw club. I'd have been more surprised to find out they weren't. They definitely look the part.

I unroll Bubba's colors to see which illustrious group he belongs to. A center patch depicting a skull with snakes crawling through the eye sockets and crossed syringes behind it has the place of honor, bracketed by "rockers," curved patches with the club name on the top rocker and their claimed territory on the bottom one. A small diamond-shaped patch with the ubiquitous MC (for Motorcycle Club) stitched into it is to the right of the center patch.

Blood red Old English script covers the top rocker with the name SPIKES & SPOKES. I've been around some of the S&S boys off and on for a number of years up in North Carolina. They are known for their total disregard for human life, and their unquenchable thirst for hard-bodied young girls and crystal meth. Hard boys, indeed. These two are sporting bottom rockers with Nashville embroidered on them.

Bubba has a couple ounces of what smells like some pretty fine dope in his bag, so I grab it, too. If nothing else, it will make for some fine trading material out on the road. Mr. Branch has a couple glossy new porno magazines and what looks like a meth rig along with some crystalline substance in a baggie. I leave all of that shit where it is and re-zip the bag. Criminal or not, I still draw a line at fucking around with meth.

Beer is a whole different matter, though. I figure nobody's going to know, and I hate to see beer go to waste, so I start taking the beer boxes out of the trunk. But whatever is in them, it isn't beer. I've had a lot of practice carrying cases of beer, and have a pretty damned good idea of what they should weigh and feel like. The first one feels wrong. So does the second one and the other three.

"What the fuck are you guys up to?" I ask the S&S hard boys.

Neither of them feels inclined to answer me, so I decide to find out for myself. Alarms are going off in my head, but there's no way I'm just going to walk away now.

I try to open the top flaps of one of the boxes, and whatever elephant snot they used for glue is some bad-ass shit. Between the glue and my fingers being damned near numb, I can't even get a corner pried loose. I fish out my Buck knife, and cut along the top of the box until I can get the top flaps off. "What do we have here?" I think, as the contents are wrapped in some kind of heavy plastic sheet. Expecting to find kilos of meth, I carefully slit one end open, and pull the plastic up so I can take a little peek.

"Holy shit!" I yell, seeing nothing but tightly stacked and rubber-banded piles of fifty-dollar bills.

Dirty, used bills, but all fifties. I yank the plastic off so I can get a better look, and start pulling out stacks of cash. There are only more stacks of fifties. I'm not going to stand around out here in the middle of the damned road, deserted or not, and count this shit. The rain is back, coming down even harder than before.

Fuck me! Now I have a serious urge to quit fucking around in case these guys have some friends following them to wherever it was they were going. I slam the trunk shut and assess my options.

Seeing as how the S&S boys are beyond my help, I figure the best thing to do is to take care of old Number One. I quickly do some mental calisthenics and decide the best thing to do is to carry the stuff I want over to the hole in the brambles and down the path a ways. I can make a cache and slowly move the stuff from there to the barn later.

The beer boxes are heavy, around fifty pounds or so each, so I make a trip for each one. A couple of them seem even heavier than the others, but I am in too big a hurry to worry about it now. Bubba's .45 goes into my belt next to my automatic, and Mr. Branch's shotgun joins the other stuff in the woods. I go back to the car once more, panting and blowing, to see if I've missed anything. I think about looking for ammo and decide that is just silly. I don't want to get caught at this stage of the game for little shit.

I doubt my fingerprints will be traceable on

the car due to all the rain, if the local cops even have the inclination to try. This looks for all the world like a simple accident and when they look in the trunk they'll find the hard boys' luggage. I open the trunk again and make sure the bags are packed like I found them, and zip them closed again. The stuff in the trunk is pretty wet, so I figure I'll leave it open. A closed trunk full of wet stuff might pique some local bozo's attention. I grab the trunk lid by the rear corners and give it a hard twist. I feel it tweak a little, and when I try to close it, it doesn't fit for shit. Perfect. I let it spring back open.

Now, what else could give me away? Something has been nagging at me since I opened the trunk lid. Jesus, the fucking car keys! It wouldn't take a mental giant to figure someone had been here if the car keys were in the trunk lock. I snag them and put them back in the switch, turning it to the on position. Bubba doesn't seem to mind; he just oozes out of the way.

I use the Maglite to make sure I haven't left anything else behind or looking out of place. I back up and that's when I see it; what a fucking dumb-ass I am. The six-pack of Miller is still on the roof of the car! I grab it, and walk back and forth a few times to see if there is anything *else* I've fucked up. Satisfied that there isn't anything to point the cops my way, I grab the beer, put my Maglite back in my slicker pocket, and haul ass away from that Crown Vic for the last time.

It takes almost three hours to get all the shit from

the cache back to the barn, and it is nearly light when I set the last beer box down. I really want to just lie down and take a nap, but there is still a bunch of stuff to do before that is going to happen.

I wash down a couple of over-the counter "pep" pills with one of the Millers, and head back to the trail through the bramble patch. I call it a trail, but mostly it's just a series of spots where the growth is less dense than the surrounding areas. It takes some doing, but you can traverse that yardage without getting carved up too badly if you know where you're going.

As I make my way back to the paved road, I look for any signs of my previous trips. The rain is still coming down like a cow pissing on a flat rock, so I'm not too concerned about footprints and such. I find a couple pieces of oilskin from my slicker hanging on branches and stick them in my pocket. There doesn't seem to be anything else and I am relieved to find the entrance to my little trail from the road completely under water.

There is a regular little creek running down the side of the road. Trusting that I have taken care of everything back at the crash site and not wanting to go back over there in the light of dawn, I decide to head back to Kenneth's to see what kind of trouble I've stumbled into.

That's when it hits me. The fuckin' boar! The fact that it's lying in the road dead (D-E-D, DEAD) isn't a problem, but the nine millimeter slugs in it might suggest, even to the local Barney Fife, that someone else has been in the vicinity, either before or after the hard boys' demise. So, I hoof it back up the road, and proceed to wrestle the heavy bastard up the road, past the Ford, because I figure any investigation will be conducted on the stretch of road preceding the crash site, not past it.

The slick-ass condition of the road makes it easier than it would've been on a dry night, but it's still a brass balled bitch to slide that heavy bastard up the road. The night is still quiet, save the noise from the wind and rain. My hands keep slipping off his back legs, and the grain of the short fur sucks, even on wet pavement. It would be easier dragging him by his front legs, but his big ol' head would drag on the road, making it even harder.

I can't believe I've been lucky enough to get as far as I have in this whole affair without someone deciding to use this road to get home from the bar without a DUI ticket. If I get through this deal without ending up in the slam, I'm going to buy some lottery tickets at the first place I come to that sells them. All these thoughts help keep my brain occupied while I'm sliding Porky off the road into a small ditch, about another hundred feet past the crash.

I roll him down the embankment then slide down after him. There's about a foot-and-a-half of water running down the ditch and a culvert under the road is sending it into a woody, tangled patch of brambles on this side of the road. I get tangled up in the whole mess, get free, and get caught up again, but manage to roll and slide the carcass under the big shit and through the smaller stuff until I figure he won't be discovered for awhile. By the time he's found, hopefully it'll look like a poaching gone bad or something not connected in any way with Bubba's last ride.

By the time I'm able to get out of the brambles and back on the road, I'm scratched-up and pissed-off. Stupid pig! Thank God the rain will hide any sign of my being anywhere near this place. I limp back down to my little hole in the woods and look back one more time. "To hell with it," I think, and slog my way back to Kenneth's barn to see what the fuck I've gotten myself in the middle of.

TWO

Christ, I'm tired. I feel like I've hiked to Huntsville and back with a cement block tied to each foot. I really could use some rest, but I need to get my shit together before the S&S boys are discovered.

I open the box that I cut open at the crash scene and dump it out. Sure as shit, nothing but bundles of fifty-dollar bills. They look legit. That doesn't surprise me as much as it would have if they'd been funny money. I can't really see the S&S getting into forgery and counterfeiting; that would take too much brain-power and skill.

I don't have any real idea of how much money is in that box, but it's a bunch. Fuck me to death! This is getting pretty heavy, pretty fast. The next box is full of twenties; old, dirty twenties stacked and banded like the fifties in the first box. If I live through this, I ought to be able to avoid an honest job and the associated tax shit for a long time. The third box I pry open is one of the heavy ones. I figure it's meth, probably about twenty keys. But no! This box is stuffed to the top with something wrapped in what looks like blue denim.

I grab a corner of the material and pull. It's denim all right, and isn't terribly clean. As a matter of fact, the contents of this box smell like a locker room after a shit fight. As the material unfolds from the box, I realize it's a club vest, a set of colors. It is rolled around a package that falls to the plank floor and gives a healthy clunk when it hits. There are oil stains and various patches sewn to the cut-off with poignant sayings such as "Helmet Laws Suck" and "Smile if you're not wearing panties." I unroll it and find, to my astonishment, that it's not S&S colors. The people who own these colors are some of the very people I'm hiding from!

The center patch is emblazoned with a pair of connecting rods with broken pistons attached. They're crossed at the center, and bound with barbed wire. The top rocker sports yellow-outlined red letters spelling PIST-N-BROKE in carnival-style lettering. The small MC patch is off to the bottom right of the center patch, and the bottom rocker says the owner is from Huntsville.

I set the colors down and pick up the fallen brown paper Kroger sack from the floor. I open it and the first thing I see is hair . . . lots of it. What the fuck? I pull on the grayish-brown locks and discover that it's a wig. I'm no authority on such matters, but I get the impression that it's a good one. It feels and looks like the genuine article.

Under the wig is a small plastic zip-lock bag full of jewelry. There are the usual swap meet skull rings, Nazi SS rings, etc., and one piece is so striking that it looks totally out of place among the trash it's lumped with. It's a Navajo squash blossom necklace, and from what I can tell is the real thing. There can't be many bikers in Huntsville, Alabama, who would wear a squash blossom.

All of a sudden, a rush flies up my spine, and I get it. Holy fuckin' shit, I get it! I pick up the PnB colors again, and verify what my eyes saw the first time and ignored. There's a small copper button on the front of the vest engraved with the slogan "How's your Aspen?" superimposed over an aspen leaf. Together with the wig, the squash blossom, and the club colors, the button makes me absolutely positive that the S&S boys had put together a disguise designed to make the wearer look like the Huntsville, Alabama, PnB chapter president, Mike "Chief" Greaves.

I pick up the Kroger sack again and pull out a Glock nine-millimeter automatic, a street map of Huntsville, and some hand-written notes in some code that I have no clue how to decipher. I go back to the box I found the PnB colors and the Kroger sack in and find two more disguise kits, each one with its own blend of hairstyle, cut-off, and jewelry.

Two more Glocks, a couple hunting knives, and a miniature propane torch are distributed throughout the kits. These two also have the PnB colors on the back of the vests, and smell like someone's been wearing them while aborting skunk fetuses. There are twelve spare magazines for the Glocks wrapped in cheesecloth lying at the bottom of the box after I've removed the disguises.

Now I'm getting wound the fuck up and forget all about the fact that my back is screaming at me. I tear into the other heavy box. Sure as shit, it's almost a carbon copy of the previous one, except for a couple of small differences.

One of the cut-offs is a very small one with the words "Property of Chief" on the center patch. It's a woman's colors, proclaiming her to be club property. By the embroidered roses on the lapels, the three-foot-long blonde French braid wig, and the small patch with the endearing "fuck off and die" sentiment, I know this disguise is based on Chief's old lady, Polly.

The way I heard the story, she got that moniker years back when she was dancing in Mobile. A black dude came onto her pretty hard and she resented it. Actually, "resented it" is a pretty gross under-statement. Raised in a white trash racist family from day one, she had no use for blacks, or Mexicans, Asians, or Jews for that matter. She proceeded to break a Miller long necked beer bottle across the dude's face, while screaming, "I don't want no nigger talkin' to me!"

Some of the PnB boys were there that night, looking for some dancers to coerce into dancing at their club in Huntsville, and Chief hollered out, "Polly want a cracker?" and the place broke up, because he's about the whitest son of a bitch I've ever seen. She ran over to where he was sitting, hiked up her right leg, and put it over his shoulder. She leaned over and asked him, "Cracker want some pussy?" That was, as they say, the beginning of a beautiful relationship. Well, a relationship at least. She's been with him ever since and is reported to be a bad-ass with a straight razor. Instead of the regulation Glock supplied with the other disguises, this one has a pearl-handled razor and a small can of pepper spray.

This is beginning to give me brain cramps. What in the hell are the S&S up to, sending a couple hard cases out with a trunk full of money and disguises designed to make the wearers look like PnB members, right down to jolly Polly? I figure that whatever the plan is, it's got to be bad for the PnB. And that is why I'm stuck on the sharp-assed horns of this particular dilemma.

Up until about three weeks ago, I was living in Virginia Beach, Virginia. I was the Enforcer for the Tidewater chapter of the PnB MC.

I know most of the Huntsville members. I spent a night at Chief's a few summers back, planning some action against some local assholes who had shown disrespect for the PnB colors. At that point, I'd been in the club for about six years. They had taken me in when I was alone and far from home and family.

I was fresh out of the Navy, riding my old Super Glide and looking for people to hang with. I met some PnB members at a titty bar in Norfolk. They seemed okay, and after a few beers, one of them invited me to a party.

THREE

That party was a turning point in my life, from ordinary ex-Navy, part-time biker to a full-fledged screw-up and criminal. I got so stoned on pot I couldn't function. I ate three or four black beauties to counter the effects of the pot, and I drank at least a case of beer in an effort to wash the cotton out of my mouth.

I was a prodigious partier during my Navy years, even making a name for myself as a serious contender in the Key West titty bar drinking wars. Partying was something I did very well, and the PnB seemed to think that was a fine attribute to have. They continued to invite me to parties, poker runs, and bars.

We went to so many bars I would have needed a journal to keep track of them. After a few months of riding and partying with them, I was approached about prospecting for the club. A prospect is a probationary member of a bike club, and doesn't get the full patch until a certain amount of time has passed, or he does something to either seal his membership or get himself beat down and thrown out.

Some prospects just never make it, and after awhile they get told to fuck off. It's normal for a prospect to get all the shit jobs like watching the bikes while the other members are inside partying and watching the dancers.

Another favorite duty for prospects is fighting. Members will start some shit then have the new guy take care of it to see how he handles himself. It's not unusual for another club brother to kick the shit out of a probie just for the hell of it. They do it ostensibly to see how much heart the prospect has, but sometimes it's just for fun or because of a personality thing.

I did my time as a prospect under the sponsorship of a club brother named Gutter Putter. He rode me like a fuckin' racehorse, and I had some disputes with some of the other members. One night in Elizabeth City, North Carolina, I'd just about taken a local scumbag's head off for trying to steal a jacket off of GP's scooter. I hit the asshole with my big-ass Maglite (like the cops carry) just at the base of his skull, and he went down like he'd been hit by lightning. I was afraid that I had actually offed the bastard, so I walked up to the door of Tops and Bottoms, a topless club we'd ended up in after a night at the flat-track races.

I leaned in and caught the eye of Skeets, one of the members, and pointed to GP. He nudged the guy next to him, pointed at Putter, then at me. The guy tapped Putter on the shoulder, pointed to me, and went back to drinking. GP gave me that look like, "What the fuck do you want?" and I just locked eyes with him and jerked my head toward the sidewalk.

He was absolutely stunned. Prospects just don't act like that with full members. I'm sure he thought I'd lost my mind, treating him like that. He came out of the door looking for trouble, thinking I'm it. Before he could even get a word out, I caught his eye and again jerked my head slightly to the side, this time toward the would-be thief. He was still where I left him, on the ground behind a Ford one-ton pickup.

GP may be an asshole, but he isn't stupid. He apparently didn't think I was stupid, either, because he changed his demeanor immediately, taking charge of the situation. He moved me back toward the door and quizzed me on what happened. He patted me on the back and said to get ready to split. He was going to tell "Nigger Bill" Samson, the chapter president, what's up.

Nigger Bill stood up, and with a few well-placed looks, got the brothers out of the place in record time. We hauled ass out of there, laid low in Roanoke for a few days, then found out from a friend in Elizabeth City that the guy I hit would live. He had no idea who (or what) had hit him. The PnB MC wasn't even on the cops' radar screen. It was time to go home.

After that, I was voted into the club as a full patch-holding member. I got the rest of my colors and had them sewn on before I went to bed the next morning. I lost the job I'd been working at a local body shop before I started riding with the PnB, but the club had some "business ventures" that kept the members in spending money. I moved into the clubhouse and took to my new life like a duck to water.

After a period of nearly four years, I was named the Enforcer for the chapter. I handled the chores needing a little brute force, some cunning, and, believe it or not, a healthy sprinkling of tact. (When senior office-holding brothers need cooling-out, it takes a mixture of all those things to get things taken care of with minimum damage.) Things went along fairly smoothly with just a few minor arrests, broken bones, and a couple of STDs to make things interesting.

But about a month ago, the shit hit the proverbial fan. A club brother named Forney (his last name was Cater, and he'd screw anything) picked up a sixteen-year-old runaway in Portsmouth and brought her to the clubhouse. He and a couple other pervs decided to turn her out, or break her in to prostitution, by taking turns at her until she was nearly comatose. After they left her in the bedroom and were discussing how much to sell her for, I arrived at the clubhouse.

It was a brisk April afternoon. I had just gotten my new bike finished and it was a beauty. I'd chopped the frame myself, and built most everything else on it at a bike shop the club owned. The black paint looked like it was a foot deep. The engine was one hundred cubic inches of bad-ass. The pipes were short, and there was no hint of mufflers.

I'd been waiting for this day to arrive, so I could finally put my plan into action. It had been hard not to do anything about some of the shit I'd witnessed (and taken part in), but I needed to wait until I was sure the bike was done and dependable before I made my move.

I backed the scooter into the curb and turned it

off—after a couple twists on the throttle, just in case anyone had missed my arrival. There are some things boys never outgrow. I took a last look at the chain, axle nuts, etc., to make sure nothing had worked loose on my ass-freezing hundred-mile shakedown cruise. Everything looked cool, so I walked up the side walkway and entered the house through the kitchen.

The three stooges were higher than hell, having been drinking tequila and shooting meth all afternoon between turns at the kid. I asked them what was up.

Forney said, "Take a look in the bedroom behind the shitter," with a big, stupid grin on his face. The other two snickered and nodded their heads.

Having a good idea of what I'd find, I walked back to the bedroom and through the open door. There was a lot to see but not what I'd imagined. Everything in the room was piled up in the middle of the floor. Bed sheets, throw rugs, and everything else that she could move easily had been shoved against the wall next to the bathroom. There was a sour smell in the air and after further investigation, I found one edge of a shag rug smoldering. She'd tried to burn the place down! The club was lucky that the rug was so dirty it wouldn't burn.

I couldn't blame her and actually admired her guts, knowing what kind of crap Forney and the twins had put her through, but this was some seriously bad shit.

"Forney," I hollered, "get your ass in here!" I could hear him grumbling and the other two laughing.

"Now, cocksucker!" I said in my best "enforcer" voice.

I'd been perfecting it for years, and it nearly always got results. If the voice didn't work, it usually got physical, and I'm one of the dirtiest fighters in the game. People who know me usually don't need more persuading than the "voice," and Forney was no different. He came down the hall with a sheepish grin on his face, thinking I was pissed about him bringing the girl here.

"You want to tell me what the hell's going on?" I asked him, real quiet-like.

He sensed that there was something going on that he didn't know about, and hurried the last few steps. He rounded the doorway into the room, and stopped dead in his tracks.

"Where is she?" he asked me.

"That depends on how long ago she left, dumbass," I said.

I pointed to the small trail of smoke rising from the pile of stuff on the floor. "She tried to burn us out, numb-nuts," I tell him, watching his face as it slowly registered the facts.

While he and the two other morons were getting ripped and watching cartoons, their helpless little runaway had indeed run away. Before she departed their hospitality, she tried to set the house on fire, and there was no telling how long she'd been gone.

The cops could be pulling up any minute. Considering their previous experiences at this address, they would more than likely bring along the SWAT team.

Even with all the feelings of loyalty and friendship that I'd developed within this organization over the last decade, I still had a serious problem with the club's manufacturing and distributing of meth. I also had serious misgivings about the recruitment and prostitution of young girls to fill the members' pockets.

I decided right then and there that this was the time to do what I'd been planning for almost two years.

It had been a hard decision, because I love motorcycles and have a lot of respect for most so-called bikers. They're just people who like bikes and hanging out with each other.

The one percent who think being a biker is synonymous with being a criminal, playing Billy Badass, hurting people, and acting like a general waste of human skin is the exception that proves the rule. They get most of the attention and press because they tend to do stupid shit and get caught at it on a fairly regular basis.

The other ninety-nine percent are mostly decent people who crave a little self-expression beyond matching bowling shirts or having the best Christmas lights in their neighborhood. They wouldn't think of pimping out some young girl at her most vulnerable, or gang-raping her. Sure, some of them would take some sixteen-year-old pussy if it was offered to them, but murder, gun-running, and drug distribution would be far out of their league.

Any group of people has a few stoners, some drunks, wife-beaters, and such, but the organized outlaw clubs are more like organized crime outfits. And the PnB MC fits that description to a tee. The only thing that matters is the Club. These guys run hookers, own titty bars where they find and turn girls into hookers, taverns where they sell drugs and hookers, a couple motorcycle shops, and even a pizza joint. Of course, you can get some dope, and even (surprise!) a hooker delivered with your pie if you know the password.

But the big money-maker, the Grand Kahuna of their criminal enterprise, is meth. Crystal methamphetamine is a substance made from cooking a bunch of poisonous chemicals (some downright deadly) together then cooling the resulting mess into a crystalline substance that, when induced into the bloodstream, makes good old speed look tame.

Meth is like speed with a supercharger. It, simply put, induces an artificial fight-or-flight response in the body as well as a high state of euphoria. You get higher faster than on almost anything else available and, as a bonus, you get addicted in record time. The shit is a nightmare, but it's relatively cheap and increasingly easy to get. You can smoke it, snort it—hell, you can even eat it—but the all-time favorite way to do meth is to shoot it directly into the bloodstream. That way, there aren't any mucus membranes, lungs, or other filtering devices in the way of getting the shit into the blood.

Whammo! The rush is incredible. As I found out the one and only time I tried it, most first-timers puke their guts out. But hallelujah, that doesn't take the shit out of the blood, or even dilute it. It just gets all the other extraneous stuff out of your stomach, making room for more alcohol. You can feel your hair growing, your vision and perceptions seem keener than ever, and you just know you could kick a grizzly's ass one-handed. You're ten feet tall and bulletproof. For awhile, anyhow. Then you need some more, because it was so cool the first time. Then more. And more. Luckily, my first experience was so powerful that it convinced me to avoid a repeat performance for fear of losing my soul.

Pretty soon you realize that you can't deal with life without the shit. You're paranoid, capable of instantaneous violence with little or no provocation. You're selling stuff, your stuff, other people's stuff, stealing stuff to sell, so you can get more meth. Women (and some men) sell themselves to get it. The longer it's been since they've had any shit, the less they charge.

They sell their asses for dope for themselves, to get their old man dope. The ones who haven't degenerated too badly dance at titty bars, selling blow jobs out back for dope or money to buy dope. Meth is a plague, an insidious attack against weak-willed and simply adventurous people alike.

That's why people like the PnB MC like it so much. It provides an ever-increasing flow of customers and cash. It helps snag and keep the young hard-bodies who dance in the clubs and sell their asses for the club's good. It fuels chaos, their old buddy and co-conspirator. They definitely like meth.

They like it so much they have their own meth labs, places where a cook adds all the noxious ingredients together and brings the whole deadly stew to the point where the crystals are formed. This is an incredibly dangerous process, and meth labs blow up, burn down, or both on a regular basis all over the country.

The fumes from the cooking are deadly, period. Bystanders or innocent people downwind can get seriously ill or die from even small exposures. But the profit is huge! So brain-dead cooks make the shit, greedy assholes buy and distribute the shit, and addicted losers use the shit. It's just a great big, ugly mess.

The labs that the PnB control are all in the swampy area south of Virginia Beach, out in places that are hard to find, easy to hide, and easy to defend. The cops aren't the only people these places attract. Others involved in the meth trade wouldn't blink an eye at killing whoever is inside a lab to get the product. It's a lot easier and safer to steal the shit from someone else than it is to sneak around to buy or steal the ingredients and actually find a place to make it yourself. These labs stink, literally. It's very hard to hide one that's close to any neighbors without serious planning. The odor from the cooking process smells like dirty socks times a thousand. So most labs are in secluded areas, or even in the back of a truck or van so they can be moved around.

The PnB's labs are overseen by a bad-ass named Reginald "Slam" Schlamme. Slam is a big boy, about six foot seven and three hundred fifty pounds. He shaves his head, and has a scar around his neck where three rednecks tried to choke him out with some barbed wire one night at a bar in Bristol. He ended up getting loose and put two of them in the hospital before the cops got there. The third one was found a week later with a broken neck, dead in the woods having "fallen off his horse." Yeah, right.

Slam takes his responsibilities seriously and anyone getting in his way is in the market for "a world of hurt" as he puts it. The labs under his care have been remarkably free from outside interference as a result of their location, Slam's diligence, and the fact that the club has eight or ten law-enforcement types in their pocket. Any time a raid is planned, the product that is ready is moved, the place in flames when the authorities arrive. It's very frustrating for the cops, as well as a source of never-ending amusement for the club brothers.

Over the last year-and-a-half, I've compiled a huge amount of information designed to put a world of hurt on the PnB MC. It's safely stashed in a locker at the airport, and only one other person has a key.

Granted, the club took me in and treated me as well as they knew how, but it just got to the point where I felt a need to do what I could to slow the influx of meth into the community I live in. The irony is that after I take action, I'll have to leave.

For ten years, I've been involved with an organization that places its members' pleasure and profit over the welfare of anyone else. I've partied with its members and fought in bars for the honor of the Club. I've hurt people to help the Club pursue its selfish, deadly aims. I'm as bad as they are.

But all of that is about to come to a screeching fucking halt.

● ● ●

Now that Forney and the Retard Twins have given me the opportunity, I'll just have to leave sooner than I thought.

I race up the stairs to my room. No need for locks here; nobody would be stupid enough to fuck with any club officer's shit without having Nigger Bill with them, and he thinks I'm as good as gold.

I open my closet, grab my sawed-off 12-gauge, then change my mind. I wipe it down and toss it back. I grab a gym bag, throw in a couple t-shirts, some socks, and underwear. I grab my toothbrush and stick it in my vest pocket. Time is running out and I need to haul ass, now!

I look around the room to say goodbye to all the shit I've accumulated, which isn't much in reality, then start tearing up old biker magazines. I get a good pile of loose pages together and wad them up into a pile right under the curtain over my barred window. I use my lighter to set fire to the paper, then to the curtain just for insurance. The flames look like they're going to take, so I run back down the stairs.

Forney and the twins are standing there, looking stupid as ever. They all have a glass of tequila and are sharing a joint. I run across the floor toward them, reaching into my right rear jeans pocket to find my brass knuckles. I put them on my right hand, and just as I reach the trio of nitwits I yell, "Look out! Fire!" as I point to a spot behind them.

They turn as a single unit and I don't give them a chance to realize their mistake. I hit Forney right at the spot where his skull and his spinal column meet. Before he even hits the floor, I've taken the Twisted Twins out, although not as cleanly as Forney. They're both on the floor moaning. I use a few well-placed kicks with my steel-toed engineer boots to put them into la-la land.

I go back into the rear bedroom, set fire to some stuff that will actually burn, and haul ass out of there. I walk as calmly as possible out to my scooter and tie the gym bag to the short bitch bar with a couple bungee cords. I look around the neighborhood and don't see a soul. That's good.

I look over at the house and there are flames leaping out of both upstairs windows that face the street and smoke is billowing out from under the carport. That's good, and bad. I'm glad the fire is proceeding so well, but I really need to make a clean escape without any interference from the gestapo or the fire department. That would screw up everything.

I kick the stroker to life, thanking all the gods that I'd spent so much time making sure it starts on the first kick, every time. I take off like every demon in Hell is after me, which won't be far wrong if I get caught.

I ride out to the area around the old amusement park at the north end of The Beach (to the locals, Virginia Beach is simply The Beach) to a little bar where all the goat-roper types hang out. There isn't much chance of running into anyone I know here. I park the scooter, and walk across the street to an Amoco station with a pay phone in one corner of the lot.

I call a number by memory, and a gruff voice says, "Narcotics, Guffey speaking."

I tell this voice, "It's Rooney. Today is the day."

It is a code we devised when I first started talking to Guffey about my plan. He told me it was stupid, not to do it, let the police handle it. I told him to fuck off, that it was going to happen my way. I wouldn't give any progress reports, wear a wire, or anything else that might expose my plans. I just told him to be damned ready to jump when I called and spoke the code phrase. He was wary, but finally gave me his private line at work, his home number, and he promised he would have the desk sergeant let him know as soon as "Rooney" called. I don't even know anyone named

Rooney, so it seemed as secure a code as I was going to be able to come up with. Now, if Guffey just hadn't spilled the beans to his fellow dope cops.

"Rooney? Oh, fuck. . . Rooney! Now? Right now?"

"Right now," I reply. "You've got the key and my sworn statement. Do it, Guffey. I just updated everything yesterday, so all the sites, maps, everything, are up-to-date. Get your choppers up, and get the labs taken down before they can regroup. They're going to be real busy for the rest of the afternoon, and that should help you get a jump on them. See ya."

Guffey yells, "Hang on, damn it!"

I really need to get my ass in the wind, but I want to make sure he's got what he needs. "I really need to go, Guffey," I tell him.

He says, "What did you mean about them being busy?"

I snicker as I say, "Turn on your scanner, cop."

I walk back across the street to my bike, and pull out of there like I have all the time in the world. After about a block, I turn up the wick and haul ass out to Chesapeake. I putt into an industrial area near the docks and park in the shade of an old tin awning in front of a seemingly deserted small workshop. I get off and look around as nonchalantly as possible.

There are people around, but none of them seems to have paid any undue attention to my arrival. I unlock the small door under the awning and, after another casual look around, push the bike through it into the room that had served as the office in some time long past. I push the scooter through the room and through another door into a space about thirty feet square.

It's blacker than Toby's ass in here. I painted both small windows in the door black over a year ago. I made sure that I could push the bike straight through the door for about ten feet without hitting anything. As I put the kickstand down and set the weight of the scooter onto it, I get the shakes.

"Holy shit!" I think. I actually made it! I turn on a shielded low-wattage light over the bathroom door, and move the bike to a spot I've prepared for it against the back wall. Things are going as well as can be expected, considering the suddenness of events, but the hard part is yet to come.

It's time to hide and watch.

FOUR

I've spent a few hours here and a few hours there, normally in the middle of the night, doing what I think might save my ass. There is a small apartment-sized refrigerator in the office stocked with enough frozen bologna, cheese, TV dinners, and burritos to keep me going for a week or so. There are cans of beans, chili, fruit cocktail, and stewed tomatoes on a shelf in the big room.

I spent nearly four hours over three different nights getting a small television antenna put up on the roof near a tangle of vents and assorted pipes above the small Vietnamese restaurant behind this space. I brought in a small television and a radio that I bought from some shady dude in an alley across from the main gate of the Naval Air Station.

There is a military surplus cot with real sheets and blankets. I'm not about to use one of those scratchy-assed military wool blankets. I'm hiding, not in jail, for chrissakes! I bought all this shit one at a time, in different places around the Tidewater area. I even broke down and got a small microwave oven, even though some people think they'll give you cancer. I figure I can cook some TV dinners or frozen burritos for a week or so, if I go into the other room while the damned thing is on without much chance of nuking myself.

I take off my riding gloves, my trusty leather coat, chaps, vest, and my boots. I put on a pair of cheap slippers, take a cold RC Cola out of the fridge, and sit down in a lawn chair I bought at a yard sale for a buck. The remote for the TV has new batteries, and I use it to turn the set on. I go to Channel 3, seeing as how they usually do the best job of reporting the flashy news stories. It's just past six p.m., and I figure things should be getting quite lively by now.

This gaudy red banner proclaiming BREAKING NEWS! is flashing away in the upper left-hand corner of the screen, and there's some bleached-blonde news bimbo standing in front of a merrily burning old house. Actually, as I expected, it's video from a couple hours ago of the PnB MC's clubhouse burning itself to the ground. The fire department is there and seems to be doing its job, but I'm guessing they won't feel too bad if there isn't enough of the old girl left to save.

The bimbo is waving her free arm around, babbling about how the mean old bikers who live in this house haven't been heard from, and the club seems to have gone into hiding following a report that a Baptist minister's daughter had been kidnapped, held prisoner, and repeatedly gang-raped in this very den of iniquity blazing away behind her.

The authorities are actively searching for any and all PnB members in an effort to determine what happened and who is involved. Especially wanted for questioning are club president William "Nigger Bill"

Samson (this with a disclaimer across the bottom of the screen apologizing for the use of the offensive word, but used at the insistence of the Virginia Beach PD), vice president Louis "Knuckles" Shackleford, and club enforcer Eric "Hammer" Thorssen. Thorssen was seen leaving the house shortly before the fire was reported.

It seems to me that the neighbors may have waited until they were sure that the house was burning truly well before they called in the alarm. I guess I don't blame them. Now Bambi the News Bimbo is gushing about how the fire department will need to wait until the fire is contained and extinguished before any search can be made for survivors or victims. She seems to favor finding victims, and lots of them. The talking heads back in the studio break in and ask Bambi if anyone knows how the fire started.

She replies, "There are rumors that the poor, traumatized rape victim may have set the fire as a diversion to aid in her escape."

"From the clutches of the Three Dumb-Asses," I think.

Now the male anchor with the plastic hair says they have pictures of the club officers and anyone seeing these people should call the VBPD right away. Sure as shit, there are booking photos of me, Knuckles, and Nigger Bill. We definitely look scary and are described as being armed and dangerous. That's only fair, I suppose, as we are definitely both of those things.

With all the attention this is getting, I wouldn't

give any of us much of a chance on the streets. I figure everyone is holed up or hauling ass for somewhere else, so it'll take awhile for everyone to check in. It will seem only natural that I stay incommunicado, seeing as how I'm being hunted by every law-enforcement type in the state. I'm hoping so, anyway. By the time the club figures out that I'm gone for good, I hope to be so far underground they'll never find me. My life depends on it.

I'm going to be here in my little hole for a while so there's no reason to get in much of a hurry, but there are a few things I feel I need to get done right away. The first thing is to change my appearance enough so anyone not intimately acquainted with me will have a hard time recognizing me. I bought a little seven-dollar barber kit at a Job Lots store in Portsmouth one day while out visiting some of the titty bars the club owns. I also picked up a box of one hundred single-edge razor blades, one of the most versatile tools in the known universe.

The bathroom isn't much, just a grease-stained sink, a toilet, and a drain in the floor, but I installed a pretty bright light and a mirror above the sink during one of my late night visits. After turning on the light and getting used to the harsh glare of the naked bulb, I set the box of razor blades and the barber kit on top of a little TV tray I'd set up next to the sink.

I open the box of blades and take one out. After peeling off the little paper safety sleeve, I grab my braid and pull it over my shoulder to where I can see it easily in the mirror. It had taken nearly eight years for my hair to reach my belt, and another few months to accomplish the same feat braided. I start hacking at it with the blade just above my right shoulder, where I have pretty good control and can see what I'm doing. I really don't feel like dealing with a bunch of razor nicks on my neck or ear, so I go slowly.

After the braid is severed, it goes into a small disposable cardboard trash can, one of a dozen I'd gotten at my local Wal-Mart. I use a new blade to start removing most of the longer hair still remaining on my head. I thought this part would be hard, cutting off all the hair and my beard that had been a part of me for so long, but it somehow feels not just necessary to change my looks, but somehow right, a catharsis of sorts.

After most of the longer stuff is in the can, I turn to the barber kit and remove the scissors. I thought they would be cheap and not hold an edge for long; that's why I started with the single-edge blades. Actually, the scissors didn't have much of an edge to start with. After much pulling and tearing—and a great deal of cursing—most of the remaining locks over about three inches long have joined the others in the cardboard can. After another few minutes of chopping and swearing, the lower eight inches of my beard are also residing there.

It's starting to look like someone sheared a Saint Bernard in here. The little cardboard trash can is overflowing, and there are strands of hair on every horizontal surface. It's time for the finish work, so I remove the electric clippers from the barber kit. There are a few different snap-on attachments that allow us do-it-yourselfers to cut hair at a relatively even length.

These things are color-coded, with each length of hair represented by its own unique hue. There are about nine or ten of them, from short to really short.

I pick out the green one because it looks to be the one that allows the hair to remain longest. I snap it onto the clippers, plug them in over the sink, and turn them on.

"Jesus Christ!" I yell involuntarily.

The fucking things make it sound like a crop duster is flying around inside the bathroom. After my nerves settle down, I hold my breath and start right in the middle, just above the bridge of my nose. I make a swath through the remaining hair all the way over the top of my head to the base of my neck.

Holy shit! That is really short! Oh well, it needs to be finished now. I use the clippers to cut my hair (and beard) to a fairly uniform length of about three quarters of an inch. Hell, I look like a fucking peanut farmer! I just stare at myself in disbelief. My hair and beard were longer than this when I was in the Navy!

With some trepidation, I take the little comb thing off the clippers and use the bare shaver to trim all the curly stuff off my neck and from under my ears. The clipper itself seems to be fairly well made and the blades are pretty sharp. If the noise just wasn't so ungodly loud! If I do this again, I'll wear earplugs.

When I feel it's as good as it's going to get, I turn off the clippers and put them on the TV table. They're hotter than the hubs of Hell and I hope they don't set anything on fire. I use some paper towels to brush all the loose hair and skin off and take a long look at the face in the mirror. I smile because I can't imagine anyone will recognize me. Hell, I don't recognize me!

I get brave and pick up the dull scissors. I trim my moustache some, along with a little hair away from my ears. I think that's it for now, before I really fuck something up. I stuff most of the hair and stuff into the can, and sweep up the rest into a sizable pile. This also gets transferred to the can, with some persuasion from my right foot.

I take one of the other cardboard cans and force it, upside-down, over the full one so there won't be hair floating around with any errant breeze. In all my stock-piling, I've forgotten plastic trash bags. Dumb-ass!

I left the TV on while I was cutting my hair, but couldn't hear a thing over the din the clippers made. Now I can hear what sounds like some news-jockey shouting over the roar of his traffic chopper. I can't make out the words so I walk over to the set and turn up the volume.

As I sit down in my lawn chair, I realize that this isn't a traffic report; it's a bust-in-progress at one of our (their) meth labs. There is one of those ubiquitous little scrolling banners at the bottom of the screen, explaining that this is part of a major move against the Pist-N-Broke MC. The ever-present BREAKING NEWS banner is at the top, alongside a flashing LIVE icon. Wow, the news types really eat this shit up. I guess it gets boring reporting the same old shit every day—murders, rapes, more murders, and the occasional rescued kitty story.

The chopper dude is explaining that this is part of a concentrated effort to smash the methamphetamine trade in the Tidewater area. I don't know how Guffey got his shit together so quickly, but he must have done some serious planning, just in case I really gave him something to use. He must've had all the judges ready to sign warrants as soon as he got locations and names. He knew they wouldn't be good for long, once the shit hit the fan.

The lab on the screen is one of the best hidden and is a huge producer. In the harsh glare of the choppers' spotlights are what look like SWAT team members swarming into the building, a rusty corrugated-tin structure about twenty feet wide and thirty feet long. There seem to be bright flashes of light through the door.

After a couple minutes during which the news dude is speculating about what is happening, there is action at the door again. Three suspects are being led out the door and toward a small clearing in front of the lab.

In the dazzling light, there is no mistaking one of the prisoners. Slam, big-assed bald fucker that he is, is at the rear of the line. He spins quickly, taking his escort by surprise, then just runs over him and through the open door. There are still people in there, having gone in as the prisoners were being led away. I'm wondering what the hell he's thinking. I don't need to wonder for long.

KA-BLAM!

The blast is so violent that it rocks the news 'copter and so bright that the camera only records a white flash, followed by flame and smoke. Slam had obviously prepared for any hostile takeover of his domain by rigging the place with explosives. It wouldn't take a huge amount, if it was strategically placed in the chemical stockpile. I'm sure there are (were) barrels of acetone and alcohol, cases of Coleman lantern fuel, and propane to fuel the burners. Maybe even some ether, just for fun. That's just the explosive shit. There's bound to be large quantities of lye and hydrochloric acid in there, as well. Anyone in there is surely dead, and anyone very close will be either dead or seriously fucked up. A world of hurt, indeed.

I start channel-hopping and it's the same everywhere. It's open season on the PnB MC. Labs are being taken down all over the area, although none as spectacularly as the first one televised. Over a dozen members of the club are in custody and the hunt is on for the rest of us (them).

The runaway's daddy is spewing fire and brimstone about these world-class destroyers of mankind. Guffey is being interviewed on Channel 4 and says the unfolding events are the result of a lot of work by the various law-enforcement agencies in southern Virginia. I'm thinking he just had a few high-ranking guys he trusted and had brought them in early enough to have a game plan formulated, just in case "Rooney" was on the level. It sure looks like the club's hired cops didn't have a clue this was going to happen.

With all the hubbub about the lab explosion and all the surrounding labs being busted, the clubhouse fire was relegated to old news. There was a rehash of the earlier story with Bambi Bimbo standing out in front of what was left of the place, now in darkness except for the lights from the news crews and the fire investigators. There were little knots of neighbors and other looky-loos around the outside of the crime scene tape, like they were trying to get their mugs on TV or just maybe see a fried rapist removed from the ashes.

One very interesting fact that hadn't been revealed earlier was that Forney and the Twins were alive. One of the Twins had regained consciousness and had hauled the other two nearly outside by the time the fire department showed up. They were burned pretty badly and were in intensive care, but were expected to survive.

I really don't know what to think . . . On one hand, I guess I'm glad I didn't commit murder, but I really don't need those three telling anyone who really set set the fire and left them there to die. Nothing I can do about it now, so I'll just proceed as planned.

Hide and watch.

FIVE

It's Saturday morning, ten days since the feces collided with the rotary air-agitating device. The news has been mostly good from my perspective. A few more PnB members have been picked up, and it seems as if most of the others have disappeared into thin air.

One notable exception is Nigger Bill. He was gunned down three days ago by a thirteen-year-old girl in Mount Airy, North Carolina. She reportedly saw his face on one of those television shows where they post bad guys' pictures and ask for tips about their location. Her mom is a truck stop whore. Where Bill met her, I don't have a clue. According to the girl, he called up and made an appointment with her mom, then showed up some forty minutes later.

When he drove up, the girl recognized him and set about "figgerin' a way to kill him for the ree-ward." When he was finished with the mother, he came out onto the little covered porch in front of the trailer. Melinda Lou Ruggles, all ninety-three pounds of her, stepped out from behind the old refrigerator on the porch, leveling a 12-gauge twice-barreled shotgun at his back while he was lighting a cigar.

Ba-boom! She cut loose with both barrels and nearly cut his dumb ass in half. He was dead before he hit the ground. D-E-D, DEAD, yessir.

The mom came running out, found out what transpired, then ran inside to call the television show's toll-free number so they could start processing the reward. After she and Melinda Lou had no doubt emptied Bill's pockets and searched the old pickup he was driving for anything valuable, they called the local sheriff's deputy and reported the fact that they had stopped one of America's most notorious desperados.

The feed from Mount Airy showed Melinda Lou and her mom, Bunny Kay Schreck, front and center, wearing their best Sluts-R-Us couture as they replied to questions from another of Bambi Bimbo's clones. They enthusiastically pointed out the spot on the porch where the coroner had "scooped up" Nigger Bill's remains.

Bunny Kay even volunteered the startling fact that it was she who had given William Samson his famous nickname.

"I'm the one that first called him Nigger Bill," she gushed to Bambi II as Melinda Lou tried her best to get her boobs to fall out of her halter top.

Seeing as how Bill was a very white, very un-African-looking American, this is something a lot of folks had always wondered about. Why in the hell was he called Nigger Bill? Of course, there are a lot of people who know, but nearly all of the television-viewing public that night had no clue. I could just see it coming; I started cracking up, but shushed myself so I could hear what was being said.

I turned up the volume just in time to hear Bambi Jr. ask Bunny Kay, "What circumstance led up to your calling him that?"

I'm sure Bunny Kay, Melinda Lou, and most of Bill's acquaintances were just waiting for that question. Bunny Kay made a fist with her right hand and maneuvered her elbow into her crotch, making a very good impression of a huge male erection.

"He was hung like Long Dong Silver!" she cackled, as Melinda Lou and the rest of us who knew the joke started howling like monkeys at Another Bambi's expression.

Even a couple of the cops in the background were grinning. I'm pretty sure her cameraman was laughing, too, because he couldn't hold the camera still for shit. Live television is a glorious thing!

Knuckles is still unaccounted for, as am I. Forney is still in pretty bad shape in an induced coma. The Twins have been identified as Rocky "Dinky" Winkler and James "Assface" Rogers, both club prospects. Assface was the one who pulled the other two to relative safety.

When they were interrogated by the cops, he and Dinky both say they can't remember what happened. They are under the impression that a piece of the roof or something had fallen on them, knocking them out. If that's what they really think, that is great news for me. I'm just a little concerned that this story is being spread around in order to make me feel safe enough to contact some of the other club members.

There is almost no way they could know about my role in the lab busts, but there are bound to be questions about my loyalty if the true story about the fire comes out. Discussions about loyalty to the club often take the form of severe ass-kickings, or worse. Hopefully, the story they're telling is what they really think.

The preacher's daughter has positively identified Forney, Dinky, and Assface as the three who abducted her and subsequently got her high and repeatedly raped her. Assface and Dinky maintain that they found her at a Denny's in Norfolk. She told them she had run away from home in order to get out from under her preacher daddy's thumb. They'd asked her if she wanted to party, and she'd said, "Hell, yeah!"

They went out to Forney's van where they gave her some crank to snort, then some cranks to blow, which she did willingly and even enthusiastically. They say that all of them proceeded to the clubhouse, where she was asked if she'd ever been involved in a gang bang. She supposedly said no, but was willing to try anything.

Things went along fine for awhile, until she asked them to stop. Of course, these three morons weren't having any of that shit. They kept at it, until they finally had her so doped up and exhausted that she quit fighting and went limp. As they told it, it was all consensual, so it couldn't be rape.

"Hell, she didn't even complain until the fourth or

fifth go-round. See, we didn't do anything wrong. Hell, if anyone should be mad it's us. She burned our damned house down! Can we go now?"

Uh, no.

Other than the occasional showing of my picture, my name is rarely being spoken on the news lately. There have been a few murders, some other rapes, a teacher molested a few kids, and Memorial Day is coming up. The biker dope fiends are old news. Things will liven up if one of us gets shot, shoots someone else, or there are any more spectacular explosions or fires.

This damned old shop is getting to me. I haven't been outside in the daylight for ten days, and even my excursions in the dark have been short-lived and few. I rigged up a hose to screw onto the sink faucet in the months prior to my self-induced incarceration, so I can take a half-assed shower. The television and radio provide some welcome distraction, but the truth is that I've got a world-class case of cabin fever.

It is almost time to boogie out of this joint. The first item on the agenda is to find a place to lie low for a spell. My old Navy buddy, Kenneth Dutton, has always said that I'm welcome any time. We've been through some serious shit together, and he can keep his mouth shut. I trust him with my life. I have to. If anyone gets wind of where I am, there will be hell to pay.

I find his number in my shaving kit under the bottom flap in a plastic baggie. I set it on top of the TV and go into the head to shower. One thing about short hair, it dries damned quick.

By the time I'm shaved and dressed, my hair is dry. I go back into the head and look at myself in the mirror. After ten days, my new look isn't as shocking, but it still takes me awhile to soak in the whole thing. I've been toying with the hair, trying to make it look a little more natural, and trimmed the beard again and again, until I finally cut it all off except for a short goatee.

I'm wearing some silly-looking yuppie khakis and a green sweater, both purchased at a yard sale over a year ago. I told the old gal they were for a Halloween costume. Brown side-zip dress boots are on my feet, and a lambskin jacket tops off the whole ensemble. The boots came from a Salvation Army store in Richmond, the coat from Sears. I look just like a million other "citizens"—the bikers' name for all the straight public.

Making sure there is money in my pockets, I pick up my keys and Dutton's phone number. By now, the pathway to the front office door is familiar and I shut off all the lights before going through the office, out the door, and into the night. It's just before two a.m. and the street is deserted.

There's a Waffle House a couple blocks away and a convenience store with a bank of pay phones next door to it. It's strange being outside. The first impression is that of silence, but quickly the myriad sounds of a city intrude. Even at this hour, the hiss of traffic and the muted cacophony of people shouting and doors slamming all intrude into the silence, somehow making the night seem safer, friendlier, more natural.

I walk up the sidewalk, dodging trash and the occasional pile of dog shit. At the corner I look both ways, all ways, and all ways again. The forced isolation is giving way to paranoia. I take a few deep breaths then punch the button to cross the intersection. Man, I think that's the first time I've done that in over ten years! I really am turning into Joe Citizen. Smiling, I cross the street against the light and walk up the block to the Kum N Go convenience store on the next block. That name always gets a chuckle out of me.

There's nobody at the phones and that makes me feel better. I open the door and the hot, stale air assaults me. After the time in the shop, the smells of hot dogs, coffee, and those little tree-shaped air fresheners all mingled together are almost too much to take. Behind the counter is a woman about thirty, and she looks relieved that her new customer looks fairly "normal." If I looked like I did a couple weeks ago, she'd be wary, ready to dial 911 at a moment's notice.

I ask her if she can sell me a roll of quarters so I can call my wife and kids back in San Diego and let them know I'm okay. I smile real friendly-like, and she decides to sell me the quarters. I take Dutton's number out and dial it, once again looking around to make sure there isn't anyone close enough to hear.

After I deposit a bunch of quarters when

prompted to do so by a recording, the phone starts to ring. It rings five times and I'm about to give up when a voice full of sleep rasps out, "Yeah, what?"

"Is this Kenneth?" I ask, not sure it's him.

"Who the fuck else would it be?" he counters, and I almost laugh out loud. Same old Dutton.

"Kenny, it's Ricky. You awake enough to pay attention? I'm in trouble."

He might be sleepy, but he's attentive at once. Nobody calls him Kenny but me. It's an old inside joke between us. He hates Kenny and I loathe being called Ricky. It's just one of those weird things that happen with good friends.

"What's up, man? Are you okay?" he asks me.

"I'm fine so far, but I'm in deep shit and need to hide out for awhile. I don't want to get you involved, but I thought you might be able to point me toward some safe hidey-hole for a couple of weeks or so."

He's talking before I finish. "Fuck that! You come here. Where are you right now? How soon can you be here? Do I need to come get you? Are you alone? What the fuck's going on?"

I appreciate his concern and all, but I really don't want to put him in jeopardy.

"Kenny, are you sure? This might get very heavy, man! I've got the cops and a bunch of very bad hombres on my ass, and it will get mucho ugly if they find me. I am alone, and I've taken some steps to change my looks, but things are very hot right now.

I'm out by The Beach. I've got transportation, something no one knows about, so I ought to be able to make it down there if something stupid doesn't happen. Is there anyone living with you? If so, just point me to a hole in the forest somewhere."

Dutton lives out in the middle of some hollow in southern Tennessee, just north of the Alabama line somewhere. That's all I know, other than the name of the nearest town—Fayetteville, or "Fehvull" as he pronounces it.

"Jesus, Ricky, just shut the fuck up about going somewhere else. Which way you comin'?"

I've thought about this a lot. If I go straight south into North Carolina, I'll be out of Virginia in no time. The only problem with that is the fact that the PnB MC spends a lot of time in northeast North Carolina partying and selling dope. US 58 heads straight west but is more than likely the route Nigger Bill took when he went to Mount Airy. It stands to reason there will be law-enforcement types crawling all over his back trail looking for other club members. I decide to take US 58 to Emporia, then head south on I-95 to Exit 138 at Rocky Mount, North Carolina. That way I'll only be in Virginia for about an hour-and-a-half, and will skirt the places where people know me in North Carolina. US 64 will take me west to Raleigh, where I'll get on I-40 and take it west all the way to the west side of Knoxville, Tennessee. From there, I'll take I-75 south to Chattanooga, then turn west onto I-24, then west again on US 64.

"I'll be coming in tomorrow on 64, from the east," I tell him.

"Stop in Winchester and give me a call," he replies after a few seconds thought. "That way I'll have plenty of time to get my shit together and make it to the highway. Follow 64 west into Fehvull, then go south on 10 for a little ways. Watch for US 431, take it south toward Huntsvull. You'll need to be watchin' for Whitt's BBQ on the left. It's only about a mile down 431. I'll order up some pork plates, and we can eat out at the house."

Good old Kenneth, I think, smiling at his total command of the situation. "It should be fairly early when I get to Chattanooga, so I'll just eat some breakfast, read the paper, and grab a few little things I need. I'll try to get into Winchester around ten or ten-thirty and give you a holler. I really appreciate this, buddy," I tell him, figuring out the timetable as I go.

"Of course you do. I'm a fuckin' saint. Now, by 'tomorrow,' you do mean Sunday, right?"

I take a second to get my mind straight and tell him, "Yeah. Sunday the sixth of May, 1990. Smart-ass!"

"Awright then, I'll see you tomorrow mornin'. Keep your head down and your powder dry, son. I need to get my ass back to sleep so's I can stay purty for the local heifers."

I laugh at the idea of Kenneth Dutton ever being "purty," and some of the tension melts away. I actually start to relax a little. I might just pull this off!

"Fine, you get your beauty sleep and I'll take a nap myself. I want to bail out of here right around the end of rush hour tonight, and I'm damned near ready to go. Watch your ass, Bubba. See you tomorrow."

I hang up, take a little look around, and go back into the store. I buy some baby wipes and a box of powdered-sugar donuts as a little treat, something to help the energy level when I get up around noon and put the last few pieces together before I haul ass. . .

It's now about eleven-twenty, and I just can't lie here anymore. I get up, fold up what clean clothes I have, including the getup I wore earlier today. Hell, I only had that stuff on for about an hour, so it'll be fine for another shift later. I put the most of the straight clothes in a gym bag, along with my shaving kit and various toiletries. I put on a pair of brown cords, a pale yellow polo shirt, and scuffed up brown loafers, all thrift store purchases. I eat three or four donuts and drink a couple RCs. My sugar level is approaching lift-off levels, so I get busy.

Against the far wall from the office is a 1982 Ford utility van, white in color, registered to the fellow on my new ID. I'd given the document's maker a picture the club had taken after I set my beard on fire drinking flaming rum. It had looked so bad that I shaved it off, and that was the only time my face had been exposed to the sun in the last ten years. The picture was taken while my hair was braided, and I'd just been wearing a t-shirt with no club insignia showing. I'd kept the picture for just such an occasion, not knowing when or why I might need it. The forger had touched it up a little with an airbrush and had taken a photo of it.

This is the photo that currently resides on the Maryland driver's license in the name of John Robert Clark in my wallet. It cost me five grand, but I got the license, a social security card, and a couple credit cards in Mr. Clark's name, all with a Baltimore address. The forger's cousin had lived there for six months while I paid the rent, taking care of all the paperwork and such.

The name and Social Security number belonged to a fellow that some associates of the forger had dispatched for transgressions against them. There are a few thousand dollars in a Baltimore bank in the same name. I'll send a change of address form to the post office when I get somewhere I plan on staying for a spell.

The van was purchased from a rental store in Baltimore in John's name and insured for a year in advance. The forger's cousin removed the engine and rebuilt it. While he was at it, he added higher-compression pistons and a fairly stout camshaft. The entire rotating assembly had been inspected, reconditioned, and beefed up before being balanced, insuring reliability. A late-model electronic fuel injection system was installed for both performance and better gas mileage. I really want this thing to look like any other old work van, so we didn't put exhaust headers on it, but I found some high-flow, cast iron exhaust manifolds from an old Mustang Cobra. The cousin installed them, along with a custom two-and-a-half inch exhaust system. The mufflers are high-performance, free-flowing models, but keep things down to a dull roar. The pipes end under the back bumper, with rusty old chrome tips aiming the fumes at the ground. The last touch was spraying the entire engine bay with a light coat of WD-40. After a few miles on some dirt roads in rural Maryland, and another light coat of oil, nobody would guess that the engine is anything but the original lump.

The interior is fitted with a custom box about eighteen inches high, covering most of the cargo area. I built it out of some old nasty-looking plywood from a waterbed that had taken a shit a few months back in the clubhouse. I painted it flat back with spray bombs, and it looks it.

In this box are all the pieces that had, until a few days ago, been my beautiful chopper. The engine went on its side near the front, with the seat, lights, rear fender, oil tank, and other smaller parts. The front end and pipes were tucked against all the small stuff. I wrapped a bunch of dirty-assed old rags and clothing around the stuff to keep the damage and rattling to the bare minimum. The wheels and the frame were wrapped up and held in place by small wooden blocks screwed to the floor and the box sides.

Also in the box are my leather coat, gloves, chaps, etc. Everything bike-related except for my colors is in the box, along with the tools needed to put it back together, padded and soundproofed. On top of the box is a piece of plywood and a queen-size mattress that covers the box as well as the wheel-wells. The plywood top is attached to the box with L-shaped brackets and drywall screws, which have been painted over with the flat black.

All in all, the effect is very satisfactory. The whole sorry-looking mess looks like it's been there forever. There are fishing poles, folding camp stools, and a propane camp stove shoved under the overhang at the rear of the mattress. There are empty RC cans, candy wrappers, and the newly-emptied donut box thrown in amid the other clutter. My bedding is wadded up on top of the bed, and my gym bag is on top of that. The trash cans with my hair and all the other garbage I've created are in the cardboard box that originally housed the microwave oven. It's in the rear, and will be discarded after a couple of hours on the road. My colors are wrapped up in a gunny sack and tied to the frame under the van, over the fuel tank where they're out of sight.

The oven and fridge are staying here in the shop, along with some of the other inconsequential stuff I don't have room for. The TV and radio will stay, too. I grab the hose from the bathroom, the hair clippers, and the last few cans of food. The hose and clippers go into the microwave box, and the food gets tossed in with the fishing stuff.

The only thing left to do is wait until the appointed

time for departure. I figure I'll take off around seven or so, toward the end of rush hour. It wouldn't do to get in a fender-bender before I even get out of the county. I turn on the TV, watch some stupid-ass game shows until about six-thirty.

There isn't anyone outside, so I open the big door and maneuver the van into the street. I go back in and wipe down everything twice with the baby wipes. I really don't think there's any way anyone will tie me to this place, but hey, I'm paranoid, okay? The rent is paid up for three months in advance, and I put a healthy deposit on the utilities in Johnny Bob's name, so there is no reason for people to come snooping.

But hey, shit happens.

SIX

The first 75 miles or so have gone very quietly. I made exceptional time from the hideout shop to here, and Emporia is just down the road a piece. I pull into a truck stop parking lot and cruise around back to where the dumpsters are. There isn't much light here, and I don't see anyone loitering around. I take the microwave box and pitch it into the dumpster that has the most grease and nasty shit all over it. I drive back around the building and back onto US 58.

After another four or five miles, I turn south on I-95 and cruise along in the right lane, about five miles an hour under the limit. In less than an hour, I turn west onto US 64 at the Rocky Mount exit, number 138. Another hour, and I'm in Raleigh, looking for the exit for I-40 westbound.

The donuts-and-RC sugar buzz is gone, and my gut is howling at me, so I pull off the interstate onto a busy-looking road and see a Popeye's across the street. I pull into a Union 76 station, fill up the van, then pull up at Popeye's drive-up window and order a box of Cajun-style chicken and a half-dozen biscuits. I bought a six-pack of RC and took a leak at the gas station, so I'm good for awhile.

Back on the interstate, I see an exit for the Benson Beltline, or the north loop of I-440 around

Raleigh. I take it to I-40, and head for Knoxville, Tennessee, about five or six hours away. Durham, Greensboro, Winston-Salem, and Hickory all fade into the rear-view mirror. Fabric and tobacco outlet stores line the freeway, and even though I don't go through Charlotte, there is NASCAR shit everywhere. It seems like there is a little racetrack every ten or fifteen miles, and there are racecars everywhere. These people take their racing seriously, and that's no shit. I pull off in Asheville at about 1:30 a.m. on Sunday and fill up the van, which I have come to affectionately think of as Vanna. I figure I'll be in Knoxville by 3:30 or so.

Strangely, I'm pretty calm. The anxiety over setting the club up for a fall and the resulting shit-storm has receded, leaving me feeling at peace with my decisions. Of course, I still need to be damned cautious.

I skirt the northern edge of the Great Smoky Mountains and cross Lake Douglas in the dead of night. This sucks! I know this is some incredibly beautiful country, and I hate to miss it because I don't know if I'll ever get another chance to see it. Oh, well, life's a bitch then you die.

As I approach Knoxville, my stomach is once again growling like a pissed-off tomcat. I see a large truck stop and take the appropriate exit. There are a lot of trucks in the lot, as you only see in the South: hundreds of the big fuckers, most idling away with the drivers asleep inside their sleepers. After filling up Vanna's tank, I pull in and park in the middle of the tourist lot where I can see her from the restaurant.

After a decent breakfast of biscuits and gravy with grits on the side, I head back to the van. Out of the semi-darkness on my right comes a shadow, moving fast. Just as I'm deciding how to take my attacker's head off, she moves into the light. It's a woman about thirty-five or so, and she's breathing hard. I look over her shoulder, looking for a pursuer. I don't see anyone, but my hackles are up, and I smell trouble.

"What's up?" I ask her as she skids to a stop about five feet from me.

"Hey, baby, lookin' for a party?" she asks me.

I realize she's a hooker, working the truck stop. She looks pretty rough in the light, and I figure she's a "tweaker" (a meth head).

"Not tonight, honey," I tell her as I start for the van again. She isn't going to give up that easily, though.

"Come on, baby! I'll treat you right. I'll blow you for twenty bucks and do half-and-half for thirty. Look at these, baby. You know you wanna squeeze 'em."

She's got her boobs out, now, showing them to me. It's like she's showing off the goods, like melons on display at the grocery store. She's got a desperate air about her, and I figure her pimp told her not to take no for an answer. Since she's over here in the "tourist" lot, I figure she's worn out her welcome in the professional drivers' lounge and in the sleepers out back. She probably stole too much, started too much shit, or both.

"Hey, babe, I'm not into chicks. Know where I

can find a dude to suck my cock?" I ask her.

It takes a second to sink in.

"Fuckin' fag! A fuckin' fudge-packer, for Christ's sake! Fuck you, you goddamned queer!" While she's squalling at me, she's tucking her tits back into her tube top.

I'm heading for the van, hoping to get the hell out of the lot before either her pimp comes over to tune up the fag, or a male hustler hears her and decides to check out my package. She's wound up like a two-dollar watch now, and is venting every bit of anger and frustration in her miserable existence at me.

"Cocksucker! Don't you walk away from me, you fucking ass-packin' piece of shit!"

You've got to give her points for variety, at least. By now, I'm damned near sprinting, and she's following me, but I still don't see anyone else.

I get to Vanna and pile in, locking the door. I really don't want to be forced into a physical confrontation with her. I wouldn't feel good about knocking her on her ass, and it might cause more attention than I care for. I get the van started and backed out of the space before she can block me, but she's staggering toward the front of the van. She's lost a shoe somewhere, and she has a definite starboard list. I drive past her, missing her by a couple inches, and head for the exit and the freeway. I feel something—either pity or disgust or a little of both—for her, but mostly I can't stop laughing. I'm glad nobody I know saw that whole fiasco. I'd never live it down, running from a truck stop whore, telling her I'm gay to get her to leave me alone.

That didn't work so well, did it? Holy shit.

From there to the junction with I-75 is about 30 miles, and I head south, still giggling about my morning's entertainment. It's about a two-hour drive to Chattanooga, and I arrive there at about seven o'clock a.m. Traffic is already heavy, so I just keep moving. It's only about an hour to Winchester, so I decide to just get there and kill some time until I call Kenneth.

I get on I-24 and drive the thirty or so miles to the US 64 junction. Taking the exit for 64 westbound, I see a group of bikers on the side of the road, taking a break. My first impulse is to park and shoot the shit—it's what I always do—did—but I remember that bikers are the last people I should be talking to right now. Nevertheless, I'm curious as to who they are and whether they pose a risk to me.

I pull off the road about a hundred feet past them, and park by a dumpster. I get out, stretch my back and legs a little, and throw my chicken box and a few RC bottles in the trash can. I glance toward the bikers, and one turns his back to me, allowing me to get a good look at his colors. Judah's Children, the top rocker proclaimed. These guys are a paradox; they claim to be a Christian group, but they're a frightening-looking bunch. Scary Jesus Freaks on wheels. No matching uniforms and cute little patches here. Most of them have shaved heads, with the occasional Gunga Dinstyle topknot or Mohawk thrown in. Lots of piercings and tattoos. No matter, they can look any way they want and do anything they feel like doing. Any outlaw clubs or cops in this neck of the woods will be more interested in them than some straight-looking dude in a white van.

I get back in the van and pull out heading west on US 64. No other distractions occur, and I pull into Winchester about twenty minutes later at eight-fifteen. I park in front of Ma's Hash House on Main Street. I sit there for a few minutes, unwinding and relaxing a little. The town square is really pretty, and the town court-house is brick, probably a couple hundred years old. There's an old Civil War-era cannon on the lawn near a small bandstand.

I'm not hungry, but I need somewhere to wait without looking conspicuous. I go into Ma's and order a piece of homemade apple pie with cheese melted on top, and a large RC. The old gal who's waiting tables chastises me for my choice of breakfast fare, but I just smile and say, "Long night."

She smiles, probably thinking I'd been out carousing with some local hussy.

"Well, that's different," she says, and hobbles off to turn in my order.

I keep forgetting that I now look like "normal" folks. The smiles and attitudes of most of the people I've dealt with on this trip continue to remind me, though. It's a pleasant change, and should come in handy. I might even get used to it. I walk over to the counter and pick up a copy of the local newspaper. My food is on the table by the time I get back.

I read the local news while eating. There's not much memorable in the paper, but I read the whole damned thing, nursing my RC and a glass of water. Feeling guilty and a little silly, I order a bowl of grits with red-eye gravy and another RC. By now, I've read every classified ad and even the Dear Abby column. I take the paper back up to the counter and pick up a Nickle-Ad and spend about an hour checking out vehicles for sale.

Finally, I figure it's time to call Dutton, so I pay my bill and leave Ma a healthy tip. I ask her if I can get change for the phone, and she obliges me with a conspiratorial wink. I'll bet she was a corker in her day! The phone is in the hallway by the restrooms, and I get an operator to connect me to Dutton's number after depositing the requisite fistful of quarters.

The phone only rings once, and Kenneth is there, asking, "Yeah, what?"

"It's Ricky," I tell him. "I'm in Winchester. I'll meet you at Whitt's around eleven, okay?"

He thinks for a second, then says, "Good enough. I'll be in a green GMC four-by-four, a '67. I'll call 'em so they'll have the grub ready to go when I get there. We probably don't need to attract any attention to us, so just watch for me and follow me when I leave. We'll go about a mile south, then take Molino

Road about eight miles or so out in the country, then some little two-tracks out to my place. If anyone is behind us, I'll go past and wait until they turn off, then go back. Sound okay to you?"

I can't think of anything wrong with his plan, and tell him so.

"Awright, then. I'll see you in forty-five minutes or so," and Dutton is gone.

It is simple enough to find Whitt's, and I pull into the lot from the tire store next door. I pull around to the far corner and back in so I can see both driveways. I hold the Nickle-Ad up so it looks like I'm doing a little reading before going in, and settle in to wait for Kenneth. After about ten minutes, a dirty old green GMC pickup pulls in and parks next to the front door.

A large, barefoot, blonde hillbilly in bib-alls and a white t-shirt gets out and goes inside. I have to smile; Kenneth looks just like I remember him. He's only inside for about two or three minutes, then he's back in the truck and backing toward the center of the lot. He sits there for a second, probably to make sure that I'm paying attention, and heads south on US 431.

I fold up the paper, start the van, and slowly ease my way onto the road. I check for traffic, pull out, and follow the GMC at about a half-mile distance. I know we need to turn onto the next road, so there's no need to follow very closely. Following Kenneth onto Molino Road, I close up the distance a little, but hang back enough so nobody will notice that we're together.

After a couple miles of garages, car lots, and such, the roadside businesses gradually thin out. There are some old farmhouses along the road now.

After a few more miles, a big sunburned arm comes out of the driver's window of the GMC, signaling a left turn. I let off the gas and coast a little so the gap grows a little more. At the corner I signal (using the turn signal) and turn left onto a little gravel road with no sign. After a few hundred yards, we turn right into the woods, and onto a little two-track that is nearly indistinguishable. We follow it for a quarter-mile or so, then head back south for a bit before the trail winds back to the north. There have been a couple other tracks heading off this one, so I'm guessing there are some other hermits out here besides Dutton. After nearly fifteen minutes of following this trail, we round a big bramble patch. There's a neat little clapboard house, and a decent-sized metal barn in the side yard. There are a couple old tractors slowly growing into the earth, and I can see a few old cars out behind the barn.

Kenneth parks the GMC next to the house, and climbs out. He motions for me to follow him, and walks toward the far end of the barn. As I round the corner, Kenneth swings open a pair of big doors in the end of the barn. He points inside, so I nose Vanna into the dark interior. My eyes adjust a little, and I see that there is plenty of room in the middle of the building. I park and shut off the engine.

Kenneth is waiting at the door, having already

swung one closed. As I walk past him, he swings the door closed and throws a big-ass beam across the pair.

He turns with a big grin on his face, and says, "Let's eat!"

SEVEN

We walk into the house and Kenneth sets a pair of greasy-looking, white paper bags on the coffee table in the small living room. The house is clean and smells like Southern cooking. The odors coming from the bags are getting to me, even though it hasn't been that long since my drawn-out breakfast at Ma's.

Kenneth walks into the small kitchen and returns with a stack of paper plates and a roll of paper towels. He sets the stuff on the table and turns toward me.

"Damn, it's good to see you, son."

He takes my right hand in his, and it feels as though he's trying to grind the bones there into dust. He lets go and sits in a big old easy chair facing the TV.

"Sit," he says. "After we chow down, we'll do some serious shit-shootin'. We'll decide what to do next, but right now this here pork is talkin' to me, and I don't want to be rude."

He lets out a throaty chuckle, and opens one of the bags. The odors coming from it make me forget any notions of not eating, and I grab the other bag and dive in. In less than fifteen minutes we are both sitting back contentedly, having devoured every last morsel of food Whitt's had stuffed into the paper sacks. We have nearly killed off two RCs apiece, and the belching and farting have begun in earnest.

Kenneth got me started on RC, back when we were both raw Navy recruits. He couldn't believe that I always ordered Coke, and proceeded to educate me on the finer points of having a Moon Pie with an ROC Co-Cola, as he called it. It hadn't taken long to get in the habit, and I still order RC if it's available. Dutton swears he won't ever go anywhere they don't have it, and I believe him.

All at once Kenneth asks me, "So what the fuck is goin' on, Ricky?"

I start at the beginning, or about the time he saw me last, anyhow. When I finally get to the part where I called him, he holds a pudgy hand in the air and says, "Stop. I can figger out the rest from there. Now what? Do you have a plan, or are you just wingin' it?"

That's a good question.

"Well, I don't have much of a plan, other than laying low for awhile. I think it'll be okay to move on within a week or so. I'd like to stay in the South, but that's just not going to happen. I figure I'll head west until I find a quiet place where there aren't any bike clubs that have ever heard of the PnB MC. I'll keep my head down and my ears open until I've settled in somewhere. I imagine I'll be able to get a job turnin' wrenches on a farm or somewhere. I just need to get away from all the low-life assholes I've been around for so long. Hell, I'm just as bad as they are! Hopefully, it's not too late to start over."

Kenneth looks at me for a couple seconds, then

says, "I was gonna tell you that you could stay here after the shit-storm blows over, but I can see that won't work. Okay, then. I've got a nest fixed up in the loft, and nobody knows you're here. We'll just keep you outta sight for a week or two, then decide where we're at. And fergit that shit about being the same as those clowns. You did the right thing, son. It took a while to see the light, but you finally did. That's what counts. We just have to make sure you stay alive to realize it."

We clean up what little mess we made and Kenneth suggests we go for a walk. I keep looking over my shoulder, afraid someone's going to pop up out of the ground and kick my ass.

Kenneth finally says, "Jesus, Ricky, calm down, willya? We'll be able to hear anyone getting within a quarter-mile of here, unless it's Dan'l Boone himself. We don't need to worry about gettin' you caught out here. I'm just going to show you a few ways outta here, in case someone actually does come around and you want to stay out of sight."

Of course, he's already thought this stuff through. He knew enough before I got here to start planning escape routes.

"Sorry, man," I say, shaking my head. "It's just hard relaxing enough to calm down. You're right. I'll mellow out, and instead of jumping at shadows, I'll let my ears detect anything I need to know about. It may take a couple days to fine tune it, though. I've been in the city and on noisy-ass bikes for a long time."

I'm laughing, and it feels good. We spend a couple hours walking around his "farm," and he shows me some hiding spots and a few trails through the brambles that will serve as escape routes in a pinch.

It's hard to believe, but I'm getting hungry again. As if he's reading my mind, Dutton kind of squints one eye and grins. "You hungry?"

"I could eat," I tell him, laughing along with him.

When we were cruising The Beach as young bucks, we had been called "power eaters" by our Navy buddies and knew every all-you-can-eat buffet in the Tidewater area. We head back to the house in search of sustenance.

Kenneth has one of those old round-top refrigerators on his back porch that he uses as a freezer. It's full of pork, chickens, and beef that he's bartered for, and he's got plenty of bread and real butter. There are lots of canned beans, new potatoes, corn, and other veggies on the shelves in the pantry. He's got one of those kitchen stoves with a grill in the middle of it, with a powered vent hood above it.

He took some steaks out of the freezer last night, and they've been marinating in the refrigerator in the kitchen. Kenneth lights a fire in the grill and hands me an RC. He points toward a net bag of onions on the counter. We both wash our hands and get busy. I skin and quarter a bunch of onions, and find some jalapeños and cherry tomatoes in the fridge. I put them into the marinade and start going through the kitchen drawers.

"Got any skewers?" I ask Kenneth, not expecting much.

He's got the steaks going on the grill, and turns around frowning. "Sewers?" he asks.

I repeat, "Skewers. You know, the little sticks for shish-kabobs."

"Well Christ, Ricky, why didn't you just ask for shish-kabob sticks? Nope. I don't have nothin' like that. Why? What are you makin' over there? I see you found those hot-ass jalapaneeno peppers I got at Piggly-Wiggly when I knew you were comin'. There's so many Mexicans around any more that they started carrying all kinds of weird food. Some of it is even written in Mexican. Fuckin' country's goin' to shit."

"Okay, no problem," I tell him, figuring I'll just toss them on the grill with the onions and tomatoes a few minutes before the steaks are done.

I've always liked hot peppers, everything from the Cuban parrot peppers in Key West to the jalapeños and habañeros of my native Southwest. (Somehow I don't think Dutton would like it out there very much.) And, of course, the cayenne peppers prevalent in Cajun food are a favorite of mine, too.

We stuff ourselves on steak sandwiches and grilled veggies then sit on the front porch for awhile before Dutton asks me, "You need me around for a week or so? There's plenty of chow, and you can either hang out here in the house or out in the loft. I need to go to Memphis to see Janie and take care of some shoppin', unless you actually need me here for somethin'."

Janie is Kenneth's little sister, and her health has never been great.

"No, man, do what you gotta do," I tell him. "I'll be fine here. I need to do some thinking about my next move. If the neighbors all know you're gone, there's less chance of anyone coming around. How's Janie doing, anyhow?"

He looks sad when he tells me, "Not too well, Ricky. She's got that damned Lupus, and she's gettin' weaker all the time. She's got a good attitude and she's tough, but it's just wearin' her down. I'm afraid she'll either have to come here or go to some nursin' home before too long."

"That sucks, man! Jesus, it's always the sweet ones who have to do all the suffering, isn't it?"

I really hate to hear this. Janie had been a sweet kid, and she'd had a crush on me back when I came down to their house once with Kenneth. She'd always been "delicate" according to her mother, but none of the local doctors had ever been able to pinpoint her problem. I guess someone finally figured it out.

"How long has she been in Memphis?" I ask him.

"Not quite two years," he tells me with a sad note in his voice. "She got to the point where I couldn't take care of her no more. There was no way in hell I was gonna put her in that nursin' home in town where Mama died. There's nothin' but old folks and veggies in there, and it woulda drove her bugshit. The place she's in is like a boardin' house and most of the people there are about her age. They have a nurse livin' there with 'em, too, so that makes it a lot better. We've damned near used up all the insurance money from the folks' passin', and I'm not sure what we'll do when it's all gone. She's lookin' at some grants and stuff, but I don't have a clue about any of that shit."

His face is lined with worry and I don't blame him; the cost to keep someone in a place like that must be staggering.

"Go ahead and go," I tell him. "I'll be fine here. I've got plenty to do for a few days. Take care of your sis, and don't worry about me."

He smiles, puts out a meaty right paw, and says, "Okay. I'll be back Sunday afternoon."

EIGHT

So here I am, wondering what the hell to do next. My plan to bury some stuff in the barn floor and haul ass out of here has gotten all fucked up. Now I have all this other shit to deal with, and it's bending my brain a little. I really feel like calling Chief to let him know what the S&S assholes are up to, just to clear my conscience. If I call without saying where I am, I might get an idea of whether or not the club is after my head. If things seem cool, I'll tell him what was in the trunk of the Crown Vickie and where to find the boxes of disguises and stuff (minus the cash, of course!). I'll use the fact that I'm wanted to avoid meeting him or any of the club. That way, I'll feel better and should be able to stay out of sight. I can drop off the boxes and haul ass for parts unknown right after.

I feel like I have the beginning of a plan. I hide everything in the back of Vanna and climb up to the loft for a snooze until Dutton shows up later.

I'm with a couple hard-bodied girls and drinking cold beer at my favorite hang-out when one of the girls turns into a big-assed woodpecker and starts tearing the pool table into kindling. Nobody else seems to notice. That's weird, because the noise is deafening and it's getting louder by the second. A piece of the pool table hits my foot, hard. I sit up, reaching for my piece as I'm trying to get the dream out of my head.

"Whoa up there, son! It's me. I tried to wake you up by beatin' on the ladder, but you were plumb out of it."

It is Kenneth. Of course. He'd whacked me on the foot with a two-by. No dummy, he'd stayed out of the line of fire on the ladder in case I came up shootin'.

"I'm goin' in the house," he says. "Get your shit together and come on in. I've got grub. But c'mon in and take a shower first, fer Chrissakes! You smell like skunko fuckin'."

After a short, hot shower and a change of clothes, I amble into the living room where Kenneth is. I sprawl out on the lumpy old couch that's misshapen from decades of sprawling by generations of Duttons.

There's a big bucket (barrel?) of chicken on the coffee table, along with a big bowl of mashed potatoes and what looks like a couple gallons of country gravy. There are paper plates, napkins, sporks, and a six-pack of RC that is slowly condensing a puddle onto the tabletop.

Pointing at the spread with my chin, I ask, "Whitt's?"

"Yup . . . thank God they're open on Sunday," says Kenneth as he fishes a huge chicken breast out of the bucket (barrel). As has become our custom, we eat in relative silence. The occasional belch or comment on the food is the only break in the quiet.

After we're both finished, we carry the bones and trash to the kitchen. I carry the trash outside and empty it into the burn barrel. When I come back inside, I sit down at the round kitchen table where there are fresh RCs and a fifth of Jack Daniels No.7.

Dutton is sitting there looking contented, gnawing on a drumstick. I honestly don't know how he does it. I've seen him eat pretty much nonstop for hours at a time, especially after smoking some weed. Which reminds me; I need to ask him if he wants Bubba's stash. I'm sure he will, if it's any good. If it's rag-weed, he can trade it off for something. I'm thinking that I'd better wait until we're through talking about the serious shit, so things don't deteriorate into a giggle-fest. And then, all at once I'm laughing.

I've just remembered that there is probably at least a million dollars in the barn if that other box is full of cash like the first two! I think our days of worrying about trading for stuff we need are just damned near over.

Kenneth is looking at me with a combination of curiosity, concern, and amusement. That just makes me laugh harder, until tears stream down my face.

"Ricky, what THE HELL is wrong with you? Are you okay?"

I can't stop, though. I'm laughing like a loon now, and wiping tears out of my eyes. Kenneth's laughing, too, the way you do when you're with someone who's laughing uncontrollably. He doesn't know why we're laughing, though, and it's pissing him off.

"Dammit, Ricky," he says between gales of laughter, "what the fuck are you laughing at? Is there something on my face? Is my zipper down? What the fuck is so funny?"

This just makes me laugh harder. I hold my hands out to him, like a traffic cop.

"No, it's not you." More laughs; I'm almost sobbing now. "Give me a minute to get my shit together and I'll tell you. Honest, man, it's not you."

He doesn't look convinced, but he doesn't look as pissed, either.

It takes a few minutes, a couple stops and starts, but I finally get over the giggles. Meanwhile, Kenneth's gone outside to make sure the garage is secure. After I tell him my story, he'll probably want to stand armed guard.

Oh, shit! I'm giggling again, picturing him out in the yard in his bib-alls with his squirrel gun, watching for interlopers. I doubt if either one of us will be able to sleep for a couple days after the whole deal soaks in. It takes a few more minutes, but I get myself under control just as Kenneth comes back into the kitchen from the back yard.

I'm trying to figure out where to start, when he pops the top on an RC and says, "Let's have it. What the fuck have you been up to? Between the look in your eyes and all the fuckin' hysterics, I'm damned near afraid to ask."

"Honest to God, Kenny, I didn't do anything stupid. I was out in the barn, keepin' outta sight, mindin' my own business," I tell him. "But something happened last night, or I guess it was maybe this morning, and you're not gonna believe this shit."

I start to tell him the whole sordid mess, but he keeps stopping me to ask questions. He must stop me at least twenty times before I even get to the wreck.

Finally, I tell him, "Kenny, please, just let me tell this fuckin' story without any more interruptions, or we'll be here for a week. Please!"

He looks perturbed, but nods. "Just don't leave anything out, dammit!" he barks, and sits back against the wall.

I start where I left off, and he keeps wanting to butt in. I hold out my hands in the traffic-cop signal repeatedly, staving off questions. He finally gets up and gets a note pad and pen from the counter by the door. He sits back down, and starts taking copious notes. It looks like he's already got a few dozen questions he wants answered.

As I predicted, he damned near falls off his chair laughing when I get to the part about the fucking boar scaring the shit out of me. We take a piss break, and I start again. When I get to the part about the wrecked Ford, the dead guys, and what I found in the trunk, he damned near goes apoplectic. His eyes get huge, and he starts peppering me with questions.

"God damn it, Kenny, let me finish this damned

thing, then I'll answer all the questions I have answers to. Please! Really, I need to get this all out while I'm in the mood to tell it. Okay? If you keep making me start over, I might forget something. You don't want that, do you?"

Kenneth Dutton may be a redneck and he may look dumber than Junior Sample, who he actually favors a little, but he isn't a bit slow. He sits there for a second, picks up the notepad and pen, and says, "If I leave you alone, how much longer will it take to tell the rest of it?"

Hell, I don't know. I look at him as seriously as I can and say, "It'll probably take a couple more hours or maybe even longer than that. This shit," I say, waving my hand vaguely toward Molino Road, "is tied in with the shit that got me here in the first place, somehow. It's a hell of a story, buddy." I grin at him, and he grins back.

"Well then, you'd better start tellin' it, don't you think?"

NINE

I wake up on the couch, feeling like someone beat me with a baseball bat. After I finished my tale, Kenneth kept us up until almost sunrise, asking questions while we tied into the JD. The Jack and RCs, combined with the late hours and too much food, have me feeling like shit. Then I remember the events of the previous day, and I spring to my feet. Bad idea: things get kinda spinny for a minute or two. I sit back down, fighting the urge to lie back down and cover my eyes.

As soon as it feels like I should be able to stand without falling down or puking, I get up and walk outside. Yesterday morning's rain is just a memory, other than some puddles. I look at my watch; it's only about seven o'clock. I figure I got about three hours or less of sleep, but there are things that need to be done and decisions to be made. I stand in the yard, breathing in the cool morning air, trying to get my brain working. I'll go into the barn and start reviewing the situation while Dutton gets some sleep. By the time he wakes up, I should be able to think more clearly and we can get some semblance of a plan together.

As I approach the barn, I hear some noise coming through the cracked doors. All of the guns are inside, with everything else. I thought I'd locked the doors, but must've spaced it out in the excitement of the moment. Now what?

I can go get Kenneth, and I'm sure there are some guns in the house, but I really don't want to be responsible for getting him hurt—or worse. Shit! I decide to check out the situation, hopefully without being spotted. I get down on my belly, and crawl up to the doors, trying to be as quiet as I can. Suddenly I feel as sober as I've ever been.

I creep over and ease my head into the opening far enough to sneak a peek into the barn. The first thing I see is a size fourteen boot coming straight for my face. As I try to back up, the door slams into the side of my head, and I hear a startled, "What the fuck?"

I'm trying to get to my feet, but between the blow to the head and the whiskey last night, I'm moving as slowly as bowels at a cheese festival. I look up, expecting to catch another boot upside my noggin, but all I see is Kenneth with this surprised, silly-ass look on his face. He starts laughing, holding onto the door for balance.

"Jesus, Ricky, what the hell are you doin' layin' in the mud? You lose somethin'?"

Another laughing fit, this time accompanied by tears. Christ, talk about adding insult to injury . . .

"Dammit, Kenny, what the fuck did you do that for? I'm feeling bad enough, without having a barn door bounced off my melon."

I stand up, leaning against the side of the barn for support. Puking is now a distinct possibility.

"Jeez, man, I just thought I'd do a little snoopin' while you were passed out. If I'd known you were gonna come out here on your belly, beggin' for breakfast, I'd have just woke you up."

More laughing. This shit is growing tired, fast, but that's what I get for the class of friends I have, I guess.

"Ha ha, asshole," I growl, as I try to see if I can stand up without assistance. Maybe. I'm swaying, a little nauseous, but it seems as if I can stand without support from the barn.

"I was just headin' for the house for some ham and eggs. Want some?" Kenneth is still grinning. Asshole.

"Sure," I say. "Now that I've had my morning beat down, I actually feel hungry."

"Good to see your sense of humor is still intact," Dutton chortles as he watches to see if I'm up to the walk across the yard.

"Yeah, it's just dandy," I retort. "I heard something in the barn, and thought I'd check it out. I guess lying on the ground and peeking around the corner of the door wasn't the best idea, huh?"

"Well, son, it might've worked if I hadn't been headin' out right then. I gave the door a shove with my foot, 'cause I had my hands full, and it smacked into something purty hard. Come to find out, it was your head!" Kenneth is laughing again.

Okay, now I get it. I just happened to be in the perfectly wrong place at the perfectly wrong moment. My head is starting to clear up some, and I realize

Kenneth is carrying some sort of package in his arms.

I ask him, "What's in the bag, bitch?"

Still chuckling, he turns and looks over his shoulder at me. "Just a little something I've been saving for a special occasion, buddy. Hang on until after breakfast, and I'll show you. Look where you're going." He nods his head toward the ground in front of me.

As I look down, I step in a puddle of frigid water about a foot deep. The sudden change in elevation confounds my balance, and I topple over, landing with both hands in a mud hole. They can't seem to find a purchase, and slide out to my sides, planting my face into said mud.

Coming up sputtering and cursing, I vow, "That's fucking IT! No more partying. I've got the whole state of Virginia's law-enforcement types looking for me, not to mention a bunch of pissed off bikers. There's probably a million bucks in that damned barn, some dead assholes killing themselves out back while they're in the middle of some plan involving impersonating some other assholes, and I can't even walk across the fucking yard without falling down. I need to get my shit together, Dutton. If I'm going to survive this shit, I need to straighten my shit out right now!"

He looks at me with his head cocked to one side, a sure sign he's being serious. "All right, then. You're right. We need to get our heads on straight, and figger out what to do next. No more booze or dope until this deal's behind us. Okay?"

He sticks out his big old meaty right paw, and I take it. We both grin, and I say, "What's this 'we' shit, paleface?"

After eating what seems like a couple dozen fresh eggs and a few pounds of home-cured ham with the biggest part of a loaf of bread toasted and slathered in real butter and homemade preserves, we adjourn to the living room with a pot of coffee for Kenneth and a six-pack of RC for me. I never got into the coffee habit, but that doesn't mean I don't need the caffeine.

Shoving the blanket and pillow from last night to one end, I sit down on the couch and ask, "So, what's in the bag?"

Grinning, Kenneth walks over to the kitchen table and unrolls the bundle he's been carrying. It appears to be a sleeping bag made of green canvas with a lining of red fabric with images of hunting dogs printed on it. Wrapped up inside are some cardboard tubes, like large toilet paper rolls. There is something in each of the tubes, and Kenneth pulls the contents from one and hands it to me across the table.

"Hand grenades? Where in God's name did you get hand grenades?"

I'm freaking out a little, but I can't help laughing. He actually has a half-dozen hand grenades wrapped up in a sleeping bag!

"They ain't hand grenades, Ricky," he says, laughing right along with me. "They're flash-bangs. You know, lots of noise and light, made to scare the shit out of people so they can't defend themselves from attack. A cousin of one of my friends is stationed at Redstone Arsenal. He sorta found these."

He's grinning like a loon, and I can't help laughing.

"What's Redstone Arsenal?" I ask him.

"It's an Army base, on the same land as the NASA Marshal Space Flight Center, just on the other side of Huntsvull. Jerry's cousin has miss-placed a few items over the years, and I got these in a horse-trade a few months back. I didn't really have any special idea for 'em, but from the sounds of things, we might be able to use 'em."

I pick up the unwrapped flash-bang, and check it out. It's about five-and-a-half inches long, and is made of a six-sided metal tube with a bigger hex-shaped block on each end. There are holes in the tube—to let the noise and light out, I guess—and there's a small handle sort of deal, along with a couple of safety pins. It probably weighs about half a pound or so, and fits really well in my hand. These might be useful, for sure, if things get hairy.

"Well, these definitely look like they might come in handy, but I need to ask you again. What's this 'we' shit? This is not your fight, and I don't want to be responsible for getting you hurt or killed. I appreciate all the help so far, but when the shit comes down, I want you sitting here, minding your own business. Not involved in some stupid shit that could leave your sis with no family at all."

After this little speech, Kenneth looks at me with that look, the one where one eye is about halfway closed, and the veins on his temples are kinda throbbing. He leans forward, resting his hands on his knees, and just stares at me for a few seconds. Oh crap!

Knowing him as I do, I recognize the signs; he's seriously pissed off, and I'm pretty sure I'm the reason for his attitude.

"If you keep up this silly-assed bullshit about keeping me out of whatever happens next, we're gonna have us a real problem, Ricky," he says quietly, which makes me even more sure he's dead serious.

When Dutton gets quiet and isn't cracking jokes, you'd better pay attention. "You're the closest thing to a brother I ever had, and besides that, you're my friend. Anything that threatens you is my business, period. Get your head around that, and let's figger out what we are gonna do next, butt-head." He's still staring at me, daring me to argue with him.

I'm not sure I can speak, what with the huge lump I have lodged in my throat. This man is the real thing, a brother in the truest sense of the word. Oh well, there doesn't seem to be an option.

"Okay, Kenny, we'll do this together, but we'll do it smart, and we'll put the money somewhere Janie can get to it, and figure out some way to make sure nobody fucks her out of it."

Dutton relaxes his face a little, sits back and almost smiles. "Glad to see you're gonna lissen to reason,

Ricky. I appreciate the thought about takin' care of Janie, and I know just the ol' boy to get 'er done. Jimbob Carter went off to law school to figger out how to be a successful criminal, and I guess he paid attention, 'cause he's the best criminal I know—and a lawyer to boot. If anyone can hide that money, and do it where we can get to it, it's Jimbob. I can't fathom any phones around here bein' tapped, but I'll go catch him at his house early tomorrow mornin' and lay it out for 'im. He's single for about the fifth or sixth time, and he and I are damned tight; I know where some skeletons are piled up, as they say," he says with a wicked grin.

I trust Kenneth, and if he says Jimbob Whoever is okay, then he's okay with me.

Seeing as how things have changed considerably since yesterday (Yesterday? Are you shitting me? It seems like a week ago when I was dragging that damned boar off the road), I've revised my plans and we bring his grungy old Minneapolis Moline tractor in and scrape the pile of dirt back into that ball-busting hole I'd been digging. Kenneth drives back and forth across the hole, packing the fill dirt and scraping more on top until we can't tell it had ever been there.

All the stuff I'd planned to put in the bottom of that hole has been spared, and is still hidden in the box under the bed in the back of Vanna. We move the van into the back of the barn, with the back doors facing the big doors of the barn, so we can keep all the beer boxes and other sundry material inside but access them easily. We head back to the house, making sure it's quiet.

We really don't want to try to explain to Kenneth's neighbors what we're doing and, by the way, who the hell I am.

We clean off the surface of the big dining table and lug it and every decent-sized table from the rest of the house into the barn and arrange them in a crescent-shaped work area behind Vanna.

"From now on, we need to keep the big doors locked, and use the people door," says Kenneth, taking a break on a sack of hog feed leaned up against the side of a small pen in a corner of the barn. "We'll keep it locked, even if we're in here. We don't need any ol' boys comin' in here and seein' all this shit. Right?"

"Absolutely," I reply. I was on the verge of saying the same thing. Great minds think alike, and all that shit. . .

"I'm starvin', dammit. Let's eat something before we get too busy figgerin' what to do next." Leave it to Dutton to have his priorities straight.

TEN

We're sitting down to lunch when a Lincoln County Sheriff's Department cruiser comes idling into the yard.

Dutton tells me, "Go on out on the back porch an' be quiet for a spell. It's Randy Miller, a kid I went to school with. I'll get him out of here before ya know it."

I hustle out to the porch and sit on the floor right next to the open window so I can hear what's being said. I hear the screen door spring and hinges protest as Dutton goes out on the front porch.

"Randy, what are you doin' out here in the sticks? I figgered you'd be wrapped around some grub somewhere this time of day."

"Don't I wish," says the deputy, about the time I hear boots on the front porch. "They got me runnin' to hell and gone tryin' to find anyone who knows anything about that crash the other night. Did you hear anything?"

"I don't know anythin' about a crash. When was this? I just got back from visitin' Janie in Memphis yesterday. What kinda crash you talkin' about?"

"A couple assholes from up 'round Nashville center-punched a big-ass oak tree over on Molino Road on Saturday night or early yesterday mornin'. Killed both of 'em. It was rainin' cats 'n dogs most of the night,

99

and we figure they lost control on the slick road. From the damage, it looks like they were haulin' ass."

"Were they drunk, ya figger?" Dutton asks the deputy, and I'm sure interested in what the local county Mounties think, so I listen carefully.

"Nah, it doesn't appear so, but they had some dope in the trunk, and they were apparently members of some bike gang. The sheriff thinks they were probably headin' south for some big biker party or another."

"So what's the problem, Randy? Why they got you jumpin' through hoops over a couple jackasses killin' themselves by wreckin' in a rainstorm?" I can just imagine Kenneth leaning forward with one eye squinted—his lissenin' pose.

"Ol' Billy Neece has some idea that the car they were in hit somethin' else besides the tree, because of some damage that don't look right to him. He wants us to check with everybody close, to see if they saw or heard anything that might help us close the investigation."

"Hell," Dutton says, "they could've hit something a week ago, or more. Just 'cause there are some other dents don't mean they all happened at once, does it? Mebbe they'd already bounced off somethin' else that night, but kept goin' until they tried to knock that ol' oak down. Why's Sheriff Billy have his panties in a bunch?"

"Hell, Kenneth, I don't know for sure, but it may have to do with him tryin' to get a bigger budget for next year. He may be pilin' up the hours on some stuff to show the county he needs more people and equipment. The way it is, we couldn't do much more investigatin' than just lookin' at the car, because a transformer blew up over by the school, and we had to go over there and deal with traffic and all the parents. Billy gave up on tryin' to keep the crash site secure for a better look, and just had Glenn Marshall come pick up the car and haul it to the impound yard. By the time the rain quit, and the investigators got to checkin' it out, it had been a couple days. I figure Billy may just be tryin' to make it look like the deal didn't get checked out right because of a shortage of manpower and equipment, instead of bad management of the people and stuff we do have.

"Well, anyhow, you weren't here, so I can cross you off the list and I might get finished up by tonight if I get lucky. Oh, hey . . . how's Janie doin'? I haven't seen her in a coon's age."

"She's still fightin', puttin' on a brave face. You know. I just hope somethin' comes along to help keep her there, where they take such good care of 'er."

I vow to myself as Dutton is saying this that we will definitely make sure Janie is taken care of, no matter what happens to the two of us.

"Kenneth, I believe the Good Lord will find a way to take care of Janie, and you take care of yourself, you hear? I'll see you later."

The deputy leaves the porch, his boots echoing on

the old wooden steps. Kenneth hollers at him before he reaches the car.

"Hey, Randy, you want a sandwich or two and a sodie pop to take along with you? I was just gonna eat when you drove up."

My head is still throbbing, and I've got a splinter or two in my ass from the old planks the porch floor is made of, and now Dutton is inviting the deputy into the house for lunch!

"Thanks, Kenneth, but I've got a bucket of chicken and a cooler fulla pop and ice water in the car. Have a good 'un."

"You too, Randy. See ya."

As the crunch of the deputy's boots gets dimmer, I hear Dutton open the screen door and then the screech and slam as he lets it close behind him. I hear the cruiser start up, and after a couple seconds, it slowly makes a half-circle in the yard and idles out of earshot.

"Awright, he's gone, Ricky," Dutton calls as he leans around the door jamb. "Let's eat. I'm hungry enough to eat the ass-end of a possum."

I'm not quite that hungry, but I say, "Sounds like a plan. I think your buddy the deputy should leave us alone. Sounds like they're just strokin' it, and if they don't get any help soon they'll just close it up as a traffic accident. That suits me just fine."

"Yeah, ol' Billy's probably hagglin' with the town council about getting more money, just like Randy figgers. I doubt if he'll get too shook up about a couple of greasy fuckers from outta town killin' themselves while drivin' like fools down Molino Road in a toad-strangler. Now that they know I wasn't here, they shouldn't be back. Now, how's about we have that lunch, then get down to business?"

We put a pretty good dent in what's left of the ham, and eat a pot of beans that was hiding in the fridge, fueling up for a busy afternoon. Dutton sets a couple of steaks in the sink to thaw out for supper, and we head back out to the barn to do some planning. Dutton is carrying a cooler with a dozen RCs, a big hunk of cheddar cheese, and a loaf of bread in it.

"Can't be thinkin' on an empty stomach, can we?" he asks, winking.

Setting down the cooler, Kenneth unlocks the door and heads into the barn. I look around the yard, and satisfied that nobody's around, pick up the cooler and follow him in and close the door.

"Lock it," says Dutton.

I say, "Give me a second, dammit."

I lock the door, and walk over to where the make-shift work area is, setting the cooler on the table farthest from Vanna. We each take out an RC.

Popping the top on his, Dutton asks me, "So, have you been thinking of what we need to do next?"

Good question. I've actually been trying to give it some thought, but between the hangover and other distractions, I haven't made much progress.

"Well, I think we need to figure out a way to get

the information about the S&S assholes and their cargo to Chief and the boys. I'd feel better lettin' them know about it. I know it probably seems silly to you, but I'd just feel better."

I realize my actions against the club will cause them a bunch of trouble, but that's a personal deal. It's because of my own feelings. Letting another club pull some sneaky shit against the PnB just somehow seems different.

"Just in case they've had some contact with the Tidewater chapter and my name came up, we need to figure out a way to do this that won't give them any idea of where to find me . . . us. We need to have a powwow with Jimbob and get the money taken care of, so if anything bad happens we'll know Janie gets it. And, most of all, we need to make sure nothing bad happens."

I look at Kenneth, and he's nodding his big ol' head, grinning.

"I like the sound of that," he says. "If anything bad is gonna happen, it may as well happen to the other guys."

"Okay then, where's the best place for us to leave the boxes of disguises, maps, and shit where Chief can get to them, without giving him any idea of where we are or which direction we came from? You know this area. I don't, so I'm gonna let you decide on a drop-off point, directions to it, and that sort of thing. We need to make it appear that the stuff came into Huntsville from a different route than it actually did, so they won't be able to know where to look, if they're looking for me."

"Ricky, you seem to be forgetting that the assholes got killed in a car crash right behind this here house, and the local newspaper will sure as hell have a story in it when it comes out Wednesday. They'll make a big deal outta the fact that a couple nasty ol' bikers carrying dope got killed on Molino Road. I'm sure Wanda will make a big thing about the name of the club and the fact that they were heading south from Nashville. It won't take a rocket scientist to figger out that they were the ones bringin' all this crap down to Huntsvull."

Shit, shit, shit!

"Damn, what was I thinking of? Of course, Chief will be aware of where the stuff in the boxes came from! I don't doubt that he'll be able to hire a snitch to tell him about the plan, and the money will come up, too," I tell Dutton, feeling like an idiot.

I think for a moment, and a story begins to take shape.

"How about this? I'll tell him I was riding south from east of Nashville, trying to get to Huntsville without running into the law. I can say I was at a rest stop and saw two carloads of S&S boys stop, head to the restrooms, then load back up into a pair of late-model sedans. I'll tell him I heard one of the drivers holler at the other car to follow him, that he knew the back way into Huntsville."

I settle in now, enjoying my own storytelling skills. "Since I wasn't wearing my colors and I was driving a black Chevy pickup I had stolen and was pretending to be asleep on a park bench, they didn't pay any attention to me.

"Then I'll tell him that one of the guys in the second car said something about 'fixing' the fucking PnB when they got there, and the little guy driving the first car laughed and said, 'Fuckin' A,' and proceeded to take off in a shower of gravel. The other car followed, and as soon as I figured it was safe, I followed, far enough back to not seem to be tailing them.

"I'll tell Chief that it was later, close to Fayetteville in a fuckin' downpour, when the first car ran off the road and hit a big ol' tree. I'd been back quite a ways, letting them go, when I saw the second car's brake lights come on and stay on. It went around a corner to the left and the lights disappeared, so I stopped and turned off my lights. I pulled off the road into a little driveway and got out of the truck. I ran down to the corner, slowed to a walk. I could hear yelling, so I slowed down even more and snuck up close enough to see the first car wrapped around a tree, and the guys from the second car hollering and unloading a bunch of what looked like beer boxes from the trunk.

"Then . . . let's see . . ." I have to think for another minute before going on. "Okay, here's the rest of the story: All of a sudden, a car came from the other direction, and they all piled into their car, except for a big dude who pointed a shotgun at the approaching car. He walked up to the driver's window and yelled in no uncertain terms for whoever was in the car to get the hell out of there, and to keep their fuckin' mouths shut. The approaching car, an old station wagon, passed me haulin' ass, and the big guy got back into the second S&S car. I'll say I guess they were spooked, afraid more traffic would come by, 'cause they hauled ass without finishing emptying the wrecked car's contents. I ran back to the truck, pulled out and took off after them.

"As they approached Fayetteville, they turned off onto Highway 10 and followed it south for twenty miles or so. There was enough traffic that I stayed back a ways and they never noticed me. They turned into a little flea-bag motel next to an intersection, and I stopped back down the road a ways, shutting off the lights and engine. After a half hour or so, the three guys came outside, and two of them walked across the street to a little dive with a Bud sign in the window. The third guy, probably a prospect, was left to watch the car. I took the lug wrench out of the truck, snuck around the back of the motel, and came up on the prospect's blind side.

"I made sure there wasn't anyone outside the bar, and no traffic coming from either direction, then quietly snuck up on the dude while he was tokin' on a joint. I dented his dome with the lug wrench, then jimmied open the trunk. I was in a hurry, hoping nobody would drive up, and worried that the two assholes across the street would come to check on their brother. I opened a couple of the boxes, and was surprised at what they held. I ran back to the truck, drove, without lights, up to the motel.

"Afraid I'd be spotted at any minute, I threw the open boxes into the truck.

"I didn't bother going back for the rest, because traffic was coming from town, a whole line of cars. Must've been a baseball game or something. I hauled ass, hid at an old girlfriend's place in Hazel Green and waited to make sure I hadn't been spotted before getting in touch with Chief. I was afraid the cops would be watchin' the clubhouse for any sign of the Tidewater PnB brothers. The pickup is hidden in an old abandoned garage, and the boxes are in a safe place." Whew! What a tale!

"Jesus, Ricky, you spin a damned fine yarn! That's pretty damned good, and we can write it down and study it. If we need to, we'll tweak it a little bit. That's a good start. If it works, we might get though this without any serious hassle. I have some pretty good ideas of hiding places we can mention that fit the bill, so we should be able to set up a drop, get the hell outta there, and be gone before they know who to look for or where to look for them. Now, let's see if I can round up Jimbob Carter and find out what he thinks is the best way to take care of the cash."

We decide the best thing to do is count the money to see exactly what we're dealing with before Kenneth goes into town to talk to Jimbob, the crooked lawyer. I'll stay here and go through the boxes and consolidate the important stuff into two boxes, to match my story about how I came into possession of them.

We open all three boxes, and one of them ends up being full of bundles of twenties. The one I opened in the rain is full of stacks of fifties, but the last box we open is the one I hadn't gotten around to. It's chock full of hundred-dollar bills, used and non-sequential.

"Holy fuck, Ricky!" Dutton is thoroughly freaking out, and I'm right there with him. "There's gotta be a million bucks here, if there's a hundred," he says, sitting back on his hog feed sack and rubbing his forehead with a bandana he's pulled from his back pocket.

"At least a million, maybe even two," I reply, starting to feel flushed and light-headed.

We make eye contact, and it's all over. We start laughing so hard I start hiccupping and snorting while Kenneth is hooting and crying at the same time. It takes a few minutes, but we finally get our collective shit together. We're both grinning like the village idiot, and are probably in what could honestly be called shock.

"Well, I guess we oughtta count it," Kenneth says, trying not to laugh.

"Yeah, I guess you're right. It wouldn't do to just guess, since you're gonna be talkin' business with a lawyer and all," I answer.

We both start up again, and laugh until our sides hurt. Dutton gets up and walks around the barn, waving his hand at me to stop. I'm seriously trying, but between the adrenaline and the silliness of the situation, I'm having a hard time. After a couple more minutes, we finally get straightened out again, and start emptying the contents of the boxes into separate piles on three different tables.

"I figger each bundle has the same amount of bills in it as the rest of 'em. We just need to count one bundle of each denomination, then multiply that amount by the number of bundles," says Kenneth.

I agree. "That sounds good to me, buddy. I'll start over on this end and do the twenties on this table, if you wanna do the fifties on that one on your end."

"Good deal. Don't bug me for awhile, and for God's sake don't make me laugh. If I have to start over, I'll kick yer ass up around yer ears," exclaims Kenneth. I start to giggle, but quickly get it reined in.

"Absolutely," I tell him.

I clear off a spot at one end of the table nearest my end, and pick up a rubber-banded bundle of twenties. Pulling off the rubber band, I start counting bills. I count the stack twice, seeing as how the bills don't lay nice and flat like new ones. There are one hundred bills in the stack, so with a little multiplication I decide that there's two thousand bucks in each bundle. I start stacking bundles at one end of the table, in stacks five high. When I'm done, there are sixty stacks, adding up to three hundred bundes. I pick up a pencil and quickly do the math . . . and do it again.

"Holy shit!' I say, before I can control myself.

I don't look at Kenneth, and he doesn't say anything. According to my math, there is six hundred thousand dollars in twenties on the table in front of me. I look at Dutton, but he's busy writing figures on a note pad. He seems to be perplexed, re-doing his figures over and over. He finally puts down his pen, straightens up, and looks at me. He's not smiling. He looks damned near shell-shocked.

"Ricky, how much dough is in that pile of twenties?' he asks me.

"Well, if my math is sound, there is six hundred thousand dollars right here," I say, my voice climbing the scale as I talk. "What about you? How many fifties are in that pile?"

Kenneth looks at his notes again, then looks me in the eye and says, "A mil-and-a-half, Ricky . . . a fuckin' million-and-a-half. I did the sums five times, and got the same amount each time. We're over two mil, without even counting the Franklins."

I look at his figures and compare them to mine; both boxes hold three hundred bundles of a hundred bills in each one. I do the math for the hundreds, assuming there are the same amount of bills in that box as in the other two. The answer is astounding . . . three million bucks in that box alone. I slide the paper over to Dutton, and let him check it out. He finally looks up and meets my gaze.

"Ricky, what the fuck were those assholes doing

with a little over five million bucks in the trunk of their car? It couldn't have been just a pay-off for some monkey business impersonating a bunch of bikers in Huntsvull. There's something fuckin' huge goin' on."

I just swallow a couple times, then say, "Hell if I know, Kenny. I'm not sure we'll ever know, unless the shit hits the fan. I hope we never know . . . I just want to get this other shit to the PnB in Huntsville, and get the fuck outta here. I hate to say it, but if there is any way in hell you get tied into this, you may need to get outta here, too, at least for awhile."

"No shit, Sherlock," he says, looking off into space.

I can imagine what he's thinking. "We'll make sure they never find Janie, buddy. I swear to God, they'll never harm a fuckin' hair on her head."

He slowly turns toward me, and the look on his face is scary. "You got that straight, Ricky. Anything happens to that little girl and there will be dead people everywhere. D-E-D, DEAD."

As Kenneth is driving off to go see Jimbob, I lock myself in the barn and start laying out all the contents of the beer boxes from Bubba Andretti's trunk. The stuff in the box with Chief's fake colors is arranged on one table, the contents of the box with Polly's vest go on another. Besides the cutoffs, guns, and disguises, there are a couple of small butane torches, four Bowie-style hunting knives, a couple maps, and a little notebook with some coded entries that I can't begin to understand.

Apparently, some hard-cases are planning to impersonate Chief, Polly, and four other PnB members, while taking care of some heavy-duty business. What their plan is, I can't begin to know, but the five million dollars involved indicates that whatever it is, it's serious.

I sit and drink an RC, munching on cheese and homemade bread. The only thing I can imagine the two outlaw clubs would think was worth five million bucks is meth . . . a huge quantity of meth. It's possible someone in the Huntsville area is encroaching on the PnB's territory, and the S&S thinks if they take out the competition while wearing PnB colors, they might eliminate both the local PnB and the other meth manufacturer. Actually, I hope that's the case, because it would serve everyone right. The meth supply in this area would be seriously reduced, and the people making it would be dead, or in jail. The only downside to this scenario is that the S&S gets away with murder and the dope. I can't let that happen.

If I tell Chief about the S&S interlopers and give him the boxes full of disguises and weapons, there will be war. Whether or not the PnB figures out the coded notebook and actually learns what the S&S plan is, they'll start killing S&S members in bunches. That will provoke retaliation, and things will get downright dangerous for members of both clubs. This makes me smile; I've been second-guessing my motives for telling Chief about the boxes and all, thinking that I really don't owe any of these people anything. Starting a shooting war between the two clubs is more to my liking. I just need to find a way to make sure it gets a good start!

I'll tell Chief the tale I cooked up about how I came to be in possession of the beer boxes, and claim to be in hiding from the law as the reason for not wanting a face-to-face meet. They'll still be thinking of me as the big dude with a braid down to his ass and a beard you could hide a nest of owls in. Even if I get sloppy and get spotted, hopefully nobody will put my new look together with the Hammer they remember.

Maybe Dutton and I can speed up the action a little. I'll suggest that the late Bubba Andretti, the esteemed S&S dwarf, was going to be impersonating Polly, so whatever they had planned was going to be executed in an area where the colors and fake members' hairstyles would be recognizable to people who were pretty sure they knew what they were looking at, but at a distance that would prevent a close-up look at their faces.

By the detail involved in the fake Chief's disguise, the person playing that part would probably be the only one who might be able to pass inspection at any semblance of close quarters. Chief's imagination will fill in the blanks, and Dutton and I will accelerate things with some of the flash-bangs and some well-timed phone calls. Feeling kind of smug, I sit back against

Kenneth's hog feed sack, after checking the doors, and take a little well-deserved nap.

ELEVEN

Dutton's Barn
May 14, 1990

I awake to the sound of a key turning in the lock on the small door. I'm instantly awake, on my feet, and have my nine pointed at the door before it's fully open.

Dutton's voice comes from behind the steel door. "It's me, Ricky, so don't go shootin' me."

I relax and tell him, "Come on in, Kenny. I've got some thinkin' done, and I think you'll like what I have in mind. How'd things go with Jimbob?"

Kenneth's voice comes from the other side of the door again. "I'll be right back and tell you what's happenin'. Don't close the door."

I remain standing at the far end of the tables, just in case there's someone out there with Kenneth. He comes through the door with a couple sacks of smoked pork loin, biscuits, and mashed potatoes and gravy, if my nose is correct. He sets the bags on one of the empty tables, and grins at me.

"I figgered we'd need some sustenance if we're gonna be out here much longer, so I stopped at Whitt's for a small repast to go."

I laugh. "We need to invest in that place. We'd be our own best customers."

"Yeah," Kenneth says, "they think I'm eatin' all this myself, or I got a fat girlfriend stashed out here."

I dig a couple RCs out of the cooler, and we each make a plate and sit on the edge of a table. As has become our normal routine, we eat without much in the way of meaningful conversation.

We've pretty well emptied both sacks and Kenneth asks, "You ready to do some brain-storming?"

"I will be as soon as I make a quick trip to the house and make use of the facilities," I reply.

I figure I'll take the cooler with me and replenish the ice and add a few more RCs.

"Good idea" says Dutton. "I'll hold down the fort and take my turn when you get back."

When we're both back in the barn, the first thing I do is to remind Dutton (and myself) that I am no longer Ricky.

"Kenneth, we both need to remember that I am now John Robert Clark, or Johnny, or JR, or whatever we decide will be easiest to remember, so we don't screw up and blow our cover."

He kinda squinches up one eye, and looks at me as if he's sizing up a hog at the sale barn.

"Well, John Robert is definitely outta the question, son," he says. "I'm kinda partial to something that'll roll off my southern tongue nice 'n easy. I think you need to be Johnny Bob, or better yet, Jonnybob, all run together. It'll seem natural around here, and when this shit is over and we hightail it to parts unknown, it'll fit in with our accents and all. Whattaya think about that?"

I somehow knew this was coming, given Kenneth's

penchant for calling everyone by their given and middle names, but it actually makes sense; it'll be easy to remember and, like he says, won't sound out of place, given our way of speaking. But I can't let him think it was that easy.

"Jeez, Kenny, you serious? Jonnybob Clark? If I'm gonna get hung with a moniker like that, I figger it's only fair that we come up with something equally awesome for you. What's your middle name, anyhow? I don't remember ever hearing it."

He just grins, and lets me have it. "I don't have one, son. My old man had a thing about 'em; neither of us kids got a middle name, and it actually was a sore spot with me for a long time when I was a kid. I think your idea's a good one, though, about maybe making it a tad harder on anyone lookin' for us. Remember what y'all called me when we were boots in the Navy?"

"Junior," I say, laughing out loud. I'd forgotten all about that.

"Yeah," Dutton says, "good ol' Junior. Y'all had a lot of fun with that, and nobody around here calls me by that name, so it shouldn't point anyone in our direction if someone hears you call me that."

It makes sense, but the thought of us introducing ourselves to people as Jonnybob and Junior is too much! The thing is, it'll work; until we cross the Mississippi, most people won't even flinch.

"Okay Junior, nice to meetcha. My name's Jonnybob Clark. I think we're gonna be good friends."

"Now that we've got that nonsense behind us, whattaya say we get down to business?" asks Kenn . . . er . . . Junior, and I have to agree that it's a good idea.

"Let's do it. I may be deranged, but I actually think this might be fun, in a scary way."

Dutton/Junior laughs out loud, and counters, "Oh, you're deranged all right. But I guess I am, too, 'cause I think you're probably right."

We get right to work, making sure all the debris from supper is off the tables and chairs. I move the trash barrel as far as I can from where we'll be working, so we don't get hungry smelling the leftover sauce on the paper.

"Okay, supposing we use the yarn you dreamed up, what's our move?" asks Dutt . . . Junior.

I don't have a ready answer. I probably should've thought more and napped less, but this undercover stuff is new to me. I used to do just what needed done, then dealt with the backlash. The club had my back, so I never thought too much about operating from the shadows. Getting right in people's faces is part of what makes outlaws successful; fear is a powerful motivator.

"We want the PnB to think someone is musclin' in on their turf, and, if necessary, is ready to do them serious damage. They need to get the boxes with the disguises and stuff in their possession, and we need to put enough distance between the pickup spot and wherever we decide to hit them that they won't think I had anything to do with it.

"Actually, we need them to believe that Hammer wasn't involved, nor Jonnybob. Hopefully, they'll never even hear his name. I think we need to scout out some neighborhoods in Huntsville that fit the profile for drug dealing, and pick a couple or three ambush spots, then do some studyin' on 'em until we decide the best spot for the hit." I figure that is a good start. "Whattaya think, Junior? Is that a plan?"

"Sounds damned good to me, Jonnybob," says my buddy Junior, winking at me. "Like you said earlier, I know some places in Huntsvull that fit the bill, and I know some lowlifes that'll be able to give me some added help, if we need it. We're gonna need to get out of here, drive down there, and do some snoopin' without anyone payin' any attention to us. I think this van of yours is the way to go, seein' as how it's in your new name and you've got a license and all that matches your new identity. The Maryland tags might catch someone's attention, but I figger we'll just take 'em off the night of the fracas, and put 'em back on as soon as we're in the clear. In the meantime, we'll just find us a mud hole and muddy up the van, plates and all. It won't look outta place, considerin' the way it rained for a couple days."

This sounds good to me, and I've actually been thinking along the same lines. The biggest concern is the money. What shall we do with it while we're driving around Huntsville, not to mention back and forth between here and there? I voice my concerns, and Junior has a ready answer.

"We'll just leave the shit right here in the barn. It'll be easy to hide the boxes under some of the shit piled up in the loft. You've gotta remember that nobody has any reason to come snoopin' around here, yet. I've never had anything come up missin' since I was a little kid, when the whole family lived here. I'll tell the neighbors that I'm headin' back down to Memphis for a couple days to take care of some paperwork for Janie, and they'll make sure nobody comes around.

"The trick will be gettin' the van outta here without anyone seein' it and wonderin' where it came from. Once we get it to the highway, we'll be in the clear. I'll park my truck in here, so anyone who does come by will figger I'm still gone."

I like this plan, and I really am starting to get excited. We might just pull this off! "We'll hole up in a motel somewhere, and I bet we can even find a decent barbecue place, so we don't starve," I say, grinning at this crazy bastard I like so much. "After all, we need to keep our strength up so we can carry off all that loot when this is over."

It hits me that we still haven't talked about what Jimbob, the crooked lawyer, had to say about the money. "Hey, I got busy eatin' and plannin' our trip to Huntsville, and forgot to ask you what Jimbob had to say. Does he think he can do us any good?"

"He had quite a few different ideas, and got right down to business. I've gotta say, he's kinda sweet on Janie, and wants to do the best he can. He knows some ol' boys in Atlanta that do this sorta thing all the time, and he thinks we could probably end up with a couple million after they launder it. It don't sound like much, but Jimbob swears it's as good a deal as we'll get. The money we end up with will be squeaky clean, and he's got a plan to make it look like there's a family trust or something that he just found out about that will take care of Janie's bills."

Junior—I still have a hard time thinking of Kenneth as Junior—makes a good point. We can't just show up with a sack full of money and give it to Janie's caregivers. It seems Jimbob is, indeed, a good crooked lawyer to have on our side.

"Yeah," I say, "but this was never for the money. If we can make sure Janie's set up for life, then I'll be happy as a pig in shit. If we end up with enough cash to start over somewhere safe, that'll be a bonus. I can't tell you enough how much I regret getting you into this. I know you're dead set on doing this, and I'm grateful. I just wish it could've happened without putting you at risk."

"Nobody's at risk yet," says my portly pal. "If we're smart, and even a little lucky, we might pull this off without any of those assholes knowin' who hit 'em. If so, things might get back to normal around here fairly fast. If not, we'll deal with it. I am not about to let you do this on your own. Get used to the fact that we're a team. I think we should go get some rest."

TWELVE

I head from the barn to the house, summoned by the Allman Brothers' Greatest Hits at about six a.m. Junior is in a good mood, and is banging around in the kitchen.

"Hey, Jonnybob, how d'ya want your eggs?" He hollers at me to be heard over the music.

Instead of competing with Dickie Betts's guitar, I walk into the kitchen and scope out what's on the menu for breakfast. There's a big package of fresh pork sausage, a basket of eggs, a loaf of bread, a tub of homemade butter, and a jar of raspberry preserves, along with a sixer of RC on the counter—all the tables are in the barn.

"Over easy, I guess," I tell the chef. "You want me to do anything? I'll make patties, if you want. Then I can make the toast while you're fryin' the eggs after the sausage is done."

Chef Junior grins a big grin, and says, "Do that, Jonnybob, old son, and we'll have us a big ol' breakfast before we get down to some serious plannin' and packin' for our little road trip."

We spend the next few minutes cooking and preparing a meal that should keep us full until lunch, at least. Maybe lunch time tomorrow. When everything is ready, we head into the living room and get settled in as best we can without any tables to set shit on. As usual, we eat in relative silence, other than the stereo, which Bubba blessedly has toned down some.

When everything is pretty much gone, we clean up and take the remains to the kitchen. I fill the sink and wash the dishes. Drying them and putting them where they belong keeps Junior busy, and he waits until the chores are done.

"Now, let's get a plan together and figger out a timetable for this assault. How's that sound?"

"Let's do it," I say. "I still think we should maybe stay in the barn and keep the noise down until we split, just in case. If someone came driving up while the music's playin', we'd get caught with our pants down. I dig the music, but I think we should go back to being careful. It should only be another day or two."

"You're right, JB," says my buddy, looking a little sheepish. "We'll be able to play the damned music as loud as we want when this deal's over. I just got a little carried away."

He walks over and turns off the stereo and the silence is total. We both look at one another, and break into smiles.

Back in the barn, we start packing the disguises back into their respective boxes. I add a small notation on each one, to keep track of which gear is in which container. We talk it over, and decide to leave the flash-bangs behind on this trip. We're just going to do some recon, and hopefully won't need them. I will take my nine mil, and I'll give the .45 I found in the Crown Vic to Cousin Junior. We can't be traipsing around the forest unarmed, after all.

I grab a stack of twenties, and shove it into a pocket of my denim jacket. I think about it for a couple seconds, then toss another bundle of twenties to Ken—Junior, dammit! "Just in case we decide we need something else, we'll have some cash to get whatever it is," I explain.

Junior's looking at me with a question in his eyes. "Good idea, but there's what, two grand in each bunch? Mebbe we oughtta take along a little more, for unexpected shit. Whattaya think? Mebbe a pack of fifties, just for insurance?"

I grab up a bundle of fifties out of the box they're in, and crawl up into the back of Vanna. I already removed the screws holding the bed to the box, thinking I was gonna bury a bunch of the stuff in it, so I lift up a corner and drop in the bundle of fifties. Thinking about it, I call Junior over and ask him to help me get the mattress and plywood out of the van.

"What're you up to, Ric—fuck! I mean Jonnybob. What've you got goin' on in that devious little brain of yours?"

I laugh at the slip . . . it's not like I haven't been doing the same thing. "I think I'll get the bike parts outta here, maybe put it back together and either use it for part of the operation or even as a decoy. It'd make a fuckin' great getaway vehicle, and I might try to figger out a way to use it for the extra mobility."

"That might work pretty good," says Junior, scratching his big ol' noggin. "Down in BT or Mason Court, where we'll probably try to set up the deal, that scooter would definitely give you an edge over cars. We'll definitely want to spend some time driving around whichever area we pick, so you can get some different escape routes figgered out."

"Good fuckin' idea, Junior, old son. Now grab hold of this crap and help me get it out of here so we can unload the rest of the stuff from this box. The space may come in handy."

Junior grins as he grabs the mattress and asks me, "How many dead bodies will fit in there, do ya figger? Six or eight, mebbe?"

"Christ, I don't know. I really hope we don't need to haul any bodies around, dead or alive. I was thinking more along the lines of the flash-bangs, Molotov cocktail fixins, shit like that. You're kinda scarin' me, bud."

At this he rears back and laughs his ass off. "Finally, I'm the one scarin' you, not the other way around!"

Whatever. "Okay, fine," I tell him. "Set that down somewhere out of the way and give me a hand with the rest of this crap."

We spend an hour or so unloading the bike parts and arranging them in order of assembly, putting the box of tools I'd included under the big table.

"We'll need to grab some engine and transmission oil, a can of bearing grease, and stuff like that at a bike shop while we're in Huntsville, and before we actually pull the job. I'll steal an Alabama tag off of a Harley so there won't be any way to tie the scooter to us. If, for some reason, the cops do get their hands on it, they'll find out it belongs to Hammer Thorssen, not John Robert Clark, aka Jonnybob."

"Good idea, son. Now, how about some lunch? I'm starvin'!"

Damned Junior could eat like a fuckin' pig, all day, every day, I do believe. But, then again, I might be a little hungry, myself. What the hell.

"You got it, Junior. When we get done, we can get loaded up and get ready to head out after dark, so nobody will see the van leave. If they do, hopefully they'll figger someone got lost and not worry about it."

After eating a fairly small (for us) lunch and taking a two-hour nap, we're back in the barn. The plywood and mattress are back in place, with a couple screws holding it down, just in case something happens and someone decides to check out the back of the van. We've each got a small bag packed with the necessities for two or three days. While we were inside, Junior called a couple of his neighbors and told them he needed to go back to Memphis for a few days, and no, thank you so very much, there'll be no need to check on the Dutton Place. Everything is locked up tight, and Kenneth didn't bother putting in a garden this spring. Yeah, keepin' up with the damned doctors and lawyers is a full-time job, and just tuckers a soul plumb out. Tell yer ol' man I said hi. Thanks again, and have a good 'un.

We were going to wait until dark to leave, but the neighbors were nice enough to provide information about their family members' activities, so we figure we'll go for it. If we get on Molino Road before anyone sees Vanna, we'll be good as gold. We pack some notebooks, Junior's Polaroid camera, pens, and pencils into a small cardboard box and toss it inside, between the seats. We've also got a small cooler packed with a sixer of RC and some hunks of cheese and jerky. It's about a forty-five minute drive, so we should be okay until we get to Huntsville before we need to find somewhere to eat.

THIRTEEN

I fish a small piece of paper out of my wallet and find Chief's phone number. I dial it and a female answers on the third ring. "Hello," she says.

I ask, "Is Chief around?"

She immediately gets cagey, not recognizing my voice and wondering if it might be the cops. This number isn't widely known, and I'm sure the mess in Tidewater has had the phone lines buzzing.

"No Chief here," she says.

I figure I'd better not let her hang up, so I make sure she knows I know who I'm talking to.

"Polly, I realize it's been a long time, and that the phone might need an exterminator, but I need to talk to Mikey, and I need to do it pretty soon. I just came from The Beach, and have some news from up there, as well as some shit being planned by some assholes in Nashville. Have him think about a place I can call him later today, where there's no chance of an eavesdropper. I'll call you back and get the number. By the time someone decides where that phone is, we'll be done."

I hope she buys this line, and I'm rewarded with, "Who is this? We have a lot of friends from The Beach."

I think for a second of a way to let her know who I am without using the name Hammer. Oh, yeah . . .

"Remember when I tie-wrapped your braid to the bleachers at the flat-track races in Elizabeth City?" She gets it, right away.

"You asshole! I 'bout scalped myself when I tried to stand up." At least she's laughing, so maybe she'll cooperate. "I'll personally go tell your friend that you're wanting to talk. I've got a number to call in fifteen minutes . . . they'll never get paper for it that fast. He'll be there, waiting for your call. I hope to see you while you're in the area. Maybe we can hit some bars."

Like hell, I think. I'm not going anywhere near these folks, at least not where they can see me. "Sounds good, but I'm not actually in Rocket City. I'll give the big man a call, and see what happens. Thanks, Polly."

She's magnanimous now, the lady of the manor. "You're welcome. Here's the number; got a pencil?" I tell her I do, and she gives it to me. "Watch yer ass," she tells me, and I tell her I'd rather watch hers. "You just might get a chance soon, cowboy," she replies, and we both hang up laughing.

I sober up right away, tell Junior what's up, and look at the clock on the wall.

Fifteen minutes later, I dial the number Polly gave me, and a gruff voice answers, "Hammer?" Let's get right to it, shall we?

I answer, "Yeah . . . it's me. How're you doing, Chief?"

"I'm doin' pretty good, but from what I can find out, y'all up north have had the shit hit the fan. Are you in town?"

There's no way I'm letting Chief or anyone else know where I am. I still don't know what my status is with the club. Are they looking for me because they know my role in the house fire or meth bust? Do they just want to find me and hide me to minimize the danger to me (and them)? I can't tell anything by the tone of Chief's voice, so I'll just have to see what I can find out.

"I'm shacked up out in the country, not too far away. Have the cops been around the clubhouse lookin' for me?"

Chief just chuckles, and says, "Yeah, those numbnuts cocksuckers were there a couple times, once with some paper. They obviously didn't find any of you from up north, and the few things they did see weren't included on the warrant, so it wasn't too bad. They're a constant pain in our ass, but we've been able to make some progress with a few of them. Polly said you were in a hurry to talk. What's up?"

"Chief, I was on a bunch of back-roads for the last few days, and came across some shit going down that I knew I had to let you know about." I proceed to spin my yarn, and by the time I'm done, Chief is apoplectic.

"Those motherfuckers!" he bellows. "We'll cut their fuckin' nuts off! The deal with the cutoffs and wigs is bogus . . . I wonder what kind of evil shit those assholes are up to. I'll get some people scouting around, see if we can turn up the other two you saw with the prospect you brained. I need to see all that shit in the boxes; when can we meet somewhere?"

I do some quick mental arithmetic, and say, "I'm workin' on my truck, and need to find some different plates and give it a shot of color. How about tomorrow night or Thursday some time?"

Chief doesn't like this much. "Why can't we get this done tonight? I'll come find you, if you're truck isn't good to go."

But I don't much care if he likes it, or not. "Chief, I've got a whole bunch of people looking for me, my name and picture are on the TV, and I'm just gonna stay put for another day or so. I'll get this done as soon as I can, and I'll give you a call. If I know where you want me to be, I'll just call your place and tell Polly or whoever answers what time I'll be there. That way, even if the cops are listenin', they won't know where to look for us."

"Remember where the club's titty bar is? We changed the name, and had to pull some shit to keep it open, but it's still in the same place, just with a new name. It's called Chubby's now."

The "gentleman's club" Chief is talking about is more of a whore house, but I guess they can't legally call it that. There's a main stage downstairs in a two-story pole-barn, with private rooms in the back and some VIP rooms on the top floor. You can get laid, blown, ridden like a donkey, or about anything else you want for the right amount of cash upstairs. You can also buy lots of dope, if you know whom to ask.

"Down by that water tower, right? On that something-or-other Parkway, next to the fireworks place."

There's a fireworks outlet next door to the north, and a small bike shop a block or so to the south of the club, along with a sign shop with a fenced yard full of old signs, sign frames, and a couple of old bucket-trucks. There's also a liquor store about a quarter mile away—bikes, liquor, naked women, drugs, and fireworks—what else could a man ask for?

"Yeah," Chief says, "that's it. Damned near to the end of the Memorial Parkway, on the east side of Redstone. Between the bikers and military types, we do pretty damned good. Every so often some college boys wander in, but as long as they don't get stupid it's okay. Polly's brother Virgil is runnin' the place for us, and we've got some pretty fine pussy workin' for us, too. I'll set you up with any of 'em you fancy after we get our business done. Give me a holler when you're ready, but for God's sake make it soon."

I agree to this, say my goodbyes, and hang up.

I'm sweating, but grin at Junior. "He bought it," I tell the portly one. "They even named a titty bar after you; they call it Chubby's!"

He snorts and flips me off, but he's smiling, too.

We make sure we've got everything in the van, and Junior opens up the big doors. I jump in Vanna and start her up. After a couple minutes, I back out and Junior closes the doors and bars them from the inside. While Vanna's warming up a little, we make sure everything is stacked and covered up with old feed sacks and such. We don't expect anyone to be in here while we're gone, but we go through the motions.

The money is in plastic garbage bags, hidden under the straw in the loft.

We go out, making sure the lights are off and all the doors are locked. Getting into the passenger's seat, Junior grins at me and points at the windshield. "And we're off!"

Laughing, I supply the rest of the silly old joke. "Like a turd o' hurdles."

I head down the two-track, watching for anyone who might wonder who's driving around out here. Without seeing so much as a possum, we make it to the paved road and turn toward Highway 431.

We turn south on the highway and pop open a couple of RCs. We're starting to unwind a little. Not a soul has paid the least attention to us, and we'll be in Huntsville by six o'clock, easy. It won't get dark for another three hours or more, so we can get a motel room, get some supper, and still drive through the neighborhoods Junior mentioned before calling it a night. We'll buy some film for the Polaroid when we stop for gas and that way we'll have some reference material to compare to notes we take while driving through BT and Mason Court. That reminds me. . .

"What does BT stand for, Junior?"

He pulls his attention from a cute little redhead in

a Mustang next to us, and says, "What?" Yeah, he's definitely relaxed, compared to earlier.

"You said there were places named Mason Court and BT we should look at for this deal. What does BT stand for?"

He sticks his index finger into his right ear and roots around for a few seconds, then answers. "Butler Terrace. Nasty place. So's the other one; Mason Court and BT are housing projects, with some decent people who are in a bad way, but also home to some serious druggies, dealers, whores, you name it. If there's bad shit happenin', it's happenin' in those two places. Either one should work pretty well for yer scheme. They're both close enough to the highway for easy escape routes, but also in areas where there are lotsa little roads and alleys where the bike should be able to shake anyone on yer ass."

"That sounds good. Any idea where we should stay? We'll need a motel where nobody much gives a shit about our comings and goings, but we don't want to be in a place where the cops troll for hookers and druggies, either."

I wish I'd paid more attention while I was in Huntsville previously, but it's too late to worry about it now. If nothing else, we can do some scouting of likely places; we've got plenty of time and don't need to be in a hurry.

"Ya know, I've been thinking about that, and I just might have the perfect place," Junior says, grinning that evil grin he wears when there's trouble waiting at the end of it. "There's an ol' gal my daddy knew just north of Mooresville who owns a truck stop. She has a few rooms out back, off the books. She lets bands playin' at the bar use 'em, that sorta thing. There's a damned good café in there, too, so we can kinda keep to ourselves. She was kinda sweet on Daddy, so I'll bet if I sweet-talked her some, we could get us a room to use, at least for this trip."

"How far is it from Huntsville to Mooresville? It's on 565, right?" The limit of my knowledge of this area is woefully low.

"Yeah, we take 565 about 20 miles to Mooresville, then north a short piece to Donna's Place. Just in case anyone actually saw us or followed us or somethin' like that, we'd lead 'em off in the wrong direction from where we came from. Whattaya think, Jonnybob?"

"Sounds damned good, buddy. This way, there's no paperwork with any name on it, and it sounds like your daddy's old girlfriend would be the type to slow down anyone looking for us. Should I just drive down to the interstate and hang a right?" As far as I remember, this is the way to Mooresville.

"Naw, don't do that. We'll be getting' there durin' rush hour, so let's hang a right on University, then we'll go south on Jordan Lane to the freeway. Hopefully, that'll get us around some of the worst traffic. Once we get to Donna's, we can get settled in and have some supper—actually, I'd rather have some supper, then get settled in. I'm starvin'!"

Junior's thinking seems valid to me, so I agree. "Sounds like a plan. We'll see if Donna's there, then you can talk to her either before or after we eat, ask her about a room, and lay a little southern charm on her. If all goes like we hope, we can get settled in and make an early start tomorrow scopin' out the terrain and the bad guys. That might work out pretty well, seein' as how drug dealers and their associates don't normally get up much before noon."

As we get closer to Huntsville, the traffic gets heavier and heavier, until we're in a steady stream of vehicles heading south at about thirty miles an hour. Just south of Oakwood Avenue NW, Junior has me get off onto the south-bound frontage road, which we follow to University Drive NW, where I hang a right and head west.

Junior says, "Get in the left lane, 'cause we'll be hangin' a left on Jordan Lane."

Okay, so far. "How far to Jordan Lane?" I ask, looking over my shoulder and watching the mirror, looking for a break in the heavy traffic to slide into.

Junior cranes his big old bushy head around, looking over my shoulder, and hollers "Move over! We gotta get in the left lane. It's prob'ly about a mile, mile-and-a-half to Jordan."

As he's pointing and yelling, I make my way into one lane, then another, finally getting into the left-most lane. My movements are accompanied by numerous hand gestures from my fellow motorists and a cacophony of honking horns of all keys and volumes.

"Damn, Junior, quit hollerin'," I tell him, peering out of the windshield, watching for the Jordan Lane intersection.

"Got ya over here, didn't it?" says my chubby friend, with a wolfish smile on his broad face. "Now just stay here in this lane, then hang a left on Jordan. It's prob'ly another six or eight blocks."

After another mile or so, I see the Jordan Lane intersection, move into the left-turn lane, and head south. As soon as I get pointed south, I muscle my way into the far right lane in preparation for a right turn onto Interstate 565.

Junior is pleased, and tells me, "Good job, Jonnybob! You might figger out this city drivin' shit yet. After we get on 565, we'll just head west to Mooresville, then head north on that little county road fer a short piece. Her joint is on the right, can't miss it. Well . . . mebbe you could, but most folks couldn't."

This last shot at my driving is delivered with a deadpan expression, but he's watching me out the corner of his eye, and doesn't notice that we're coming up on a traffic light. I've been watching it, gauging when it might turn yellow. When it does, I check to be sure it's relatively clear behind me and I ease up ever so slightly on the gas pedal. Junior is still watching me for a reaction or retaliation of some sort, and doesn't snap to my plan. I wait until the last moment, then jump on the brakes hard, dislodging my portly companion from his comfortable sitting position, while also prompting a chorus of honked horns and shouted epithets from those behind us. It's a silly thing to do, but the look on his face makes it worth it. His eyes are large as half-dollars, and his face is red. He's sputtering and cussing, and my laughter isn't helping matters any.

"You did that on purpose! You dumb-shit, what in the hell's the matter with you?"

His memory needs a little refreshing, so I inform him. "Hey, you were the one telling me I don't know how to drive in the city. I guess you're right, it is kinda hard. Sorry if I scared you."

He squints one eye, and leans toward me. "Okay, mebbe I deserved that, but we really should think about keeping a low profile. We surely don't need a police report with this van's description and license number, not to mention your new name on file in this damned town." He grins and adds, "You got me, son! Let's call a truce until this deal's over, whattaya say?"

Just then, I hang a hard right onto the entry ramp to 565, making him lean toward me pretty hard. "Sure, we can have a truce, but quit tryin' to kiss me, for God's sake!" I say this as he's trying to regain his balance, and he's trying hard not to laugh.

As the van settles back into a more normal position, he straightens up in his seat and pulls his shirt tail down from where it had ridden up during his gymnastics. "Very fuckin' funny, butt-head. As soon as this deal is over, and the truce is officially a thing of the past, you should watch yer ass very closely, 'cause I don't get even, as you well know. I'll get so far ahead you'll never catch up."

Laughing, I move into the middle lane and concentrate on my driving. He joins in, but reminds me, "I'm serious. You are gonna be in deep shit when this is over."

Oh, I know that, for sure. This man is a serious prankster, and has an evil streak that has no equal in my experience. I've never had him looking for ways to fuck with me before, but I've seen plenty of people suffer payback of one sort or another at his hands. I will definitely need to watch my ass, but I'm afraid it will do no good; he'll just wait until I get complacent and then it will get ugly. No need to fixate on it now, as our temporary truce will keep me safe for the immediate future. Whatever happens later, happens. And I do deserve it, so what the hell.

FOURTEEN

Junior has been stewing for awhile, and I've been watching the signs on the side of the interstate. I just took the Mooresville exit, and am heading north on Limestone County Road 71.

The town itself is south of the highway, but the tourist-friendly, historical theme of downtown Mooresville is evident in the businesses surrounding the intersection. As I head north, the businesses thin out rapidly, and within a mile, I spot a small—by today's standards—truck stop with an attached bar and restaurant on the right side of the road. There's a large sign out front, on tall posts so it can be seen for a long way. It must have been grandfathered in when the town fathers started trying to make all the businesses look alike, so as to convince the tourists that the town of Mooresville looked just like it did in the late 1880s.

For whatever reason, this sign has survived, and I'm glad. It's easily twenty feet tall and forty feet long. It's bright yellow, and in lavender letters at least eight feet high, proclaims "DONNA'S PLACE". Under that, there's a phone number and the usual listing of services available: GOOD EATS! TRUCK REPAIRS! FUEL! FULL BAR! There is a small building out back that looks like it was once a six- or eight-room motel, complete with a small drive-in alcove next to each room. It is also the retina-searing yellow of the sign, with lavender trim and doors. No missing this place, for sure.

"Damn, son, lookit that," chortles Junior as he straightens up in his seat and leans forward to check out the whole deal. "I 'member Daddy talking about how Donna had got herself crossways with some of the local big shots. She's in the county, not city, so her place isn't subject to all the rules they got in town.

"They tried to get her to tone her place down some, take down that big-ass sign. She fought 'em tooth and nail, got the sign back-doored somehow. Then just to twist their tails, she painted the whole place that bright-ass yellow.

"Lots of the locals took her side against the town guys, and she's been here for at least thirty or forty years, so business must be good enough to keep the place open. You know, word-of-mouth gets around, and all the local (and not-so-local) people who don't necessarily fit in south of the highway congregate out here to raise hell and thumb their noses at the snobs in town. Truckers hear about the place, and stop for the food and a good time. She keeps her fuel a dime cheaper than the guys south of the highway, too."

"Well, it looks like whatever she's doing is working, 'cause the lot's pretty full," I say. "Let's see just how good this food is, and see if she remembers you. We just need to keep the use of your real name to a minimum. Try to get her to call you Junior. I imagine you'll be able to think of something, seeing as how you're so full of bullshit."

"Bullshit? Me? You wound me, Jonnybob. I'll do my best to figger out a way to convince Donna to call me Junior if you'll kindly stop hurtin' my feelings." Unable to keep a straight face, Junior starts laughing, and I join in.

I wheel Vanna into a parking space near the rear of the main building's north side, and we enter through a door just behind the kitchen. As we walk down a short hallway, the smells of home-style cooking are nearly maddening. I hadn't realized just how hungry I am until I was assaulted by all these wonderful odors. Junior is just ahead of me, and approaches a woman bussing tables.

"S'cuse me, hon, but is this the place to eat some of that wondermous food we been smellin'?" She turns around and I'm smitten. My pulse increases a couple of points, and I have an incredible urge to take her in my arms. I think better of it. While maybe not beautiful, she's a striking woman. She's thirtyish, probably five foot seven or eight, with shiny hair the color of midnight, and the bluest eyes I've seen in a long time. She's wearing a blouse of the same yellow everything else seems to be, and jeans that aren't ragged, but appear to be a hundred years old. Her eyes crinkle up, and she favors Junior with a smile brighter than the exterior of the building.

"Why, it surely is!"

Her voice is something out of Everyman's wildest

fantasy: sexy, but not overtly so and with a hint of delight to be speaking to the listener. Oh yeah, I'm smitten, but Junior is ruined. He's suddenly unable to speak, much less flirt, and it's wonderful to behold. I'll be able to rag him about this for years to come! Combined with the stunt at the yellow light, this should press Junior pretty hard for suitable retaliation.

I step around Junior, and tell the waitress—Judy, according to her lavender-lettered name tag, "My friend is so hungry he's plumb tuckered out. He doesn't seem to even have enough strength to ask where you'd like us to sit. We need to get some food in him before he passes right out."

She turns to me, and her smile doesn't waver a bit. I'm sure every man who comes through here flirts with her, and I wouldn't be at all surprised if a fair number of women do, too.

"Well, we'd better get him set down before we have to carry him, don't you think?"

I think she's probably had the same effect on a fair number of people before, and is trying to make light of the fact that my buddy is still transfixed and nearly unable to take his eyes off of her.

"Follow me, boys," she tosses over her shoulder as she walks toward a booth next to a window that overlooks the section of parking lot we're in. She noticed which door we came in, and seats us in a position to keep an eye on our vehicle. I can tell she's been doing this for a long time. The easy banter, the reflexive seating arrangements, the way she talks to the other customers as we pass their tables makes me believe she's been working here for a long while.

Stopping near the booth, Judy turns to Junior and asks, "Will this be okay? I'll have a couple of menus over here in just a shake, so you can get something in your belly before you pass out."

Junior just grins goofily at her, mumbles something about this being fine, and slides onto the bench nearest the kitchen.

I smile at Judy and tell her, "This will be just dandy, and thanks for putting us where we can watch the rig. Junior, here, will be fine just as soon as he gets some food shoveled down his neck." And as soon as you walk off he may become coherent again, I think, but don't say out loud.

"What would you boys like to drink? I'll bring them to you with the menus and some water," Judy says, trying not to look my dopey friend in the eye.

"Sweet tea," says Junior, and I second it.

She walks off, and Junior watches her. He turns back to me and says, "I been 'witched."

"It does seem so," I tell him, laughing at his predicament. "She is one fine-looking woman, for sure."

Junior shakes his head. "It's not just that. When she looked me in the eye, I couldn't think. I couldn't talk. Hell, son, I'm not sure I was even breathin'. She's fine as frog hair, for damned sure, but there's somethin' else there workin' on me. I ain't sure what it is, but it's powerful strong."

Just as Junior is saying this, Judy returns with the menus, some tea in a pitcher, and two cut-class tumblers. "Just give me a holler when you're ready, and I'll take your order. The special today is fresh-caught catfish, beer-battered and fried, with hush puppies, coleslaw, and fresh baked oatmeal bread. You two look damned hungry, so I'll make it all-you-can-eat for five bucks a head."

Junior and I both produce ear-to-ear grins, and I tell her, "That sounds just like what the doctor ordered. Junior here just might live, after all."

While we're waiting for the food, we take turns visiting the men's room and wash up. Just as I'm sitting back down in the booth, Judy appears with a large platter of fried catfish, a basket of hush puppies, a bowl of coleslaw, and a loaf of hot bread with a tub of butter on the side.

We thank Judy, and she aims her response right at Junior. "If you need anything else, just whistle. I'll leave you boys to it. Enjoy."

We attack the food with a vengeance, and soon there's nothing left but a platter with fish bones, some cornmeal crumbs, maybe a tablespoon's worth of coleslaw, and a piece of bread about the size of my wallet. Junior's eyeing the bread.

Judy has been by and switched our tea pitcher for a full one, and now returns. With a low whistle, she observes, "Y'all must not have had anything to eat for a few days."

We both laugh, and I'll be damned if Junior isn't blushing!

"Actually," I tell her, "we already ate twice today, although lunch was kinda slim."

She's laughing along with us now, and tells Junior, "You can't have any dessert until you finish up what's left. We've got pecan pie, baked this afternoon, and some ice cream to put on top, if you're interested."

Junior grabs the bread, tears it in half, and hands me a chunk while spooning the remaining coleslaw onto the piece in his hand. In two bites, it's gone, and I follow suit and finish off my portion of the bread.

With a big grin, my chubby buddy tells his new best friend, "We'll have some pie, with ice cream on top. And I'd like a large ROC Co-Cola with lotsa ice."

"Me, too," I chime in.

Judy picks up most of the plates and walks off. She's back in a minute to clear the rest of the detritus off the table. "You boys surely know how to make food disappear," she says, wiping the table with a damp cloth.

Not wanting to talk too much about ourselves, I resist the temptation to tell her some of our history as power eaters in the Navy. "Yeah, we try not to leave any food on our plates. We don't want it getting lonely."

She laughs, and heads off to get our dessert.

"Jonnybob, old son, I think I may need a nap.

Damn, that was some fine chow! I've been watchin' the other waitresses, and have tried to see if anyone else working here might be Donna. I haven't had any luck yet. Mebbe she doesn't work on Tuesday, or not at all. She might just sit at home and count her money. Hell, I don't know . . . I guess I'll just ask that cute waitress, if I can talk to her without freezin' up."

We both laugh at this, and just then Judy shows up with two huge slabs of pecan pie smothered in French vanilla ice cream. "Think this'll hold you over until breakfast?" she asks, and we both nod, grinning like fools.

"Yes'm, I do believe this just might keep us until daylight," Junior tells her. He looks up from his plate, sorta checking her out from the corner of his eye. "Does Donna still work here, or does she let someone else run the place these days?"

Judy explodes into laughter, causing everyone in the dining room to look our way. "Lordy," she exclaims. "Momma would bust a gut if she heard that. She won't ever leave this place until she's dead or comatose."

Junior and I have one of those "holy shit!" moments, looking at each other across the pie and ice cream.

"Donna's your momma?" asks Junior, now fully looking at Judy, regardless of the consequences.

"Sure enough. I've been working here since I was about six, picking up trash and such. Do you know

Momma?"

Junior looks back at me and I give him the barest of nods. "Well, not really," he says, "but my daddy knew her and I came here a couple times with him. I was hopin' I might talk to her, if she's around."

Not only is she around, but Judy says she's in her office behind the bar, and offers to go tell her we're here while we eat our dessert, which we've pretty much forgotten. She gets our names (Junior tells her his last name is Dutton) and walks off.

Junior looks at me and says, "Good thing we were nice to that lady. If we'd pissed her off, our plans woulda been screwed right from the git-go. We'd better eat this pie before she gets back, then we'll see what Donna's got to say."

As we're sopping up the last of the ice cream, Judy comes back from the bar and says, "Momma said to bring you around to her office when you're done. Dinner's on the house. Your daddy must've been special. She hasn't smiled like that in a long time."

We dig for tip money, but Judy won't hear of it. "You're gonna make me mad if you keep acting like that, and you won't like me when I'm mad." I believe her.

We thank her profusely, and tell her the food was excellent. She suggests we give the tip money to the cook, and we agree this is a great idea. We each pull out a five and leave it on the table.

Judy says, "Follow me," and heads around the corner into the bar.

The bar is fairly small, with seating for probably forty people. There's a sliding section of wall that allows for overflow into the dining room during dances, parties, etc. There are a couple of pool tables, a shuffleboard game, and a couple honest-to-god pinball machines. The bar itself is about thirty feet long, with stools arranged down its length. There's a beautiful old mirror behind the bar, probably eight feet by twelve feet.

Off to the left end of the bar, there's door with a sign on it that says "Private: Keep the Hell Out" in saloon-type lettering. Judy leads us to this door, gives a rap, and walks right in. We follow her into a room about twelve feet wide and maybe fourteen feet deep. There's a love seat against the near wall, a couple armchairs, a small TV on a stand, and a gorgeous old oak desk in the far corner.

The woman sitting behind the desk is in her late fifties or early sixties, wearing a pair of rhinestone-studded reading glasses attached to a chain around her neck. She would be easily recognized anywhere as Judy's mother, as they could be twins born thirty years apart.

She stands up, and shows off a figure many women half her age would kill for. She's also wearing the obligatory bright-as-the-sun yellow blouse, brown corduroy jeans, and lizard skin western boots. She has rings on every finger, diamond studs in both ears, jangly bracelets on both wrists, and a huge turquoise pendant hanging from a silver necklace. Maybe those aren't rhinestones on her glasses, after all. Her hair is also as black as her daughter's, probably with help from a bottle. She cuts a fine figure, and I imagine every man in three or four counties has chased her at one time or another, or at least thought about it.

"Kenneth Dutton! I do declare, it's been a very long time since I heard that name. Your daddy was a very dear friend of mine, and I remember him talking about you and your sister. He was so proud of you kids! I was heartbroken when I heard about his passing."

Donna takes Junior's right hand in both of hers and looks him right in the eye. I can tell he is going to cloud up.

He swipes at his eyes for a second with his left hand, and tells her, "I'm mighty obliged to hear you say that, Miss Donna. Daddy thought the world of you, too. It made me a mite testy when he wouldn't let me come in when we stopped by here, seein' as how he always spoke so highly of you, and talked about how pretty you were—are."

Donna reaches out and hugs Junior to her, and says, "Kenneth, your daddy helped me through some things that a young boy shouldn't be exposed to. Every time he stopped by was to take care of something for me, something that I couldn't do alone. There wasn't any foolishness going on, no hanky-panky, if that's what you're thinking. Suffice it to say I have secrets, and so did your daddy. We helped each other through some hard times and there was a bond between us stronger than most family ever feels.

"Just know this: I wouldn't have any of this without your daddy's help. Not money, not any shenanigans in bed, nothing that would take anything away from his wife and kids, just some assistance with things that got plumb outta hand. I promised him I'd never tell anyone, especially his family, what all he did here. But know this, Kenneth Dutton, your daddy was a hero, and never did anything that would make you feel less than proud to be his son."

Junior by now is holding on to this remarkable woman and smiling his big old goofy grin, tears rolling down his cheeks. "Miss Donna, I surely do appreciate your telling me all of that. I always wondered, especially as I got older, if you and Daddy had something going. Momma never acted like it bothered her, though, so mebbe Daddy had told her enough to set her mind at ease. It hurt me to be left in the truck, but it was probably for the best, according to your account of things."

"Well, trust me when I tell you that nothing— nothing—ever happened sexually between your daddy and me. He and my late husband were involved in some moonshinin' together and became best friends, and those two had a bond stronger than any two humans I ever saw. Your daddy was there when Leroy died, and promised he'd take care of me. And, if you know one thing, Kenneth, it was that your daddy always kept a promise. Please, don't ask me any more questions about what all happened back then, because I made a promise, too. It's so good to see you!"

At this, she lets go of Junior, and he lets his arms drop to his sides. Donna steps back a step or two, and turns to me. "Who's this good-lookin' fella with you? I understand you two could eat a truck-load of groceries all by yourselves."

Junior turns to me and says, "This is my best friend in the world, Jonnybob Clark. We were in the Navy together. He's visitin' and wanted to come down and check out Huntsvull. I figgered while we were here, I'd take the opportunity to come by and say hello. And, to be completely honest, I remember Daddy sayin' you had some rooms out back you let bands and such stay in. Seein' as how it's a Tuesday, I was hopin' you might have an empty one we could use for a couple days."

"Well, I do still have those rooms out back, and it is definitely Tuesday, so there's nobody out there, other than Sammy the cook, who lives full-time in one of them. But I think maybe you two have a secret or two, as well. Why would two young studs want to stay out in the middle of nowhere in a rented room behind a truck stop, rather than in a motel in Huntsville, close to all the clubs and such? Why would you park in the back of a place you'd never been to before? Why would Kenneth here decide after all this time to pick now to say hello and inquire about said room in the middle of nowhere?" Donna looks at Judy, who, unbelievably,

I'd forgotten was in the room. "What do you think, Judy? Are these two on the level? Should we trust them?"

I guess we should've known how this would look. I'm feeling embarrassed and can tell Junior is as well. "I'd like to say something, if I may. Kenneth here is for sure the best friend I've ever had. I've gotten myself into some trouble, and called him for a place to lay up for awhile."

Kenneth looks at me with this weird, confused expression on his face. I can't blame him; I'm confused, too. These two women have just removed all thoughts about deceiving them from my mind. I truly believe they can be trusted with our secret—hell, with our lives.

"It's a long story, and we've taken some steps to protect our whereabouts and identities, so I'd appreciate it if you'd call Kenneth 'Junior' in public. I'd also be very obliged if nothing I tell you goes beyond this room."

Donna and Judy look at each other, then at us. It's silent, other than a grandfather clock in the corner ticking softly.

"You boys go out and have a drink," Donna tells us. "Give us girls a few minutes, and we'll come find you."

FIFTEEN

"Okay, spill it," says Donna.

She and Judy are on the love seat, and Junior and I are sitting in the armchairs. We never saw either one of them walk through the bar, but there is a tray with pitchers of sweet tea, a few pastries, and four glasses on it. There is a door in the side wall, which I'd taken to be a closet. I guess it must lead into the hall or somewhere in the dining room.

Junior and I have just spent thirty minutes or so in the bar, talking about just what we should tell these women. We won't lie; we've agreed on that. But there is disagreement on how much to tell them. I don't want to put them in harm's way, and neither does my buddy. He thinks they can be of enormous tactical value, if we'll just let them know what it is we're planning, especially since we want to get this done pretty quickly.

It's been three days since the wreck on Molino Road, and with my theft of the stuff from the S&S boys, we need to strike pretty quickly. I finally gave in and am now prepared tell our story to these two women we just met.

"First off, I just want to tell you I can't believe we're actually going to do this. We've been plotting for days about how to keep this a secret, and here I am, about to tell two perfect strangers what we're up to.

Something that could get us hurt, even killed."

At this, Donna and Judy look at each other, and Donna takes Judy's hand in hers. "Okay, are you running from the law?" This from Judy, who's staring at Junior.

"I am. Kenneth's not. I guess the only way to do this is to start out at the beginning and go from there. When I get finished, if you want me out of here, I'll leave. Just that easy. Kenneth hasn't done anything illegal, and I've tried to get him to stay out of the whole mess, but he won't have it."

I look at Junior/Kenneth, and he cocks a fist like he's gonna smack me in the chops with it, but he's smiling, and finally, I am too.

I tell the whole story. One or the other of the women keeps interrupting, and finally Kenneth says, "We'll never get done at this rate. At my house, I ended up taking notes and asking questions when he was done. Mebbe y'all should do the same thing. It'll go a hell of a lot faster."

Judy jumps up, finds a couple of small note pads and a glass of ink pens. After making sure they each have a pen that works, they nod at me, and I start over from Nigger Bill's untimely demise. It takes quite a while, and when I'm done, Donna and Judy both have some questions. I do my best to answer them, and finally we all seem to be on the same page.

Kenneth speaks up (funny, in this room I've started thinking of him as Kenneth, again) and declares, "I'm hungry." We all have a good laugh, and he continues, "No, really. Those little doughnut deals were okay, but my belly's rumblin'. Could we get a sandwich or somethin' from the café?"

Donna looks at the clock; it's 11:35 p.m. "Hell, boys, I've gotta be up at 4:30 to make biscuits, so I think I should all call it a day. Most of the rooms are unlocked out back. Pick a couple of the open rooms other than number six, and make yourselves comfortable. There are sheets and pillows on the beds, and blankets in the closets. Each room has a little half-bath.

"Judy, would you be a peach and take these boys through the kitchen so they can grab a snack, then show 'em the rooms?"

Judy gives her mom a hug and kisses her on the cheek. "C'mon, boys, I'll show you where we can make a sandwich. I think I'll join you for a snack, then we can get you settled in out back."

In the kitchen, Judy whips up some roast beef sandwiches and finds half a cherry cobbler in the walk in refrigerator.

While we eat she asks, "So what is the plan for tomorrow? If I understand you correctly, you want to go into Huntsville and do some scouting around for a place to make your move on the PnB. Why don't I go with you? We can get a lot more done that way. I'm familiar with the town, and know a lot about the different neighborhoods and all.

"My ex rode with a small club that hung around

the PnB in Huntsville; I left him when he got jacked up on meth and almost killed a girl in a topless bar over there. He's doing twenty years in the state pen, and I say good riddance. That damned dope turned him into a mean sonofabitch, and he scared the hell out of Momma and me before we finally got shut of him. A bunch of his club brothers wanted the shit he left here, but Mom got the local cops to run 'em off. If you do decide to put your Harley together for this deal, you might find some of the stuff you need in the little shop out behind the cabins."

"Well," I say, swallowing a bite of sandwich, "that's all well and good, but I can't see getting you involved in this mess. It's bad enough I can't get Kenneth to stay out of it, but I really don't want anyone else putting themselves in danger for my little vendetta. Somebody might recognize you. You're not exactly homely, you know." Judy waves this off, and Dutton and I just grin at each other. "On top of all that, the van only has two seats."

Judy levels a look across the kitchen counter at me and says, "Bullshit. Y'all are fightin' a fight I want to be a part of. This is my home, dammit. Those damned people selling crank are killin' people, and messin' up a bunch more.

"As for somebody recognizing me, don't you worry about it. I'll take care of that, and we'll take my car, so there'll be plenty of seats. You're all paranoid that people are gonna know we're up to no good, but think about it, Jonnybob. To everyone out there we'll just be three folks driving down the road in a twelve-year-old Malibu. It'll attract less suspicion than that child-molester van you guys are in, and it runs like a striped-ass ape. Jimmy, my ex, worked at a shop that built roundy-round cars, and built the 377 for my car. He wasn't good for much after he started using crank, but he was a hell of an engine builder when I met him.

"We used the Malibu for a number of less-than-legal enterprises there for awhile, and it's a great sleeper; stock hubcaps, quiet mufflers, stock baby-crap yellow paint, the whole deal. The windows are tinted as dark as they can be without attracting the cops' attention. I think we should get an early start, check out whatever it is you want to see, go from there."

Kenneth and I have been eating and glancing at each other during Judy's monologue, and I'm pretty sure we're both thinking the same thing: this woman isn't just a cute piece of fluff in tight jeans. She's smart, knowledgeable about things we need to know, tough, and stubborn.

"Don't you have to work tomorrow—I mean, today?" I ask her this in a last-ditch effort to keep her out of it, but honestly, I know she's gonna come along, whatever I say.

"I'll call Darla, a girl that fills in here. She'll be glad for the hours and tips. I'm not on the schedule until one tomorrow, so I'll have plenty of time to call her at a decent hour."

Her logic is sound, and I tip her an abbreviated salute to acknowledge that I'm beaten. We all eat in silence for a while, except for the sounds of chewing and clanking forks on our plates.

"What time do you think we should leave?" I ask her.

Kenneth seems content to sit back and let Judy and me hammer out the details.

"I think we should be out of here by six at the latest," she says, picking up dishes and putting them in a small pile by the dishwasher's station. "That way, we can cover a lot of ground before most of the lowlifes are awake. We'll have plenty of time to check out some likely places for our play before dark."

"Well, if we're gonna be leavin' here in a little over five hours, I think we should get some sleep," says Kenneth as he stretches and yawns. "We'll need to eat some breakfast before we leave, and transfer a few items from the van into Judy's car, not to mention hittin' the water locker for a quick shower."

Judy and I agree, and I go outside and back Vanna into a carport between cabins three and four. As I walk around the van to the right side to open the sliding door, I see Judy and Kenneth strolling across the parking lot.

I sure hope I don't get either one of them killed!

SIXTEEN

The first thing Kenneth and I learn is that BT and Mason Court aren't places the PnB MC would be hanging out. These housing developments are full of blacks, mostly, and the drug of choice is crack, not meth (or, as the tweakers call it, "crank"). We still might use some of the stuff we learn later, but there's no way the bikers are gonna come here looking for meth so also muscling in on their action. It's just the wrong part of town.

Judy has already thought about this. "I knew this was the wrong part of town for what you had in mind, but thought it would be better to show you and let you decide for yourselves. We need to look for a place in the southwest. The PnB have a kitchen set up down by Redstone somewhere, in a small industrial park, from what I could get from Jimmy. I think we should concentrate on finding it, do as much damage as possible as quickly as we can, then haul ass. I've been thinking, and hitting them at Chubby's might be a good idea. If we can get most of the major players there for a meeting about what you 'found,' we might be able to take a big chunk out of their money-making operations like whores and meth at the same time. I don't see us having anywhere near the impact that you did in Tidewater, but we can definitely make life uncomfortable for them.

"If we can find the place they're cooking the meth, and sic the cops on it while we're hitting Chubby's, we can make a big-ass dent in their operations. And, from Chubby's we can head south to Laceys Spring, then take Alabama 36 and 67 to I-65. We take a right, and its less than ten miles back to Momma's. From Chubby's, the whole trip will only take about thirty minutes, if we have any luck at all. I know that route really well. That's how Jimmy and I went to the races and back; the Speedway is only a couple miles southeast of Chubby's."

This woman is sharp, and thinks like a criminal, to boot. I like her more all the time. Her strategy sounds good, and I can tell Kenneth is thinking the same thing, if the awestruck look on his face is any indication.

"That sounds like a much better plan," I say, "and by doing that we can stay out of downtown Huntsville. There won't be nearly the chance of discovery down there, and it sounds like you have a good idea for an escape route. I probably won't need to use the bike now that we won't be operating in residential areas, so that'll save time, too. Whattaya think, Kenneth?"

Kenneth turns his shaggy head toward me and says, "Kenneth? I thought I was Junior. I wish you'd make up yer mind, son. I shorely do."

I just laugh, and tell them both, "Judy makes a lot of sense. People around here don't know you, and they don't know what we're up to. If we can pull this off without getting busted by the cops or grabbed by the bad guys, nobody will know who to look for or where to look for them. If we do get caught, using an alias probably won't do much good. As for me, I still need to use my new identity, because all the cops in Virginia and a bunch of pissed-off outlaw bikers will still be looking for me, even if they don't know I'm part of this. My future is tied to John Robert Clark, for good or bad."

They're both nodding their heads, so I continue "Judy, let's go down by Chubby's and get the lay of the land. From there, we can look for the meth lab. You have a fair idea of what part of town it's in, and I have a pretty damned good idea of what to look for, so we might get lucky. If all else fails and we don't find it, we can get the information we have to the cops and let them find it after we hit the PnB at Chubby's."

Judy cocks her head, and looks at me with a weird expression. "Jonnybob, the cops know where it is. There's a good number of corrupt cops on the HPD, if you believe the gossip. Whether the cops are dirty, or just lazy, or have a plan of their own, for some reason they haven't hit the lab. There's no way they don't know where it is."

"Well, I might be able to do something about that, if we can find out where it is. I know a guy—the cop I gave the info to in Virginia Beach—who could probably get the attention of someone in this state who *does* care about meth bein' cooked in Huntsville. Now that we know we can't trust the locals to help, we can also assume they may be turning a blind eye to what's happening at Chubby's. That could be good for us, meaning the club might spread the word to stay away during my meeting with Chief and his boys."

Bang! It hits me right between the eyes; I'll call Guffey now, and let him get on the horn and do some investigating of his own. He can use the busts in Virginia Beach as the reason, asking for help from the DEA or whoever, saying the lab and meth trade here ties in with the big labs up north. It just might work!

"Pull over somewhere so I can use a pay phone, Judy. I think I know how to get this taken care of without driving all over southwest Huntsville."

I tell them what I've got in mind, and they both agree that it's our best bet.

I dig Guffey's number out of my wallet, and dial the number. I shove a bunch of quarters that I just got from the clerk at the liquor store in the mini mall into the phone and wait. A desk cop answers the phone, and tells me Guffey is in a meeting.

"Just tell him Rooney is on the phone, and has something he wants to hear," I tell the doughnut-eater. He tries to brush me off, but I'm not having any of it. "Listen, this is something tied into the events of the last few days, and I'm on a pay phone. Get him, and get him in a hurry. He'll be very pissed off if you screw this up! Got me? This is urgent!"

He mumbles something about trying to find Guffey, and puts me on hold. I'm shoving more quarters in, getting low on change, when Guffey comes on the line. He's breathing hard, and sounds like he just ran a mile.

"Rooney? Sergeant Fisk tells me you have something for me, and you're on a pay phone. Give me the number, and I'll call you right back, so we won't get cut off when the money runs out."

I read him the number off the phone, and hang up. He'll know where I am, but that can't be helped. Hopefully he won't put me in a position to get my tit in a wringer, seeing as how I've been feeding him good intel.

I pick up the phone when it rings. "Guffey?"

I'm rewarded with, "Yeah, it's me. What've you got? Where are you, and what's going on?"

If I want him to do this, I need to be fairly straight with him. "Okay, Guffey, I know you're recording this, so just let me talk without a bunch of questions. I don't know how long I can stay here on the phone.

"I'm in Huntsville, Alabama, and I have some information about meth in the Rocket City that you may be able to act on. The local PnB chapter is cookin' meth and sellin' it out of some place they own. I've been told by a reputable source that the local cops know where the lab is, but haven't moved on it. I think you can probably use the action up there to get someone interested in doing something here. I've got a plan for something that will keep the PnB busy while you hit their lab, but we only have until tomorrow—at the latest—to do something about it. If you're interested in doing something, you need to get moving right now. Get someone on the phone down here and convince them that I'm on the level."

Guffey pauses for a couple seconds and says, "Jesus, Rooney, I don't know if I can do anything that fast. I do have an old buddy in the State Police down there, but you're asking a lot."

I tell him, "I'm not asking for anything, Guffey. I'm telling you what's going on, in case you want to try to do something about it. I'm going to do what I need to do, then I'm getting the hell out of here."

He sighs into the phone. "And we appreciate it. I just don't know how quickly we can put something together. Last time we had a pretty comprehensive plan to fall back on when you called. This deal is out of the blue, and I don't have enough contacts down there to guarantee we'll be able to get something happening that fast. I'm betting the DEA or ATF has the PnB in their sights, so maybe if I can reach the right person, we might be able to convince them that now is the time for action. I'll do my best . . . I promise.

"As for this other deal you're talking about, whatever it is, I'm going to advise you to forget it. You've already done more than your share, and there's no need to get anyone else hurt. You hear me, Rooney? Stay out of it."

I look around the area where the phone is, then wave at Kenneth and Judy in the Malibu a couple of parking spaces away. "Guffey, I appreciate the concern, but you wouldn't even know any of this if I hadn't told you, so do me the favor of letting me do what I need to do. I'll call you back with an idea of when to expect my diversion as soon as I know when it will be. If the locals can put together a bust on the lab, great. If not, well then I guess shit happens. One way or the other, I figure we'll be talking again soon. Get busy, cop."

I hang up, and walk over to the Malibu, still looking around the parking lot. I don't know what I'm looking for, exactly, but figure I'll know it when I see it. Kenneth is in the front seat on the passenger side, so I slide onto the rear seat and sit kinda sideways, so I can look out the front and rear, as well as the passenger windows.

Judy gets out of the car and heads for the pay phone to call Darla about working her shift.

Kenneth leans across the seat back and says, "Jonnybob, Judy and I are thinkin' that mebbe we should head up to the farm and get all the stuff from there, so we'll have it with us if the shit hits the fan. Whattaya think?"

I've been thinking about this, too. "I think that's a great idea. I'm glad I have you two to keep focused on what's important."

Kenneth grins and says, "Judy thinks, since we ate so late last night and skipped breakfast before we left, mebbe we should stop somewhere for a late breakfast, early lunch, before we head out. This might be one of the last times we can eat without bein' in a hurry, ya know?" I love this guy!

"Judy thought all that, did she? I'll bet she had to twist your arm something awful to make you agree." We're both laughing.

"I told you he wouldn't believe that story," says Judy, who's just returned from the phone. "Although I do think it's a good plan. What do you think, Jonnybob?"

I think it's a great idea, and tell them so. Judy says she knows just the place, a place Donna has told her about, so I sit back and keep a watch out the windows for whatever it is I'm looking for, while the two up front jabber about food.

The place Judy picks is in a place called Booger Town, off Governor's Drive between a used car lot and a tattoo parlor, which is closed at this hour. Fat Bob's Diner is one of those places you can find just about anywhere; six or eight tables with Formica tops and chrome legs, matching chairs with vinyl covering the seats, and a counter about fifteen feet long. The stools are bolted to the floor, and match the chairs. The aromas coming from the kitchen are wonderful, and the place is clean. The sole waitress is about forty, with whore-red hair and a big, friendly smile.

"Just sit anywhere, and I'll be with you in a second," she tells us, then returns to trading insults with a skinny guy at the counter. He's probably fifty, with a slicked back pompadour and a horse face. He's got on an honest-to-goodness plaid sports coat, and he's wearing white shoes.

"You figger he works next door?" Kenneth nods his head toward the used-car lot, with a huge grin on his face.

As we're pulling out chairs at a table in the corner, we all crack up, trying not to let the two at the counter know what we're laughing at. Judy is hiccupping, trying to stop, and failing miserably. Kenneth and I are trying to keep it down, but not having much success.

The waitress comes over as soon as we're seated carrying a tray with three glasses and a pitcher of water. She's got menus in her other hand, and is still smiling that big smile. "It's good to see people having fun," she says, setting the glasses, menus, and pitcher on the table. "Too many people walkin' around with a frown on their face these days," she observes, cocking her head a little to the left and looking at Judy, who's still fighting the hiccups.

A couple of taciturn dudes at one of the other tables glower at her good-naturedly. It seems she may have been aiming that remark at them. One of them, a big guy with long greasy black hair and a Wild Bill Hickock moustache keeps looking over, like he's trying to place us . . . or me.

"Can I bring you folks some coffee?"

Kenneth sits up straight, and answers the waitress

with a straight face. "Not for me, ma'am. I'd appreciate an ROC Co-Cola, please."

Now she's the one laughing. "Sure thing, hon. How about you, sweetie?" She's looking at me and I tell her I also would like an RC.

Judy says, "Coffee for me, please. Black, and as strong as you've got. Keepin' up with these two has got me plumb worn out."

April is the name on the name tag on the waitress' apron. She says, "They surely look like a handful. I figger either one of 'em would be plenty tiring, but both at once would be a chore. Fun, but a chore nonetheless."

As this sinks in, we're all choking and sputtering, and Judy's hiccups are back. April winks at me, and spins around on her heel, heading back to the window behind the counter. After she brings our drinks and takes our order, the place starts to fill up a little, and pretty soon she is busy. It seems she is, indeed, the only waitress, as well as the cashier and bus-girl.

After a meal consisting of a ham steak the size of a Frisbee accompanied by a pound of hash browns and three eggs with biscuits and gravy on the side, I'm sitting back in my chair, contentedly watching my friends finish up their breakfasts. Kenneth is on his third RC, and thankfully, Judy's hiccups have subsided. She is finishing up a huge Denver omelet with a shovel-full of grits. She thought the biscuits and gravy looked intimidating, so she had whole-wheat toast. Problem is, they serve it four slices at a time. Dutton had a short stack of hotcakes, grits, *and* hash browns, with a New York Strip almost as large as my ham. Oh, yeah, he had three eggs, too.

The grouchy dudes get up and head up to the counter to pay up. I mention that Wild Bill has been checking us out, and Kenneth says he was probably just checking Judy out. I guess he's probably right, but as the pair heads to the door, I get the distinct feeling that Wild Bill is trying to figure out if he knows me. I cross my fingers and hope he keeps moving.

April has been back by a few times, making sure everything is okay. Now she wants to know if we'd like pie.

We all three groan, and I tell her, "Next time, April, I swear."

This seems to appease her, and she heads over to another table. Wild Bill and his buddy are gone. I let out a sigh, and relax.

As we wait for the check, I ask Kenneth "You figure anyone in Fayetteville will need to be told what's going on, with us showing up in Judy's car? And we should probably give most of the cash to Jimbob so he can get it taken care of. We'll keep enough to get by until we can get everything behind us and meet up later."

Just then, April is back, with our check. I take it, and turn it over to see what the damages are. All it says is "Have a nice day!" with a big smiley-face.

I get up and walk over to where April is wiping down the counter and say, "While I surely do appreciate the sentiment, I believe you forgot something."

She looks sideways at the check in my hand, and says, "Nope, that's all there is. Bob said to tell you it's on the house. He wouldn't think of charging Donna Miller's daughter and friends for breakfast. Y'all have a nice day, hon, and come back for that pie."

I return to the table, and tell my partners in crime what just transpired.

"What?" exclaims Judy. "How in the world did they know who I am—and who's Bob?"

April, who is now bussing the table behind Judy, leans over and tells her, "Honey, anybody that didn't know you're Donna's girl would have to be plumb blind. That, and your momma was in here a while back, talking about your baby-shit yellow Malibu. From what she says, it'll haul ass! Too bad about that worthless old man of yours getting on the dope and all."

Judy is flabbergasted, and Kenneth and I are just confused.

"Okay," Judy allows, "I know I look like Momma, and the car would give it away to someone who put the two together, but who's Bob? Is he Fat Bob, the owner?"

April is enjoying this a lot, and addresses all of us. "Yes, indeed he's the owner of this place and a few others on this block."

She waves a hand vaguely, sort of encompassing

most of the block.

Judy still looks confused, and asks April, "But if he's been cooking this whole time, when did he see us? I haven't even seen him look through the window in the kitchen. The only person I've seen is the black lady in the chef's hat."

Now April is in stitches; she's pounding her hand on her thigh, laughing until her face is red. The other diners look over, but soon lose interest. They're probably used to April's antics. "Honey," she says, choking back laughter, "Fat Bob isn't cookin'! He's the owner! He doesn't even work in here. I run it for him, and only see him at mealtimes. He was in here when you walked in, and told me who you were. He said to put your meals on his tab, and he'd settle up with me later."

Holy shit! The skinny guy in the plaid coat was Fat Bob, and he knows Donna.

Kenneth can't resist. "Does he own the car lot next door? I might be needin' a new truck."

Judy and I look at him like he's lost his mind, but he keeps a straight face.

April looks at him sorta crossways, and says, "He does, but he's not over there much. He's got his nephew watching the place for him. Give him a call, and he'll meet you over there. The number is on the sign, and it's in the book, too. I'm sure he'd make you a good deal, if you're serious." At this, she gives Kenneth a searching look, no doubt trying to decide if he's just making fun of her boss.

"Oh, I'm dead serious," Kenneth replies, "I've been needin' a truck to replace my old GMC, and I think I just might be able to do it pretty soon. I'd just as soon give my business to someone who bought me and my friends breakfast."

This seems to tickle her, and she gives us another big smile. I stand, and pull out my wallet. Kenneth follows suit, and Judy stands up and gives April a hug.

"Tell Bob we're grateful for the breakfast, and we'll be back as soon as we get some business taken care of. I'll be sure and tell Momma hi for y'all, and tell her how well y'all treated us."

April is beaming, and turns to me. "You just put that wallet away, before I bounce an ashtray off your head. I done told you that there's no charge for the food."

I think she might actually do it, but I pull a fifty out and put it under my water glass. I tell her, "The food may've been paid for, but I always tip a waitress. The better she is, the better the tip. I want you to take this without a fuss, and know that you're the best waitress I've had the pleasure of meeting in a damned long time. Thank you."

While I'm giving this little speech, Kenneth has peeled off a fifty and put it under his plate.

Judy has been watching him, and smiles at us both. "We'd better get moving," she says. "We need to put some miles behind us before dark."

The three of us head for the door, and one at a

time tell April goodbye. As we exit onto the sidewalk, we're all about to bust a gut. We pile into the car, and Judy gets us the hell out of there before April finds the bill Kenneth left and starts a scene.

Judy hangs a left and drives up to Governor's Drive. She hangs another left and drives west a few blocks, then takes the entrance ramp onto I-565 heading northeast. At the intersection with Memorial Parkway, she takes the ramp and heads north toward Fayetteville. At Hazel Green, we stop for gas and Kenneth hits the restroom.

I'm standing next to the car, stretching, when I notice three chopped Harleys parked next to the gas pumps at the convenience store across the street. The feeling I had earlier is back, although the fact that three bikes are sitting at a gas station shouldn't necessarily be cause for alarm. Nevertheless, I slide back into the car and pull my nine mil out from under the driver's seat, where I'd stashed it this morning. I slide it under my belt in the back, and let my shirt tail hang down over it.

"What is it?" Judy's seen what I'm up to.

I hand her a fifty and tell her to go pay for the gas and get Kenneth out here as soon as possible. She takes off at a fast walk, and I turn back to watch the bikes across the street.

Now there are three hard-cases standing there next to the bikes, and one of them is gesturing and pointing different directions. The other two are nodding, and they finally mount the scooters and head out . . .

in three different directions.

All three are wearing PnB colors, and I'm pretty sure Chief has them trying to find me and get things moving, regardless of how much time I want to work on my fictitious truck. It's a good thing we're heading out in a couple of minutes and they're chasing wild geese.

I wonder if this means the club knows about my part in the fire at the clubhouse or the meth bust, or both. Maybe Chief's just in a hurry to get the stuff I told him about and try to figure out what the S&S assholes are up to. Whatever, it shows that changing my appearance and name was probably a damned good idea.

"Let's get the hell outta here," says Kenneth, sliding behind the steering wheel. "Crawl up here and ride shotgun, so's I can talk to you without gettin' a crick in my neck."

I look at Judy, and she nods. "Kenneth knows his way around up here way better than I do, so we figured he should drive."

I get out and Judy takes my place in the rear seat. I slide onto the front seat.

Judy leans over the seat rest. "Get my .45 out of the glove box and hand it to me, would you?"

I just give her a wry grin, and do as she requests. It's a nice piece, and smells of gun oil. There are a couple of spare clips lying there, so I hand them to her with the pistol.

"Thanks," is all she says, and proceeds to put the clips in her purse and the auto in a pocket on the door panel.

Kenneth has had the .45 I gave him in his jacket pocket all morning, since we decided to drive through BT and Mason Court.

"What's the story with those three bikers back there?" Kenneth asks, looking at me through the shades he bought back at the gas station. "You figger they're lookin' for you?"

I think that's exactly what they're doing. "Yeah, I reckon they're trying to find Hummer's hidey-hole. I don't know whether Chief's just antsy to find out what the S&S are up to, or they know what I did at The Beach. Either way, I'm glad they don't have a clue where we actually are. We don't need a hassle with anybody; the more we stay off the radar, the better."

"Well if we get in and out of my place without a hitch, we'll be on the home stretch, as far as anyone who knows any of us is concerned. You been thinkin' about what all we need to bring with us?"

Kenneth has a good point. If we can get our stuff and get out of the Fayetteville area without anyone seeing him in this car, it will be another thing we won't have to worry about.

"What about getting the money to Jimbob?" I ask him.

He scratches his head for a second, then turns toward me and says, "I'll drive my Jimmy downtown with the money. Y'all follow me. After I give the cash to Jimbob, I'll meet you somewhere. Hell, I'll just walk down to Tinker's Place, order a beer, then walk out the back door. The bathroom's back there, next to the alley, so nobody'll miss me for awhile. Even if they do, they'll figger I'm out back smoking a joint. From there, I'll just walk a block down the alley to that Qwik Stop convenience store on the corner. Soon as nobody's watchin', I'll slide in and we'll get out of town. Shouldn't be hard."

Judy agrees that this seems like a good plan and settles down with her eyes closed. "I'm gonna take a short nap. Wake me up when we get there."

Kenneth and I grin at each other; she's cool as a cucumber. I'm really glad she came along. She's easy to look at, but her main strength is her strategic thinking. She'd have made a good military officer. The three of us make a pretty damned good team!

SEVENTEEN

We get to Kenneth's place around half-past noon without anyone recognizing him. He backs the Malibu up by the small door on the side of the barn, and as soon as the door's unlocked, Judy takes the keys from him to open up the house and hit the bathroom. She woke up about the time we turned down the two-track that leads to the house.

Kenneth's watching her walk across the yard. There's no exaggerated motion, just a very nice ass moving the way it's supposed to. Kenneth isn't the only one watching, I have to admit.

We're both grinning, and he says, "Ain't she somethin'?"

She is indeed somethin'. "She's a hell of a woman, old buddy. I'm really glad you thought of going to her mom's. Things are going much better than I'd imagined, and a lot of that is because of Judy. She's got grit."

He nods, and says, "She shore does, at that."

We go into the barn and make sure everything is where we left it. It is, and we take a couple of minutes just to get our heads around what we're going to do. Judy comes into the barn and throws the keys to Kenneth.

"Is this your scooter?" she asks me as she walks over to the table where all the bike parts are laid out.

"It looks like it was real nice . . . did you hate to tear it apart?"

I turn around from where I've been digging the box of flash-bangs out of its hiding spot, and tell her, "Well, it sucked, but I knew it had to happen. There was no way I was going to try to get away on it. And if I'd just put it in the back of the van, any cop pulling me over for any little thing might've gotten suspicious, given the fact that a bunch of bikers were being sought for meth and rape charges.

"My new ID and look wouldn't have done me a lot of good if Hammer's bike had been found in my van. So, yeah, it was hard, but now I really don't even care if it ever gets put back together. It's in Hammer's name, and I should probably stay away from the biker scene for a while, anyhow. Who knows? Maybe some day I can go back to riding and hanging out with bike people, but it'll be awhile, and may need to be a long ways from here."

"Too bad, but I guess you know best. If you decide to stash it somewhere else until you decide what to do with it, we can mix it in with Jimmy's stuff. Nobody's gonna mess with that stuff, and he'll be in the Bessemer pen for a good long while. There are a couple frames there that I have titles for, so you could put it together, then I could 'sell' it to you, so you'd have clear title in your new name."

"Well, that's definitely an option. We'll talk about it after we get this other deal behind us. Thanks for the offer, Judy. I really appreciate it."

For someone I've just met, Judy has made quite the impression on me. She's smart, gutsy, and is seriously good looking, as a bonus. If Kenneth wasn't so obviously interested in her, I'd probably be tempted to make a run at her.

I turn to Kenneth, who's digging through some tools over in the corner, and ask, "So, what all do you figure we ought to take with us, old son?"

"You don't have a shovel in the van, do you?" He looks up at me as he asks this, and shows me a couple of military "entrenching tools" and a big, thick iron bar about five feet long.

"No," I tell him. "I don't, but that's probably a real good idea. I think we need to take all the boxes with the disguises and shit in 'em, and the flash-bangs, for sure. We'll throw in the shovels and that big-ass bar. What else?"

Judy speaks up from where she's looking through the box with Chief's name on it. "What about these guns? Do we want to leave them in the boxes with all the other stuff? Or should we take them with us, in case we get into a firefight and need the extra firepower?"

I look at Kenneth and raise an eyebrow. What does he think? I hadn't thought about taking the guns, but if things go according to plan, the PnBers won't get a look into the boxes anywhere near us. By the time they realize that part of what I said was in the boxes is missing, they should be busy dealing with the results of our assault. I don't plan on giving them time to react.

"Well, hell, I think Judy's right," says Kenneth, scratching his ass through his jeans. "We sure as hell don't want those assholes to have 'em, and we just might need 'em. What do you think, son?"

I don't see much sense in disagreeing. "Once again, Judy's got the right idea. Let's get the pieces and all the ammunition out of the boxes, and we'll stash 'em around the car. We'll grab that straight razor, too, just in case."

We spend a half-hour or so digging through the boxes, removing the guns, spare clips, hunting knives, the small propane torch, and the razor and mace from Polly's disguise kit. The three of us spend another thirty minutes stashing the weapons in various places in the Malibu. We don't bother putting any of them in the trunk, as we probably won't have a chance to get in there after them if things really go to hell. If the cops bust us, we're toast. The boxes with the disguises, the box of flash-bangs, the shovels, and the big iron bar fit easily in the trunk, without needing to remove the spare tire.

Finally, we're packed and ready to hit the road. We load the newly-repacked boxes of money into the back of Kenneth's GMC and throw an old horse-blanket over them. He throws his handy-man jack on top to hold the blanket down as I open the big door. He starts the truck, and lets it run for a minute or two before backing it out of the barn. He parks it next to the Malibu and shuts it off.

"Do we need anything else from the barn or the house?" I ask Kenneth, looking at him and Judy both.

Judy holds up a Piggly-Wiggly sack, full of what appears to be groceries. "I threw some canned goods and crackers together, just in case we get stuck hiding somewhere for a day or two. I told Darla she could have my shift until I got back. Hearing you two talk about Whitt's, I thought we might get some barbecue to go.

"I'll call them from town when we see Kenneth leave Jimbob's, then we can pick it up on the way out of town. As long as Kenneth doesn't go in, we should be okay. We'll stop at a Qwik Stop on the way into Fayetteville, and I'll go in and buy a case of RC, so you guys don't go into withdrawals or get the heebie-jeebies or something."

Kenneth and I are both laughing, and it's apparent Judy's probably the smartest one of the three of us.

She and I get into her car. I'm wearing my boonie hat, which I found laying on the table next to the bike parts. Kenneth locks up the house and barn, and takes a second to look at the place he's lived his whole life. I wonder if he's thinking he may never see it again.

He turns to us, and hollers across the roof of his truck, "And we're off!"

Before I can answer, Judy yells back, "We're all off, that's for sure. But that's why we're so lovable!"

We all crack up, and Kenneth motions for us to go

first. He'll follow us and deal with any neighbors that might happen by.

Judy fires up the Malibu and makes a wide u-turn into the driveway headed out of the yard. Kenneth follows suit, and follows us to the paved road without any of us seeing so much as a rabbit. So far, so good. Judy points the nose of her Chevy toward the highway and jumps on the throttle for just a couple of seconds. That long-rod 377 pulls like a freight train, and she leaves Kenneth in a haze of tire smoke.

"Whoa, girl," I yell over the sound of the engine. "We're supposed to be flying under the radar, remember?"

Judy eases off the gas, and grins at me with just a hint of contrition on her face. "Sorry, JB. I just needed a little mental health moment, you know?"

I grin back, thinking how damned much I like this woman. In different circumstances, I would . . . well, it doesn't matter what I'd do, because I need to leave her alone. Feeling a little guilty, I take a look over my shoulder at the road behind us. Kenneth is back there, just shaking his head. I don't see anyone else, and there's no traffic coming from the east, so I guess the throttle pedal exuberance is no big deal.

"No biggie . . . I'm just jumpy. I guess we all need a mental health moment."

The trip to town is uneventful, and Judy pulls into the Qwik Stop on College Street and parks the Malibu around on the side with no windows, toward the back of the building. Kenneth drives by and hangs a left on Nelson, where Jimbob's office is. Judy hops out and walks inside as I step out and lean against the car. Traffic is pretty brisk, and the Qwik Stop's lot is busy with vehicles coming and going.

Judy comes around the corner of the building with a case of RC and a plastic bag full of jerky and candy bars. "See anything interesting?"

I grab the passenger door and open it up so she can put the groceries in the back seat. "No, but I didn't really expect to. Nobody should have any interest in us, other than checking you out."

Hey, it's the truth. Anyone with a pulse would check her out. She punches me on the shoulder, and leans up against the car where I'd been. I pick a spot against the wall, about six or eight feet away. From here, I can watch for Kenneth without appearing to be doing anything other than talking to Judy. Of course, I also get to look at her. Looking can't hurt, can it?

"I don't think it should take Kenneth very long at Jimbob's," I say, "so we should probably be ready to go when he drives by. Have you got Whitt's number, or do we need to get it out of the phonebook?"

"I got it out of the book at Kenneth's," she says, leaning back so the sun shines on her face. The sunlight also causes the highlights in her hair to shimmer, almost like a living thing. "Have you got any suggestions about what I should order?"

Oh, I've got suggestions, all right, but not about

barbecue.

"I guess it should be something that won't be too messy to eat while we're on the road. Maybe some of those chicken breast strips with fries. Kenneth will be disconsolate, not getting any gravy, but I guess he'll live."

I'm trying to watch the traffic for Kenneth, but I spare a moment to look at Judy, who's laughing. I wonder how this exceptional woman is still unattached. Just watching her laugh taxes my resolve to leave her alone.

"Hell, we'll just get some small containers of gravy to dunk the fries in. That should keep him happy, and won't be too messy. There he is," she says, pointing toward the west where Dutton's old GMC is poking along with the left turn signal blinking lazily.

He turns north on Bellview Avenue, ignoring us completely. Judy heads to the pay phone on the corner, and I watch Kenneth turn right on Edison Street, heading to Tinker's place, his favorite watering hole. There's an empty lot between the house on the corner and the alley, so I can see him pull into the lot at Tinker's. He parks around the side under a big ol' oak tree and walks into the bar.

Judy comes trotting up, and says, "We're all set. Is he already inside?"

"Yeah, he just went in. I figure five minutes or so, and he'll probably come along that fence just west of Tinker's, on the far side so nobody from the bar can see him. Then he can just mosey across the road and along that hedge. Let's get the car turned around and parked over there by that dumpster, so we can get him in the car and we can get out of here without him needing to cross the parking lot."

Judy nods, walks around and gets behind the steering wheel. I slide into the shotgun position, and pull the door closed, keeping my hand on the door handle. She pulls the car over by the dumpster, and we open both doors, giving the impression that we're cleaning trash out of the car.

We both surreptitiously check out the area we expect Kenneth to come from, and in less than five minutes, I see him emerge from under some low-hanging tree limbs on the far side of the road. He crosses the road like he's got all the time in the world, and ambles along the side of the hedge that borders the east side of the corner house's yard. I hold the passenger door open and he crawls into the back seat, slouching down against the driver's side window, facing me.

He's grinning like a damned fool. I grin back at him as I get in and close the door. Judy's already in the car and has the engine fired up and puts the stick into first gear. We ease around behind the Qwik Stop to College and merge into east-bound traffic without much heartburn, considering the amount of traffic at this time of day.

Judy looks at Kenneth in the mirror, and says, "Kenneth, if you don't mind, how about waiting until we pick up the food and get headed to Huntsville before telling us what happened with Jimbob? That way, I won't miss anything while I'm in Whitt's."

"Sure thing. We've got a bit of time before we get to Huntsvull, and I'm starvin'. We can talk about it after we're done eatin'. What'd you order?"

"I got a bucket of chicken tenders, a tub of fries, a dozen biscuits, and a quart of gravy with some cups to put it in for dippin'. When this is over, I need to eat vegetables for a week, just to catch up."

Judy's laughing, her hair blowing in the breeze coming through the window. I can't help but think about the danger I'm putting her in, but we've been through this a few times and she's determined to see it through.

"Hell, sounds like you've got it under control, then," says Kenneth, playing with a piece of lint on his shirt and grinning his goofy grin. "I see you got some RC, so I guess I'll live."

Judy slows down and turns right onto Main Avenue, which turns into the Huntsville highway. She was right about us blending into the background. Just a couple of scruffy rednecks with the ol' lady driving. I'm not gonna tell her that, though. I'm not stupid.

When Judy pulls into the parking lot at Whitt's, I hand her a fifty. As soon as she's out of the car I turn to Kenneth.

"I think we need to cut Judy in for a share of the money, don't you? She's putting her ass on the line, same as us, and she's been a big help."

"I was just about to suggest that very thing to you, son. That girl's got spunk. She thinks quick on her feet, and besides that, I like her a whole bunch. And on top of all that, she's damned good lookin', which don't hurt nothin'. I actually told Jimbob to see what he could do. We actually checked you two out with some binoculars from his roof, in case one of you needs to get in touch with him after this thing's over. Just in case, ya know?"

Before I can say anything, Judy comes out of Whitt's carrying a good-sized cardboard box filled with food. I jump out and grab it from her so she can open her door. She takes a bucket of chicken and a tub of French fries out of the box, and hands them to Kenneth in the back seat, and he sets them on the seat next to him. She keeps handing him stuff until the box is empty, then walks over and tosses the empty box into the dumpster. It seems like we're spending a lot of time around dumpsters today, but at least we still haven't done anything to call any attention to ourselves. We get in the car, and Judy pulls out onto 431, heading south toward Huntsville.

EIGHTEEN

Huntsville, Alabama
May 16, 1990

Coming into Huntsville, I tell Judy to head on down the Memorial Parkway to Chubby's, so we can get a good look at the layout before it gets dark. Kenneth has been telling us about what Jimbob is planning with the money.

It seems one of his "clients" makes a lot of dirty money and has a few different places he uses to launder it. He is willing to make us a really fine deal if we help him with a problem he has. His youngest daughter is eighteen, and he hasn't seen her for more than six months. Three days ago, he was informed by a girlfriend of hers that she's been hanging out in Huntsville with some PnB asshole named Smutly, dancing at a titty bar the club owns. The father and his associates have yet to verify this information. They made a few trips to the club, even once yesterday, but haven't seen her or had any luck getting anyone to talk to them about the teenage dancer named Chastity. Her real name is Shirley Bennett, and she was a straight-A student, went to Sunday School, all that stuff, according to her dad. He can't imagine why she's tormenting him and his wife with this behavior.

I'm pretty sure the story is the same old sad one about a pretty girl who was smothered by her parents, a "bad boy" on a motorcycle, and huge quantities of alcohol and drugs. By the time the naïve girl figures out the dashing biker isn't in love with her, she's strung out on dope, dancing and whoring for the club. She's afraid to run, ashamed to call friends or family for help. She's been told repeatedly that, in case she tries to leave, she and her family will be killed or worse. (Trust me, there are a lot of things worse than death.) So, she stays high, tries not to make any waves, and moves any notions of escaping to the very furthest recesses of what little rational thought she has left.

"What does he want from us?" I'm sympathetic, but we're going to be very busy.

Kenneth grins at me and says, "This is the best part, son! Old man Bennett just wants the PnB asshole who dragged his innocent baby off to the whorehouse punished—severely punished. He told Jimbob that if we grab his little girl and make this guy Smutly's dick accidentally fall off or otherwise rendered inoperative, he'll swap us clean money for the money in the beer boxes, straight across. Dollar for dollar. Damn, we can do this! They don't know me. I can get in there and check out the lay of the place this afternoon. I'll pretend I've been drinkin' already, have a beer and ask 'em if they've got any young pussy for sale. Sorry, Judy." He grins at Judy, who brushes off his apology with a snort. "Anyhow, I'll play it cool, see if they keep the young stuff in a certain part of the building or whatever. That way, tonight when we hit 'em, we'll have a pretty good idea of which exit to be watching."

"That would probably work, but do we really care enough about the money to get into this, on top of what we're already planning?" By the time I've said this, Judy and Kenneth are shaking their heads, and I know why. "You're right . . . money or not, we need to get that girl out of there. She's Kenneth's hometown girl, and finding this asshole, Smutly, who turned her out, and putting a kink in his dick will be a pleasure, not to mention a public service. How far are we from Chubby's, Judy?"

"We'll be there in about ten minutes. We need to dirty Kenneth up a little, make him look like one of the guys from a local garage or something. I'll pull into a little self-serve carwash I know of right up here on the left, and you can spread some dirt on your clothes and hands, Kenneth. Don't overdo it, just make yourself not quite so clean. We want you to be able to clean up later, in case anyone is going by a description of the dude who came in the bar looking for young pussy. Sorry, Kenneth." She's batting her eyelashes at Kenneth in the mirror, and I almost cough up a lung.

She's something else, for sure.

"I don't mean to sound simple-minded, but if I get my clothes dirty, it's going to take more than a little rub to clean 'em up." We're sitting at a red light, and Kenneth leans up over the front seat, pointing across the intersection at a laundry/dry cleaner's shop. "Pull in there. Most of those places rent uniforms to gas stations, mechanics, and such. I'll bet they have some that are too worn out to rent that they sell cheap. I'll get some pants and a shirt that come close to matching. I'll wrinkle 'em up and get 'em dirty at the carwash. That way, when I leave, I'll change. It ain't much of a disguise, but it's better than nothin'."

Judy leans over, grabbing Kenneth's head in both hands. She plants a big, loud smooch on his forehead, saying, "You're a genius, Kenneth Dutton! See if they've got a hat while you're at it. That way, you can cover up part of your face with shadows, making it even harder for them to recognize you later."

"Light's green," I tell Judy, who turns back forward, waves out her window at a guy in the turn lane, and smiles her thousand-watt smile.

He lets us crowd over in front of him, and Judy hangs a left, then turns right into the driveway for the little strip mall where the laundry is located. She waves at the guy again as he drives by, craning his neck to get another look at her. She parks across the driveway from the laundry, facing the parkway.

I open the door and let Kenneth out. He saunters over to the sidewalk and makes a slow lap up and back, finally going into the door of Ruthy's Kleen Rite Laundry and Dry Cleaning. I giggle, thinking about getting him Martinized, whatever that means. Judy looks at me with a quizzical look on her face, and I wave her off. No need to make a bigger ass of myself than I already have.

"You like him a lot, don't you?" She's looking at

me with her head sorta cocked to one side, smiling.

"Yeah, I do. He and I have been through a lot, and although I hadn't seen him in almost ten years, I still consider him my best friend. You know he's sweet on you, right?" Now it's my turn to give her the quizzical look.

"Of course I do. He's sweet, and I like him a lot. If he's half the man his daddy was, a girl could do a lot worse, according to Momma. What about you? No girl back in Virginia?"

"Nah. I decided early on I didn't want to subject a woman to that life. There were quite a few who were interested, but most of them just wanted to be *with* a club officer, so they could lord it over some of the others. That type didn't interest me. Oh, sure, I screwed a bunch of them, but just didn't want to get tied up with one of them. And the type of woman I'd like to spend time with wouldn't put up with that shit." I point over the back of the seat, and tell her, "Here he comes. I know you won't hurt him on purpose."

We trade a smile, and Kenneth's at the door.

"Let me in, Jonnybob," he says, holding a plastic bag full of clothes.

I jump out and hold the seat back forward so he can get in. He crawls in, and proceeds to dump the bag's contents onto the back seat. There's a khaki shirt with a spot over the left pocket where the material is darker than the rest, where a patch of some sort has been removed.

There is also a pair of khaki work pants with some frayed cuffs and a few stains scattered across them. He pulls a couple of ratty old shop rags out of the bag, grinning like a loon.

"Man, they've got a big ol' box full of odds and ends that never got picked up or just got too worn out to rent out. They just let me grab what I wanted, then weighed the pile. I got the whole mess for three bucks!"

He looks so proud of himself that I don't tell him that I figure he got robbed.

Judy smiles at him over the seat back. "Good job, Kenneth! I'll drive over to the car wash I was telling you guys about, so we can dirty them up some."

"Damn straight," says Kenneth, nodding his bushy head up and down decisively. "I'll get 'em good and grubby, so the assholes at Chubby's will just figger I'm from one of the garages or welding shops around here. Pull over by that Qwik Stop and let me use the bathroom to change, and I'll just wear these so's I can rub up against some dirty stuff and kneel down in the dirt; that way the dirt will be in the right places. Right?"

This cracks me up. Here we are, planning to do some serious shit later, and Kenneth is concerned about making his dirty disguise realistic. He's laughing too, and Judy joins us.

"You know," she says, "I'd have just rubbed them with dirt. I would never have thought about getting the dirt in just the right spots. Kenneth, you really are a genius . . . Isn't he, Jonnybob?"

"Well," I say, "genius may be just a bit much." At this Kenneth sticks out his lower lip and makes a really convincing pouty-face. "Don't cry, big fella," I tell him, grinning at Judy. "While maybe not genius, it's a really good idea and it makes sense. Little details can make or break a disguise. Just look at the trouble those S&S pukes went to, even down to Polly's razor."

Judy pulls around the strip mall and heads south down the alley for a couple of blocks, to a little neighborhood mom-and-pop convenience store next to the car wash she'd mentioned earlier. The building was apparently a gas station earlier in its life, and the restrooms are on the outside. Judy pulls up to the curb next to the restrooms, and shuts off the engine.

"I'll go in and get the key," she says. "That way, nobody will notice Kenneth. Just in case."

Once again, she's thinking ahead. She hops out of the car and heads around the corner to the front door of the store.

Kenneth bumps the back of my seat on his way out the driver's door, and grins. "I'll be right back."

Judy comes back with the key and hands it to Kenneth. She laughs at the look on his face as he notices the word WOMEN on the key chain.

"I couldn't very well ask for the MEN's key, could I? I'll stand watch here so you won't get embarrassed." She turns and winks at me, and we're all laughing.

I lean toward their side of the car and tell him through the open door, "Hell, Kenneth, I remember you streaking the Wave's barracks at NAS Fallon. This shouldn't be too bad!"

He just mumbles something about smart-asses, and unlocks the women's restroom. He carries his bag of clothes in and slams the door. Judy and I are cracking up.

After a minute or two, an old gal wearing about six or seven sweaters and a few pairs of sweat pants wanders around the corner of the building from the alley. She squints at us suspiciously as she nears the restroom doors.

"You waitin' in line?" she asks Judy, who only shakes her head.

The old gal walks over and grabs the door handle on the women's room door, and gives it a yank. No dice. She balls up a bony fist and smacks the door twice, three times.

"What?" comes Kenneth's cranky voice from inside.

"Hurry up, I gotta crap!" The crone is leaning against the wall, hollering at the door.

Judy and I are losing it, but really don't want to have her turn her attention to us. We're looking everywhere but at her, and not doing a very good job of not laughing.

"Judy, this ain't funny," Kenneth bellows. "Leave me alone, and I'll be out in a minute. I almost got my clothes changed."

"If you're just changin' clothes, open the damned

door and let me in before I shit my pants!" The old woman beats on the door again.

Judy and I are making choking noises, trying not to laugh out loud. Just then, the door opens, and Kenneth comes storming out.

"Dammit, this ain't funny! Here I am in a girl's room with a Tampax machine on the wall, and . . ." He sees the old raggedy-ass woman just as she slaps him upside the left side of his melon.

"Get outta the way, you fuckin' moron! Next time use the men's room, or I'll by-God call the cops!" She pushes him out of the doorway and flees into the restroom, slamming the door behind her.

The look on Kenneth's face is priceless, and it's just too much for us. Judy's leaning against the car, howling and hiccupping. I'm lying across the car seat, pointing at Kenneth and laughing so hard my ribs hurt.

"What the . . . I thought . . . dammit, you two, quit laughin'! What the hell was that, anyway?"

Kenneth is red-faced, and keeps looking over his shoulder at the door the old witch went through, like he expects her to reappear. He's wearing the khaki work clothes, and is carrying his clothes in the bag he got from the laundry.

I'm having a hard time breathing, and have to get out of the car and walk a few paces away, to get myself under control. Judy is wiping her eyes and trying really hard not to laugh. She's having limited success.

"You two are a real pain in the ass, you know

that? I'm gonna walk over to the carwash next door and get some dirt on these clothes. I'd shorely appreciate it if you two would try to get your shit together by the time I get back. Jesus!"

Kenneth gathers as much dignity as he can, sets the bag of clothes on the hood of the Malibu, and walks down the sidewalk to the alley. He turns right and walks down the alley toward the carwash. Judy and I look at each other and break into new gales of laughter.

She says, "He'll think it's funny, later. You don't think we really hurt his feelings, do you?"

"He may be butt-hurt for awhile, but I'm sure he'll be fine as soon as he realizes there's nothing we could've done," I tell her, wiping my eyes with my shirt tail.

"Nothing, other than chasing her off, warning him, or not laughing," Judy tells me with a mock-serious look on her lovely face. "It just happened so fast," she hiccups again, "and it really *was* funny!"

I grab the bag containing Kenneth's clothes and put it in the back of the car, on the floor. I crawl in after it, and lean my back against the side of the car, watching the restroom doors.

Judy leans in the driver's door and says, "Chicken shit! You're not gonna leave me out here alone to deal with her, are you?"

"Hell, get in the car," I tell her. "Kenneth will be here shortly, and hopefully she'll still be in there."

"I need to wait and take the key back up front.

The guy in there was real nice, and I don't want to be responsible for that old witch running off with his key."

She has a point, but I really don't feel like dealing with it.

Kenneth walks around the corner of the building with a sheepish look on his face. "Sorry I yelled at y'all. I thought you two were just messin' with me until I came outta there. That old bitch scared the hell outta me. And she packs a pretty good wallop, too."

"Oh, Kenneth, I'm sorry . . . it just happened so fast. And once you came out, it really was hilarious. I'm sorry if I hurt your feelings, but if it had been me, you'd have laughed. No way around it." Judy gives him a hug, and he's grinning like a fool again.

"You're right, and it's okay. Let's get outta here before she comes out. I shorely don't want her smackin' me again."

"We've got to wait until she leaves so I can get the key and give it back to the man up front," Judy says, reaching out and resting her right hand on Kenneth's left shoulder. He reaches up and puts his right hand on top of hers, for just a second.

He turns to me and says, "At least one of us is a nice guy, huh? " He looks around, then at me. "Where's my bag of stuff? The key's in it."

Sure enough, I look in the bag and see the big plastic tag displaying the WOMEN logo. I fish it out and hand it to Judy, who's leaning in the driver's door.

"I'll be right back," she says over her shoulder as she hops up onto the sidewalk.

Kenneth comes around to the passenger's side and gets into the car, leaving the door open.

He turns half-way around and looks at me. "Some shit, huh, Jonnybob?"

He waggles one eyebrow, and I crack up. Some shit, indeed. We have a good laugh, and Judy is crawling into the car.

"You tell him about my friend?" Kenneth asks, winking at me over the seat back.

"I'm not *that* nice a guy," Judy tells us

As she backs out and turns onto the street, we're all in pretty good spirits. I can't help thinking that it may not last long.

NINETEEN

We're heading south on Memorial Parkway, or "the Parkway," as the locals call it. Chubby's is just a few blocks further south, and we've decided to drop Kenneth off a block or so away, so he can walk up to it without Judy and me making an appearance yet. We don't want anyone noticing the car, her, or me. I don't think anyone down here would recognize me in my new guise, but I don't want to take the chance.

We've been talking about it, and agree that Kenneth should be fine for a couple of hours, as long as he doesn't get too blatantly curious and get his ass kicked. I don't figure this time of day should be too bad. There won't be many patrons, and the ones who are there, hopefully, won't be all liquored up and looking for trouble. The people running the club shouldn't be a problem unless they think Kenneth's a cop or a relative of one of the dancers looking to stage an intervention.

Judy and I are going to cruise around a little, checking out alternate routes, just in case the road south to Laceys Spring doesn't work when the shit hits the fan. I also need to give Guffey a call, so I can get an after-work-hours number to call. I also want to see what kind of progress he's making toward taking down the PnB meth lab.

Kenneth looks pretty grubby in his dirty work clothes. He seems to think they'll be good and dry by the time he walks a block or two, and he'll brush off the loose stuff before he walks into Chubby's, a very believable action. Just a working man dusting himself off before heading into his favorite watering hole. Never mind the fact he's never been there before; I doubt they'll pay much attention to him at all until he decides to ask about some young stuff. This is the weak spot in our plan (plan? I'm not sure that's a good word for what we've got), but we're just winging it. I sincerely hope nobody gets hurt that doesn't need hurt.

Judy pulls over into a parking lot in front of a small carpet outlet, and shuts the engine off. "I just had a thought. Kenneth, instead of just leaving you to your own devices while we're driving around killing time, what do you say Jonnybob and I stay put somewhere with a pay phone, so you can reach us when you've learned what you need to know?

"And, Jonnybob, your cop buddy in Virginia— Guffey, right? He can call you back if you need to leave a message."

I think about this for a second or two, and come up with an idea of my own that I think might work even better. "You know, I think we need to slow down a little. The PnB doesn't know where I am or what I look like. They don't know about this car or either one of you two. If we can give Guffey more time, it will help him get some people together to take down the meth lab. Hell, if he can get the local DEA or state drug cops interested, they may know of more than this one lab. It might turn into a big area-wide bust if we can stall our play for a couple of days."

Kenneth is looking at me like I've grown a third eye. "I am shorely confused! First we were in a hell of a hurry, and now we're not. What happened to make you change your mind?"

Judy is slowly nodding her head, with just the beginnings of a small smile on her lips. "I think I get it. Tell us what you're thinking, JB."

"It's been bugging me for awhile that we might be rushing this, but didn't know why. All of a sudden it kinda clicked. Nobody knows where we are, except for our friends. The PnB wants to talk to Hammer, but they think he's in Hazel Green or somewhere out that direction.

"They think there are some S&S assholes out there that Hammer stole the boxes of disguises from, but there are no such assholes. The S&S in Nashville will still be wondering what happened to their stuff, and they'll be confused and pissed off. Both clubs will be disorganized, edgy, wondering what's going to go to shit next. I think we oughtta let 'em stew for a while.

"I'll call Guffey and let him know we've decided to cool it for a few days. Maybe that'll give him time to get some cooperation from the cops down here. He doesn't know anything about what I look like or where I'm at, other than the fact that I called him from

Huntsville. Even if he feels inclined to, he can't give any of the local cops anything that'll help 'em find me, or us. He doesn't even know there is an 'us'. I think I should give him a call and let him do what he can.

"I might even call Chief and stir him up some. The longer we wait, the crazier he'll be, and he'll have all the club brothers stirred up, too. People in that state of mind make mistakes. Hopefully, we can take advantage of that."

When I finally shut up, Judy and Kenneth just look at me, then at each other, then back at me.

Judy looks at me, and speaks up "That all sounds pretty good, except for one thing . . . what about Shirley? She's still in there being drugged and whored out. We need to do something about her as soon as we can, even if we lay off the club for a few days."

"She's right, Jonnybob," says Kenneth. "Like you say, they're gonna be all wired up, waiting for trouble. Anything could happen. We need to take care of business, get her out of there. If we have to wait for awhile to put some knots on some bastard's noggin while we're de-ballin' him, I guess we'll just have to wait. But he won't get away. . . I promise you that. If he's too tough to de-ball, I guess I'll just have to make him dead. D-E-D, DEAD, yessir."

"Kenneth," I tell my friend, "We really don't want to have to kill anyone. That really ratchets up the heat from the cops. We'll fix that asshole, I promise. For a guy like that, being unable to use his dick as a weapon will be worse than death. When we get done with him, he won't ever use his for anything other than pissing— if that.

"Now, let's find us a quiet pay phone so I can call Guffey. We can talk about our next move and decide what to do about Shirley while he's doing whatever it is he's gonna do about the meth shit."

Judy and Kenneth both nod, and Judy fires up that long-rod Chevy engine, making the pipes bark. She looks over her shoulder and pulls out onto the Parkway. "I figure we want to head into town, where there are more people and more cars, try to blend in. Is that okay with you two?"

Kenneth and I both grin at her and I give him a wink. He just gives her the "go-ahead" motion that traffic cops use, and she pulls out and across to the northbound lanes, accelerating almost gently. As the blocks slide by, we all exhale a sigh, almost as if we've been holding our breath.

TWENTY

"Booger Town is what they call the old part of southwest Huntsville, around Merrimac originally. Nowadays, a lot of people don't know the boundaries for sure, and are likely to call anything between the freeway and Merrimac Booger Town," says Judy. "It was quite the poor shanty-town for a long time. The people who grew up there are very loyal, and there are still lots of them who refer to themselves as Booger Town Boys. There's even a band named that. Seems like they must all be around a hundred years old. I remember listening to them when I was little, and they seemed old then."

We're cruising around in the Malibu, looking for a quiet spot with a pay phone. Kenneth is off on one of his learning binges, peppering Judy with questions about Huntsville. I'm watching out the window, subconsciously looking for trouble, I guess. We pull up to a stop sign on Seventh Avenue, and there's a pay phone catty-corner across the intersection in front of an abandoned gas station. Convenience stores are slowly killing off what few real gas stations remain, and I can't help but wonder what everyone will do for minor car repairs when they're all gone. I guess we'll all have to go to tire stores for flat repairs, garages for tune-ups, and exhaust shops for mufflers and the like. I worked at one as a kid, and the thought of them being obsolete makes me sad.

"Let's see if that phone works, okay? I'll see if I can get a message to Guffey. If they don't think we can get word to him tonight, I'll call later at home. If he's not answering, I'll call later with a number where he can reach us in the morning. If they think they can get him to call back pretty soon, we'll hang out and wait. Is that okay with you two?"

Judy responds by hanging a left, then immediately turning right into the old station's driveway. She makes a wide turn and ends up facing the corner at an angle so we can pretty much see any traffic coming into the intersection. I hop out of the car and walk over to the phone, halfway expecting it to be out of order. The heavy glass panels on either side of the open-air phone are both spider-webbed and sagging from constant abuse. There's no phone book, only the chain it was attached to. There are gum wrappers, pop cans, and even a used condom lying on the ground around the pole supporting the phone. I don't even want to think about it.

I've still got some quarters, and I put one in the phone to make the call. A recording comes on and tells me to stick a few more in so the call will go through. I do, and it only rings twice before a bored-sounding cop says, "Virginia Beach Police Department."

I tell him Rooney needs to talk to Guffey, and am astounded when he replies. "Yes sir, I'll have Sergeant

Guffey on the line in just a moment."

I'm still trying to digest the difference of this guy's demeanor from the one I got earlier, when Guffey picks up his extension. "Rooney?"

"Yeah, it's me," I tell him. He sounds frazzled. "I'm at a pay phone, number's 256-555-7267. Get that?"

I can hear him scratching with a pencil or pen, and he reads the number back. I tell him that's it, and hang up. It doesn't seem like it's a full minute before the phone rings.

Guffey's talking before I can get a word out "Rooney, I'm doing all I can, and it looks like I'm making some progress, but there's no way I can get anything done tonight or tomorrow. Is there any way I can persuade you to wait for another day or two before you do whatever it is you've got planned?"

"Actually," I tell him "I just called to tell you that I'm going to give you a couple more days. Things have changed here, and if you can get something happening in the next two or three days, I'll wait and make my move at the same time. It sounds like you're having some luck making people listen. What's up?"

He doesn't say anything for a few seconds, and I wonder whether he's looking around the room to make sure nobody's close enough to eavesdrop. I've been thinking he's recording all of our calls, but he may have an agenda of his own. Hell, maybe he doesn't trust his co-workers any more than I do.

"I've been talking to some people in Alabama, as well as here, and I think we've got a plan. The DEA has been watching the big PnB lab for a while, and were about ready to do something. I think this may jump-start their plan and it might help whatever you're up to as well.

"There are two or three other smaller labs they plan to hit at the same time . . . we're just trying to get the manpower gathered up and staged without tipping our hand. The consensus is that there are quite a few HPD personnel on the PnB pad. This is being planned and orchestrated by the feds . . . I don't even have an official horse in this race. They're letting me hang around because of the busts we made up here, and the intel I've been giving them. Intel I get from you, of course."

"Be sure they understand that if they cut you out, they'll be on their own. I'm not breaking in a new guy at this point. I don't trust the feds."

I'm slowly pivoting my neck, checking out the sur-rounding area. There's no way they can trace this call unless Guffey is in on it, and I really don't think he'd burn me . . . yet.

Maybe when everything is said and done, he might figure I'm expendable to further his career, but not yet—I hope. I don't see anything out of the ordinary, and Judy is watching the north and west entrances to the intersection as Kenneth watches the south and east routes.

Guffey's talking and I snap back to attention. "You hear me, Rooney? I said don't use the same phone twice. It would probably be better if you didn't even stay in the same part of town. I can't prove the feds are tapping my phone, but I wouldn't put it past them. I'm on the phone in the juvenile booking area, so I don't think they could've predicted that. They want to talk to you, really bad. I told them I don't know for sure who you are, but they have a good idea, and I do, too. I don't care, because you've already been a big help shutting down these assholes, but the feds aren't as forgiving as I am. Watch your ass."

It seems Guffey and I are on the same wavelength. "Have you got a projected timeline?" I ask him in hopes the answer will help us with our own plans. "Anything you can tell me that might help make my life easier?"

Judy hops out of the car and walks over to me. "Just a minute, Guffey," I say, and turn toward her. She looks worried.

"There's a black Crown Victoria, no markings, but lots of antennas on it . . . Kenneth noticed it twice. It seems to be working a grid coming down Seventh. It might not have anything to do with us, but we don't like it. Are you about done?"

"Yeah," I tell her, slowly turning my head so I can see the area of Seventh Avenue east of where I'm standing. I don't see the Ford, and I'm glad. Maybe we can get out of here before they get to this point of their search. "I'm done. I'll be there in a minute."

I can see Kenneth rummaging around, probably getting guns situated where we can get to them quickly.

"Guffey? I've gotta go. Now. I'll be in touch."

I hang up before he can say anything, and walk over and jump into the Malibu. Judy immediately heads north across the lot, and turns west on Seventh, then north onto the next road. We cruise through the houses and up to Governor's Drive. Traffic is pretty heavy, and she has to wait a minute, but finally she gets a hole and blasts across Governor's, still heading north. She hits a couple right-left combinations, drives under the interstate, then hauls left and heads west on Holmes, constantly watching the mirrors. Kenneth and I are looking every direction, but mostly behind us, and still haven't seen the Crown Vic.

Kenneth says something we've all been thinking. "Maybe it was just the Huntsvull PD lookin' for a dope dealer or somethin'. They might not even be lookin' for us. I can't hardly believe they could've found us that quick, even if they are tappin' that cop's phone."

I told them what Guffey said as we make our way out of Booger Town.

Judy takes her eyes off the road for a minute, and looks across the seat at me, then at Kenneth in the mirror. "Maybe this has nothing to do with that cop. I'm wondering if maybe those cops are on the PnB payroll, doing a little trolling for Hammer. What if that guy this morning over at Fat Bob's really did think he recognized you from somewhere, and finally figured out who he thought you were? Even if he wasn't sure, he might've told Chief or someone else and they told Chief. If that happened, Chief might've called one of his pet cops and asked him to keep an eye out for a baby-shit yellow Chevy with a couple guys and a gal in it somewhere in Booger Town. If that's the case, we need to get the hell out of here and decide what to do about transportation."

Her theory may not be even close, but it might be right on the money, and it does make sense. "You figure he heard any of that conversation about who yer momma is?" Kenneth is leaning up across the back of the front seat, talking to Judy.

That's a damned good question. If so, Donna could have some PnB assholes camping out and asking questions.

"What we need is some of them phones you carry around on your belt, like I read about in *Popular Science*," says Kenneth, looking at me. "They're small, about the size of a sub sandwich, and you can clip them on your belt. They've got a battery in 'em, and you don't need a phone line or nothin'. They work off of satellites, kinda like some of that military communication shit. But I guess it'll probably be a couple or three years before the public can get them."

"We'd better call Donna and see if anybody's been hanging around, looking for this car or checking to see if they recognize anyone," I say, looking over at Judy.

Judy immediately pulls into a convenience store parking lot and jumps out. "I'll call Momma and be right back," she says through the window as she turns and heads to the pay phone on the wall.

"Dammit!" I explode. "This is bullshit! If they've found out who Judy is, and do anything to hurt her or Donna, we just might have to put some fuckers in the ground, bad idea or not. I'm really sorry I got you guys into this, Kenny. I should've just hauled ass in the middle of the night and left these assholes to the cops."

Kenneth just looks at me with one eye half closed, and drawls, "Horseshit. If you'd run away in the night without doing what you figgered is right, you wouldn't be my brother. We'll get through this, I swear it, son. If we need to, we *will* put some fuckers in the ground, and not feel bad about it. But you've gotta realize, Ricky . . . Jonnybob . . . this could all be bullshit. They might not know anything at all. Let's find out what's happenin' before we get all worked up. We need to stay calm, and just do what needs done."

Of course, he's right. I'm starting to feel the pressure, and I need to get my shit together if I hope to pull us through this escapade without anyone on our team getting hurt or worse.

"You're right, man. Sorry for the fit. Here comes Judy," I tell him, nodding my head out the window.

"Momma says there hasn't been anyone in the bar or the store looking for anyone special, and no outlaw bikers have been there at all. She's had a few run-ins with them, as I told you, and they stay away for the most part. I also talked to Darla, and she's good with working as many shifts as Momma will let her. Momma said she'd get someone to cover for me, and if anyone asks she'll tell them I'm taking a short vacation."

She gets in and starts up the engine, then looks over at me. "What do you think, Jonnybob? Shall we head out to Momma's and check it out? If anyone sees me, it's no big deal. So far, I've only been gone one day, and that happens every now and then. We can decide what we need to do, and get some groceries into Kenneth so he doesn't just wither away and die."

At this, Kenneth falls over onto the back seat and pretends he's starving. "I cain't see . . . I think the lack of nutrition is affecting my eyesight, I shorely do!"

He sits up and looks at both of us in turn, settling on Judy. "I think we should head out there by back roads, sneak up on the place, and see if anything looks wrong to you. If everything looks cool, we can ease into the back where the van is, and park your car around behind one of those cabins for now. I still think we may want to do something about changing cars, though."

I have a thought, but I'm not sure how it will be accepted. "Judy, what's your favorite color?"

She just looks at me, and sorta frowns. "Are you messing with me?" she asks, then looks at Kenneth. "Are you two up to something?"

Kenneth just looks confused. "If we are, I don't know what it is. Are we up to somethin', JB?"

Actually, I think he may have a pretty good idea of what I'm getting at. We both look at Judy.

"Well?" I smile at her, and she finally relents. "I guess I'd have to say blue. Why? What in the world does my favorite color have to do with anything? Are you planning on buying me a dress?"

Now we're all laughing. Judy is driving west on Highway 72, and traffic has lightened up a little from what it was like in Huntsville. No black Crown Vics in the rear window, and now that we've found out that things seem normal at Donna's, we're all relaxing a little.

"Not a dress, but I am thinking of doing something nice for you. I realize you're probably attached to this wonderful color on your car, but I'd be willing to paint it any shade of blue they have at the tractor supply store in Athens, just because I like you. Actually, I think it might be a good idea, just in case anyone decides to look for you. This car runs damned good, and you wheel it around pretty well, too. I'd like to keep using it, but this baby-shit yellow sticks out like a turd in a punchbowl. Would it bother you a whole lot to paint it?"

"Hell, I've been wanting to paint it forever. But we probably shouldn't paint it blue, because I've told everyone that I'm going to have it painted blue some day. How about black? We can sort of scuff it up and get it good and dirty after it's black, and it'll look like a hundred other Chevys in a hundred different trailer parks. This is a good old car, but it won't bother me any to put a temporary paint job on it. When this deal is over, I'll be able to get it done right."

"Where are we gonna paint it?" Kenneth is leaning up over the seat again, and has a big grin on his face.

I look at him, then at Judy, then back at him, shrugging.

"Let's do it at my place," Kenneth says. "We can hole up there, and you know how many people come around, Jonnybob. I've got a compressor and an old paint gun we used to spray farm equipment with. It's not great, but it'll work to make this a different color. On the way in, you can drop me off and I'll get my truck from Tinker's. That way we'll have transportation if something happens, and I can leave it at the farm when we leave, and there won't be any questions about it sitting at the bar if we're gone for a few days."

Judy's nodding, and she looks at us with a grin on her face. "When we sneak out behind Momma's, you can get some sandpaper, masking tape, that sort of thing out of Jimmy's shop. While you two get whatever you think you'll need out of the van and the shop, I'll put some stuff together for myself for a few days, just in case. I'll fill Momma in on what's going on. Come on in through the kitchen when you get done. I'll tell the kitchen staff to ignore you, and you can go through the back door into Momma's office. We'll eat some supper, then head up to Kenneth's, to minimize the time we're here."

We all agree this is a good plan, and Judy points the Malibu south on Sparkman for awhile, then hangs a right on some mostly untraveled little roads. After a few left-right combinations, we turn right on the Old Madison Pike, heading west.

"I figure we'll be there in a half-hour or so," says Judy. "I'll take the Pike to where it turns into Brown's Ferry Road, then work our way south and west until we're on the old Highway 20. It'll come out on the Mooresville Road just south of Momma's. I always use the main highways, and everyone knows it. They'll never expect us to come in on the old 20."

While Judy is wending her way through the countryside, Kenneth and I make a list of stuff we'll need to paint the Malibu. Paint, thinner, masking tape, sandpaper, Scotch-brite pads, a disposable air filter to put on the spray gun. We'll also need some cheap dust-masks, a bunch of rags (Kenneth says he has drawers full of them at his place), a way to spray the barn floor down with water to keep the dust down, some cheap plastic drop cloths to cover up everything we don't want to get overspray on. When we buy the paint, we'll grab some stir sticks and strainers. I don't mind doing a fast and cheap job, but being sloppy is something else.

TWENTY-ONE

Limestone County, Alabama
May 16, 1990

Kenneth and I are so busy making our list that we haven't been paying any attention to where we are. Suddenly, Judy jumps on the brakes, and both of us are thrown forward. Kenneth crashes into the back of the front seat, and I bang my right ribs into the dash.

"Sonofabitch!" Judy lets off the brakes and is cranking on the steering wheel, first right nearly into the fence alongside the road, then back left. She's on the gas now, trying to get the Chevy back on the pavement before we get stuck in the muddy ditch.

Kenneth and I are both looking out the left side of the car, trying to see what the hell she almost ran into. At first, I don't see anything other than the skid-marks she left on the road. Then I see it. Kenneth must've just seen it, too, because we both start laughing at the same time.

Judy's furious, and tells us to shut the hell up. "It's not funny, dammit. I could've killed him."

The "him" she's referring to is a scraggly-ass puppy, maybe a Border Collie cross of some sort. He's standing at the edge of the weeds on the other side of the road, and looks scared, even from here. He's trying to decide whether to run away or hide. His tail is so far between his legs, he looks like he doesn't have one. I'm glad Judy didn't hit him, but I'm gonna be nursing sore ribs and the wrist I tweaked on the windshield. Kenneth and I both stop laughing, and Kenneth tries to mollify Judy.

"Sorry I laughed, Judy. You just scared the shit outta me, and when I saw what you swerved around, I guess I was so relieved that I started to laugh. I'm pretty sure Jonnybob laughed just to be mean, though. You know how he is."

Having regained the pavement, Judy is watching her mirrors for traffic. There isn't any behind us, and only a couple of cars are coming the other direction. Before I can protest Kenneth's slanderous remark, she's out of the car and walking back toward the dog. He's torn between wanting to run and needing some attention. Attention finally wins out, and I don't blame him. If Judy was talking baby-talk to me and begging me to come to her, I'd surely do it.

"Looks like Judy's got a soft heart, Jonnybob." Kenneth is watching her as a parent would a favorite child. "Maybe that's why she's watchin' out for us. Lord knows you need someone takin' care of you, and I guess it wouldn't hurt for me to have a guardian angel, either."

By now, the puppy's in Judy's arms, and she's waiting for what little traffic there is to go by.

"It appears we have a new companion for the rest of our ride to Mooresville," I tell Kenneth, pointing to Judy and her new friend. The puppy is slobbering all over her face and neck and she's smiling like a new bride. I'm smiling myself.

"Looks like you've got some competition, buddy."

"Hell, I bet he can't cook," he tells me. "He's a cute little bastard, but if he starts messing with me, I'll drop him in a well."

"Kenneth Dutton!" Judy has heard my friend's careless statement, and is not too happy about it, or him. "Would you rather walk back to Fayetteville, Tennessee? I can't believe you'd say such a mean thing about a poor little puppy!"

"Judy," I say, "I really don't think he meant it, but you know how he is."

Kenneth's face is red and he's sputtering like an old one-lunger John Deere. He doesn't dare mention my remark about the dog being in competition with him for Judy's attention, and she's staring at him, waiting for a reply.

"Well, hell, I was just bein' silly . . . you know I wouldn't hurt no damned dog. Fer Crissakes, Jonnybob, tell her I wouldn't hurt no damned dog."

He's pleading with me, and as much as I'd like to make him suffer for awhile, I just can't do it. "Kenneth's not the kind of person to hurt a puppy, Judy, and I'm pretty sure you'll admit it when you get over bein' mad. He's just a poor country bumpkin who hasn't had any decent civilized company in so long that he just isn't any good at tellin' jokes." I look at Kenneth, trying to keep a straight face. "How's that, buddy? Any time you need me to help, just ask."

Judy's calming down some, and the puppy is licking every piece of bare skin he can find. I make eye contact with Judy, then Kenneth. Everyone grins. We'll be okay.

"If you're not gonna make him walk," I tell Judy, "I think maybe we should get movin', before someone calls a cop for a broken-down car sittin' in the middle of the road. That wouldn't help our surprise trip to your momma's any."

Judy pushes the dog over the seat to Kenneth. "Hold on to him while I'm driving. If he so much as whimpers, *you're* walking."

She shoots me a conspiratorial wink, and shifts the transmission into first gear. As soon as the car starts moving, the puppy starts racing back and forth across the back seat, looking first out one window then the other. He's trampling Kenneth's nuts about every third trip. But he doesn't say anything for fear of being pitched out of the car.

It's a little after seven p.m. when we get to the intersection of Old Highway 20 and the Mooresville Road.

There are a couple pickups heading north, and Judy waits for them to pass before pulling out. Both drivers wave to her. I'm not sure if it's because they recognize the car, or if they just wave at everyone.

She waves back, and says, "Just local farmers. I don't see any vehicles that look out of place. I'll take the north entrance into Momma's place, so we can see all the different parking spaces as we go around to the back. I'll go slow enough that we can see the south and front lots on the way by."

Donna's is fairly busy, and there are probably twenty cars scattered around the place, with six or eight eighteen-wheelers parked along the south side of the lot. Judy is cruising the lot slowly, looking for anything that looks wrong. As we pull past the front entrance, we all see them at the same time—a pair of choppers parked nose-out against the corner of the building. Kenneth and I instinctively put our hands on the pistols.

Judy takes a closer look and says, "It's all right. That's my cousin Bobby Ray's red panhead on the right, and his uncle Travis's green knucklehead next to it. Travis is Bobby Ray's momma's brother, and he lives over by Decatur. Bobby Ray lives with him, at least whenever he's off for a month or so. He's a union pipe-fitter and travels all over working on power-plants and the like. They always come over when Bobby Ray's in town to see me and Momma."

As we roll past the rest of the vehicles in the north lot, I'm still a little rattled. Seeing those bikes got my adrenalin pumping. Judy doesn't see anything else that looks hinky, so she pulls in on the north side of the farthest cabin and we all pile out of the car. Other than the traffic and the faint sound of music coming from the bar's jukebox, it's quiet.

The puppy is running around, sniffing everything.

He hikes a leg and pisses on everything that doesn't move, and even tries Kenneth's right shoe. Judy and I crack up, but His Chubbiness doesn't see the humor.

"Damn, this dog hates me," he says. "He stepped on my jewels five or six times, and now he's pissin' on my shoe."

Judy picks up the pup and scratches his ears, regarding Kenneth with an evil grin. "I guess he heard you threatening to drop him down a well," she says, watching Kenneth for a reaction.

"Hey, dog, I was just kiddin', honest." He's bent over, staring the puppy in the eyes, when the dog darts his tongue out and catches Kenneth right in his open mouth. "Jesus! That's disgusting! I was just tryin' to be friendly. No need to get all nasty about it." He's wiping his tongue on his shirt-sleeve and spitting.

"If I was you, I'd think twice about licking that shirt," I tell him. "It's hard tellin' what all was on the wall and floor of that carwash." Now he's gagging, unable to decide which one of us he wants to smack, me or the dog.

"Yeah, I've seen people wash horseshit and cowshit out of trailers in those places," adds Judy. "I wouldn't be surprised at all if some of it gets splashed on the walls."

Her eyes are dancing in what light there is out here. Kenneth is mumbling under his breath about all three of us. He's had a pretty weird day, for sure. I decide to take it easy on him, for once.

"Kenneth, why don't you go take a shower and change while I go through Jimmy's shit? When you're cleaned up, I'll take a quick shower while you move whatever we need from the van and the cabin into Judy's car."

I turn to Judy, who's snuggling her new buddy. "What are you gonna do with him?" I point at the dog with my chin and reach inside the car for my nine mil that I'd had layin' on the seat between me and the door.

"I'll leave him with Momma. She loves dogs, but especially Border Collies. This little guy looks just like one we had when I was in grade school. Maybe that's why I got so shook up earlier. You think Kenneth will forgive me?"

"Forgive you?" I ask her. "Because you got mad at him for talking crap about that puppy? Hell, he'd forgive you if you bit one of his fingers off. He'll be so tickled that you're not mad at him anymore that he'll be just fine.

"If you'll unlock the shop with Jimmy's stuff in it, I'll get busy. When we're both cleaned up and have everything in your car, we'll come in through the kitchen, like you said, and find you. That should give you plenty of time to tell your mom what's going on."

"First off, I'm going to go over to the cabin where I keep some of my clothes and stuff and take a shower, myself. I think he," indicating the puppy, "will be fine. After I've changed, I'll pack some clothes for a few days. I've got enough makeup in my purse. If I have to, I can stop at a store somewhere."

Makeup? I have to grin, hearing this woman thinking she needs makeup. She's one of those lucky women who look better without trying than most of the others look after a couple hours primping. She catches me smiling.

"What? Are you laughing at me?" I don't feel it would be productive to tell her what I was thinking, so I tell her, "Smiling, not laughing. You and that mutt make a cute couple. If you'll unlock that door, we'll see you in forty-five minutes or so."

Judy stares into my eyes for just a few seconds, trying to figure out what it is I'm not saying. She shifts the dog into her left arm and reaches into the car for her keys. She shuffles through them, picking out a plain square-headed key.

"Here. This is the key to the shop. We don't worry too much about locked doors. All the lock is good for is slowing down someone intent upon getting in. I've got one in my purse, so you keep those until we're done." She snuggles the puppy, and says, "Say good-bye." He tries to lick my face from where he is, and both of us laugh. "Good boy." She turns to me and says, "See you boys in a while. No hurry. And be careful."

She turns and walks off toward the cabin on the west end. I watch her for a couple of seconds, enjoying the view, then decide I should get busy. I unlock the little shop with all of Judy's ex's stuff in it, turn on the overhead light, and step into the room. The place is full of bike parts, tools in boxes, cardboard boxes, and wire milk cases full of all manner of man-stuff. There are repair manuals stuffed in an open suitcase on top of a bookcase full of porn.

There are cartons full of photographs from Daytona, Sturgis, Laconia, and a lot of other bike rallies all over the South. There are probably people I know in some of those pictures, but I don't have time to snoop, even if I felt like it. There are what amounts to hundreds of motorcycle magazines lined up on one shelf, dating back to the early seventies.

Over in the corner near the back door is a metal locker with dribs and drabs of multi-hued paint dripped and splashed all over it. Bingo. I climb over a few bike frames to get to the locker door. Inside is a collection of paint guns, both siphon-fed and gravity-feed. Good quality stuff. I figure I'll take one with us to paint the Malibu. There is a box of disposable water-separator filters for use with paint guns, and I put the whole box of six on top of the locker.

There are sleeves of wet-or-dry sandpaper in various grits, as well as most of a box of maroon medium-grade Scotch-brite pads. These work really well in tight or weird-shaped spots, where sandpaper is too stiff or easily torn. I've seen people paint a bike using only different grades of Scotch-brite.

There are three or four sanding pads, and a dual-action air sander, commonly called a DA. There are some boxes of six-inch round sandpaper disks for use on the DA, and if Kenneth's air compressor can handle the air requirements, this will make things a whole lot easier and faster.

It looks like Jimmy or somebody put all of his shit in the shop when he found out he was going away. It's small, but would be a nice little shop without all the crap piled on the floor. I spy an empty Pabst box over by the little bathroom, and bring it over to the locker, where I load it up. I thread my way back through the maze to the front door, where I set the box containing the paint guns (I couldn't resist bring a couple of the nicer ones), sandpaper, filters, and sander. This is going faster than I thought, and I haven't heard anything out of Kenneth, so I decide to see what other usable stuff I might find.

Judy was right; there are enough parts in here to build at least one bike. Looking through some small chrome pieces in a wire milk crate, I see a cylindrical tube about six inches long, with a clamp to fasten it to the frame of a bike. I'm not sure why, but I pick it up and unscrew the cap. Normally, these are used for registration and insurance papers, or as a stash box for dope.

Inside this one is a military-spec "pencil flare" launcher, with a half-dozen flares that fit it. I've had a few of these over the years, pilfered from the parachute-riggers' shop in my squadron. They're small, with a spring-loaded button on the side. You just pull back the button and move it sideways a fraction of an inch to lock it in the "cocked" position after you've screwed a flare onto the threaded end. When you're ready to shoot the flare, you simply use your thumb to move the button back in line with the slot. The spring slams the firing pin against the flare, and whoosh, off it goes. They're a lot of fun to play with, kinda like bottle rockets on steroids.

I'm guessing Jimmy carried these around as a goof. There aren't really many legitimate uses for them, other than the one they were intended for—attracting rescue personnel after you've exited your aircraft in an emergency. They're also highly illegal, but that's a minor consideration unless you get caught actually using them for nefarious purposes. What can I say? I figure they're too tempting to pass up, and put them back in the tube. Screwing on the top, I hear footsteps on the wooden steps. Kenneth walks in and I pitch the tube to him. "Catch," I say, and he does.

"What's this?" he asks, looking around. "What do you want me to do with this? Jesus, what a bunch of stuff." He looks at the chrome tube.

I tell him, "It's full of fun . . . put it in that box, would you? It's a pencil flare launcher and a bunch of flares. Remember that time on The Beach, shooting pencil flares at the Shriners?"

Kenneth starts laughing so hard he's got tears in his eyes. "Yeah, I remember. How could I forget? That one skinny dude tripped over the plaster donkey in front of that Mexican food joint and landed right on his melon, shoving that little red hat down over his ears and eyes. I thought I was gonna throw up, I was laughing so hard."

Just thinking about it makes him start again, and now I'm laughing just as hard as he is. That was definitely a night to remember!

After we get our collective shit together a little, I tell him to look in the box of paint supplies by the door and see if there is anything else we need to look for. I dig around in the piles, but don't see anything especially interesting. Kenneth says we've probably got most of what we'll need to paint Judy's car. The sun is going down behind the trees across the road, and it's a beautiful evening. Things probably won't be this peaceful for long, but it's a pleasant sensation for now. I decide to go clean up and leave Kenneth to go through Vanna and the cabins for anything he thinks we can use.

"I'll be back in a few. Would you go through the van and the cabins and grab whatever you think we might use? Judy was gonna clean up, change, and meet us in Donna's office. If there's a bag of her stuff in the car, she's already over there."

Stepping over all the boxes and piles, I work my way over to the door. Kenneth steps outside, and I follow him, turning off the light and locking the door behind us.

I go into the cabin I used last night, and take a quick shower. I brush my teeth, run my fingers through the short-ass hair on my noggin, and get dressed in jeans and a plain black t-shirt. I look around the room, throw my dirty clothes into an empty Wal-Mart bag, pick up my stuff, and head out to the car. The sun is fully down now, and it's starting to get pretty dark. Kenneth is nowhere to be seen, but I hear him rummaging around in the back of Vanna. At least I hope its Kenneth.

TWENTY-TWO

Kenneth comes stumbling out of the side door of the van with a paper grocery sack in his hand. He sees me and says, "I got that roll of fifties out from under the bed, just in case. I already put our bags of clothes and stuff in the Chevy."

That explains what the noise was; he was wrestling the plywood and mattress out of the way to get the money we stashed there yesterday. That's probably a good idea, considering we probably won't be back here for a couple days.

"Good thinkin', Kenneth," I tell him, putting my hand on his shoulder for a second. "It's been a long day, hasn't it, buddy?"

"Damned long, and it's gonna be a damned sight longer before we get up to Fehvull and get my old truck back to the house. Let's see what kinda grub Judy's got rounded up. My belly button's rubbin' against my backbone."

We walk off toward the kitchen door, chuckling. No matter how this whole deal might turn out, we can still laugh, and that makes me happy. We walk through the kitchen and the people working there pay us no attention at all, other than the dishwasher scooting out of our way with a nod of his head. Judy said she'd pave the way, and it appears she made it abundantly clear to the kitchen help to ignore us. Passing through the swinging door into the hallway, we head to the door leading into Donna's office.

I knock on the door and, after a couple seconds, it's opened by a scruffy-looking dude about fifty years old. He's probably six-two or -three, and close to two hundred fifty pounds. His hair is black, shot through with some silver strands, as is his beard, which starts at his lower eyelids and hangs to about six inches above his belt. The belt's an old Harley primary chain, three links wide, with a buckle made from a pair of chrome-plated brass knuckles. There's a gold chain attached to a stud in his left ear at one end and a piercing in his left nostril on the other end. He's wearing a rolled up ban-dana around his head with the words FUCK YOU printed on the front. My kind of guy—as long as he's not affiliated with any of the people looking for me.

"C'mon in. We've been waiting for you guys," says Hairy with a surprisingly high-pitched, almost musical voice. Kenneth and I enter the office as Hairy looks up and down the hall, to make sure nobody is snooping around. He closes the door and locks it from the inside, which, I imagine, is how Donna keeps out unwanted visitors.

"Are you two hungry? I've got a pot of chili and a couple loaves of fresh-baked bread over here on the table," says Donna.

She's wearing another blindingly yellow blouse and enough jewelry to sink a battleship. Judy is sitting in an easy chair against the far wall, talking to a guy dressed head to toe in black leather—boots, pants, patch-covered vest, and ball cap. He's probably in his early thirties, has a Fu Manchu moustache and sparkling blue eyes. His hair is short, though not as short as mine, and also black. The fact that he's related to the ladies is apparent. This must be Judy's cousin Bobby Ray, rider of the red panhead chopper out front. Hairy must be Travis, Bobby Ray's uncle and the owner of the gorgeous green knucklehead parked next to Bobby Ray's scooter.

Judy jumps up and grabs Kenneth's arm, turning him to face Bobby Ray. "Kenneth, this is my cousin Bobby Ray Miller. Bobby Ray, this is Kenneth Dutton, the son of an old friend of Momma's and the one I've been telling you about." She beckons to me, and says, "This is Jonnybob Clark, Kenneth's best friend. He's the one that took on the PnB assholes in Virginia."

This kinda bothers me. How many people are going to be told about what we're up to? I trust these women, but I'm afraid things might spin out of control if we just keep letting people in on our/my secrets.

"Jonnybob, this is my cousin Bobby Ray, and that's his uncle, Travis Petty. Don't worry," she says, noticing my slight hesitation. "These boys are fully in agreement with what you did, and what we want to do. They're totally dependable. I'd trust both of them with my life, and Momma's life, too."

This is a pretty convincing recommendation, so I

step forward to shake Bobby Ray's hand. Kenneth is right behind me, and we both turn to Travis and repeat the process.

"Donna," I say, "I assume you filled these guys in on what's going on."

She nods, and I turn back to the others in the room. "You must've been here for awhile already to hear the whole story. Have you filled them in on what we found out today?" I ask Judy, and she's visibly relieved that I've accepted the inclusion of Bobby Ray and Uncle Travis into our circle.

"I hit the high points, about like Momma did with what happened in Virginia. If they need any other details, you can provide them as you see fit. Come over here and get a bowl of chili while it's hot, and we'll compare notes after you eat. We had a bite while we were waiting for you. I hope you don't mind."

This last was directed to Kenneth, who is already busy filling a bowl with steaming hot chili. He's got pretty close to half a loaf of bread on a plastic tray, and he sets the bowl next to the bread to free up his hands for silverware and a glass of sweet tea.

"Fine with me," Kenneth tells her, taking his tray to a chair next to a small table in the corner of the room. "This way, there's not a line to wait in."

Everyone laughs, and finds a seat while I make a tray of my own. The bread smells delicious, and the chili is thick with meat and kidney beans. Lots of onions and tomatoes float in the mix, as well. The aroma has been making me crazy since Travis opened the door, and I can't wait to tie into it. I also pick up a sweating glass of tea from the table, and find a small chair in the corner next to Donna's desk. I set my tray on a small footstool and get myself settled in. I figure this seat was left open for me on purpose, so I give my full attention to Donna.

"I appreciate your letting Judy come with us today. She's a huge help; I don't know what we would've done without her. Thanks."

Donna just smiles at me and says, "*Let* her? Young man, there's no way I could have stopped her. I know to pick my battles, and this one was a lost cause. She would've gone, whether I thought she should or not. Now eat your supper, and we'll talk when you're finished."

I smile my thanks to her, and pick up my tray. Setting it on my lap, I proceed to finish off the bread and chili in a pretty good hurry. Kenneth is already on seconds, and I'm not far behind him, filling my bowl and piling bread on my tray for the second go-round. The chili is excellent. Even Kenneth likes it. It's spicy, but not so hot that he's complaining, although I think it would be a very cold day in Hell before he would complain about anything to these women.

Bobby Ray and Travis step out the door into the bar, and close the door behind them.

"They'll be right back," says Donna. "I imagine they went out to the bar for a shot or two. Sweet tea isn't really their speed. Don't you two drink?"

"Oh, we're no teetotalers, for damned sure. We just decided to lay off the liquor until this deal's over," says Kenneth. "I think it's a good idea for us, trying to keep ourselves focused on what we need to do. I don't begrudge anyone a drink, and I figure Jonnybob and I will pound down a few right outside that door when this is over." At this, he turns toward me and gives me a wink.

"I'm sure Kenneth's right about that. We've never been shy about beltin' back a few." I smile at the three of them, while stacking my empty plate on top of Kenneth's.

As I walk back to my chair, there's a soft rap of knuckles on the door to the bar. Bobby Ray and Travis come back in and shut the door.

"We want to help," Bobby Ray says to me. "Travis and I go to Chubby's every now and then, so we won't look out of place. Travis just called Randy, a friend of his who built that place, and he knows about a hidden staircase in the back. Randy told us how to open the door to the staircase from the storage room at the back of the upstairs hall.

"We figger we can get upstairs for a lap dance—or whatever, take care of whatever idjit they've got watchin' the girls, and take the one named Chastity down the stairs and be gone before they can do anything about it. Hell, the guy named Smutly may be the one up there watchin' the girls. If we stage it about the time you're doin' the meeting with Chief, there should be enough time to get plumb gone before they even know we've been there."

"And I thought you two went up front for a couple of shots," says Donna. "You've been busy, for sure. It makes sense to me. What do you think, Jonnybob?"

"It's a damned sight better than anything else we've come up with. I like it a lot, except for one thing. They know you guys. They'll come after you when they finally figure out what you did. I have made peace with the idea that I'll have to leave and not come back, and Kenneth knows the same might happen to him. But I'm not sure I want to get a bunch of people in the position where they might have to give up everything they know."

"Hell," says Travis in his high-pitched voice, "they don't know us, other than as a couple saddle tramps who stop in Chubby's for a drink and a lap dance every so often. We've been pretty careful not to give too much information to those assholes, so they wouldn't come lookin' to rip us off."

"But somebody in the club is bound to have a pretty good idea of where you two are from," says Kenneth. "Hell, this isn't that big of a place. I agree with Jonnybob that they'll be able to find you, and will shore as hell want to, after you take Shirley out of there, unless we can make it look like you did it in their best interest."

He's taking turns looking at each of us, looking for an argument. So far, there isn't one, so he continues. "How about this? We call JB's pet cop, have him tell the HPD to send some boys in the front door in a fairly noisy fashion. These two," says Kenneth, nodding toward Bobby Ray and Travis, "can always say they took Shirley out of there to keep the club from gettin' busted for havin' an underage dancer. Hell, they could just knock on all the doors, sayin' there's a bust, and if any of the girls are underage or have warrants, they should haul ass. Then show 'em the back way out . . . they may even know about it already. By the time the boys downstairs know they're gone, you guys could have Shirley in a car and be outta there."

"That oughtta work," says Bobby Ray. "We'd head south to Laceys Spring, then take Highway 67 west to Decatur. We go under I-65 and across 31, then it's only a short piece up Beltline Road to Old Moulton Road. Turn left, and ten minutes later we're at Travis's house."

"How are you going to get her to go with you?" This, from Judy, has been niggling at me, too. "She's going to be afraid to leave, for fear the club will find her and kick her ass. Also, she'll be worried about her family. We need to come up with something that will convince her you're on the level. Something that will make her believe you and get in a car with you. She may be young, but I'll bet she's not stupid. As long as she's been with the PnB, she's bound to have smartened up some about matters of survival." Judy says this slowly, with passion.

She makes sure we're all paying attention. It's something we'll need to think about carefully, because we surely don't want to screw up what will probably be the only chance we'll have to get the girl away from the PnB.

"Hell," says Kenneth, "I'll call Jimbob and have him tell her daddy what's goin' on. He can have someone she knows and trusts waitin' out back, and just put Shirley in the car and haul ass during the confusion. That way, she's clear, and Bobby Ray and Travis can stay there, milling around so's everyone sees 'em. With a little luck, by the time they decide to look for her we'll be makin' their lives so miserable, they'll be too busy to worry about one less teenage dancer."

"Get on the phone and tell Jimbob what we're thinkin'," I say, "and I'll call Guffey and see what he can do about a distraction."

I'm starting to like this idea. It seems to be taking on a momentum of its own, and I always seem to work best when I'm on a roll, not sitting and thinking.

"There's a pay phone in the front of the restaurant, and another pair of 'em by the restrooms in the bar," says Judy. "But for some privacy, there's a phone in my cabin out back. Kenneth, why don't you use it to call Jimbob, and I'll unlock the garage and show Jonnybob where the phone is in there. The mechanics are gone for the day, so it'll be quiet and he can talk to the cop in private."

Kenneth heads out the back door of Donna's office with Judy and me right on his tail. Travis and Bobby Ray are sitting up close to Donna's desk, comparing notes and ideas with her. At the kitchen, Kenneth heads left toward the back door, and Judy heads down the hall to the dining room. We walk straight across the room, and exit through the side door into the parking lot. There are probably six or eight trucks parked in the lot, with their engines quietly idling to provide power to the refrigerated trailers and sleeper compartments.

Walking up to the office door at the nearest corner of the truck repair shop, Judy reaches behind a tin sign advertising batteries and pulls out a key on a six-inch-long piece of wire. "I've got keys hidden all over the place, because I hate carrying a bunch of them around in my pocket, and I very rarely carry a purse, unless I'm heading somewhere away from here." She unlocks the doorknob, and we walk into the small office.

There's an old bus seat against one wall, for customers to sit on while they're waiting. A counter about four feet long is in front of the door into the work bays, and there's a pop machine in the corner. I imagine most of the people waiting for repairs to their rig would walk next door and wait in the café or bar. There's a phone on the counter, and Judy slides it toward me.

"Go ahead and call that cop. I'll go see what Momma and the boys are talking about. I'll meet you and Kenneth back in Momma's office when you're done. Just lock the knob and pull the door closed when you leave." And she's gone, closing the door.

She hangs the key on its hook behind the sign, then I reach for the phone. There's light from the parking lot shining through the windows, allowing me to see well enough to dial without turning on the desk lamp. I figure there's no need to advertise my presence in the closed shop. I dig Guffey's information out of my wallet and dial the number for his home phone.

The phone rings twice, and he's on the line. "Yeah, Guffey here," he says.

"Nice greeting," I tell him. "This is your friend in the South. Should I wait for you to go someplace else and call you back?"

He sounded unsure earlier as to whether the feds would be bugging his phone at work, and I can only imagine that they would bug his home phone, too, if a judge let 'em.

"No, we're good," says Guffey. "I've got an acquaintance who is very good at detecting bugs and that sort of thing. He came by a little earlier and pronounced the house clean. If I remember right, you were asking me about a timeline when you hung up so abruptly this afternoon. You have a problem?"

It takes me a second, but I remember starting to ask him about his progress when Judy told me about the black Crown Vic in Booger Town. I hesitate for a second, but finally decide to trust Guffey for a while longer. He's still our best bet for some backup during our move on the PnB.

"I don't think so," I tell him. "There was an unmarked car trolling the area we were in, but I'm not sure it had anything to do with us. They didn't appear to see us, and we got out of there without any sign of being followed."

I think about telling him we're changing vehicles, but decide not to push my luck. My gut tells me he's on the level, but my basic mistrust of cops wins out.

"Well," he starts out, "I've been in meetings all day with different groups, mostly the DEA. They're willing move on the club's labs as soon as Friday night, if you give the word. They don't want to wait too long, in case someone notices all the extra personnel or vehicles in town. They're keeping the locals in the dark, other than the mayor and a couple of his trusted people."

"Friday night will be great," I tell him. "I've got a couple things to do, but that should work out real well."

I start to tell him about our plan to grab Shirley and any other jail-bait that wants to go, when I have a really devious thought. We don't need Guffey's cop friends to provide us with a diversion—we won't even need anyone else who's not already involved. I'm going to think about it some, but decide not to mention it to Guffey. It is, after all, extremely illegal. That is part of what makes it so appealing.

"You got any idea what time you want to pull this off?" Guffey hasn't noticed my day-dreaming, apparently. That's a good question. If my new plan works out, I'll call Chief and wind him up real tight. The longer he stews over it, the sloppier he'll get.

"I figure around midnight will work," I tell Guffey. "It'll be good and dark, and if I do my job well, the PnB will be confused and anxious. You guys hit the lab while I twist their tails."

"I don't know what you've got in mind, but I hope you and your friends think it through. It would be a shame if any of you got hurt bad or killed just to piss on the PnB's shoes. We'll take care of their labs, and put a serious dent in the meth trade in the Rocket City."

Guffey thinks this is still all about meth. Of course, it started that way. But now there's Shirley, not to mention her fellow "dancers," and the PnB jackass we need to take care of . . .

Hell, it's beyond the need to stop the meth; now it's personal.

TWENTY-THREE

The door to the dining room is locked, and the CLOSED sign is in the window. As I walk back around to the back door of the kitchen, I'm feeling pretty pleased with myself. I can't wait to tell the rest of my conspirators about my new plan. I'm giggling to myself as I walk through the kitchen. Even the cook and dish-washer are smiling. At the hall, I make a right and walk down to the back door for Donna's office. I give it a couple of raps and wait, in case they've got it locked.

I hear someone fiddle with the doorknob and Judy opens the door. I walk into the room and, to my surprise, she's the only one in the room. Even the dirty dishes and remaining food are gone. Judy laughs at my confusion, and grabs me by the hand.

"Everybody else is out in the bar. It was deader than dead out there and Momma had Elroy put the PRIVATE PARTY sign in the window and lock the door. She told him and Sally, the waitress, to go on home and they'd get paid for the rest of their shift. It was getting kinda close in here, you know what I mean? Out there, we can have a little room, and not be tripping over each other. Kenneth even talked Momma into having Sammy whip up a bunch of pigs in a blanket. She's had a long day, and went on home, but she wanted me to tell you that anything you want is yours. Like it or not, Jonnybob, you're family now."

She's still holding my right hand in both of hers, and pulls me a little closer. I'm not entirely comfortable with my feelings about this. Any other time, any other place, any other woman, I'd be ready for anything. But this is Judy, my new friend, and Kenneth's new object of desire. I shouldn't have worried, because all she does is lean up and kiss me on the cheek, kind of like a sister or spinster aunt might. Thank God. I sure don't need any more distractions right now.

"Come on, we've been waiting to see what you found out. Kenneth wouldn't tell us anything until you got back."

She tugs me toward the door to the bar, opens it, and pulls me through. Kenneth is sitting at the bar with a pitcher in front of him. He sees the question in my eyes, and picks it up and waves it in my direction.

"ROC Co-Cola, nectar of the gods," he says, laughing at my expression. "Grab one of them there frosted mugs and pour you a slug before I drink it all."

Travis and Bobby Ray are shooting pool at the table closest to the bar, and the little round table next to them is naked except for an ashtray. Each of them has a long-neck in his hand, and Marshall Tucker is asking me if I can't see what that woman is doin' to him. Everyone seems so relaxed, for a second it feels like any night in any bar in the South.

"I'll get you a mug," says Judy, moving behind the bar and reaching into a freezer full of frosted mugs.

"As soon as Kenneth gets his wienies, we'll sit down and compare notes. It shouldn't be long. Sammy said he'd just take some biscuit dough and wrap up some little smokies. I figure it'll be another ten minutes or so. Sit down and relax for a spell, it's been a hell of a day."

There's no doubt about that. This has been a long day, filled with instance after instance of misconceptions, fits and starts, plans made, discarded and modified. Surprises, threats both real and imagined, and moments of pure hilarity have all conspired to make this one of the strangest days of my life, if not the strangest.

Just as I'm about to answer Judy, something grabs my right leg right above my boot top. Jumping about a foot up and to the left, I make a noise perilously close to that of a pre-teen girl having just opened a Christmas present. Everyone turns to see what the fuck is wrong with me, then they all start laughing. Kenneth is pointing at me with his head thrown back, bellowing like a maniac. At my feet is that goddamned puppy Judy almost killed earlier. He's humping my leg for all he's worth.

Shaking him loose, I holler "Jesus! Get off me, you fuckin' idjit."

Now everyone is holding their sides, laughing at me. The dog is just wagging his tail and trying to re-mount my leg while I dance around in a circle to fend him off. Travis is having spasms of some sort, and I'm a little afraid he might vapor-lock. Bobby Ray is standing there, beer in one hand and wiping tears off his face with the other. Dutton's pounding on the bar and making noises like the laugh track from *Hee Haw*. Judy's trying to get to the puppy, but is having a hard time, with the two of us going round in circles. She's trying hard not to laugh, but isn't having much luck. Finally, I stop long enough for the puppy to catch up with my leg, and he jumps up on my boot and goes to town. Judy grabs him by the scruff of his neck and pulls him off of me. He's squealing like he's being murdered, everyone else is still laughing, and I finally lose it. I'm bent over the top of a bar stool, laughing like a loon. Good thing nobody else is around. I'm sure we look like a bunch of morons, but the moment provides some relief from the strain of planning our assault against the PnB.

Judy's finally got the dog in her arms and settled down, although I can tell he's still lusting after my leg. She's scratching him behind the ears and cooing to him between hiccups. It seems she's prone to them when she laughs too hard. I won't forget that.

Travis walks over to them and gives the dog a scratch. "What's this little feller's name?" he asks in that weird high-pitched voice of his.

We all try to rein in our laughter to hear Judy's response. I haven't heard her call the damned thing by a name, and kinda figure she hasn't had a chance to work one out yet.

"Kenneth and Jonnybob both called him by the

same name. So, I guess we'll go with that," says Judy, with this look I don't much like on her face. I have a feeling this is going to turn out badly.

"What, yer gonna call 'im Idjit?" asks Kenneth, still red-faced and wiping tears from his cheeks. We all crack up again, but it's short-lived. We're all laughed out, I guess.

"No, Kenneth. I am surely not going to call this sweet dog Idjit. I was referring to what both of you said as he was showing you affection, first to you in the car, and now to JB here in the bar." She looks at both of us in turn, with that smirky smile I'm not too fond of, then asks the room at large "Anyone?"

Travis looks up from scratching the damned dog and says, "Jesus. That's the closest thing to a name Jonnybob said to him, other than Idjit. I didn't hear what was said in the car earlier, but that'd be my guess."

Judy's beaming. "Right on the first try, Travis," she says, leaning over and giving him a kiss on the cheek, er, beard.

It seems that's her favorite way of expressing her affection for people. I know I have no right to, but I feel a little twinge of jealousy. Judy's just one of those women who makes everyone around them love 'em at least a little.

"I figure he'll fit right in around here. Jesus, get off my nuts! Jesus, watch out. Jesus, get out of my breakfast. Jesus, quit humpin' my leg. That sort of thing. What do think, little guy? Are you my little Jesus?" The stupid dog just snuggles tighter against her chest and licks on her chin. I'm jealous again. "It's settled, then," says Judy. "This is my new baby Jesus,"

"If you say 'baby Jesus' very loud, you're liable to have every religious nut in the state in here, thinkin' he's channeling the Lord," laughs Bobby Ray. "I'm not so sure that name is a great idea. Sure we all think it's funny, but there's a bunch of people who won't."

"Fuck 'em," says Judy, and Kenneth and I just about swallow our tongues. "He's my baby, and I'll call him whatever I please. My friends here named him for me, and I'll not change it just to make our holy-ass neighbors feel better."

I'm sure there's a story (or a few stories) behind that attitude, but now is not the time to pursue it. If she feels that strongly about it, then who are we to try to change her mind?

Just then, Sammy walks around the corner with a pizza pan balanced on one hand and a big tray in the other. The pizza pan is piled high with little smoked sausages wrapped in biscuit dough and baked to make pigs in a blanket, one of Kenneth's favorite snack foods of all time. He and I used to make them in a toaster oven in the barracks. The tray is full of cheese chunks, a bowl of spicy mustard, and, God bless him, a bowl of pickled jalapeño peppers.

"I asked him if he had any hot shit," says Kenneth, already reaching for the sausages as Sammy sets the trays on the bar. Good old Dutton, watching out for his buddy.

I walk around the corner into the hall and dig a fifty out of my wallet. As Sammy comes around the corner, I hand it to him. "Thanks, man. We really appreciate the effort."

He just grins and pulls another fifty out of his shirt pocket. "Your friend already tipped me. It's too much, but he wouldn't listen." Sammy looks embarrassed, but pleased, too. It's not often a cook in a truck stop gets any tips at all, much less a fifty-dollar tip.

"It's worth it to us. Keep it, and this one, too." As I try to stuff this bill I have in his pocket, he backs away.

"No, sir! I did it for Miss Donna and Miss Judy. I surely can't take any more money from their friends for such a little favor." He looks pretty damned serious, but I can't just let it go.

"Sammy, my friends in there and I are going to be up to a little mischief . . . I don't imagine that will surprise you any." He nods, and I continue. "We're planning a little excursion that just might get some of us hurt." He's starting to bristle up, and I know why. "We are all gonna do our level best to keep Judy from getting hurt, but she is insistent about going along. I'll bet money you know that when she makes up her mind, there's no changing it. Am I right?"

Sammy looks me in the eye, and I can tell he's trying hard to decide whether or not he can trust me with his friend's well-being. "Seein' as how Judy and her momma both seem to trust you and yer buddy, I'm gonna take yer word fer it, but just so's ya know, if anything happens to that little girl, me and you are gonna have us a little talk. She's been a sister to me fer a real long time, and if she gets hurt, someone else will, too. You got me?"

I like this guy! Damn, these two women are just surrounded by loyal, courageous folks. I can see why Kenneth's daddy did what he had to, to help Donna when her husband died. And I truly believe her when she says there weren't any shenanigans. She has too much integrity. Integrity is something all these people have. They may not be on the school board or the city council, but they know what's right and what isn't.

"I got you," I assure him. I feel the same way. If any of those people, and a few others I know, get hurt, people are gonna pay, hard. "I promise you we'll do our damnedest to keep Judy out of harm's way. Now take this, and use it to do something nice for someone else if you won't keep it. It's just a thank-you from us for being someone worth knowing. Okay?"

Sammy hesitates, but finally takes the bill. "I'll give it to Jason the dishwasher. I'll tell him you guys gave it to him for takin' care of the extra dishes and all. He lives with his momma, and they ain't got much. She sells vegetables in season, and takes in sewin' jobs. This'll be a big help to 'em."

Damn, it's hard to give money to people around here!

"Whatever you decide is fine with me," I tell him.

"Thanks again for the food, and hopefully, the next time we see you, you can join us for a drink or two. By then, this should be over, one way or the other."

Sammy nods, and sticks out his hand. I take it, and we shake. He leaves without another word, and heads back to the kitchen.

I walk back into the bar, and Travis is holding Jesus, while Judy seems to be kicking Bobby Ray's ass in a game of eight-ball. Kenneth is about a third of the way through the pigs in a blanket, and the others have little paper plates on tables near them with cheese chunks and wienies with mustard on them. Only Travis has a couple jalapeños on his.

"Where you been?" Kenneth is waving a mug of RC at me, wanting me to come over and sit down.

I grab a plate and pile some cheese and peppers on it. I spoon some mustard onto the plate, and take the stool nearest the tray of sausages. They're still warm, and I put a few on my plate.

"Just talkin' to Sammy for a minute," I tell Kenneth. "He's worried about our pretty friend."

"What did you tell him?" Kenneth's serious, now. The laughter and jocularity are gone, just like that.

"I told him we'd do everything we can to keep her safe, but there's no way we're gonna talk her into stayin' out of it. I didn't give him any details, just mentioned some 'mischief' we were planning. He knew something's up. He's not stupid; none of these people are. They're all in love with these two women, and loyal as hell. He'd be a good man behind you in a tussle."

"That's about what I figgered," says Kenneth, looking over his shoulder at the pool game. "I had a hell of a time makin' him take a tip. He said he did it fer her," he nods at Judy, then continues. "I like to needed to twist his damned arm to make him take a fifty. Told him to buy somethin' nice for his momma, but he says he ain't got one. Donna's been lettin' him live out back and work here for about twenty years or so, and he says she's as close to a momma he's ever had. Real close-mouthed, fer sure. It shows, though, how much he loves these women. I think they're the only family he's got, Jonnybob."

I'm about to say something when Judy sinks the eight ball with a whoop. "You owe me a beer, Cuz! I'll collect some time when I can sit down and do some serious drinkin', between kickin' your tail at the pool table." She gives Bobby Ray a punch on the arm, and walks over to where Travis and Jesus are. She gives each a scratch behind the ear, then comes over and sits next to Kenneth at the bar. "I hate to be a party-pooper, but we should probably get down to business, now that we're all here."

She shoots me a short inquisitive look, like "where have you been?" I just wink at her, and pop another pepper in my mouth.

"No wonder you ain't never been kissed, son," says Dutton. "I can't imagine any purty gal wantin' to get that nasty-ass flavor on her lips."

Judy leans around Kenneth and asks me, "What do you think? Shall we push a couple tables together, where we can all sit down and talk?"

"Sounds good to me," I reply, following this up with a drink of RC. I stand up and motion to Bobby Ray. "Give me a hand, would ya?" I ask him, and we slide a couple of the square tables together to make one table about three feet by six feet.

We arrange five chairs around the outside, and Kenneth walks over with the pizza pan and the pitcher of RC, which he's just refilled. Judy grabs the tray of goodies and brings it over. She puts the plates of cheese and peppers on the table, as well as the bowl of mustard. She produces a stack of paper plates and slides the sausages onto one of them, freeing up the pizza pan. She walks over to the bar and sets down the trays, then leans over and throws the switch, shutting off the jukebox.

"Anybody need anything before we get started?" She's pointing toward the bar, and we all take stock of our beverage situation.

Travis is sitting at the chair nearest the pool table, and has the puppy at his feet. He picks up his empty beer bottle, looks at it, and says, "I'll just have a Coke, Judy."

"Me, too," says Bobby Ray.

Now that things are getting serious, it seems we're all going to stay away from the alcohol. That's probably a good thing.

"Heathens," says Kenneth, referring to their choice of soft drink. "Why anybody would choose to drink that stuff when there's ROC Co-Cola available is beyond me. I think you must've been brought up wrong."

He just sits there, shaking his shaggy head with a mournful look on his face. It's all I can do not to laugh. I just refill my mug from the pitcher and shake my head, too.

Judy reaches over the bar and pours herself a glass of soda water and dunks a lime slice in it. She comes back over to the table with a handful of napkins and sits between Travis and Kenneth.

"Kenneth, you want to go first? I had a talk with Guffey and came up with something I think might work out," I say. "But I think it might be better to see what you found out first, to make sure they fit together."

"Shore, I'll go first," says Dutton, wiping biscuit crumbs off his face. "Jimbob called Shirley's daddy and asked him if he knew someone who might talk Shirley into a car without any fuss. I think he knows she might balk at having him rescue her, and he suggested a couple girls Shirley used to hang out with in Fehvull. They all went to school together, and they're worried about her. One of 'em is the one who called Shirley's folks, and she says Shirley's called her a couple times, and has sounded scared of gettin' caught on the phone. She's pretty sure she can get Shirley in a car without any hassle, once she's outside and away from the PnB assholes."

"Who's gonna drive 'em?" asks Judy. "We can't have some teenage girls sitting in a car in Chubby's parking lot. That could cause some problems all by itself."

That's for sure. This might be the chance we've been looking for to keep Judy out of the line of fire.

"I think it needs to be someone they think they can trust," I say. "Someone they'll feel comfortable with. I'm no psychologist, but I'm pretty sure they'd feel better if it was a woman, especially Shirley. She can't be feelin' real safe around men right now. I think we can take care of the problem of her friend sitting in the parking lot by using my van for the extraction. It just looks like a work van, and shouldn't attract any undue attention. I think Judy should be in it."

She's already leaning forward as I say this, starting to protest. I hold up my hand in a stop motion, hoping she'll let me finish. She sits back a little, but she doesn't look happy.

"Think about it, Judy. You know your way around. You also can take care of yourself, and if Shirley sees you, she won't be as tempted to bolt as if it were an unknown man waiting for her. I think Kenneth," I say, nodding vaguely toward the table, "should drive you and the friend to Chubby's. When Travis and Bobby Ray come out with Shirley, they'll get her to the van and the friend can get her in. Nobody will recognize the vehicle, and Bobby Ray and Travis won't be under suspicion, and—most importantly—the girls will be safe."

"Now wait just a goddamned minute, Jonnybob." Kenneth leans across the table toward me, with that what-the-fuck frown on his face. "If this is some bull-shit way of tryin' to keep me outta this fight, it just ain't gonna work. I'm not gonna be drivin' those girls around the countryside while you're havin' all the fun. I told you from the get-go that I was in this deal until the end, and I meant it. I still feel the same way. No sir, no way I'm gettin' stuck drivin' a taxi cab." His face is getting progressively redder, and he's startin' to spit a little.

Travis breaks in. "I realize I'm one of the new guys, but I'd like to say that I think you're both a little wrong-headed about this. Jonnybob's right about Judy bein' the right choice to be in the van." He looks sheepishly toward Judy, and shrugs. "I agree that she is the one least likely to make that girl bolt. I disagree about having Kenneth drive, though. The girl will probably recognize him from around town back home, and might think her daddy hired him. That might spook her, even if her friend is in the van. Time will be short, and we can't have people standing in the parking lot arguing." He looks at us all in turn.

Judy still doesn't look convinced, but at least she's not interrupting. Kenneth is sitting back, somewhat mollified by Travis's observation that he shouldn't be driving the "taxi".

"There's an old Chevy van out behind my sister's house. She lives next door to us," says Bobby Ray, looking at me. "I'll grab the plate off it and put it on yours so it'll look local. After we're done you can put yours back on and there shouldn't be any problem. Judy, I'm sorry, Cuz, but I agree that you should be the one to take the girls home. I don't know that we need to send anyone with you, unless things go to hell and we need to fight our way out. If you can get away without any problem, I have no doubt that you'll be able to handle it by yourself. You're tough, smart, and you drive better than any of us, I reckon. We still need to find the asshole that talked Shirley into goin' to Huntsville and persuade him that doin' that kind of shit is bad for his health. I figger Kenneth will want a piece of that, seein' as how Shirley's from his neck of the woods."

"Well, it looks like I'm out-voted," says Judy. "What you say makes sense, but I can't help feeling like you're sending me off on this errand to 'protect' me. As I said, most of your arguments make sense, especially the part about me being able to out-drive any of you." She's actually smiling a little, which makes me quit holding my breath. "I can indeed take care of myself . . . but I really hope this doesn't degenerate into a running gunfight, because it will be hard to keep a couple of teenage girls settled down, drive, and fight at the same time. If things go to hell at Chubby's, who's gonna jump in the van and help?"

"Bobby Ray," says Travis, without any hesitation. "We've already eliminated Kenneth as a choice, and we all know Jonnybob ain't goin' anywhere. One look at me and those girls would run hard and fast. I look too much like the people we're tryin' to get her away from. Bobby Ray is a damned fine hand in a fight, and can drive awful well, himself. Those two girls couldn't be in finer hands. If I had a daughter that needed rescued, I'd feel real comfortable with you two doin' the rescuin'."

Bobby Ray doesn't say anything. I have a feeling he and Travis have talked about this earlier. He grins at Judy, and she grudgingly smiles back—a little smile, but a smile nonetheless.

I've been sitting here, letting them thrash it out. As Travis said, one thing absolutely clear is that I'll be in the middle of the mess at Chubby's until it's over, one way or the other. I'm really glad Judy has agreed to be in the van and take care of the girls. With any luck, they'll get away in the confusion, and be able to drive off without a fuss. One by one, they all turn to me.

It's Kenneth who speaks first. "Okay, buddy, we seem to have that ironed out, at least for now. There are some details we'll need to figger out, but the main part's decided. Now, how's about tellin' us what happened when you talked to yer cop up at The Beach?" He's full of piss and vinegar again, now that he's not the one nominated to drive the van to safety.

"Guffey says the feds will be ready to hit the lab

Friday night. I told him that would be good, that we had a couple of things to do first. We'll also let Chief stew about not hearin' from me. By the time I call him Friday, he'll be spittin' nails. I'll arrange for him and his officers to meet me to look at the boxes of disguises we got from the S&S boys. He still thinks there are some of the S&S bunch in the area, and between watchin' for them and lookin' for me, he'll be shook up good and proper.

"We can take Judy's car to Kenneth's and get it painted, then make our move."

"Hang on a second, says Travis. "Judy told us about the plan to paint her car, and I think I have an idea that'll help. I've got a paint shop out behind my house where I paint scooters and the occasional car, mostly race cars. Why don't Bobby Ray and I take it home tonight, and we can have it painted by early tomorrow evenin'. Seein' as how you just want a half-assed job, mostly to change the color and make it look commonplace, we won't need to get real picky about prep work. When this deal is done, I'll take it back and do it right. That way, you won't need to go up to Fayetteville and take the chance that some of Kenneth's neighbors might get nosy. I've got everything we'll need, and people are used to seein' cars go in and out, so there won't be any undue attention paid. Bobby Ray can grab that plate off of Raeann's van and when we get back here tomorrow, we'll be ready for Friday." He sits back, and waits to see what we think.

It sounds good. He's got the equipment, the know-how, and a place set up for painting. Nobody will give it a second thought, since he does this all the time. While he and Bobby Ray are taking care of that chore, we can be spending our time making sure we're ready.

"That sounds like a great idea. Thanks," I tell Travis. "Everybody agree?" I look around the table, and the others are all nodding. Kenneth is killing off the last sausage, and Judy's chewing on a chunk of cheddar. "Okay, I guess that's settled. Let us grab a few things out of the Malibu, then you guys can take off. Travis, have you got a phone?"

"There's a phone in the shop," says Bobby Ray. Travis is busy trying to take a bite of jalapeño without having the juice squirt all over. "It's got an answering machine hooked to it, so we'll be able to know if you call, even if we miss it at first."

I look at my watch, and see that it's only a few minutes before midnight. "All right, then. It's almost midnight. You guys should get on the road. Wait a second . . . what are you going to do with your bikes?"

"We'll just stash 'em in that ol' shop with Jimmy's shit," says Travis. "Give us a hand and it'll only take a couple minutes. Judy and Kenneth can get whatever you need out of her car, and we can be gone in a half hour or less."

TWENTY-FOUR

Kenneth and I are sitting in the restaurant, waiting for our breakfast. By the time we got everything squared away last night and sent Travis and Bobby Ray on their way, it was almost a quarter to one. We agreed to get an early start, so we both got up, showered, and met here in the dining room at seven a.m. Judy's taking care of some stuff with Donna, and Darla is working her shift this morning.

Kenneth's drinking RC with a glass of ice water on the side, and I've got a huge glass of sweet tea in front of me. I guess we're hoping the sugar buzz will wake us up a little. We grabbed our clothes and a few handguns out of the car, one for each of us to carry and a couple stashed in our rooms. We left everything else in the car, seeing as how it'll be back later today or in the morning.

Having Travis volunteer to get the car painted was a godsend for us. I know we would have been stressed out trying to get that done and get our shit together by tomorrow night if we'd gone to Kenneth's.

"Hey, I just remembered . . . What are you gonna do about your truck?" I give Kenneth a napkin to mop up some RC he's got puddled up in front of him.

"Last night," he says, "I told Jimbob to have his cousin Bernard grab it with his wrecker and put it behind his station until I come get it. It's been there before, so I don't figger anyone will take any note of it."

"Good." I'm glad that detail has been taken care of. "I've got something I need to bounce off you," I tell him, making sure nobody's close enough to hear us. What I'm about to tell him isn't for public consumption.

"As long as it ain't the sugar bowl," he says, chuckling. "What have you got on that devious little mind of yours?"

"I was going to ask Guffey to help talk some of the locals into providing a distraction for us. As I was talking to him, I was thinking about who to use. I even thought of the fire department. All of a sudden, I realized we don't need a fake distraction." I stop and take a sip of tea—just for effect. "I'm gonna start a fire in the fireworks outlet next door."

This gets Kenneth's attention. He looks around and leans across the table, nearly spilling his drink again. Just as he's getting ready to say something, Darla comes out of the kitchen with our breakfast on a rolling cart. I put my finger to my lips, and start making room for my plate. Kenneth gets the hint, straightens up, and plasters a big ol' grin on his face. As he moves stuff out of the way, Darla sets my plate in front of me. "Ham steak and three eggs, sunny side up, with grits and biscuits."

I thank her, unfold my napkin, and put it in my lap. Kenneth's got a place cleared, and she sets his plates down. "A double order of biscuits and gravy, with a side of hash browns and a cheese omelet. Anything else I can get you boys?"

Darla's a cute little gal, probably close to Judy's age. She's a little chubby, but not unpleasantly so. Of course, she's wearing the obligatory yellow blouse, and it is doing its best to restrain her ample bust. Kenneth is mesmerized, which seems to happen a lot around here. There must not be any attractive women in Fayetteville, or something. She fills out her jeans pretty nicely, too. I tell her I think we'll be fine, and she tells us to holler if we need anything. Kenneth doesn't do a very good job of discreetly watching her all the way to the kitchen.

As soon as she's gone, Kenneth leans across his plate and says, "Are you fuckin' nuts?"

I just grin at him and say, "Your breakfast is gonna get cold. Let's talk about it after we eat, okay?" He just glares at me before he attacks his biscuits and gravy.

"You did that on purpose," he says between mouthfuls. "You tease me with somethin' like that, then make me wait until after breakfast to find out what kind of silly shit you're plannin'."

"We could talk about it if you want, but I didn't figure you wanted to let your chow get cold," I tell him with a big grin.

"Awright, I know you're fuckin' with me. But as soon as we're outta here, me and you are gonna have us a talk." He nods his big ol' head, then again for emphasis. We both tie into our breakfast and don't say another word.

After we've emptied our plates, Darla comes by to make sure we don't want anything else before she clears the table. No check. I know where this is going. I'm getting used to it, and I can tell Kenneth is thinking the same thing. Neither of us is very good at not paying our own way. I imagine Donna (or Judy) has told Darla not to charge us, but there are ways to make things right.

"Could we please have the check?" I smile my best smile at Darla, and I'm rewarded with one of her own.

"It's on the house—Donna's orders." She's picking up our plates, and under mine is a hundred dollar bill. She does a double-take, then points at it and says, "Don't forget your money."

"That ain't my money," I tell her with a straight face. "It must've been left there by the last people who sat here."

"But you're the first customers today to sit at this table," says Darla, who seems a little flustered. "It must be yours," she says, looking from one of us to the other.

"It's not mine," Kenneth says, just as seriously as he can. I pick it up and hand it toward Darla, who makes no move to take it.

"I guess someone just left it here," I say. "If they don't come back for it, it must be yours." She's giving both of us a look that says she thinks we're messing with her. "But I can see why they'd leave it," I tell her. "You're a great waitress. Maybe they just wanted to leave you a big tip, but didn't want to embarrass you.

Which reminds me—here's your tip. We wouldn't feel good riding on the tails of whoever left you that Franklin." I pull a twenty out of my pocket and lay it on the table.

I'm sure she knows what we're up to, but is having a hard time deciding how to handle it. Kenneth stands up, leans over, and whispers something in her ear. She smiles, nods. He picks up both bills and hands them to her. As she puts them in her pocket, she suddenly gives Kenneth a squeeze and a kiss on the cheek. Picking up the tray full of dishes, she heads to the kitchen.

"What was that about? What did you tell her that made her take the money? And how come I didn't get a hug?" I don't really care about being left out—well, not much—but I'm really curious what he said to make her take the tip.

"Let's go on outside, and after you tell me what hare-brained scheme you're plannin', I'll tell you."

At that, he turns and heads down the hall and through the side door. He's sitting on a railing that runs the length of the building, picking his teeth when I walk outside. I sit down a few feet away, and lean back against the wall.

"Something's been naggin' at me about that fireworks outlet," I start out. "While I was talkin' to Guffey, it came to me. When I was down here before, I remember the club brothers talkin' about owning a fireworks warehouse. That's got to be it, right there next door to their titty bar. Around here, those places are only open for a month or two out of the year, if I remember right. They were talking and laughing about using that building to store some of their, shall we say, 'sensitive' shit, like firearms and explosives. The place doesn't have any windows, except for right in front. It's a perfect place to keep shit you don't want people to see. I figure we can get a couple flash-bangs in there, make a big mess. The fire department and some cops will show up, while we take Shirley and the other girls down the stairway in the back of Chubby's. Everyone will be watching the fireworks next door—pun intended." Kenneth's making a face at me, but makes the go-ahead motion with his hand.

"With any luck," I continue, "we'll be able to do some damage to Shirley's asshole boyfriend and some other club business while things are goin' crazy. If not, we'll single him out and take care of him later."

"What about Chief?" Dutton's got his "thinking" look on his face, and is chewing on his toothpick. "How are you gonna set up a meeting with him, blow up the fireworks place, *and* get away? It seems to me that you've got a whole lot of shit to do, all at once."

During breakfast, I've been thinking about this very topic. Chief obviously wants to check out the boxes of disguises, and has had his boys out combing the countryside for Hammer. I still don't know whether he knows anything about my part in the events in Virginia. It's been long enough now that something might've been said. If any of the three stooges actually remembered anything about what happened at the clubhouse, my life wouldn't be worth a plug nickel. I'm not sure what advantage there is to actually meeting with Chief face-to-face. I don't actually give a damn what the S&S assholes were up to, do I? Wait a second. Who really would care about the fate of those disguises?

"Kenneth, you just hit the nail on the head," I tell him excitedly. "I don't see any reason we should meet with Chief at all. I think we should set up a meet between him and some people that would really like to get their property back. Let's give the Nashville S&S chapter a call, tell 'em we have their property. Let 'em think we're willing to sell it back to them. They sure as hell won't want the PnB to get their hands on it.

"They're probably thinking that has already happened. They lost two members, a car, their boxes of disguises and weapons, and, oh yeah, about five million bucks. They'll be at least as crazy as Chief and his goons. They might make a mistake if we can convince them that we have their shit and haven't told anyone about it yet."

"Damn, son," interrupts Kenneth. "I think you might be on to something. We can try to get all those assholes in one place while we're hitting Chubby's and the fireworks store. The feds will be taking down their meth lab at the same time, so if we pull it off, they'll be seriously fucked."

I think about this for a minute and totally agree. "Seriously fucked is right," I exclaim. "Those assholes won't know what hit 'em!"

"What assholes would these be?" Judy just exited the side door. "You two might think about moving somewhere less conspicuous if you're going to be holding conversations about seriously fucking assholes. People who don't know you might get the wrong idea." She's grinning ear to ear, obviously pleased with herself for startling the two of us.

"Damn, Judy, you scared the hell outta me," says Kenneth.

He's red-faced, either from excitement about our conversation or because of Judy's appearance. She gave me a little scare, too. She's right. We shouldn't be sitting here talking about this stuff.

"Glad to see you," I tell her. "How much of that did you hear?"

She's shaking her head side to side. "Not much, just you saying those assholes would be seriously fucked and wouldn't know what hit them. Who are you talking about?"

We're all on our feet now, and we're walking across the lot toward the cabins. I look back, making sure nobody else is within earshot.

"Kenneth and I were talking about something that might work out pretty well if we can pull it off. Where do you think we should talk, without worrying about being overheard?"

Judy stops, and we stop alongside her. "I was just going out to my house to water my plants and get some clean clothes. I've about gone through what I had here in my cabin. Come with me, and we can talk while we're gone."

"Where is your house?" asks Kenneth. "And how are we gonna get there?"

That's a good question. I suppose we could take Vanna, but I'd just as soon not take it out in public before we're ready tomorrow night.

"I've got a little place just up the road a little, on the other side of Belle Mina. The nearest neighbor is about a quarter of a mile away, so it's really peaceful and quiet. I was going to take Momma's car. Come on, it's parked out front. I came out this way to tell you guys where I was going—and I wanted to avoid everyone in the restaurant. We'll never get out of here if I have to stop and talk to everybody." She heads out toward the front of the building with Kenneth and me in tow.

"Have you got a phone out there?" I ask Judy. I've been thinking about what Kenneth and I were talking about, and have just had an idea about how to implement it.

"Of course I've got a phone," says Judy sarcastically, looking over her shoulder. "Most everyone does, these days. Even here in Alabama. Here's Momma's car."

We've turned the corner and sitting there by the front door is a new Cadillac Eldorado, shiny as new penny. It's black, with dark tinted windows and chrome wire wheels. Judy unlocks the driver's door and opens it. She reaches in and hits the door lock switch, unlocking the passenger-side door.

"I'm surprised it ain't yellow," says Kenneth and we both chuckle—I was thinking the same thing.

Judy smiles, and says, "Don't encourage Momma. She drove a lemon yellow Camaro before she got this."

I crawl into the rear seat, and Kenneth sits up front. Judy fires up the Caddy and it purrs like a kitten. After a minute or two, we back up and head out of the lot to Mooresville Road, where Judy turns north and runs the speed up to sixty or so. She handles the Caddy like it's a part of her. The big car just floats along like it's not even touching the ground.

"Okay, this will take about ten minutes, so I guess we might as well talk about your new idea on the way. You seemed pretty excited about seriously fucking up some assholes, which brings me to my original question. Which assholes?"

"I was telling Kenneth about an idea I had to get the Nashville S&S chapter down here to pick up their property."

She looks over her shoulder at me like I've suddenly grown a third eye.

"Hang on, it'll make sense in a minute," I tell her. "If we can get them to believe we have their stuff and haven't told the PnB about it, they'll sure as hell come after it. If we can get Chief to show up in the same place at the same time, we could definitely start some shit. Do this at the same time we're blowing up the fireworks warehouse and hitting Chubby's, and the feds are taking down the meth lab, and the PnB will be seriously fucked. As a bonus, we get to screw with the S&S at the same time."

I watch her in the mirror, expecting her to tell me how smart I am. She just looks at me as is I'm some new species of insect.

"Blow up what fireworks warehouse? What the fuck are you talking about?" Her voice climbs about an octave as she's talking. Maybe she doesn't think I'm so smart, after all. "Kenneth, do you know what he's talking about? I'm lost. It sounds like your crazy friend wants to turn this county into a war zone. Jesus Christ! What have I got myself into?"

She turns her attention back to driving, and gets on the brakes pretty hard to make a left turn onto Fennell Road. I tell her I'll wait until we're where we're going before I explain what I'm talking about, so she doesn't drive us into a ditch. More dirty looks.

After a short distance, we take a right on County Road 95, then a left on Fennell Lane, according to the road signs. I wonder if there are any other roads named Fennell something-or-another around here.

We head west about an eighth of a mile and turn into a driveway next to a small, but well-kept, little house. There's a small garage in the back, and a clothesline stands next to it. Judy parks next to the back door, and we all pile out of the car. The silence is complete, save the muted sound of a tractor in a field somewhere off to the north.

"This is a right nice spot," says Kenneth. Ass-kisser. "I'll bet this is a lot like home . . . no traffic to speak of, and everybody watches out for one another without bein' a pain about it."

"It really is nice," says Judy, stretching her arms over her head. The motion is so natural, yet its sensuality makes Kenneth's eyes widen and he looks all love-struck again. Not surprisingly, my reaction is more like lust.

Judy doesn't seem to notice and walks over and opens the back door. "All my neighbors will be wondering who the two men I brought out here were, but they'll be too polite to just come out and ask. I'm going to pack a small bag. You two can either come in or hang out here in the yard. I'll make a pitcher of lemonade and we can talk about Jonnybob's new plans to start a biker war in Huntsville." More dirty looks. I'm starting to get used to them.

Kenneth and I stand there for a minute, looking around the yard, enjoying the cool morning weather and the solitude of the Alabama countryside. There's a little metal-framed, round table with a pebbled glass top and an umbrella standing though the hole in the middle of it. Around the table are scattered four lawn chairs and a couple tiki torches with citronella candles to keep the bugs away in the evening. Overall, a very nice place to spend some time. We settle into a pair of the chairs, and stretch out our legs. We can hear Judy through the screen door, the sound of her shutting the door on the clothes washer followed by the sound of water running into the steel drum. Domestic sounds, quite unlike anything I've experienced for a long time. Soothing.

"Lemonade okay, or would you rather have an RC, Kenneth?" Judy's leaning around the screen door, and has a bandana tied around her hair. Domestic, indeed.

"Lemonade would be just fine with me, Judy," says Dutton, looking over at me. "What about you, Jannybob, lemonade okay with you?" Bless him for including me, in the wake of Judy's obvious slight.

"Lemonade sounds wonderful," I say, looking around Kenneth to smile at Judy.

She sorta frowns for just an instant, then says, "I'll make a pitcher and be out in a few minutes."

TWENTY-FIVE

Judy's Backyard, Belle Mina, Alabama
May 17, 1990

Kenneth appears to be napping when Judy pushes the screen door open with her hip and comes down the steps with a large pitcher of lemonade and ice in one hand and a small tray with glasses and cookies on it in the other. When the door slams behind her, he starts awake, looking sheepish. Judy sets the pitcher and tray on the table then settles into a chair where she can face both of us without looking around anybody.

She leans up on her elbows and looks right at me. "Sorry for my snotty comments earlier. I guess the reality of what we're actually going to do has finally set in. I've been irritable and bitchy all morning, and took it out on you. I'm truly sorry. It has nothing to do with you personally, really. I guess it's just stress."

"There's no need to apologize. Christ, you didn't even know me forty-eight hours ago. Since then, as you say, I've planned a biker war and the blowing up of a fireworks warehouse."

It's hard to believe we've only known this incredible woman for a little over a day-and-a-half! In that amount of time, we have all become friends, even close to family. Her momma and the other family and friends have all entrusted her to Kenneth and me. It's mind-boggling. Two days ago, her biggest worry was fending off the occasional drunken idiot while waiting tables. Now we have her involved in some shit that might turn seriously ugly. People will definitely get hurt. Some might die. What are we thinking?

"Judy," says Kenneth in a manner about as serious as I've ever seen from him, "I think I can speak for Jonnybob when I tell you that we would be surprised if you weren't stressed out. Hell, I know I am, and I'm pretty sure my buddy here is feelin' it, too. We surely don't wanna get anyone hurt, especially you or your momma. JB's been tellin' me when you're not around that he's worried about that."

She's watching both of us, and her eyes are starting to get moist. She's doing her best not to tear up, but I have a feeling she's going to lose the battle.

"But," continues Dutton, "he feels, and I agree with him, that if we're gonna do this, we should cause maximum damage while we're at it. He's got an idea that sounds good to me, and might actually make it safer for us, 'cause it'll make the PnB assholes take care of three or four things at once, spreading them out."

He looks at me for my reaction, and I reach over and put my hand on his shoulder, giving it a squeeze. He looks back at Judy, and she's smiling. The tears never came, and she nods her head once, twice.

"Okay, I guess I'm ready to hear this new plan," Judy says, reaching for the pitcher. "Grab a glass and a cookie or two. We might as well enjoy this beautiful morning while we're at it."

She pours each of us a tall glass of lemonade and

passes around the tray of freshly baked cookies. Oatmeal cookies. Homemade. Delicious.

"Kenneth and I were talking at breakfast, and I think we came up with something that might make this whole mess work out better for everyone—other than the bike clubs involved. I remembered that the fireworks warehouse next door to Chubby's is owned by the PnB, and they use it to store a lot of their property, mostly guns and explosives. What would make a better diversion while we grab Shirley than a full-fledged conflagration next door?"

I'm excited, and I guess Kenneth is, too. He's leaning forward, acting like he can't wait for me to stop so he can talk.

"Yeah, and on top of that, there'll be a big-ass fire and explosions, too!" It takes a second, but it sinks in that he's screwing with me for using the word conflagration, and I crack up. Judy does, too, but Kenneth just sits there with a smirk on his face.

"Okay, I get it now," says Judy, still laughing at Kenneth. "I guess I over-reacted when you said something earlier about blowing up a fireworks warehouse. It actually sounds like a good idea, but how do you expect to get in there? I've been in those places, and they're locked up like Fort Knox. If the club is keeping illegal guns and explosives in there along with the legal fireworks, it'll be locked up even tighter."

"Hell," says Kenneth, grinning, "we'll just need a cordless drill and some driver bits. That building is just a bunch of tin sheets screwed to a steel frame. We can just remove a few screws, bend the tin out of the way, and knock a hole in the insulation big enough to lob a few flash-bangs inside. If we sorta aim them toward different walls, we oughtta hit something that'll burn."

Something's been nagging at me, and I finally figure out what it is. "Remember what I found in Jimmy's shit? That pencil flare gun and a few pencil flares should work really well to get something started, and it'll be easier to get through a small hole in the wall. We might even be able to get it aimed through the gap between the roll-up door track and the door jamb. It won't take much of a hole, because the flares are only about a half inch in diameter. Whattaya think about that?"

"That'll work, son!" Dutton is excited, but Judy looks confused.

"We found a chrome tube in Jimmy's shit that had a military flare launcher and some flares in it," I explain. "The launcher isn't very big, about the size of a jumbo Magic Marker, and the flares screw onto the end of it. They're about the size of my little finger. It will be a lot easier to make or find a gap to shoot them through than those flash-bangs."

"I remember seeing that stuff," Judy says, leaning forward with a grin on her face. "I wasn't sure what it was, and Jimmy was as fucked up as a soup sandwich at the time, so I couldn't get a coherent answer out of him. You say they're military? He must've got that stuff from one of his buddies at Redstone."

Kenneth is sitting back, drinking lemonade and munching on a cookie. He's got his "thinking" face on, listening to Judy and me. Both of us realize he's quiet for a change, and look at him at the same time.

He just grins, and asks "What?"

"You're looking kinda smug over there," I tell him. "What are you thinking about?"

When Kenneth gets quiet, things can get interesting in a hurry, and I still can't always predict which direction they'll turn.

"I was just sittin' here enjoyin' the fact that you two are back on friendly terms. I realize this isn't the time for such happy thoughts, but even if all we're talking about is startin' a big-ass fire and kidnappin' a little girl and causin' a whole bunch of trouble for some low-life sonsabitches, it still makes me smile to be spendin' time with my two favorite people in this screwed up world. It's a beautiful morning, the lemonade is sweet, the cookies are down-right delicious, and we seem to be gettin' our shit together for our little attack on the outlaw biker butt-heads. Excuse me for sayin' so, but life is sweet!"

Judy and I look at each other, and bust out laughing. Leave it to Kenneth to make me laugh during what could be defined as a war council. And even though it's funny, his point isn't frivolous. Here we are, planning something that could easily get any one of us hurt, arrested, or killed, but we're relaxed, and I believe that's a good thing. If we were all keyed up, the anxiety and stress could keep us from thinking clearly or cause any number of wrong assumptions or bad decisions.

"Well, I guess it's time to stir the shit a little." I turn to Judy and ask, "Is it okay if I use your phone to make a couple long-distance calls? I need to find someone who can put us in touch with our friends in Nashville."

She's already standing up and motioning for me to stay put. She goes into the house and returns with a cordless phone and one of those little spring-loaded metal address books. She sets the phone down on the table in front of me, and slides the little pointer on the side of the metal case to the letter she's interested in, and pops the lid open. She scans the entries on the page, then hands the book to me.

"If that number is still good, the last entry on the page should get you close. One of Jimmy's old running mates is riding with the S&S up there, and last I knew, he was the one in charge of putting together their poker runs and stuff like that. He should be able to get you in touch with Slippy, the club president, in a hurry."

TWENTY-SIX

I dial the number listed in Jimmy's address book for "Roscoe," and sit back while the phone rings. Seven times.

I'm just about to give up when a voice thick with sleep, drugs, or both answers. "Yeah . . . what?"

I hear a bottle or glass ashtray hit the floor along with some cursing and coughing. I guess I shouldn't be surprised that I woke him up; after all, it's only ten in the morning. Middle of the night for some of these guys.

"Is this Roscoe?" I hear some more thrashing about, and hear him light a cigarette and take a big drag. "Hello? Roscoe? You there?"

"Yeah," he replies, and starts coughing again. "Who's this?"

It's easy to see why Roscoe is in charge of the "charity" poker runs and such—his phone skills are second to none.

"This is important, Roscoe, so I want you to listen closely. I have some news for your Pres, and he won't want you to fuck this up. Are you listening, asshole?" I figure a little name-calling might clear up the cobwebs in his brain, and I'm not disappointed.

"Asshole? Who you callin' asshole? Who the fuck is this? What fuckin' news?" Roscoe sounds more alert, so I go into my spiel.

"Roscoe, as I said, I need to talk to Slippy, not some flunkie like you. He will be extremely pissed off if you screw this up. I'll give you five minutes to get yourself woke up, then I'll call back. Be sure you have some paper handy, and something to write with. If you fuck me around, I'll find another way to get this message to the Slipster, and I'll make damned sure he knows *you* dropped the ball. Get your shit together, and don't fuck with me. Five minutes, Roscoe."

I click the phone off, and sit back with a big grin on my face. Judy and Kenneth are both chuckling.

"Damn, son, that should wake his sorry ass up," says Kenneth. "What are you gonna tell Skippy?"

"Slippy," I correct him. "I haven't decided for sure, yet. I figure I'll let good ol' Roscoe stew for a few minutes while we talk about it. Any ideas about where to set up a meeting between the clubs, Judy? You know this area, and also know what we're wanting: a place that both clubs will accept as a plausible secret meeting spot, yet neutral enough for everyone involved to feel they're not on enemy turf.

"Both clubs need to think they're meeting with a single person or a couple people at most; the PnB will think its Hammer, and the S&S will be coming to meet their secret informer. We need to keep them separated until the last moment and, hopefully, the resulting shitfight will keep them all busy for a while. If a bunch of them get fucked up or killed as a result," I shrug, "so much the better."

Before Judy can answer, Kenneth says, "You know, I think I know of a good place to send all these assholes. There's a place out east of Fehvull on the Winchester Highway where folks go for monkey business. There's a bare dirt lot out behind the Eagle Snacks warehouse that would be perfect. It's out of town, in a place where no innocent bystanders will be likely to get involved when things go to shit. I'll call up my deputy buddy, Randy, and tell him I saw a bunch of shady characters headin' out there about ten minutes or so after the time you set up the meeting. He's liable to make a big bust and make that damned sheriff, Billy Neece, happy. He may even get the assholes still standin' put in the county hotel for awhile. And on top of all that, they won't be anywhere near where we're at, makin' things that much easier for us."

What he's saying makes sense, but I hate to send all this drama to his home town. Thankfully, the place he has in mind is out in the country, and if we play our cards right, nobody but the bad guys will get hurt. There's nothing to tie Kenneth to what's happening, so the fact that the meeting happens in his back yard shouldn't get his tit in a wringer in any way. But I still don't feel quite right about him being the one to call Randy.

I'd rather keep his name completely out of the records, since he lives right next door to where Bubba Andretti and Mr. Branch bit the big one. When the shit hits the fan and the sheriff's department ends up arresting a bunch of S&S and PnB members, Sheriff Neece will probably figure out that it has something to do with the two bikers killed on Molino Road with S&S colors in the trunk.

"Kenneth," I start, "I think that'll work, maybe even better than we could hope. There's just one thing I'd like to change, though. How about if we get Jimbob to call Randy or whoever's working tomorrow night instead of you? When this mess gets tied in with the S&S boys wreckin' out behind your house, I'd really rather your name wasn't mentioned. If Jimbob calls as a concerned citizen, you'll be left out of it, and the result will be the same. And when Jimbob lets Shirley's dad know that the assholes that've been pimping his daughter out are in the local lockup, we may not even have to take care of that limp-dick Smutly who took her to Huntsville. We'll just make sure he knows that we are responsible for dropping the asshole right in his lap, so we still keep him happy. He may even like this better, as he can hand out whatever justice he sees fit, personally."

"And if Smutly doesn't go to Fayetteville," adds Judy, "we will definitely take care of his sorry ass down here. Bobby Ray and Travis can figure out whether he's in Chubby's when they arrange to go upstairs."

"I guess I'd better call Roscoe back and convince him to put me in touch with Slippy. Just so I don't screw up, you say the empty lot is out behind the

Eagle Snacks warehouse?"

Kenneth nods. "East of Fayetteville on the Winchester Highway. Just east of the Lynchburg Highway, take the first right, then the first right again, drive down the lane behind the plant. Got it?"

I nod my head as I'm making notes.

"Okay, here goes nothin'."

It's been more like ten minutes since I called, but I figure Roscoe will be sitting next to the phone in order to avoid getting his ass kicked if I call the next person on the list and tell him Roscoe shined me on. The phone rings once, and Roscoe's there. "Yeah."

"I see your vocabulary hasn't improved since the last time we talked," I say. He just snorts, then coughs for a spell. "Are you ready to write this down?" I ask, waiting for him to catch his breath.

"Write what down? You still haven't told me what this is about. Who the fuck are you, anyways? I don't appreciate bein' woke up and fucked with by some ass-hole who won't even tell me who he is."

Roscoe actually can string more than one or two words together . . . imagine that.

"Look, just write this down and don't fuck it up, or Slippy will probably de-nut you." That should get his attention. "Tell Slippy that I need to talk to him, no-body else. It's about some boxes that were in the trunk of a Ford in Fayetteville." A noisy intake of breath, followed by more coughing. I wait until he's done. "I have them, and if he wants them back, he needs to talk to me. Get him to your place, but don't fuck around all day. I'll call back in an hour, and if he's not there, I'll call Chief in Huntsville and see if he's interested. One hour, Roscoe . . . talk to you then."

We're all laughing when I hang up the phone, imagining the shit-storm Roscoe's going to start when he gets in touch with Slippy. It's obvious he knew what I was talking about. Hopefully, he'll light a fire under the rest of the club. The more they're wound up, the better for us. I want them ready to kick some ass when they drive into the empty lot behind the potato chip place in Fayetteville.

TWENTY-SEVEN

Over the last forty-five minutes, the three of us have been working on the best way to get the two clubs to the meeting place, at the same time, without either group figuring out that I'm not the one they're meeting. Chief and his boys will be looking for Hammer, and Slippy and his bunch will be looking for an unknown person with their property.

Judy put together a lunch of roast beef sandwiches and fried potatoes, and we've been eating while we have a chance. In between bites, Kenneth has a really good idea: tell each group to only bring one vehicle. That way we can convince them that the person they're meeting is in the only other vehicle there. Since they'll be expecting a lone occupant, each group should feel confident, and that might just make them a little less cautious.

Judy says the PnB crew has a nondescript Chevy van that looks a whole lot like Vanna that they use to haul dope and other goods. I'll tell Chief to come in it, so there will be room for the boxes and his crew on their way home from the meet. I'll make it clear that if I see any other vehicle in the vicinity, the deal's off and he won't see the contents of the beer boxes.

Seeing as I know what vehicle the PnB contingent will be in, I'll call Slippy first and tell him I'll be in a white van, and find out what he and his crew will be driving. I'll give him the same speech about only bringing one car, blah, blah, blah. After I know what he's driving, I'll call Chief and tell him what vehicle to be looking for. I'll explain I "borrowed" it from a parking lot to explain the Tennessee plates.

By the time I'm finished with lunch, the hour I gave Roscoe is up, and I really want to get this part of the deal settled, so I call him again.

The phone rings twice, then a different voice says, "Yeah?" These guys need a new writer for their material.

"Is that the official phone greeting for the S&S MC?" I ask this new person, who I'm hoping is Slippy. "It seems that no matter who answers the phone, that's all they've got to say. Is this Slippy?"

"Yeah, this is Slippy. This had better be good, or I'm gonna find you and teach *you* some fuckin' manners," says the S&S cub president. "R-Dog says you've got some information for me about some of our property. Who is this, and how did you get our shit?"

R-Dog? Holy shit! It's all I can do not to break out laughing.

"Who I am isn't important. What is important is that I'm in possession of some cardboard beer boxes that were in a black Crown Vic that hit a tree outside Fayetteville a few nights back. The contents of these boxes would make a certain motorcycle club in Huntsville very angry, if they came to the same conclusions I came to."

I hear him take a couple of deep breaths, and there is some muffled cursing.

"What is it you want?" he asks.

I think I detect some malice in his tone. He doesn't seem to like me much.

"I want to help you out," I tell him. "I have no use for that bunch of pussies in Huntsville, and I've always been treated good by you and your brothers." Let him wonder about who the hell I am—it'll keep him confused. "I want to give you back your goods, and I want to be accepted as a prospect in the S&S." This last bit just pops out, and I'm having a hard time not giggling.

"How do I know you're not full of shit?" he asks. "Give me a little idea of what's in the boxes, and while you're at it, how the hell you came to have these boxes in your possession."

"Okay, fair enough. There are some articles of clothing that would make some dandy Halloween disguises, if a group of un-named people wanted to impersonate some un-named biker types from a certain city in northern Alabama. These disguises are very detailed, right down to the hardware. There is also a bunch of high-grade paper, banded together into small stacks. Sound familiar?"

It sounds like poor ol' Slippy is about to have some sort of asthma attack or something. He's wheezing and sounds like he might actually be strangling. Bummer for him.

"Okay, so I believe you've seen the inside of these boxes . . . how do I know you actually have them? And I still want to know how you got your paws on 'em."

I can hear Slippy telling Roscoe and whoever else is there to shut up so he can hear me. It seems the whole bunch is wound up; the rest of 'em must be listening on an extension.

"Oh, I've got 'em, all right. As for how I got 'em, that's easy. My second cousin and I were comin' home down Molino Road when we came up on that Crown Vic wadded up agin' that tree. We got out and went over there to see if everyone was okay. The two dudes in the car were dead, and while I was wonderin' what to do next, Wend—er—my second cousin went around to rummage through the trunk, which had popped open in the wreck. We grabbed all the boxes, thinkin' we'd go through 'em later. We didn't figger out who they belonged to until we saw yer dead bros' colors in their bags. By then we were freakin' out, and just hauled ass.

"After we got back to my place, we went through the boxes. I'm sure you'll understand that we were surprised by what we found. Wen—damn—my second cousin wanted to keep the money and the hardware and just pitch the rest of it.

"Like I said, I've always respected the S&S, and wouldn't go along with that. We ended up drunk and fightin' about it. I caught him tryin' to swipe some of the cash the next mornin', and we got into it again. I don't want to get into a lot of detail, but he won't be causin' anyone any more trouble. That's partly why it took me so long to get ahold of you. I had to make sure he wouldn't be found before I did anything else. I just got back late last night, and wanted to rest up a mite before I called."

Whew! Kenneth and Judy are hangin' onto each other with their hands over their mouths. I give them that look, like *Don't make me laugh!* That just makes 'em laugh harder. They finally go around the corner into the other room.

Slippy seems to have bought the whole damned thing. He says, "Well, you done real good, bubba. You sound like just the kind of man this club needs more of."

There is a flurry of muffled voices; I'm guessing the other club members on the extension are surprised to hear this ringing endorsement of someone who's got 'em over a barrel and is just plain rude, to boot.

"Why don't you bring our stuff by the clubhouse, and we'll have a party. I'm sure nobody will object to making you a prospect after you took care of our property, and your cousin—ha, ha—for us."

More muffled exclamations, followed by Slippy tellin' 'em all to shut the fuck up.

"Well," I say, "I'm kinda ashamed to say this, but I don't have a car or anything to drive. My old Honda is down with a busted chain, and I couldn't haul all those boxes on it, anyhow."

Gnashing of teeth! A fuckin' Honda!? Slippy is

hollerin' in a whisper, the others are all going bugshit. Madness.

"I'm off work tomorrow night, and I know a good place to meet here close to home . . . I mean in a neutral location. I can borrow Wende—my second cousin's van. Nobody's missed him yet, and it's parked out front of my place. I'd just be afraid to take it as far as Nashville, since the right front wheel fell off about a week ago. We got it back on there, but it's kinda sketchy."

Laughter. Pandemonium. Slippy whispering, yelling, again, to shut the fuck up.

"Okay, man . . . what is your name, anyhow? We're all friends here, right? If you're gonna join the club, we'll need to know what to call you."

Muffled snickers, chuckles, and downright laughter from the extension.

"My name's Jer, uh, well, everyone around here calls me Monster."

I have the good sense to sound ashamed of myself as I say this. The peanut gallery at R-Dog's is about to go into mass hysterics. I plunge ahead, as if I can't hear all the background noise. "Anyhow, there's a place just east of Fayetteville on 64, the Winchester Highway." I consult my notes and plunge ahead. "Headin' east, you'll go past the Lynchburg Highway intersection, then hang a right on Industrial, where the Eagle Snacks warehouse is. Go south behind the warehouse to the first little dirt lane on the right. It'll take you to an empty dirt lot. I'll meet you there tomorrow night at midnight. Wen—my cousin's van is a white Chevy, one of those child-molester vans with no windows. What'll you be drivin'? I'm kinda spooked, which I figger you can understand, so I don't want to see more than one vehicle down there. If there are any other cars or whatever in the area, I'll take off, and you won't find me. I don't live in Fayetteville or anywhere like that, so you won't know where to look." Muffled snuffles and giggles.

"Okay, Jerry—I mean, Monster," Slippy is tryin' hard not to laugh out loud. "We'll see you tomorrow night at midnight in the dirt field behind the Eagle Snacks warehouse. We'll be in a Dodge van, kind of a dark blue color with a Harley sticker on the side. I understand your caution, but you'll find out there's nothin' to worry about. Hell, you're our new prospect. We won't let anythin' happen to you, right?" Now the chorus is in high gear, and they actually hang up the extension, or put something more substantial than someone's hand over it.

"Cool," I say, not trusting myself to say much more. "See you then, bro."

I hang up, and the three of us are all in tears as I relate the parts of the conversation that Kenneth and Judy didn't hear.

I'm sure Slippy and his bros are rollin' on the floor, laughing at the dumb-ass Jerry or Jerome, with a second cousin named Wendell or something like that, who just went missing and left his white Chevy van with a wonky front wheel at his cuz's place. Monster! Holy shit, that's just hilarious. The kid probably works at the Kum-n-Go, fer Crissakes! No need to look for him before the scheduled meet and attract any undue attention. It'll be simple to get the boxes from the dweeb, then dump him and his van somewhere out of the way. By the time someone finds him, the S&S will be long gone.

Monster! Ha!

TWENTY-EIGHT

Things have settled down quite a bit. None of us has laughed uncontrollably for at least five minutes, and the giggles, chuckles, and hiccups are tapering off, too. This next call won't be as easy, or as comical.

Chief knows Hammer well enough to spot a total bullshit story, so I'll have to make him believe whatever yarn I spin. It will need to mesh with the one I told him the other day about how I came into possession of the S&S property. Luckily, Kenneth and I made notes before I called Chief the first time, so I have some idea of where to go from there.

I dig out my list of phone numbers and call Chief's house, figuring I'll get Polly, if anyone. She picks up the phone and says, "Hello," just like last time.

"Polly, this is your pigtail-pullin' buddy from up north," I tell her, and I hear her breath quicken just a little.

"The big man is wantin' to talk to you right away," she says. "He's been kinda cranky since the last time you two talked." I can only imagine.

"That's why I called. I'll call him at that number I used last time, unless you think somewhere else would be better."

I figure it can't hurt to be conciliatory at this stage. There will be plenty of time to be an asshole later.

"No," she starts, "that'll be fine. You still have that number?" I tell her I do. "Okay, give him about thirty minutes. I'll need to go talk to him in person. Just don't fuckin' make him any madder, will ya?"

"What I've got to tell him should make him happy," I say, and almost mean it. "Things have been weird. I'll call him at one o'clock. Take care, Polly." And I'm gone.

She sounded worried enough to go straight to wherever Chief is and tell him I've surfaced. She'll probably even tell him I'm going to make him happy. She can only hope that he'll be mad at me instead of her for that little bit of bad information.

"You must've changed your story, if you plan on makin' that asshole happy," says Dutton with a grin on his face. "Last I heard, he was prob'ly gonna be a mite unhappy."

Judy is smiling at the two of us, and nodding her head. "Yeah, JB, what's going to make him so happy? Or were you just maybe lying to that sweet woman?"

Dutton just snorts, and we all have a good laugh.

"I may have misled her just a little," I tell them, looking for my notes to refresh my memory before I call Chief.

Judy and Kenneth wander outside while I study, after I promise to let them know when I get ready to make the call. I go through my notes, nursing a lemonade and snacking on a few cookies.

At five till one, I go to the screen door and crack

it open. "Okay, you two, I'm about ready to call Chief. Please, if you get tickled or whatever, try to get somewhere out of my line of sight. That last call was nuts, and those clowns were too busy laughing at Monster to realize I was screwin' with them. But Chief is gonna be on guard, and there won't be anything funny from his perspective."

They both nod, and look appropriately sober. Hopefully, we can pull this off without making Chief any more paranoid than he already is.

I dial the number I called last time, and Chief picks up damned near before the first ring is complete. I think he may just be a little antsy. If so, that may or may not play into our plans.

"Hammer," he growls. "Where the fuck have you been, man? I've been goin' nuts, waitin' to see what those S&S pukes are up to. I thought you said you'd call me yesterday."

This accusation is about what I expected; he's on edge and not in the mood to be polite.

"I said either yesterday or today, if I remember right," I tell him, not groveling as he had probably hoped. "I've got my own problems. I saw your boys ridin' around up here," (let him think I'm around Hazel Green), "and that pisses me off. I told you I'd be in touch when I was ready. I don't appreciate bein' hunted for, like some fuckin' prospect with a hangover." That should make him definitely unhappy.

"Hey, we're worried down here. You tell me the

S&S is plannin' to fuck with us, usin' disguises to make 'em look like our officers, and then you make me wait for a couple days like some fuckin' punk." Yeah, I think he's unhappy. "I can't worry about your ego, Hammer. I need to do what's best for the club. Yeah, I sent a couple members up to Hazel Green to try flushin' you out. Get over it." Now, this is getting better all the time.

"I'm not gettin' over anything, my friend. Or maybe I should say former friend?" That should get a rise out of him. "Not only were your bros up here advertising the fact that they were looking for me, there were three S&S assholes doin' the same damned thing at the same time. Maybe you're all in this—whatever it is—together." I can hear him take a big breath, getting ready to let me have it. "Hang on, let me finish," I tell him before he can speak. "I'm wanted by the fuckin' cops, the feds, who knows who else, and instead of helpin' me lay low, my club is throwin' my name around all over the fuckin' countryside. On top of that, the S&S is lookin' for me in the same place at the same time. I have to ask myself, 'How do they know about me, and who told them where to look?' It seems to me that someone in my club ratted me out, and I can't figger out why, unless the two clubs are workin' to-gether on something. Is that what's happening?" I can hear him breathing, and can almost feel the rage and confusion through the phone line.

"I don't know anything about any S&S members in Hazel Green. Believe it or don't, but that's a fact.

I'm pissed that you would accuse us of selling you out to those pricks. I'm even more pissed that you think we would do business with them. I'm just looking out for this club, and yeah, I might've fucked up sending men looking for you. No offense, Hammer, just doin' what I thought was best at the time. Let's meet somewhere so I can get that shit from you, and we'll get you somewhere safe from the cops and the S&S, or whoever else might be lookin' for you."

He's making quite an effort to calm down, so I'll give him what he wants. He doesn't have a clue that I've already made up my mind to avoid him at all costs. He thinks he can talk me into believing that he has my best interests at heart. Bullshit.

"That's why I called." Let him think I've softened up a little. "I found a place where I can be sure I'm not bein' ambushed. There's a place just east of Fayetteville, Tennessee, on Highway 64 called Eagle Snacks." I can almost hear his next argument forming. I press on before he can interrupt. "It's just east of the Lynchburg turn-off, on the south side of the road. Turn on the little road next to it and drive south to the back side of the warehouse. There's a little trail headin' back to the west that ends up in a little clearing. I'll meet you there tomorrow night at midnight."

He busts in, not wanting to hear any more. "No, damn it, I told you we'd meet at Chubby's." Little does he know that I'll be at Chubby's, but he won't. "We can have a party after we're done with business, and you can get some pussy from any of the dancers you want. I've got too much shit goin' on to drive around the fuckin' Tennessee countryside like James fuckin' Bond. Just meet me at Chubby's."

My turn to interrupt. "No, Chief, that's not gonna happen. If you want this shit, you'll meet me where I say, when I say. I still don't know what's goin' on with you guys. I've gotta watch out for myself, so we'll do it my way. Midnight behind the Eagle Snacks warehouse east of Fayetteville, tomorrow night. Don't bring more than one car, or you won't see me. I've had time to scope the place out, and you won't be able to sneak up on me, so don't even try. One car . . . what'll you be in?"

He's pissed; I can tell by the way he's breathing and by how quiet he is.

"Okay. We'll do it your way, but we're gonna have us a long talk when this is over." He thinks so, huh? Yeah, right. "I'll be in a white Chevy delivery van. It should fit in with the warehouse and all. What are you gonna be drivin'?"

Judy called it. The white delivery van will be just what the S&S bunch will be expecting.

"I grabbed an old Dodge van from a parkin' lot in Tullahoma next to the Air Force base. It even has a Harley decal on the side. It's dark blue, no windows. Sounds like we might start a fad."

I let myself chuckle. Let him think I've lightened up a little. Maybe he'll drop his guard, if only a fraction of an inch. Any little bit might just turn out to be deadly.

"All right, Hammer, tomorrow at midnight. Just you and me."

Like he really thinks I'd believe that shit. That van will have at least three or four of his club bros in there with him.

That's okay, let the S&S deal with 'em.

TWENTY-NINE

After I fill in Kenneth and Judy on the conversation they missed, we all sit around and discuss our individual ideas about how things are progressing.

"Son," Kenneth begins, "I think you've come up with a way to keep all of those guys out of the way while we hit Chubby's and grab Shirley. Not to mention the fact that the feds'll be bustin' up their lab at the same time. Speakin' of which, when are you gonna call your cop buddy?"

"He's not my buddy!" I proclaim, with just a touch of annoyance. Dutton's grinning like a damned Cheshire Cat, and I realize he used that phrase on purpose, just to get my goat. He knows me too well. "He and I just have a common goal right now, that's all. You're right, though. I need to call him and give him the timetable we've set up. Midnight should work pretty well. There'll be a crowd at Chubby's, so that'll help Bobby Ray and Travis. That time of night, there shouldn't be much traffic down in the neighborhood where the lab is. And Chief, Slippy, and all their butt-head buddies will be at least forty-five minutes away, dealing with each other—and the cops—if things go according to plan. You need to call Jimbob and get him up to speed, too."

Judy chimes in, "I'm kinda worried about the place you set up the meeting, Jonnybob. What if some local kids are out there, partying? There might even be some couples parking out there."

Crap. I hadn't even thought of that.

"Hell," Kenneth says, "I'll mention it to Jimbob, and he and Randy can figger out some way to keep the locals away without spookin' the boys in the vans. Jimbob really is one of the most devious sonsabitches I ever met. He'll come up with somethin', I guarantee it. I'll call him directly, just as soon as you get off the phone with yer cop from The Beach."

Hell, if Dutton has that much faith in the crooked lawyer, who am I to question him? Judy looks mollified, as well.

I guess it's time to call Guffey and give him at least the main parts of what we've got so far.

I've got his office number memorized by now, and I try it first. When I ask for Guffey and tell the desk cop it's Rooney, he says, "Just a minute," and puts me on hold.

I'll give him about thirty seconds, then I'm gone. After Guffey's warning, I don't want to give them long enough to trace the call. Before the second hand has traveled past three of the little numbers on my watch face, Guffey answers. He must've been in the room.

"Give me a number. Hurry."

I read Judy's number off the handset and hang up. I'll just have to trust Guffey for a while longer. We won't be here long, anyhow. In about seven minutes, the phone rings. I turn on the handset, and it's Guffey. "Okay, I'm in the room they let lawyers use . . . no bugs. What's up?"

I figure there's no reason to waste time, so I get right to it. "Are you guys still thinking about hitting the lab at midnight tomorrow?" He says they are, so I continue. "We've got a couple things going on that'll spread the PnB boys out and make your job and ours easier. There are some things going on that you don't know about, and don't need to know about. If everything works out as planned, I'll be done, and you'll have your bust. This might even make the happenings at The Beach look small by comparison."

Maybe, maybe not. This gets his attention, though.

"Rooney, you need to stay low. The feds would just love to nab you in addition to busting up the club's big lab. I told you, they've got some other labs that they're going to hit at the same time. This will be plenty big enough without you putting yourself and whoever's with you in harm's way."

"Nice speech," I tell him, "but like I said, there is shit going on that you don't know about. It is shit that needs to happen, and will happen. None of us has a death wish, and we're hoping to get through this unscathed, but we're prepared to do what needs done. There are factors at play other than the drugs, Guffey. You do your job, I'll do mine, and hopefully, we won't end up in the same place at the same time.

"This will probably be the last time we talk, so I want you to know something. You're the only cop I ever trusted. I hope things work out so you can rub your success in the faces of the fuckers who've been giving you a hard time."

"Rooney, you have restored my faith in people who aren't in law enforcement or part of the system. You've done more good from your side of the street than a lot of the cops I know combined. Be careful, and give me a holler someday when all this is a distant memory.

"Oh, yeah, one more thing . . . *Hammer* those assholes."

He's gone, and it takes me a second to realize what he was telling me: he does know who I am. Luckily for me, Hammer has disappeared, never to be resurrected.

THIRTY

Now that we're down to calling Jimbob to let him know about the meeting in Fayetteville, I figure we should take a few minutes to make sure we don't forget anything. Judy suggests we make a list, and Kenneth and I agree that this is a very good idea. That way, we won't have to play phone tag later, trying to tell Jimbob about stuff we forgot the first time.

"Okay," says Kenneth, stifling a belch after polishing off the last cookie and the remaining lemonade. "Here's what I've got so far. First thing, Jimbob needs to call Shirley's daddy and let him know we're gonna make our move tomorrow night. Old man Bennett needs to get Shirley's best friend to Huntsvull, so she can coax Shirley into the van. I'll tell Jimbob to make sure Bennett understands that he or his goons can't be there. Hopefully, they'll want to be around when the shit-storm happens in Fehvull."

"Yeah," says Judy, "it's hard tellin' what Shirley might do if she saw some of her dad's employees waiting for her. Maybe it would be best if the girlfriend's mom or somebody brought her down."

"I'll make sure Jimbob gets the message across. Next, Jimbob needs to call Randy and let him know something is gonna happen out behind the Eagle Snacks warehouse, without gettin' any more specific than he needs to. I'm sure he'll spin a fine yarn. He's a lot like you in that regard," he says, looking at me. "He'll need to convince Randy that it's serious, and they can figger out a way to keep the locals away."

"You know," I start, "I think I may have an idea about a way to do that. What if Jimbob calls Randy this afternoon, and tells him the basics? He can voice his concern over the chance of innocent people getting hurt, and suggest that the sheriff's department patrol that lot real frequently tonight. In a small town like Fayetteville, the word'll get around pretty damned quick that the cops are rousting people out there. The deputies can also let it slip around town that they're gonna be patrolling out there real heavy for the next few weeks, trying to put a stop to underage drinking and such."

"That'll work!" says Kenneth. "Those county mounties hit the bars and convenience stores with that story, and none of the locals will get close. Since they're so damned hard up for money, ol' Billy Neece has been a real hard-ass about fines and such. People will eat that story up with a spoon. That should keep the place clear of everyone except the assholes we want to be there."

"Back up a second," says Judy, with a concerned look on her face. "When and where are we going to meet the girlfriend? And what's her name? We need to know something about her so we can make her feel as comfortable as possible in the circumstances. You've got to realize that she's very likely to be freaked out, being told she needs to come down here and break Shirley out of that place. And, what if her parents won't go along with it? What do we do then?"

Kenneth is scratching the back of his neck, thinking about Judy's questions, and I have to admit that I hadn't taken the time to think of those things, either.

She looks back and forth from one of us to the other, and finally says, "Well?"

"I hate to sound like a broken record," says Kenneth, "but I really think Jimbob will be the one to get all that sorted out. He's a damned sly old bastard, and he knows where everybody's skeletons are hidden. At least we have the rest of today and a good chunk of tomorrow to get the whole mess figgered out. If it takes a few phone calls back and forth, I guess that won't hurt none—as long as it's just me and Jimbob on the phone."

"I don't know the man, but I'm inclined to go along with Kenneth's gut feeling, Judy," I say. "Kenneth will just make sure he knows our concerns, and let him see what he can come up with. The only part that might be a problem is his being able to call us. We're not sure where we'll be over the next twenty hours or so."

Judy gathers up our dirty glasses and plates and walks over to the sink. "We really don't have anywhere we need to be for the next little bit, so why don't we just stay here until Kenneth and Jimbob either get everything ironed out or decide on a time for us to call him back?"

"Yeah," says Dutton, leaning forward with a grin on his face. "Ol' Jimbob's got one of them pager doo-dads he carries around, so we can always give him a call and wait for him to call back. The number we're at will show up on his pager, so he won't need to know in advance where we'll be. And, if he's not in his office, he'll still know we called. As a matter of fact, it's gettin' kinda late on a Friday afternoon to count on him bein' in his office. Just in case it takes a while for him to call back, I'd better give him a call and get the ball rollin'."

THIRTY-ONE

On the Phone with Jimbob, the Crooked Lawyer
May 17, 1990

Luckily, Jimbob is still in his office. Kenneth has been talking pretty much nonstop for the last ten minutes or so, telling him about our plans and what we'd like him to do as our back-up. Judy and I are not being overly attentive, since we've already heard all this before. I'm looking out through the screen door, watching the breeze move the leaves in the trees, just enjoying the chance to relax a little. Judy is picking up what little mess we've made, and seems to be humming some tune really quietly while she works.

It gets all quiet for a few minutes, and I realize that Jimbob must be talking, addressing our thoughts and suggestions. All of a sudden, Dutton snaps his fingers at us, and we both turn toward him to see what's up. He's pointing at the pad where he's been scribbling down notes. There's a name there, underlined, with some more heavily printed notations under it. The name is Melody, and it says that she's Jimbob's niece. Below that, heavily underlined, is the phrase *Shirley's best friend*. Kenneth is back to scribbling, and he writes, "the one who said Shirley had run off to Huntsville with bikers," then adds, "willing to help, parents no problem."

Judy is leaning over Kenneth's shoulder, reading as he writes, and her eyes meet mine for a second.

She's grinning ear to ear, and gives Kenneth a kiss on the top of his head to let him know she thinks this is good news. Kenneth's face turns bright red, and it's a good thing he isn't trying to talk, instead of listening to Jimbob. He makes a few more notes, then asks, "So you're pretty sure you can get Billy Neece to pay attention?"

As he listens to the answer, he's nodding, and gives us a thumbs-up. It sounds like Jimbob is going to come through in a big way, just as Dutton said he would.

Kenneth asks a few more questions, answers a few more, and makes sure we can reach Jimbob by way of his pager. After a couple okays and a heartfelt, "have a good-un," Kenneth hangs up and scoots back from the table, nearly crushing Judy's toes in the process.

She bats him upside his noggin and says, "Hey! Watch where you're going, there."

Kenneth looks sheepish and apologizes profusely. He suggests we get a drink and settle down to discuss what Jimbob had to say after he's hit the head.

After we've all visited the bathroom, poured ourselves a glass of sweet tea, and adjourned to the patio table once again, Kenneth fills us in on his conversation with Jimbob. As far as getting the sheriff's office to help, the lawyer is fairly sure he can make them pay attention and do what they can in order to keep locals away from the meeting spot tomorrow night. He won't tell them that we planned this shit fight in their jurisdiction; rather, he'll tell them that he has information from a very good source that the two groups are planning the meeting in Fayetteville as a neutral spot. That should work. Kenneth's cop buddy won't have any idea we're involved, and Jimbob seems like the kind of guy that can keep his mouth shut.

As for the problem of keeping Shirley's daddy and his goons away from Chubby's, Jimbob said not to worry. He will make it abundantly clear that any such intrusion could very well screw up the whole deal to the point where Shirley might not get away. He also informed Kenneth, as Judy and I inferred from the notes Kenneth took, that Shirley's best friend Melody is, indeed, his niece. His sister, Melody's mother, is pretty much entirely supported by Jimbob, and he says he can guarantee that she won't be a problem as far as getting Melody to Huntsville. He plans to bring her down himself, and will park a couple blocks south of Chubby's so he can tail Judy and the girls back to Donna's. He won't do anything to spook Shirley, and will stay out of sight until Melody can convince Shirley that he's her best bet to broker a peaceful reunion with her family.

"That sounds like a great idea," says Judy, just beating me to it.

I agree. I'm sure Jimbob will use his participation in the rescue as a lever for increased business dealings with Shirley's dad. Maybe I'm too cynical; he may just want to do the right thing. Or, maybe it's a little of both. No matter, his help is going to make things much easier on all of us.

"Jimbob's no slouch in a tight spot, either," says Kenneth.

"He'll come in handy if someone decides to follow Judy. I'm feelin' better about this all the time."

"Me, too," I tell both of them. "That takes care of a few different things I've been worrying about. Did you discuss when and where to meet them before we go to Chubby's? If so, I missed it while I was daydreaming."

Kenneth is shaking his head back and forth, and Judy is looking at his notes, doing pretty much the same thing, indicating that she can't find any reference to that discussion.

"He said to just give him a call and tell him when and where, when we get it figgered out," says Kenneth. He finally seems to have relaxed after the marathon telephone conversation and checking of his notes. "He said that he'll have his pager on him all the time, and shouldn't ever take more than five or ten minutes to get back to us. He's gonna have Melody at his place from noon on tomorrow, waiting for our call. He says she's really concerned about Shirley and that she'll do whatever we ask her to do in order to help."

I can't wait to actually meet Jimbob; he seems to be damned good at anticipating what needs to be done and what he can do to make it happen. No wonder he's a good lawyer, crooked or not.

Dutton has that *I'm hungry* look on his face, and I can pretty well anticipate what he's about to say.

"Since we can call Jimbob from about anywhere, and seein' as how it's damned near supper time, how about we go to Donna's and have us a meal? Travis and Bob-by Ray are gonna meet us there whenever they get Judy's car done, so we'll need to go there sooner or later. Then you won't have to cook," he says, grinning at Judy and batting those big ol' puppy-dog eyes at her.

We all have a good laugh, and I volunteer Kenneth and me to do the dishes while Judy makes sure all of her plants are watered and does anything else that needs to be done while she's here.

She agrees, and Kenneth says, "I'll wash, you dry Nobody'd want to eat off of anything you washed."

THIRTY-TWO

Donna's Place, Mooresville, Alabama

May 17, 1990

After making sure everything is ship-shape and locking up her house, Judy is back behind the wheel of Donna's Caddy, and we're flying down the road toward Mooresville. We got the dishes washed, dried, and put away without breaking even one piece. We're all in a good mood, content with the progress we've made today.

As we speed south, I'm starting to pay more attention to traffic, any cars parked on the side of the road, anything that might seem wrong. I'm pretty sure Judy is doing the same thing, and Kenneth is actually being quiet, so it's hard telling what's floating around is his big ol' noggin. So far, I haven't seen anything to make me suspicious, but it just seems that things are going too well. I keep thinking that something bad is bound to happen any time now.

As we approach Donna's, I say, "Judy, let's make a lap around the lot, see if anything looks out of place."

She just looks over her shoulder with a smirk on her face and nods her head, once. Of course, she had already thought of that! We're damned lucky to have her on our side.

"Sorry," I say. "I guess I'm just keyed up."

She just shoots me a smile, and gives her head a shake. No worries.

There's a pretty good crowd at Donna's, if the parking lot is any indication. The café side is packed, and the bar side only has a few open parking spots. Just as Judy is about to pull in, a semi pulling a tanker trailer comes through the lot at about twenty-five or thirty miles an hour and pulls out into the southbound lane without so much as a glance in our direction. Judy's on the horn, flying the one-finger salute out of the driver's window.

"Asshole!"

She manages to get the Caddy slowed down and misses the trailer, but I get the impression she's about to chase the truck down and give the driver a good ass-kicking.

We're all watching to see if he's going to stop or pull over, but he shows no sign of doing either. He just motors on down the road toward the entrance ramp onto the interstate.

"Jesus, what a clown! I can't believe that idiot came through the lot that fast and never even looked before he pulled out into the road. Truck drivers as a whole have gone to shit." Judy's shaking, either from anger, adrenaline, or both.

Kenneth and I are both agreeing with her and adding our own opinions about inept truckers as she begins her lap around the café side of the parking lot. We're all looking for suspicious vehicles, but nothing looks hinky, at least not to me. Neither of my comrades says anything, so I guess they don't see anything out of place, either.

As we drive around to the bar side of the lot, we're all looking for a black Malibu, hoping Travis and Bobby Ray have gotten it done and brought it back. No luck.

I ask Judy a question that just occurred to me. "Is your mom still here? I guess she must be, since we have her car. If so, we should probably say hello before we head into the dining room for supper. I'm sure she's curious about what we've been up to since this morning."

Judy and Kenneth both agree. Judy backs up and parks over by the cabins, away from the congested parking lot. She's still muttering under her breath, and her eyes are flashing. I can tell she's still seething about the wayward trucker.

We go in through the kitchen, and we all say our hellos to Sammy, Jason, and a couple other kitchen hands I don't know. Sammy locks eyes with me, and I give him a thumbs-up. He smiles just a little, and goes back to his work.

Jason is nearly bowing as we pass. I guess he got the money Sammy said he'd give him, and told him where it came from. It looks like we've made a friend for life. I give him a squeeze on the shoulder as I pass, and say hi.

We make our way out of the kitchen and down the hall to Donna's office. The door is locked, and Judy uses a key on the Caddy's key ring to unlock it. She gives a rap on the door, and opens it. We are all struck nearly dumb by what we see. Travis, Bobby Ray, and Donna are seated around a card table playing what appears to be Rummy. The three of us start talking at once, and the three at the table are laughing at the expressions on our faces.

Bobby Ray speaks up first. "Didn't see it didja? I was pretty sure you would, but Travis said there was no way. I guess he was right. Good on ya, Unk!" He tips his head toward Travis, who, I'm pretty sure, is sporting a shit-eating grin behind all that beard.

Judy looks confused, and so does Kenneth. I imagine I look the same way. I didn't see any black Malibu, and I was looking especially for it.

"Okay, where is it?" asks Judy, finding her voice. "We looked for it as we drove around the building, and it's not out there. Is it in the shop?"

All three of the card players shake their heads. Nope.

"Did you park it behind the cabins or somewhere out of the way?"

Again, three nopes. They're all about to bust, grinning like lunatics.

"Come on, and I'll show ya," says Travis, scooting his chair back and standing.

We all step back as he walks past us and out the door into the hall leading to the kitchen. Donna and Bobby Ray bring up the rear of our little procession, giggling like little kids. Judy shoots them an annoyed look, but doesn't let Travis gain on her. I can tell she doesn't much like being messed with like this, and if the other three were anyone but family, they'd probably get an earful.

We go past the kitchen, through the dining room, toward the side door. There are a lot of greetings from the diners for Judy and Donna. They graciously return them, but don't appreciably slow down. We all exit the dining room into the parking lot, and Travis starts across the lot to the far side.

Judy has had enough. She has her hands on her hips and clearly isn't taking one more step. "Travis, where in the hell are you going? I can plainly see that my car isn't out there. I'm getting tired of being laughed at, and if this is another reason to laugh at me some more, you might want to re-think your strategy."

Kenneth and I keep our yaps shut. This has all the markings of a family spat, and we both are smart enough to stay out of it. Donna and Bobby Ray have no such compunctions . . . they're both snickering and receiving glares in return from Judy.

We've walked out to the last row of cars and pickups, where Travis stops and turns to Judy. "I'm not tryin' to piss you off, Judy. We thought you wanted to keep the fact that we painted your car a secret, so nobody would recognize it. We parked it over here so there would be a fair amount of other cars around it, wanting to see if you'd notice it as you drove in. The fact that you didn't tickles the hell out of me. It means Bobby Ray and I did a good job."

"Yeah, Cuz," says Bobby Ray, still trying, without much luck, to quit giggling. "We didn't do it to piss you off, Judy. We just want to see if you thought we did as good a job as we thought we did."

I've been looking around the lot while the family has been squabbling, and have finally seen the Malibu. Genius! I nudge Kenneth, and point at it with my chin. Judy is too busy staring at Bobby Ray and Travis to notice that we're not paying attention. Kenneth looks where I'm pointing, then back at me with a raised eyebrow. I just wink at him and point to the same spot again. He gives me a weird look, but turns and watches the lot again. I know the precise instant that he sees it. He barks out a laugh, and turns to me with a big smile on his face.

It's too much for Judy. She wheels on Kenneth. "I'm glad this amuses you, Kenneth Dutton. Would you like to explain to me why you've decided to gang up on me with these three?" Kenneth would burrow into the ground if possible. His face is a bright red, and he won't look Judy in the eye.

"Judy, he wasn't laughing at you," I say, being rewarded with a look that could bend glass. "I saw where your car is parked, and called his attention to it. He was just amazed at what these two," indicating Bobby Ray and Travis, "accomplished. I'm blown away, too, but I'm really glad I didn't let on, because I'd hate to have you jump down my throat like you did his. Nobody's picking on you. These guys just wanted to prove a point."

Travis and Bobby Ray are nodding their heads vigorously. "If we had all trooped out here to your car, any chance of keeping its new look secret would've been blown. By coming all the way out here, we can scope out the entire lot, seeing if we can spot it while not letting everyone else know what we're looking for, or at."

I can see that Judy is following what I'm saying, and she is starting to look a little sheepish, too. I don't want to make it too hard on her, though, because we need her, and we need her happy.

"I'm gonna tell you a part of the lot to look at. The rest of us will be milling around, not staring at your car. When you see it, you'll see why these guys are so proud, and why Dutton and I got such a kick when we finally recognized it. Okay?" Judy nods, with an anxious look on her face. "Look over there on the north side of the lot, between the newspaper machines and the side door," I tell her. "I think we'll know when you figure out which car is yours."

Judy looks at the part of the parking lot I indicated, but soon looks back at the rest of us with one eyebrow raised. I just point back that direction with my chin, and she reluctantly turns back to try again. I think she still feels that we're messing with her. Then she sees it. Bingo!

"Damn!" she exclaims, turning back toward the rest of us. "I never would have thought that was my car! It doesn't even look like the same kind of car! How did you do that?"

She turns back and stares at what used to be a baby-shit yellow Chevy Malibu. Now it's a nondescript, washed-out green lump that's faded to a light green in spots. Travis has used the two colors to muddy up the body lines, and has somehow given the paint a weathered finish that makes it look like it's been sitting outside for a very long time. But the crowning glory, the part that made Dutton bark, Travis and Bobby Ray proud, and Donna and me laugh quietly, are what ap-pear to be rained through partition of body cancer along the rocker panels and around the fenders. If I hadn't known that Judy's car was out here somewhere, I never would have thought that this rusty-looking pile of crap was her pride and joy. No wonder these guys couldn't wait to see her reaction, even if it meant getting yelled at in the process.

"We probably shouldn't stand around out here staring at it," says Donna, trying to wake us all back up to the fact that this is a secret. "Let's go back in and I'll get Sammy to whip something up for supper. I can't hang around too awfully long, but I want to hear the latest." She squeezes Judy's arm. "Are you happy now, Punkin?" I see a bit of a flush start up Judy's neck and cheeks.

Punkin? Dutton chances a look at me, and grins, but not for long. Punkin. Oh boy, I can't wait for the perfect time to use that. But now isn't the time, unless I want Judy yelling at me next.

I'd rather eat.

THIRTY-THREE

Donna's Place, Mooresville, Alabama
May 17, 1990

Donna stops off on the way back in to talk to Sammy about supper for the six of us, reminding him to allow extra for Kenneth and me. She seems to think we eat more than normal people.

While we've been sitting here in Donna's office waiting, Travis and Bobby Ray have been picking at us for not seeing the Malibu in our way into the lot. Judy's been trying to convince them that the asshole trucker is the reason she missed it, that if it hadn't been for him, we would have noticed it right away. We all know this is bullshit.

"Well, Judy," I start in, "you may have recognized it, but there's no way I would have. Travis, the way you used the lighter green to disguise the body lines is perfect. Nobody seeing that car will be able to give much of a description of it, other than being a rusty, old, green car."

Travis is beaming, obviously pleased that someone recognizes the effort he put into disguising Judy's car, way above and beyond the effort required to just scuff the yellow paint and squirt it black.

"I sprayed it with the dark green first. It's acrylic enamel, and I thinned it with lacquer thinner to make it dry fast and not look too glossy. As soon as it was dry, we scuffed it up with Scotch-brite, and I started fogging on that pukey light green color. All the paint was left over from some other jobs. I just thought that if we were gonna try to disguise that car, we might as well try something other than just a color change. I pretty much added the light green color to spots that would be faded first by the sun, but sorta messed around with the body lines, adding some here and missing some there. When that dried, we scuffed it up again, then wet-sanded where the light green is to make it blend more evenly."

He's justifiably proud, and I just wish Judy would give him and Bobby Ray the credit they deserve. It may be overkill, but it's damned effective.

"Well," says Kenneth, "I don't know shit about any fancy paintin', but I've gotta tell you that I was just plumb fooled. I had to look a couple times, and wouldn't have ever recognized it if I hadn't known it was there, and if Jonnybob hadn't pointed me in the right direction. How the hell did you get that rust on there? From where we were, it looks damned real. I'm just a dumb ol' country boy, but you definitely got me. Good job."

Travis is grinning, but Bobby Ray is just plain vibrating, smiling so hard I think he might hurt himself. Travis tells us why. "The rust was Bobby Ray's idea," he says. "He took some sand and metal shavings from the blast cabinet, and stuck the mixture to the body with some of that spray adhesive you use for fabric. Then he sprayed some rattle-can red and black primer lightly on and around it to make it look like rust. I wasn't real sure what to think when he started, but I've gotta say that it turned out cool. I'll keep that trick in mind in case I ever need to make something else look old and junky. Some of these guys around here are building what they call 'rat bikes', and they make 'em all oily and dirty. Makes 'em look like shit in my opinion, but I guess if someone comes around, wanting to pay me to make their bike look like shit, what the hell do I care?"

Bobby Ray is just about to bust, but we all know what would put him over the top—some recognition of his contributions from his gorgeous cousin. Judy's been listening, and finally breaks into the technical discussion of how to make a nice car look like shit.

"Okay," she says, "maybe I didn't appreciate the skill it took to make my car so hard to recognize, and from what I'm hearing, I've been an ungrateful bitch. I'm sorry for the hassle I gave you guys, but I just thought you were screwing with me. Do you forgive me?"

Like there was any question. We're all putty around Judy, and one of her most endearing traits is that she very rarely takes advantage of it. We all tell her she's not a bitch. Of course she's forgiven, blah, blah, blah.

Donna comes back in and asks us if Bobby Ray has told us about his great job of making rust from dirt and glue. Poor guy just can't get a break. He smiles at her and says that yes, everyone is thoroughly impressed, thank you very much. We all share a good laugh, and

Kenneth wants to know where supper is. I'm surprised he hasn't fainted dead away from malnutrition. But come to think of it, I'm damned hungry myself. Just as I'm thinking this, there's a knock on the door, and Sammy and Jason wheel in a couple of carts loaded to overflowing with food and pitchers of beverages.

"Damn, that smells good," Kenneth says, trying to get past everyone to be first in line. "I thought I was shorely gonna die before we got done monkeyin' around and ate."

Whatever is on the trays does indeed smell good, and everyone seems to move toward them at once. Sammy is uncovering dishes and trying his best to keep Kenneth out of the way until he's finished.

"If I'd known we were gonna be mugged, we would've worn armor or somethin'," says Sammy, laughing at Dutton's efforts to get around him to the chow.

Jason has given up, and is just doing his best to stay out of the way. Donna puts two fingers in her mouth, and whistles so loud we all stop and stare at her.

"Let these two do their job, dammit! Kenneth, you just sit down and stay out of the way for a minute, and the rest of us will do the same. Sammy, please arrange the food and drinks over there on the table. We can use the card table and a couple of these other little tables to eat on."

It is something to behold; Kenneth Dutton sitting impatiently, waiting to be told when he can move, while food is being placed within ten feet of him. The rest of us are having a good laugh at his discomfort, but I think everyone in the room will be glad when we can tie into the grub. From what I can see, there is some sort of roast, mounds of biscuits, a big bowl of mashed potatoes, and I'm pretty sure I smell gravy. There are a couple pies, and pitchers of water, what looks like iced tea, and something dark, probably RC for Kenneth.

It only takes a couple of minutes and the food is off the carts and on the table. Sammy and Jason head back out the door into the hall, and the rest of us all look expectantly at Donna.

She laughs, and tells Kenneth, "Okay, have at it."

He's on his feet before she's through speaking, and the rest of us aren't far behind him. After everyone has filled a plate (or two, in Kenneth's case), we situate ourselves around the tables, except for Judy and Donna. They're both seated at Donna's desk. For a few minutes, the only thing I can hear is the sound of six people enjoying some great food. Before I'm through with my plate, Kenneth has finished both of his and is loading up with large wedges of both apple and cherry pie.

Noticing that most of us are watching him, he grins and says, "This gettin' ready to blow shit up and rescue teenage girl stuff just starves a man plumb to death."

There's a lot of laughter and good-natured ribbing, and the rest of us refill our water and sweet tea glasses as we decide on which kind of pie we want. There's some small talk, but we seem to be waiting for the meal to be over before we get back to business.

THIRTY-FOUR

After Bobby Ray and I gather up all the plates and take them to the kitchen, we all settle down with drinks—Kenneth has another slice of apple pie. Donna won't stay around long, and we want to let her know the basics of what we're up to. Since Bobby Ray and Travis have already told her what all they did, we want to fill everyone in on what we accomplished on the phone while we were out at Judy's. We can hear the rest of the details from Travis and Bobby Ray after Donna heads home.

"Well, we got quite a bit done today," I start out. "I called the cop in Virginia Beach, and he says the feds are good to go tomorrow night at midnight. They have ID'ed a couple other meth labs in Huntsville that they're gonna hit at the same time as the big PnB lab."

Donna and the boys are nodding and grinning at this news. The bar next door sounds like things are getting an early start; there's a bunch of hollering and the music suddenly goes up a few notches in volume. Donna frowns, and goes through the front door of her office into the bar. There's an unspoken agreement between the rest of us to wait for her to return before we continue.

Judy gets up and heads toward the bar, too. I get the impression that the commotion we heard isn't a normal occurrence. Travis heads Judy off, and tells her he'll go see what's going on, that she should just wait with her friends. I'm starting to get a little uncomfortable . . . what had been almost a party atmosphere has suddenly turned into something else. There's a feeling in the air of trouble. Trouble is something I'm pretty good at, but now isn't the time, or the place. The noise next door gets much louder all of a sudden, and there's a loud crash. All thoughts of us sitting in here go out the window and we all jump for the door. Travis is into the bar first, closely followed by Judy, me, and Bobby Ray. Kenneth was pretty comfortable with his pie and didn't get as good a start as the rest of us, but he comes barreling through the door looking for trouble.

The sight that greets us makes us all skid to a halt. There's a big, burly dude upside down against the juke-box. Donna has got him by an ear, and is telling him in no uncertain terms what she thinks of his conduct. The bartender has a sawed-off, double-barreled shotgun trained at three other guys backed up against the wall on the far side of the pool table. A few other customers are watching in what seems to be amusement.

Judy marches over to the trio pinned against the wall. She's standing there with her hands on her hips, jaw thrust forward, reading the riot act to these three big ol' rednecks. "How many times do you morons need to be told? You can't just come in here and go behind the bar to turn up the damned jukebox. We heard you arguin' with Merle from next door! Momma is just flat gonna ban you if you don't straighten your shit out. Is that what you want?"

Donna is still giving hell to the fourth one, who is still upside down in the corner.

Kenneth and I look at each other and grin. It doesn't appear that the ladies are going to need any assistance from us. Of course, the twice-by pointed at the three against the wall probably makes a little difference. Bobby Ray has leaned up against the bar, and Travis is about three paces behind Donna, not about to get in her way, but there if the big dude decides to get belligerent with her.

Donna turns to Travis and tells him to help the big guy up. "Have Bobby Ray or Jonnybob help you get him up and out the door. Merle," she says to the bartender, "if any of these 'gentlemen' so much as spit, blow their damned legs off."

She turns to the three "gentlemen" against the wall and points them toward the door. "And don't come back in here for at least a couple damned months. You boys surely try my patience. Now go."

And they go, just as meekly as you please.

Travis and I herd the big dude out the door right behind his three buddies. The other patrons applaud, and Donna curtsies. She motions for us to all head back into her office.

"Come on," she says. "Show's over. Merle, see if you can get the jukebox back on; I guess I shouldn't have pitched Hogbody into it, but he really ticks me off some times."

Hogbody? Now, there's a great name!

As we file back into the office, Judy asks, "What did he do this time, Momma? Grab your ass?"

At this, we all turn to Donna, who's trying to get a few errant strands of hair tucked in where they belong. She just laughs and shakes her head, making a few more strands fall loose.

"No, this time he tried to tweak my tit. No matter how many times I dump him on his head, he just won't take a hint. He and those three inbred brothers of his are going to push me too far one of these days, and I'm gonna have Merle ventilate one or two of 'em. The damned sheriff's office would probably give him a medal, and make this place a historical landmark."

Kenneth is sitting there with his mouth open, looking confused. "You're the one who knocked that big ol' boy down? I figgered one of those other three clowns did it. How'd you get him on the ground?"

I've been wondering about that, too.

"Judo," says Judy. "Momma has been taking classes since before I was born. Anyone else who knows her wouldn't mess with Momma unless they had a gun. She flips old Hogbody ass-over-teakettle about two or three times a year. I think he must enjoy it, because he just keeps coming back for more. One time, about three or four years ago, she busted three of his ribs and a collar bone. He hit the door just as someone was opening it, and it jacked him up pretty good."

The mental picture of Donna throwing that big redneck upside down against the jukebox had me tickled, but this last installment does it. I'm laughing all of a sudden, and everyone joins in. Dutton is red in the face, and he's laughing so hard he's crying. Judy's got the hiccups, and the rest of us just keep laughing harder because the whole situation is so goofy.

As everyone winds down, Kenneth asks Donna the question I was about to. "Who are those guys, any-how?"

From what little I've heard so far, those four are lucky Donna hasn't pressed charges, instead of just throwing them out every now and then.

"Hogbody's real name is Sam Miller. He's an ornery old bastard, and I've known him since grade school. My husband, Leroy—Judy's daddy—was his stepbrother. The three knuckleheads with him are his brothers, Danny, Charlie, and Fritz. Their daddy adopted Leroy when he married his momma. Leroy's daddy got killed in a knife fight at a roadhouse over in Tennessee, when Leroy was only about five or six. When his momma married old man Miller, he adopted Leroy, so he and those four all had the same last name.

Sam thinks that if he tries often enough, I'll let him take Leroy's place. He's the reason I started the Judo lessons in the first place. I'm just about to the point of callin' the law on him, if he keeps it up. Either that, or I'm gonna let Merle shoot him." She chuckles, still fussing with her hair. Then she says, "Let's get back to our monkey business, so I can get out of here and get some sleep," as we all sit back down around the card table. "Hopefully, there won't be any more interruptions."

Just as she's saying this, the jukebox starts back up, but at a level comparable to the period before Hogbody and the Redneck Trio came in.

"Let's see," says Judy, sipping at her sweet tea. "JB was just telling you guys what the cop up in Virginia had to say about the meth labs, if I remember right. Their taking down the labs at midnight will keep a whole bunch of the local cops busy, so we shouldn't have much trouble with them at Chubby's. The cops up in Fayetteville just might be busy, too. Tell 'em about your plan, Jonnybob."

She sits back with a wink for me, and gives Kenneth a sideways grin.

The other three look at me expectantly, so I tell them about the shit storm we're trying to start between the PnB and S&S boys.

"If it works, and they both show up out there without knowing who they're actually going to meet, it should get pretty interesting. Jimbob thinks that the county cops will have all the locals scared off, so there won't be any innocent bystanders around, and there's a good chance that they'll be able to make some arrests after the fireworks are over."

"Speakin' of fireworks, tell 'em about what we're gonna do for a distraction at Chubby's," says Dutton, leaning forward across the table and grinning like a loon. "You guys are gonna *love* this!"

Travis puts up a hand in a stop motion, and gives me his attention.

"Before you do that," he starts in that weird voice, "tell me a little more about Monster. Is this a real guy, or did you make him up? I'm not real clear on that, and if he's real, don't you think these guys might fuck him up?"

Judy, Kenneth, and I all smile, but Judy beats the two of us to the punch.

"He's a figment of Johnybob's twisted imagination," she tells the others. "As he was spinning that yarn, Kenneth and I were about to blow a gasket. We had to go into the other room because we couldn't stop laughing. When he told Slippy that his Honda was broken down, I thought I was going to wet myself."

Dutton can't stand waiting, so he butts in. "Yeah, this guy Skippy must be a total dim bulb, 'cause he swallowed the whole deal, according to what I could tell. They think they're coming to Fehvull to meet some wanna-be biker kid. They're gonna shit when they realize who's really there."

His chuckles dissolve into chortling, and he's soon crying again. Judy's hiccups haven't returned yet, but she looks close.

"Yeah, Monster is just a guy I put together from all the goofballs I've met over the last twenty years or so who think they want to be outlaw bikers. Most of them don't have even the slightest clue what's involved, they just see the bikes, the chicks, the drugs, and think it looks like a good time. Granted, I made him more comical than strictly necessary, but once I got going, I couldn't stop. Good thing Slippy's not real bright, or he might've figured out that I was funnin' with him."

Everyone is grinning, and Travis is giggling in his high-pitched way now that he knows Monster isn't some real kid that we're gonna feed to the wolves.

"Tell 'em about the fireworks, Jonnybob," says Dutton, still trying to quit chortling or whatever it is he's doing. It's a weird sound, whatever it's called.

"Okay, you guys know that we're needing a distraction to get Shirley out of Chubby's," I say, watching them all nod in agreement. We'd talked about it before, but hadn't really decided what to do. "Kenneth and I are gonna shoot some flares into the fireworks outlet next door to Chubby's, and the result should be a dandy distraction."

Dutton is back to laughing, and the looks on the others' faces range from confusion to dawning hilarity. But Donna looks pensive.

"I realize you need some way to get everyone's attention away from the girl," she says, "but it seems a little selfish of you to burn down someone's business just to create a distraction. You're going to take away somebody's livelihood, and I don't think that's fair."

Judy leans forward, suddenly serious, and takes Donna's hand in hers. "Momma, the fireworks place is owned by the damned club, the PnB. That's why it's such a great plan! Not only will a fire next door get all the customers and such outside watching, but the club members there will be freaking out about their place burning down. They store guns and stuff there, too, we think, so they'll be thinking about making themselves scarce when the fire department and cops show up. We're not going to hurt anyone who doesn't need it, believe me."

Donna's nodding now, taking it all in. She grins at me, and gives Judy's hand a squeeze.

"I should've known you wouldn't do anything that selfish. I guess I'm just tired and not thinking straight. I'm going home to bed, and I'll get the rest of the story from you tomorrow or whenever I see you next. Goodnight, Punkin." she says, giving Judy a hug around her neck, then she gets up, grabs her purse, and heads out the door into the back hallway.

Kenneth jumps up and runs out behind her, then returns in a minute or two. "We done forgot to tell her where we parked her car," he explains. "I didn't want her to be out there wanderin' around lookin' fer it, in case those four idjits came back."

We all smile, and Judy says that was terribly sweet of him. I think for a few seconds that he may swoon. He's never going to be the same, after meeting Judy. Hell, that's probably true of most folks. I know it is with me.

"Well, now," says Bobby Ray, "that sure sounds

like fun, and I think it should work fine. Travis and I will be in the bar, and just before midnight we'll go upstairs for a lap dance or somethin'. When the shit hits the fan next door, we'll find and grab Shirley and head down the back stairs. Judy's gonna be in your van . . . that reminds me, we've got the plate off the rear of Raeann's van to put on yours. It's right over there, by Donna's desk."

I look over, and leaned up against the wall is the distinctive Alabama license plate, with the two hearts and the Heart of Dixie logo on top. The stickers are even current. If anyone pays any attention to Vanna, they'll think it's a local vehicle, and it shouldn't stand out like the Virginia plate would.

"Thanks," I say.

"Okay," continues Bobby Ray, picking up where he left off. "Judy's gonna be out there where the back stairway comes out. Did you get the girl's friend to ride along?"

Judy chimes in before I can answer. "Shirley's best friend is going to be here, and the crooked lawyer, Jimbob, is bringing her down. He said he'd drop her off, then park down the road a ways and follow us back here after we get Shirley in the van. It'll be nice having someone following us, just in case. Kenneth says Jimbob is a real stand-up guy, and I tend to believe it. From everything I've heard, I think he'll be a good person to have on our side."

"Jonnybob," says Travis, "what are you and

Kenneth going to be doing after you start the fire next door?"

Kenneth looks at me with that what-the-fuck look on his face that I know so well. I'm sure he's wondering the same thing. We haven't talked about this at all.

"We're gonna be in the Malibu," I say, "and after it gets dark we'll scoot back into the woods there behind the fireworks place. We'll have some goodies with us, besides the flare gun and flares. We'll start the fire a couple of minutes before midnight, and as soon as the fire department shows up, we'll start adding to the confusion.

"I figure we'll lob some flash-bangs under some of the bikes in the lot with PnB member decals on them. By then, everyone's attention should be on the north side of Chubby's so that should help you guys get Shirley and anyone else that wants out down the stairs and into the parking lot where Judy is. We're gonna park the Malibu on the north side of the fireworks place, so we have a straight shot at the highway when we leave." Now comes the good part. I can't wait to see Dutton's face when he hears this.

"After we've got the fireworks place burning, and have blown up a couple bikes, Kenneth and I are going to make sure that some people see us. We're gonna make damned sure they see us, and see which way we go."

Kenneth is looking at me like I've grown a third eye, and only Travis seems to understand what I've got in mind. He's grinning, and elbows Bobby Ray in the ribs.

"Right!" Travis exclaims. "You guys make sure some of the firemen and club members see you over there, acting suspicious. They'll think you guys started the fire, so when you leave and head north, they won't even think about following anyone heading south from the other side of the building. That's genius!"

I'm not so sure Kenneth agrees with that assessment, but he does seem to be coming around. A big ol' smile is starting to spread across his face, and he scoots his chair right up against the table.

"You shorely are a sneaky bastard, Jonnybob Clark. No wonder you wanted Judy's car all disguised and hard to remember . . . you're hoping that anyone tryin' to tell the cops what it looks like will have a hard time gettin' it right. Travis and Bobby Ray done such a good job that it'll be even harder."

He's got that shrewd "thinking" look on his big ol' mug, now. "Where the hell are we goin' from there? I'm purty damned sure we ain't goin' through downtown Huntsvull, runnin' from the law. What've you got in that sneaky head of yers?"

I wish Donna had stayed, so I could be sure this next part is feasible, but we can talk to her in the morning.

"I've got an idea about that, but there are a couple pieces to put together first. I suggest we all get a good night's sleep and we can meet tomorrow morning to hammer out the last details."

Grumbles, mumbles, dissension. None of my co-horts seem to like this development.

"Really, I'm not trying to be evasive, but I just need to talk to a couple of people in the morning before I'm sure if my idea will even work. Please bear with me. We've got almost everything else buttoned up, and we've got all day tomorrow to put this last little bit together. How about it—can we wait until morning? Give me until then, okay?"

They don't like it, but all four of them seem like they're going to let me get away with it.

"C'mon, Travis, let's get goin'," says Bobby Ray. "We can be to your place with the scooters pretty early, then come back in the mornin' in my truck. We'll need a ride tomorrow night, so that'll work out pretty good."

I'm glad Bobby Ray thought of that. I hadn't thought about what they'd drive. Travis stands up, gives Judy a hug, then shakes Kenneth's hand, and mine. Bobby Ray does the same.

"We'll see you in the morning," says Travis, looking me right in the eye. "If anything comes up before then, call us."

He and Bobby Ray head out the back door, and Judy stops them. "Do you need a hand getting your bikes out of the shop?" She is heading toward the door, and they wave her off.

"Naw," says Bobby Ray, "we got 'em in there where it'll be easy to get 'em out. See you tomorrow."

And they're gone. Judy walks back over to the card table and starts picking up dirty glasses and such. Kenneth and I pitch in, and it only takes a few minutes to make the office ship-shape once again. We fold up the card table, and slide it into a closet next to the front door.

Outside, it's really quiet, other than the muffled sounds from the bar. After giving both of us a peck on the cheek, Judy heads over to the little cabin she uses, and Kenneth and I walk over to ours. I stop alongside him before he goes inside, and he looks at me and grins.

"Okay, son" he says, "what's on that devious mind of yers? I know you well enough to know that you're not gonna wait until mid-mornin' to decide what to do next."

I grin, give him a punch on the arm, and say, "Keep Judy busy tomorrow until I get back. Try to convince her not to be pissed off, okay?"

I think he's going to argue, but he decides to let it go. "Be careful, dammit, and don't keep us waitin' all day." With that, he goes in the cabin and shuts the door.

I walk over to the truck shop, find the key behind the sign, and let myself in. There's enough light filtering through the windows to see the phone without turning on a light. I dial a number I memorized in Donna's office earlier, hoping it's not too late.

THIRTY-FIVE

The call to Donna went pretty well, considering the fact that I woke her up. She listened to what I had in mind, gave it a couple seconds of thought, then agreed to help me.

"Only thing is, I'll have to go in early and make the biscuits, so we can be there by six, when they open," she'd said. "If you want to help, we can get it done easy."

So, I met her in the kitchen at four-thirty, and we got the eight dozen biscuits made up and put on baking sheets to rise. She called the early cook and told her to come in a little early to put them in the oven, because Donna wouldn't be there to do it.

She suggested we take her car, and I agreed instantly. Nothing wrong with some serious comfort every now and then. On the way to Huntsville, we talked about what I had planned, and she seemed to think it was worth a try.

So here we are, sitting in the small office of Fat Bob's in Booger Town, talking to Bob, the skinny used-car dealer and café owner. He was waiting for us to walk in the door when April unlocked it. Both of them seemed really happy to see Donna, and made me feel welcome, too.

Donna introduced me to Bob and gave them the short version of what Kenneth and I were up to with our new-found friends and conspirators. When she explained who Kenneth's daddy was, they both perked up and paid even more attention. It seems as though that connection bought me more credibility with them. I'd like to know more about him and these people who regard his memory so fondly, but that's a story for another time and place.

The three of us, minus April, came back to the office for some privacy. Fat Bob's is one of those places that fills up early with working people gearing up for their day with a big home-cooked breakfast. No need to worry about anyone hearing us talking about what we've got planned for this evening.

"Donna, you know I'll do anything you ask, so what do you need from me?" Bob has turned out to be an intelligent, funny guy with one of those low-key deliveries that takes awhile to get used to. I think he may wear the used-car dealer uniform as a joke, but I'm not about to ask him about it.

Donna reaches out and gives his hand a squeeze, letting her hand rest on his for just a few extra seconds. She smiles at him with just a touch of wistfulness, and I just know there's another story there that I'll probably never hear.

Hell, they might not tell me even if I asked, and I'm not about to do that.

"Jonnybob has an idea about how to get him and

Kenneth away from the club, the cops, and anyone else who might look for them after they leave Chubby's," she tells him, inclining her head toward me as she's speaking. "I'll let him tell you about it."

They both look at me expectantly, and I tell Bob, "Judy's Malibu will be damned near impossible to give a good description of in the dark, but I just want to make sure nobody gets lucky. It would suck if we had a flat, or blew a radiator hose, or something, after all the effort Travis and Bobby Ray have put into making it anonymous. Once we get away from the immediate area without incident, I think there's little or no chance of anyone recognizing it. The main thing is to get away without being followed and park the car somewhere out of the way until the heat dies down."

Bob is grinning, and breaks into my tale. "So you're wondering if I'll let you park in the car lot, right?"

Donna smiles at him and says, "That's right. What do you think, Bob? Could you maybe hide a key or something for them?"

"Hell," he says, "I'll do better than that. You know, they're racing out at the Speedway tomorrow night, and they have the track open for test-n-tune tonight until eleven or so. There are always a few of the racers and employees who hang out after the time they make 'em quit using the track, drinkin' and shootin' the shit. A trailer leavin' that area with a beat-up old car on it wouldn't get any attention at all."

He's getting a little excited, leaning across the table toward me. What he's saying makes sense, too. But something is bothering me and I need to voice my doubts.

"I love the trailer idea, Bob," I tell him. "My limited knowledge of this area causes me a little concern, though. Isn't the road that heads out to the track just a quarter-mile or so north of Chubby's? What if someone sees us turn, and follows us?"

"I thought of that," he says, "just as you started talking. If you drive about a mile north on the Parkway, you can hang a right on Green Cove Road. You should be able to haul ass, 'cause all the attention will be focused south-bound. Once you get on Green Cove, drive east about a mile and turn south on the Ditto Marina Parkway. It'll be on your right just before Green Cove turns left and heads north. Hang a right on Ditto and go about a quarter of a mile, and there will be a turnoff on your right. It leads to a parking lot for boat trailers and such. There shouldn't be many in there, but it won't matter, anyhow. They don't allow camping down there, so there probably won't be anyone hanging around."

"I like it," I tell them. "It won't take long to load the car on a trailer. I'd like to look at the trailer, get an idea of where the ramps are, how they're attached, all that. Wait. What will we use to haul the trailer? This is getting a little complicated. I hate to be such a pain in the ass; I know the only reason you're helping is because of Donna, and I don't want to cause any hard feelings for anyone." Donna's shaking her head, about to say something, but Bob beats her to the punch.

He holds up a hand to stop her, and asks us, "Anyone ready for breakfast? I'm starvin'."

He's already reaching for a pad on the desk, and I guess there's no need to fight it. I smile and nod, and Donna just laughs.

"Damn," she says, chuckling, "All this crew does is eat. Well, why not? I'll have some biscuits and gravy, a half-order, and a side of hash browns with grilled onions. I'll just keep drinking coffee."

Bob had brought a large carafe of coffee in for Donna and himself, along with a pitcher of iced tea for me.

"What about you, my friend?" Bob's looking at me with an expectant look, pencil poised above the paper. "You need a menu?"

"No, I won't need a menu. I'll have one of those ham steaks, like I had the last time I was here. Grits, with biscuits and jelly, no gravy." I pat my belly. "I need to watch my girlish figure."

Bob chuckles, writing down my order. He scribbles a couple other notes on the pad, and gets up.

"I'll give this to Ruby and tell April that we're gonna still be awhile. I'll be right back."

He goes out the door and closes it behind him, but not before I see something that doesn't make me real happy.

Wild Bill is sitting at a table with a buddy, right in the small part of the room I can see while the door is open, and he's looking right at me. I see the flicker of recognition again, and it bothers me. After all the luck we've had, I'd hate for our plans to get screwed up at this point.

"You look like you've seen a ghost," says Donna, looking toward the door as it's closing. "What's wrong, hon?"

"There's a guy out there that was here when we were in here Wednesday. He acts like he knows me, but I can't imagine that. I look so different from the way I looked the last time I was down here, it would be a miracle if someone actually recognized me. The thing that bothers me is the fact that right after he saw us, we saw a cop cruising Booger Town, like he was looking for someone."

She's looking concerned, kinda like I feel. "I'll ask Bob who he is when he comes back."

Just as we're starting to wonder where Bob is, he comes back in—and Wild Bill is right behind him! Christ! I'm reaching for my nine mil, and my mind is going a thousand miles an hour trying to figure out the best way to get Donna and me out of here.

Bob puts his hands out, and hollers, "Hold it, Jonnybob! Don't go nuts on me, son. Close the door, Bo."

Donna's got me by the arm, and I'm having a hard time deciding what to do. I don't want to hurt her or

Bob, but what the fuck is Wild Bill, or Bo, doing in here?

Suddenly, I just relax. If this is it, I guess that's just too damned bad. I deserve whatever happens, I suppose, but Donna sure doesn't. I look at her and smile, letting her know it's okay. She relaxes her hold on me, and I sit down, defeated.

By now, the door is closed and Bo is leaning against it, staring at me. I don't know if it's because he realizes he came pretty close to being shot, or because he's hoping for a reason to shoot me.

"Jonnybob, what the hell is wrong with you?" Bob is agitated, and I guess I can't blame him. It was pretty apparent why I was reaching into my belt under my shirt tail. "What happened while I was gone for five minutes to make you want to pull a gun on me?"

He's kinda shook, but not as much as most people would be. He's a pretty cool customer, yes sir.

"I think I can answer that," says Donna, trying her best to defuse the tension. It'll take some doing, because I'm still pretty sure the shit is about to hit the fan, as far as my situation is concerned. "Jonnybob was just telling me about seeing someone in here the other day, who acted like they recognized him. He saw that same person when you opened the door to take our orders to the cook. From his description of this person, I'm pretty sure he was talking about Bo, here."

Bob and Bo look at each other, then at Donna, and finally at me. Bob rears back and laughs so hard it scares Donna damned near off her chair. My ears are getting hot, and I feel my temper starting to take over. If things are going to hell, that's one thing . . . but I'm not gonna sit here and be laughed at by anyone.

I grab the arms of my chair, and start to get up when Donna grabs my arm, again. I start to shake her off, then remember myself. This woman has done nothing but help me; I can't do anything to endanger her. But if I get a chance to take care of business without putting her at risk, these two are gonna regret pissing me off.

"Whoa up there, my friend," says Bob, sobering up. "I'm not laughing at you. This whole damned thing is just fuckin' hilarious, that's all."

As classy as Donna comes across in most circumstances, the language doesn't faze her. Come to think of it, I've probably been guilty of using the same phrase. Her owning a bar and putting up with the likes of Hogbody and his brothers have probably made her immune to rough language. I get the impression that when she was younger, her circle of friends was pretty wild. More stories for around the campfire sometime.

Just then, April knocks on the door and brushes past Bo when he opens it. She gives Donna a big smile, and tips me a wink. That small gesture calms me, makes me settle back into my chair a little, ready to at least listen. I wink back, tip my tea glass at her. She sets the food down on the desk and heads back out, closing the door quietly behind her.

Bob passes out the food, including a plate for Bo, who still hasn't said a word. He hasn't smiled yet, even when Bob was laughing his ass off.

"Can we all," asks Bob, "go ahead and eat our breakfast before it gets cold? I swear nobody in this room is going to hurt you, Jonnybob. I really hate cold oatmeal." I hadn't paid any attention, but that's all he's got in front of him, other than a couple slices of whole wheat toast. He sees me looking, and explains. "Damned cholesterol. Doctor says I've gotta get it down or my heart'll explode."

He chuckles again, and I decide that whatever is going to happen can wait a few minutes. Maybe the time spent eating will defuse some of the tension in the room. We all get settled in, arranging our silverware and such.

"I can't imagine," I tell Bob, "how hard it would be to stay on that kind of diet. I'd probably never be able to stick to it."

Bo's nodding his head. At least we have something in common.

"Staying on the diet is easy," says Bob, pausing with his spoon halfway to his mouth. "If food tastes good, you spit it out."

It takes a second, but we all get it at about the same time, and all of a sudden we're all laughing. Breakfast proceeds in a fairly jovial mood, but I'm still watching Bo pretty closely. He still hasn't made a sound, other than a snorting laugh at Bob's joke.

When everyone has eaten, and all the dishes have been piled on the window sill, Bob suggests that whoever has the need of the facilities should do that now, before we get down to business. Donna excuses herself and goes through the door into the café. I make sure my shirt tail is out of the way, just in case. Bob notices my movement, as does Bo. Things get tense again all of a sudden, now that Donna is out of the room.

Bob leans across the table and says, "I want you to trust me, Jonnybob. Bo, here is no threat to you or any one of your friends. I'm not sure why you got so riled up when he came in here, but it's probably not a coincidence that he called me over and told me a story about you when I went out to order our food. Somehow, he got the wrong idea about you, and I'm guessin' whatever it is about him that's got your back up is probably just as wrong-headed. I told him that you're a stand-up guy, and whatever he thought was wrong. Honest, you have nothing to be concerned about from anyone in this place. I assure you we would never do anything to hurt Donna or any of her family or friends. Okay?"

He sticks out his hand, and I shake it. Bo is a little more reticent about it, but finally puts his big ol' paw out across the table, and I take it almost as cautiously.

"Now that the pissin' match is over, I need to go before I make a puddle right where I stand. Can you two promise not to do anything rash while I'm gone?"

Bo nods, and I do, too.

"I'll be right behind you," I tell Bob. "That iced tea is runnin' right through me."

We head out the door, and I check out the dining area while Bob is in the head. I don't recognize anyone, and nobody seems to be paying me any attention at all. Good.

Donna comes out of the ladies' room, and seems surprised to see me.

"It's cool," I tell her. "I'm just waiting my turn."

She smiles and walks over to where April is wrapping silverware in napkins. They're giggling when Bob comes out of the head, I go in, do my business, and return to the café. Bo is there, patiently waiting his turn, with a smile on his face. Imagine that! I wasn't sure he knew how to smile, but he probably feels the same way about me.

Bob is over at the counter with Donna and April, and they head toward the office when they see Bo leave the restroom. We all go back into the office, and I notice the dirty plates are gone. There are fresh pitchers of water and iced tea, as well as a full carafe of coffee. There's a plate of fruit and another piled with pastries. I fill my glass with tea and throw a couple cherry turnovers and a slice of watermelon on a plate.

"You're not worried about your figure, any more, huh?"

Bob gestures at the turnovers, and I just flip him the bird. I'm smiling, though, so he will know I'm just kidding. He and Donna laugh, but Bo looks puzzled.

He wasn't in here earlier, so he's not real sure what's going on.

As we all settle back into our chairs, Bob walks over and makes sure the door is locked. Time to get down to brass tacks, as Kenneth would say.

THIRTY-SIX

"Okay, Jonnybob," Bob starts, leaning back in his chair, "how's 'bout you tell us what made you reach for your piece when Bo and I came back in the room?"

I immediately feel picked on, wondering why he's starting here. He must see the change in my body language or something, because he continues before I can get started, "I know Bo's story, and I really feel things will be clearer if you start out, Jonnybob. Just humor me, okay?" He waits a couple seconds, and adds, "Please."

Who am I to argue with politeness?

"All right," I say, turning toward Bob and Bo, "I came in here Wednesday with my friend Kenneth and Donna's daughter Judy." Bob is nodding; he's heard all of this. "While we were here, I noticed Bo at another table, and felt that he was paying too much attention to us, or me. I was afraid he had recognized me, but I really didn't know how that could happen. I didn't look anything like I do now as recently as a few days ago."

They're both paying attention, and they share a knowing look, as if something has suddenly become clearer. I decide to continue my story.

"While we were eating, April was talking to Judy about her car, how Donna had mentioned the color in here at some point. After we left, we saw a Huntsville unmarked cop car cruisin' Booger Town, like they were looking for someone. I was pretty sure they were looking for us, and I thought Bo was probably the one that had called them, although I didn't know his name at that point. The people I'm avoiding have some local cops on their payroll, and I was afraid Bo had called someone who sicced the dirty cops on us."

More nodding, and a trace of a smile on both faces.

"When I saw him sitting out there this morning," I continue, "I kinda freaked out. I told Donna about how I recognized him, and my suspicions, just before you guys came in the room."

Donna says that's exactly what happened, and heads start nodding once again.

"That's why I reacted the way I did. So convince me I was wrong."

Now even Bo is smiling—sort of.

"When Donna called me last night and asked me to meet you two here this morning, she gave me a little idea of what this was about. From what I've heard this morning, I definitely think you're on the side of the angels. I told you I'd do whatever Donna asked me to do, and I meant it.

"As for my nephew here," he indicates Bo with a wave of his hand, "he was up north a while back, picking up some cars I'd bought at an auction in Knoxville. While he was in a truck stop getting some fuel and a snack, he saw a lot lizard trying to scare up some business."

Oh, shit! I start chuckling. Donna looks at me with that what-the-fuck kind of look on her face.

Bob resumes his narrative. "The guy is tryin' to get her to leave him alone, then finally tells her he's queer. She goes bugshit, starts smackin' him around and screamin' at him."

Now I'm starting to giggle, remembering the silliness of that encounter. Donna looks totally confused, wondering why I find this so damned funny.

"So ten days later or so, Bo sees a guy in here that looks familiar from someplace, but he can't quite figure out where from. After this guy and his friends leave, it hits him; it's the queer from the truck stop.

"The guy didn't act all girly, but it was definitely the guy from the truck stop that had told the hooker that he was gay. So imagine Bo's surprise when he sees this same guy in my office this morning. He called me over, asked who the hell you were, and tells me where he knows you from."

Donna's looking at me, then Bob, then Bo, then back at me. Bo still looks belligerent, like he expects me to deny that I'm that guy from the truck stop. Bob's just grinning his ass off. I'm shaking my head, probably looking pretty silly and embarrassed.

"If Jonnybob's gay," Donna starts out, getting a little riled, "I'm a Shriner's donkey. I've seen how he looks at Judy, and Darla, too. April even said he was flirting with her, and between her and me, we've got a few decades of dealing with men, so I think our impressions would be pretty reliable. There's no way he's the man Bo saw in that damn truck stop parking lot. Tell 'em, Jonnybob."

She looks right at me, and I'm having a real hard time not laughing right in her face. There's no option but to get it over with.

"Actually," I tell her, "it *was* me."

She's speechless. Bob's laughing at the look on her face, and Bo looks vindicated.

"I was on my way to Kenneth's when I stopped, and I was hoping not to attract any attention. When that hooker came on to me, I just wanted to get her to leave me alone so I could get back on the road. I finally told her I was gay just to get her to give up. I never thought she'd go crazy like that. I imagine everyone out in the lot heard her. I was glad nobody I knew had witnessed it, and I never imagined I'd meet someone here who had."

I look at Bo, and tell him, "I apologize for the way I acted earlier. I guess I'm just paranoid."

Bob and Donna are chuckling, and finally Bo joins in. He's snorting that weird laugh, and when he finally speaks, I'm surprised. His voice is as low and raspy as Travis's voice is high and squeaky. Bo's voice sounds like the guy who sings bass in those gospel country bands, only lower. It actually seems to make the glasses on the table vibrate.

"I trust Donna and April's instincts," he says.

"Sittin' here listenin' to you, watching you, I'm pretty sure you're not queer. I'll bet it surprised the shit outta you when that whore started beatin' your ass and screamin' at you. It sure tickled me. I was laughing and she heard me. She started comin' over to where I was, and I got in the truck and hauled ass before she got there. I guess I'm as big a chicken-shit as you were." He starts snorting again, and the other three of us are laughing along. "Sorry I made you nervous . . . Like Uncle Bob says, I'll do what I can to help. I know how much he respects Missus Miller, and from what he's said, she thinks a lot of you. So count me in, if you can use me."

Bob kinda cocks his head to one side, looking at me to decide what I think. I get out of my chair and extend my hand to Bo again. This time, there's no hesitation; he grabs it and gives it a shake. The atmosphere in the room is definitely friendlier than it was a short while ago.

"I've gotta go" says Bo, heading toward the door. "I need to open the lot, and get some work done on a couple cars. Let me know what you need, and I'll do what I can. I don't need to know all the details. Maybe you can fill me in over a few beers later. See you in a little while, Uncle Bob. Missus Miller." He nods at us, and heads out, closing the door behind him.

Bob refills his coffee cup and offers some to Donna, who puts her hand over the top of her cup.

She asks for a glass of water, Bob pours her one and sets it in front her. He looks at me and I just shake my head. Any more tea and I'll be pissing my pants.

Bob walks over and makes sure the door's locked, then returns to his chair and sits down. It's much more relaxed in here since we got all the misconceptions sorted out.

"If I remember right," says Bob, "you were wanting to look at the trailer you'll be using to haul Judy's car back to Mooresville." That's right, I was. I am. Whatever.

"I had another idea while we were eating breakfast," he continues. "What about using my roll-back? That way, you won't need a separate truck and trailer; you can just load that Chevy on the roll-back and tie it down. The result will be the same. Nobody'll pay any attention to a car on a roll-back with a towing company name on the door."

A roll-back. Yeah, that'll work.

"I like that idea a lot," I tell him, and Donna's nodding in agreement. "If I can get a little practice before we take it over to the marina, I'm sure we'll be able to get the car loaded and be out of there in five minutes or less. That'll work great, and like you say, nobody will pay any attention. That's a great idea, Bob."

He's beaming, and gives us a mock bow. "I think I know how to make it work even better," he says. "We'll ask Bo to load up one of the cars from the lot and drive to the marina parking lot. He can unload that car and leave the bed extended so you can drive right up to it. He can hook up the winch, pull it up on the bed, and tie it down in just a couple minutes. He does some repo work for me, and he's damned quick at loadin' up a car and gettin' the hell out of Dodge. As soon as he gets you loaded, he'll drive off in the car he hauled over there. While you're over there talking to him, he can give you a crash course in operating the roll-back. It's easy. Hell, if I can do it, anyone can. I'll stay here and visit with Donna for a few minutes. I know April would like to visit a little, too."

Well, that makes things even easier. This just keeps looking like it might work out, after all. I guess I'd better get things moving and get back to Donna's so I can tell my co-conspirators that the last piece of the puzzle is in place. I'm sure Judy will be pissed, but hopefully Kenneth was able to keep her calmed down.

"That's even better, for sure," I say to Bob who looks relieved that I feel so confident in his idea. "I'll head across the street and talk to Bo. You guys can visit for a while, then we'd better head out so a certain young woman doesn't kick my sorry ass when we get back."

Bob and Donna both laugh at this, and I get up from the table. I give them both a little salute, and head out into the café. The room's full, so I just wave at April and go out onto the sidewalk.

There's not much traffic, but the parking spots on

the street are pretty much full. I wait until it's clear, and run across the street to the car lot. As I walk into the office, Bo is coming through a door joining the office to the shop next door. He's wiping his hands clean on a rag, and actually seems glad to see me. That's a good sign.

"I saw you coming," he says, motioning me to a chair next to the desk. He sits in the one behind it, and leans back to put his feet up on top. "You got something I can help you with?"

No beating around the bush with this guy.

"Your Uncle Bob had an idea to make things easier for us tonight, and suggested I come over and ask you to give us a hand. I realize you don't know much about what we're up to, but what Bob came up with shouldn't put you in any danger."

He just looks at me and twists that big ol' moustache, and says, "Go on."

"We need to get the vehicle we're going to use someplace where nobody'll pay any attention to it," I explain. "Bob came up with the idea of putting it up on his roll-back truck, down by the race track. He thinks that will work, hiding in plain sight, so to speak. I agree. An old Chevy on a roll-back leaving the area next to the Speedway shouldn't get a second look from anyone, and even if it does, it won't look suspicious. We've done some stuff to the car to make it hard to describe, and if we're lucky, the people who will be lookin' for us won't know for sure what kind of car they're even looking for."

Bo's nodding, and seems to be following my disjointed explanation pretty well.

"So," he says, "where do you want me to take the truck and wait for you? And where do I need to take the car once I get it loaded?"

Well, that makes it obvious; he understood exactly what I was saying, only went a step further than we had planned.

"There's a parking lot on the Ditto Marina Parkway, not far from Green Cove Road, where people park boat trailers and stuff," I tell him. He's nodding along and waves his hand for me to continue. "Bob says that we can load a car from the lot onto the roll-back and take it to that parking lot. You can get it unloaded, leaving the bed extended so we can get our car loaded in a hurry. We'll take the truck and head out, and you can drive off in the car you hauled over there when you leave."

He just sits there, twirling his moustache. "That's it?" he asks. "You just want me to put a car on the roll-back, drive to the marina parking lot, unload the car, load your car, and take off? Is that right? That doesn't sound like much help."

Maybe not to you, Wild Bill.

"Believe me," I tell him, "that will be a great deal of help. It might just be the difference between a clean getaway and getting in a bunch of shit. If this works like we think it will, you will have made things a lot safer for us. It may not sound like much to you, but it's real important."

He takes his feet off the desk and leans forward to rest his elbows where his feet recently were. "That sounds easy enough. When do I need to be there?"

I'm glad he agreed to do this so easily. We really are getting a little pressed for time, and I'm glad I didn't have to spend time persuading Bo to help.

"You should be there and have the car unloaded by midnight, because we should be there shortly after twelve. I'd appreciate it if you'd show me how to operate the roll-back, so I can unload our car when we get to where we're going. We'll have it back here by Sunday afternoon, if everything works out right."

He gets up and motions for me to follow him. We go through the shop into the fenced yard where the roll-back is kept. It's no thing of beauty, but Bo says it's a damned good truck. I hope so, because if something goes wrong, Kenneth and I might be in for a wild ride.

THIRTY-SEVEN

After a quick rundown on how to operate the roll-back from Bo, I walk back over to the café to thank Bob again. April puts a bag of cinnamon rolls in my hand as we leave. There are hugs all around, and the trip back to Mooresville is uneventful. Donna and I compare notes, and we both laugh about how things turned out.

Pulling into the lot at Donna's Place, I see Judy and Kenneth sitting on the rail along the parking lot, watching Jesus acting like a puppy. They're both laughing, whether at the dog or at something one of them said. Man, I hope neither of them gets hurt tonight. Donna must have an idea of what I'm thinking, because she reaches over and gives my arm a squeeze.

"Y'all will be just fine, hon. Just remember that you're the good guys in this deal. No regrets, okay?"

No, I don't have any regrets . . . yet. The thought of any of these remarkable people getting hurt because of my personal war with the meth trade just about makes me sick. But it's out of my control now.

All of them have their own reasons for doing this; it's not just my crusade anymore. My main responsibility now is to pull this off without putting anyone at more risk than necessary.

"Donna, you're a damn fine woman, and I'm proud to know you," I tell her, squeezing her hand back. "I feel really lucky to have met you and everyone else here since Kenneth and I arrived on your doorstep. Hopefully, you'll feel the same way about us tomorrow. Now, I guess I'd better face the music and go say hello to Judy and Kenneth. Wish me luck."

Donna pulls up in front of my friends sitting on the pipe rail, rolls the window down, and greets them with a sweet, "Good Morning."

They both respond in kind, and, as I get out of the car, Kenneth says, "'Bout time you got here. We were beginnin' to think you'd run off and hid somewhere."

Well, at least he doesn't seem pissed off. Good.

"No," I respond, "I just decided to take this pretty lady out for breakfast."

Donna smiles at me, waves at all three of us, and pulls her Caddy over into its normal parking spot. She gets out and heads into the kitchen to see how badly things have gotten screwed up in her absence.

Judy is watching Jesus acting like a dumb-ass as I walk over and shake Kenneth's hand. She finally acknowledges my existence, squinting one eye as she looks over at Kenneth and me. Jesus notices nobody's watching him and comes over to sniff my boots. Having seen this movie before, I keep an eye on him lest he decides to either piss on my boot or hump my leg. He seems to lose interest fairly quickly, and runs back over to a clump of weeds and starts chasing something I can't see. What a retard.

"Well," says Judy, "are you going to tell us where you've been and what you've been doing, or not?"

She doesn't seem especially hostile, which I'm grateful for. I imagine I've got Kenneth to thank for that. He knew I was up to something, so I'm sure he wasn't surprised, unless by the fact that I took Donna with me.

"We're all set," I tell them, sitting down on the rail a few feet from Judy to the west, so she doesn't have to squint to look at me. "Donna and I went over to Fat Bob's this morning and had a long talk with Bob. He's willing to do whatever he can to help, mostly because Donna asked him. His nephew Bo, the one who runs the car lot, is going to run an errand for us that'll make things a lot easier."

Judy looks surprised, as does Kenneth at first. But now they're both grinning and looking like they're satisfied that my errand wasn't one for fools.

"Well, come on out with it," says Dutton, chewing on some kind of vegetation he's pulled from a clump at his feet, "What's the scoop?"

I don't want to have to go through the whole thing any more than necessary, so I'd rather have Travis and Bobby Ray present when I explain what I've got planned. I haven't seen them yet, and wouldn't know Bobby Ray's truck if I saw it.

"Are Bobby Ray and Travis here yet?" I ask Judy, and this, at least, makes her smile.

"They're in the café stuffing their faces," she says. "They got here about an hour ago, all excited to hear your plan. When they found out you were AWOL, they decided to have some breakfast and flirt with Darla. That girl is loving all the hours she's getting, as well as all the attention. She'll be really disappointed when I get back to work."

Good for Darla.

"Have you two eaten?" I ask Judy.

Silly question, as far as Kenneth's concerned. He's never gone this late in the day without food unless he was passed out.

"Kenneth was in there when they opened," Judy says, giving him a push that almost makes him fall off the rail. "I wandered in there a couple hours ago and had a cup of coffee and an egg sandwich. Why? Didn't Bob feed you?" She's grinning at the silliness of her question. Sorta like asking Kenneth if he's eaten yet. "We've just been out here playing with Jesus, waiting for you and Momma to get back. I must say, I was surprised to hear that you two had come in so early and got the biscuits ready, then hauled ass before any of us were awake. You're a sneaky shit, Jonnybob Clark."

She's smiling as she says this, so I don't feel bad. And besides, she's right. I *am* a sneaky shit.

"Let's wait for Travis and Bobby Ray, so I can tell everyone at once. In the meantime," I tell Kenneth, "maybe you should call Jimbob and set up a place to meet him and his niece."

He and Judy share a grin, and he chuckles. "Already done, son. I called him about an hour ago and we decided that he'd just meet Judy at that car wash we were at the other day. That way, Melody can get in the van with Judy, and Jimbob can ease on down past Chubby's and find a place to park around midnight, so he can pull rear guard after Judy drives by. They're gonna be there about 11:30, so nobody will be in a hurry. They'll have a half-hour to drive a few blocks and get in position. You and I can park the Chevy over by the fireworks place, and the boys can get themselves in the bar in time to work out their deal. Speaking of the boys, here they come."

I follow his gaze and see Bobby Ray and Travis exiting the door at the end of the rear hallway—the one that goes past Donna's office. They're both laughing, and give us a wave as they approach.

"What are you two laughing at?" Judy quizzes them, good naturedly. "I hope it's something about Jonnybob, and it's good enough to share."

And she thinks *I'm* a shit . . .

Travis is first to speak, in that weird high-pitched voice that I've grown accustomed to. "Actually, we were talking to your momma, and she was telling us about her trip to Huntsville with JB this morning."

Uh oh. She wouldn't do that, would she? Sure, she would. Crap.

Bobby Ray is grinning like a sugared-up ten-year-old. He can't wait for the bombshell. He's like a kid waiting for Santa Claus. He can't look me in the eye, and Travis is having a hard time keeping his shit together.

Double crap.

"I think we should find some place with some privacy to discuss our plans," I say, trying to head off what's coming, at least for awhile.

Judy and Kenneth seem to sense my discomfort, and are watching me pretty closely as the other two continue to giggle and shuffle their feet.

"Let's go out to my place," says Judy. "We can get comfortable and Jesus can run around for awhile without me worrying about him getting run over." She looks at Travis and tells him, "We were waiting for you two so Jonnybob would tell us all about his plan. It sounds like you two have something to tell us, too."

More giggling, shuffling of feet. Snickers. Dammit!

"C'mon, JB," says Dutton, "let's give that ol' rusty Chevy a test drive. Nobody's even looked at it twice since we parked it. You boys," he says, looking at the Tickled Twins, "can meet us out there."

Before they can resist, I jump up and head over to the Malibu. "Sounds good to me. Do we need to go by the store or anything before we head out there, Judy?"

Anything to postpone the recitation of *Jonnybob's Shame*. Judy's looking at me kind of weird, as is Kenneth. Travis and Jonnybob are both still snickering, but have started moving toward a nice-looking black Dodge Ram pickup parked up by the front of the building.

"I suppose we could go by the Mini Mart and pick up some snacks. You can fill up the car with gas while we're there, too."

She gathers up Jesus in her arms, and tells us to wait while she tells Donna where we're going. Oh no.

"You can call her from your house, right?" I definitely don't need her to come back from a confab with Donna laughing like the other two. "She's probably busy, seeing as how she got here late. You'll have plenty of time to talk to her before tonight."

Please . . . please don't go in there.

Judy stops and thinks about it for a few seconds, then heads toward her car. "You're probably right. Let's get everything ironed out, then I'll talk to her before we leave. Why don't you drive, JB? You should probably get used to my car before tonight, just in case you need to do some serious ass-haulin'."

Whew. Thank God for small favors. She tosses me her keys, and I get in on the driver's side.

Judy heads over to the passenger side of Bobby Ray's truck, hands Jesus to Travis, and says, "Here, you two take him with you. I want to ride along and show JB some stuff as we go."

Travis doesn't look real thrilled, and I can't blame him. That damned puppy will probably trample his nuts the whole time they're on the road. But he's not about to argue with Judy, so he takes the dog and closes his door. Judy comes over to the Malibu, gets in, and buckles up.

"We'll meet those two," nodding at the black Dodge, "out at the house. When you leave the lot, hang a left. We'll take some back roads so you can put my baby through her paces. Just in case, you know?"

Yeah, I know. I really hope we won't need to use all the car's capabilities tonight, but it's a damned good idea to be prepared.

"Okay boys," she says, looking over her shoulder at Kenneth, "buckle up tight, 'cause we're gonna have a little fun."

THIRTY-EIGHT

As we pull out of the lot at Donna's onto County Road 17, Judy yells, "Punch it!"

I do, and the tires spin for a couple seconds before hooking up, and I'm shifting gears, trying to keep the engine revs in a reasonable range and the car pointed in the general direction I want to go. This damned thing pulls like a freight train, and we're soon over a hundred miles an hour, before we even reach the overpass to cross I-565. I let off the gas and get on the brakes.

I'm thrown forward against the seat belt.

Kenneth exclaims, "Dammit!" from the rear seat.

I look at Judy, and she's grinning. I can see that she really loves this car, and enjoys showing people what it'll do.

"Holy shit," I say, breathing for the first time in a few seconds. "This thing hauls ass! And it stops damned well, too. What all have you had done to it?"

I slow down to the limit, and we head toward the little town of Mooresville. Judy points at the next intersection and tells me to hang a right. I do, and she directs me onto the shoulder. I pull over, put the tranny into neutral, and leave my foot on the brake. Kenneth and I are all ears.

I'm wondering if Judy can give me any specific details about the car. Knowing what the Malibu is made of might make things a little easier to figure out.

Judy looks at me as if she can read my mind. After a few seconds, she grins and punches me on the shoulder. "I think I told you earlier that I've got a 377 long-rod motor in 'er. It's got gobs of torque, but it takes a little practice to get used to it. You need to sort of squeeze the throttle, not mash it all at once, 'cause she'll turn around on you in a corner when the cam comes in. Pretend there's an egg under the gas pedal and try not to break it. It takes some finesse. The trans is a close-ratio Richmond five-speed, and is damned near bullet-proof. The front A-arms are all tubular, and we've got coil-over shocks on all four corners. The brakes are disks on all four wheels, with big rotors and calipers. Jimmy built this thing like a race car, and it runs and handles like one. The tires are Hoosier street-legal radials, and they grip really well."

Okay, I was wrong. I should have known Judy wasn't "normal" in the sense of women and machinery. She's consistently thrown around terms and nomenclature in a manner that should have made me expect her depth of knowledge about her "baby". I look at her with a combination of surprise, admiration, and that other feeling I've been trying to ignore—lust.

Again seeming to read my mind, Judy colors slightly. She says, "I know. I've heard it a hundred times. 'Girls' shouldn't know so much about cars and bikes. Just be glad I do know what I'm talking about, and have such a bad-ass car you can use for your shenanigans tonight."

We all laugh, and my doubts fade away like smoke in the wind. Kenneth looks a little apprehensive, but Judy's grinning ear-to-ear with anticipation of the fun to come.

She takes a breath, looking over her shoulder—for cops, I imagine. "This road we're on is the Old Highway 20. There isn't much out here, no crossroads. Jimmy called it the Mooresville Grand Prix, and it was his favorite test track. There's a pretty good straight stretch ahead, then there's pair of pretty good forty-five degree left-handers. After that, there's a long straight where you can really wring 'er out. There's a mild left-hand kink down toward the end of the straight, then a hard left. From there, I'll give you a heads-up on what's coming up next. Okay?"

Damn, there's no doubt she's spent a lot of time with racers. She obviously knows what she's talking about. Contrary to my thoughts of a few minutes ago, there's a pretty good chance that there are a lot of women in this part of the country who know as much, or more, than she does. Stock car racing is a fairly family-oriented sport, and I guess everyone in the family learns everything about the race car, if only by osmosis. Judy simply enjoys the machinery, the parts that make things happen, in a big way. Just another thing we have in common. If not for Kenneth's attraction to her, I would definitely try to spend some time getting to know her better.

I've spent some weekends hanging around some of the roundy-round guys back at The Beach, and my uncle Jim raced when I was a kid in Colorado, so I understand the lingo. One of the PnB members had a road-race Mustang that he ran at a small membership-type track in Tidewater. On track days, a few of us would take turns driving it, trying to improve our times. Hoping I remember some of what I learned there, I pull my belts tight. I give Judy and Kenneth a thumbs-up before pushing the shifter up into first gear. Hopefully, I can impress my passengers while keeping the car right side up and out of the ditch.

I check the mirrors, look over my shoulder to make sure nobody's snuck up on me on a bike or something, and pull out onto the road. I ease into the gas to get the car rolling, then start squeezing—not mashing—the throttle—like there's an egg under the pedal. The Malibu takes off like a rocket, and we're soon coming up on the first left-hander. I downshift from fourth to third, keeping the revs up, cut down to the bottom of the apex and accelerate out toward the next one. I do the same drill, this time harder on the throttle as I exit the corner. Squeeze, shift, squeeze, shift, now hard on the gas as we haul ass down the straight. I take the kink in fifth, then immediately start downshifting—fourth, third, down to second, hard on the brakes to make the hard left-hander. We come out of it with the tail hung out and the Hoosiers smoking.

"Hard right," yells Judy, but I've already seen the

sign and am in third gear, then hard on the brakes. Back down to second, hard right, ease on the gas, back to third, fourth. "It gets a little twisty through here," says Judy, raising her voice above the noise of the engine. No shit, Sherlock.

There's a kink to the left, another, then a left-right combination. It's all fourth gear through here. Now we're on a short straight, and I wind it up pretty tight, but stay in fourth gear.

I go through another fairly tight kink to the left and Judy hollers, "Big one-eighty right up here! It's really tight."

I'm glad she said so—the sign for this corner is missing. I'd probably have put us out in a field if she hadn't said anything. The right-hander is definitely tight. I'm down to second. Squeeze, shift, squeeze, shift, all the while negotiating a left-right-right combination of corners.

We're headed toward the interstate and Judy says, "Good. Slow down and pull over up here."

I lift off the throttle a little, let the car settle down, and pull over onto a wide spot on the side of the road. I take a couple of deep breaths, and give my heartbeat time to slow back down to something approaching normal. Kenneth is hooting and hollering, making a hell of a racket. Judy's grinning ear-to-ear, probably happy I didn't wreck her car or hurt any of us.

"I think you've had all the practice you need," she says, laughing. "Where did you learn to drive like that?

I think you've been holding back on us." She reaches back and ruffles Kenneth's hair. "How 'bout you, Kenneth? Are you ready to take a turn?"

"No fuckin' way," Dutton blurts, his face red as a tomato. "It's scary enough with someone drivin' who knows how. With me at the wheel it would be purely terrifyin', for all of us." We all crack up, and I offer to let Judy drive back.

"You go ahead," she says. "Just take it a little easier on the way back so you still have some tread left on the tires for tonight."

I bang a u-turn, and we head back toward Mooresville at a more reasonable speed. That was a lot of fun, but I hope our little escapade this evening doesn't require any driving similar to that. Daylight, out by myself with a navigator, is a whole different deal than racing through the dark on roads I don't know, without anyone to warn me about upcoming corners or obstacles.

As we proceed back the way we came, we see evidence of our passing in the other direction. Especially at the exit of that first hard left-hander, there are prodigious black tracks weaving back and forth across the road.

"You got on it a little too hard, too fast, on that one," says Judy, "but you figured it out after that. I'm impressed."

I brush off the compliment, but it feels good to have Judy happy with something I've done. That hasn't been the case very often lately. I can't wait to see what Travis and Bobby Ray think of my plans for hiding the car in plain sight. Hopefully, they'll be as upbeat as Judy is.

THIRTY-NINE

We stop on the way back through Mooresville at the Mini Mart to fill up the gas tank and pick up some snacks and lunch stuff. Not one person pays a bit of attention to Judy's car. As I'm checking the oil and water levels, Judy and Kenneth come out of the store with bags of foodstuffs. There are six-packs of RC, a pair of boxes full of fried chicken, and assorted other packages of stuff I don't recognize. At least we won't starve.

We pull into Judy's driveway, and Bobby Ray peeks around the corner of the house. He comes toward us, laughing. I figure he's still laughing at what Donna told them about my experience at Bob's this morning, but when he starts telling Judy what's going on, I realize I'm off the hook . . . for a while, at least.

"That is one chicken-shit dog you've got there, Cuz," he says between gales of laughter. "He ran under my chair and hid when you pulled into the yard, and he won't come out. Where've you guys been? We were just talkin' about comin' and lookin' for ya, but didn't know for sure where to look."

"You leave that puppy alone," says Judy. "He'll be just fine as soon as he figures out he belongs here."

She hands Bobby Ray a couple of bags full of grub

and leans the seat back forward so Kenneth can crawl out. He hands out the bags he has in back, and unfolds from the back seat, grinning. I don't know whether he's grinning about Judy's dog being a chicken-shit or something else, but if it's the former, I hope he keeps it to himself. I'd hate to see Judy tie into him again.

"We went out on the Mooresville Grand Prix to see how Jonnybob did with my car. I tell you, the boy's a natural. I feel a lot better knowing how well he drives. If things blow up, he and Kenneth will have a good chance of getting away from anyone in pursuit.

"Speaking of which, as soon as we get the food in side and everyone gets a plate, we'll hear the new developments from this morning."

At this, she aims a pointed look at me, but all I can see is Bobby Ray starting to turn red before he heads back around the corner. I hear him and Travis start laughing at about the same time, but I don't have any idea how to postpone the inevitable any longer. I follow Judy and Kenneth into the back yard.

Travis is seated at the patio table, and Jesus has crawled up in his lap. He gives us a wave and goes back to scratching the dog's ears. Bobby Ray helps Judy carry the bags from the Mini Mart into the house. Kenneth flops into one of the lawn chairs, and I lean up against the clothesline post, enjoying the gorgeous morning and soaking up the quiet. I've been so busy plotting and scheming that I haven't taken the time to enjoy much of anything.

Kenneth fills Travis in on where we've been, and I can hear Bobby Ray and Judy joking around in the kitchen. Jesus has hopped down from Travis's lap and is nosing around the yard.

All of a sudden, Judy's laughing, really hard. She's telling Bobby Ray he's full of shit, and he's telling her he sure as hell isn't. They're both laughing their asses off, and before you know it, Judy's hiccups are in full song. I'm pretty sure I know what (who) they're laughing at.

Judy comes busting through the screen door, and grabs Kenneth by the shoulder. "How come you didn't tell us that Jonnybob is a little light in the loafers, Kenneth? It's no big deal, but it would've been nice to know. I could've introduced him to some local boys."

She's getting a real kick out of this, and Travis has joined in the hilarity. Kenneth has a confused, what-the-fuck look on his face.

"Okay, y'all have your fun, but it seemed like a good idea at the time," I say.

This cracks them up even more, if that's possible. Kenneth just keeps looking from one of us to the other, waiting for an explanation.

I look at Dutton, and start in. "I didn't tell you about this, because I didn't need the bullshit, but I can see that everyone else knows, so here goes." I move from the clothesline to an empty lawn chair. "This happened on the way from The Beach to your place. I was at a truck stop out by Knoxville when . . ."

I tell them the tale, from my meeting the tweaked-out hooker to the standoff in Bob's office this morning. By the time I'm done, the hilarity has given way to occasional chuckles and the rare clapping of hands at a particularly silly spot.

I finish my story and tell them that now Bo is on board as a fellow conspirator.

Judy says, "Hold on. Let's get something to eat and drink before you start. Holy shit, that was fun! We got so busy listening to your story that even Kenneth forgot to eat anything."

She gives him a punch on the shoulder and ruffles his hair to show him she's only kidding. Travis says he needs to visit the facilities, and Bobby Ray starts chasing Jesus around, making weird cat-like noises. That puppy is definitely a chicken-shit.

After everyone has taken their trip to the bathroom and fixed a plate in the kitchen, we go back outside to the patio table. Kenneth has two plates, one full of chicken and potato salad, the other full of chips and cookies.

He notices everyone staring at him and he laughs. "Hell, we been so busy planning fires and ass-kickins and such, I've plumb forgot to eat a couple times. I need to build up my strength before tonight."

Everyone gets a good laugh out of this, and we all settle in to lunch.

"Go ahead, JB," says Travis, munching on a pickle. "I think we can listen while you tell us how you and Kenneth plan to avoid bein' followed when you leave Chubby's."

The others nod, and I take a bite of chicken, then wash it down with RC.

"Okay, but I'll be takin' a break every now and then to get a bite down my neck, okay?"

More nods. Jesus is trying to dig a hole to China over by the flowerbed, and that's the only noise to hear, other than chewing.

"Before Bo came into the office with Bob, we'd been talking about a way to stash Judy's car somewhere so we wouldn't have to drive all over Huntsville in it, disguised or not. I asked Donna to set up a meeting with Bob so I could tell him what we were up to, ask him if we could stash the car in his car lot."

Everyone is following along, nodding and chewing. I take a couple bites of chicken, eat a little potato salad, and wash it down.

"Bob was willing to do that," I continue, "but he had a better idea. He originally suggested using a trailer, driving the Malibu up on it, and hauling ass. As we talked about it, he had an even better idea. He's offered to let us use his roll-back wrecker truck."

Travis grins from ear to ear, as does Bobby Ray. Kenneth's nodding his head decisively, and Judy looks interested, too. They are all familiar with the type of truck I'm talking about. The long, flat bed of the truck slides back on rollers and tilts at the same time, basically turning into a big ramp. A winch is installed at the front of the bed, making it easy to pull a disabled vehicle up the ramp, then the whole deal tilts back down and rolls forward before locking into its original position. A good operator can load or unload a car in a hurry, by himself, without all the hassle using a wrecker entails.

"He's going to have Bo load up one of his used cars on the roll-back and take it over to a place called the Ditto Marina Parkway. Donna and I picked up a map at a gas station on the way back, and I've got the route memorized. Bo will unload that car and wait for us. We'll put the Malibu on the roll back, tie it down, and drive down to the road that goes by the race track. When we head out to the Memorial Parkway, I'm hopin' nobody will pay any attention to a junky-lookin' old car up on a wrecker. We'll head south, past Chubby's, so we can sweep the escape route, just in case any of you or Jimbob has a problem."

Travis is the first to react. He slaps his knee with his hand and hollers, "Perfect! If you make it to Green Cove Road before anyone gets fired up and follows you, you'll have it dicked. That little parking lot will work out great; I've been there a bunch of times, and at that time of night it should be damned near empty."

Bobby Ray agrees enthusiastically, and even Kenneth has quit chewing long enough to chime in. "I like it. That way, we won't have to be traipsin' all over the damned countryside, hopin' to get away from the cops, fire department, biker club, and titty-lovers."

Well, that pretty much says it all. I laugh along with the others, and take another swipe at my lunch.

"I like the idea of following the same roads we're gonna take," says Judy, "but the thought of you driving right by Chubby's kind of bothers me. What if someone recognizes you, or the car?"

Travis speaks up with what I was about to say. "There's no way anyone there is gonna tie the two cars together. They'll see JB and Kenneth head north, then a few minutes later, a roll-back with an old car on it will come from the direction of the Speedway and head south. There are dozens of cars on trailers and roll-backs that do that every weekend. Seein' as how they're havin' test-n-tune tomorrow night, there'll be a pretty steady stream of them all night. These guys'll blend right in. I don't think anyone will give them a second glance."

"I agree, Judy. I wouldn't do it if I didn't think it'd work. The people out there in the lot at Chubby's won't get enough of a look at your car to even know what model or make it is. Then when we come back from a different direction with it up on the wrecker, it would be a miracle if someone put the two together. I just don't see it happening." I take a breath and a drink of RC.

"I think I know a way to make sure," says Bobby Ray. "One thing that will definitely make them think it came from the track is numbers on the doors. My buddy, Kevin, has one of those machines that cuts stickers out of plastic for signs and such. He's been makin' signs for semi doors, numbers and other stickers for the racers, and all kinds of other signs. I'll call him and tell him I need a couple numbers made for a stock car that Travis is painting. It's short notice, but I'll bet I can talk him into it. I'll call him right now."

He jumps up and bangs through the screen door. Jesus yelps, and runs under Judy's chair. What a pussy.

The rest of us are talking about the merits of Bobby Ray's idea, when he pokes his head out of the door and says, "He said he'll do it, as long as they're only one color. What number, JB?"

Hell, I don't know. It doesn't really matter, as far as I'm concerned.

"Nine," says Judy. "Put one right-side up on one side, and upside down on the other. That will be even more confusing if anyone's paying attention."

"Cool," says Travis. He's clearly enjoying this twist. "Tell Kevin to make 'em white; that's the most common. Is that okay with you, JB? Kenneth?"

Kenneth looks pleased to have been consulted, but just shakes his head. "Naw, I don't think so. That'd be too shiny, too new lookin'. I think a bright blue or somethin' would be better. It'll show up in the lights—and flames." He gets a fit of the giggles and takes a minute to straighten up before continuing. "But they'll pretty much disappear in the dark. We don't need anyone remembering some guys putting bright white number nines on a car at that boat trailer parking lot."

That makes sense, and I'm nodding along, content to let the others make the decision.

"That's better," says Bobby Ray. Travis agrees, and so does everyone else. "I'll tell him and we can pick them up in a couple hours."

He's gone, and the screen door bangs. The puppy flinches, yelps, and tries to burrow farther into Judy's lap. Lucky little shit.

"I think I'm gonna take a little nap, if that's okay with y'all," says Kenneth. "I think I know everything I need to know, and we can have us a skull session later, right before we head for Huntsvull. Is that okay with you, son?" He's looking at me, and I really can't think of any reason to disagree with him.

It's been a long day, already, and a nap is probably a damned good idea.

"Sure, we've got plenty of time, and I think we've got everything covered. I agree a short strategy session before we split up and head out is a good idea. Bobby Ray and Travis will have to be there before any of the rest of us, seein' as how they're gonna hang out in the bar for awhile before they make their move upstairs to find Shirley. What time do you think we should sit down, Travis?"

As I'm asking him this, Bobby Ray comes out of the house. Slam. Flinch. Yelp. Jesus.

"I figger the more we talk about it, the more we'll muddy it up," says Travis in that high-pitched voice. "I think a short meeting to hit the high points would be a good thing, though. How about nine o'clock, at Donna's? That way, stuff will be fresh in our minds, and we can all split up to do our part."

That's just about what I was thinking. We can check out the vehicles, do whatever we need to do to get ready, before having a short skull session to get psyched up for tonight's action.

"That sounds real good to me. What do you guys think?" I look at each of these remarkable people in turn, and everyone gives me a thumbs-up.

Now all there is to do is spend the next nine hours making sure we're rested, ready, and equipped to do what needs done. I'm sure we'll all fill our guts with chow, if we can find room among the butterflies.

FORTY

When we got back from Judy's, Kenneth went to his cabin and crashed. I think the stress finally caught up with him, no matter how much he might deny it. Judy went into the café to talk to her mom, and spend some time with people other than us, I think. She half-heartedly volunteered to help me, but I figure she needs some time to recharge her mental capacities and take her mind off of the night's activities.

I went through the Malibu, checking tire pressures, fluid levels, belt tension, all the sort of stuff that can bite you in the ass at the most inopportune times. Everything looked just dandy, so I took all the weapons out of it, as well as all the ones from Vanna and the ones I was carrying into my cabin and cleaned them. I also made sure they were all full of ammunition, and had spare clips, full and ready to go. I put the sawed-off shotgun and a Glock back in Vanna for Judy to arrange as she sees fit. She has her hand-cannon in her purse, having retrieved it from the pocket on the door. I also returned two of the Glocks to the Malibu glove box, and stuck my nine mil back in the waistband of my jeans. Kenneth still has the .45 in his pocket, and I stuck Polly's straight razor in the door pocket that Judy's automatic had recently vacated. The flash-bangs are in the trunk, the pencil flare launcher and flares are in the glove box, and the small propane torch is there, too, just in case we need more help getting a fire started somewhere. I toss in a small canvas tool bag I found, figuring it might come in handy.

When I was finished, I went to my cabin and stretched out on the bed, trying to decide whether or not I'd forgotten anything. At some point, I actually crashed and had a decent nap devoid of bad dreams, for which I'm extremely grateful. I really don't need any bad vibes before things even get going.

As I'm coming out of my cabin after my nap and a shower, I see Kenneth and Judy back on the pipe railing at the edge of the parking lot, watching Jesus being his normal dumb-ass self. They're sitting there, enjoying each other's company, and I feel a quick stab of jealousy. I'm ashamed of myself for it, but it's there, all the same.

Kenneth sees me and hollers, "Hey, sleepyhead, it's about time you got up. We were afraid you'd decided to chicken out on us."

Judy laughs, and the dog takes a look at her before returning to his pursuit of an ant or something in the grass along the rail. I smile, head over, and sit down on the rail next to Dutton.

"I got all the guns cleaned and checked out," I tell them. "The car's ready to go, and Vanna is, too."

They both nod, and Kenneth actually has the good sense to look a little sheepish. "If you two want to check out your weapons," I say, "I have some oil and stuff in that cabin, and boxes of ammo, too."

Judy chuckles, and says, "Great minds think alike, JB. I cleaned my .45 and put the spare mags in my purse right before I met Kenneth."

I'm not surprised. She's no slouch when it comes to planning ahead.

Kenneth looks even more sheepish as he stands up and heads to my cabin. "I'll be back in a couple minutes," he mumbles, "even though I can't imagine that the damned thing has gotten very dirty since we left my house. Damned perfectionists."

Judy and I laugh, and enjoy the silence while Kenneth's gone. She's watching Jesus do his thing, and I'm just relaxing, trying not to let anxiety get hold of me. Now that we're alone, I don't know what to say.

"You hungry?" Judy's talking to me, and I snap out of my thoughts. "I told Kenneth we should wait for you, so he's only been snacking. That man is something else!"

She's grinning, thinking of my goofy buddy, and I can't help smiling along with her. Dutton is one of a kind, and I'm thankful that he's decided to help me out. He's rude, always irreverent, and even downright disrespectful at times, but I love him like a brother. And the boy can definitely eat!

Just as I'm about to answer Judy, Kenneth comes out of my cabin and heads over to where we're sitting. "Okay, you were right; I feel better now that I made sure my gun's clean and ready to go. Can we go get some supper, now? I'm hungry enough to eat Spam."

Judy hops up and takes Jesus over to her cabin, telling him what a pretty boy he is. Yeah, right. She rejoins us, and we all head over to the rear door leading into the hallway between the kitchen and Donna's office.

As we're passing Donna's office door, it slams open and Donna comes bursting out, running into Judy and knocking her and Kenneth into the opposite wall. She's agitated, and her hair looks like she's been combing it with a broom.

"Damn!" exclaims Judy, as she's nearly howled over. "Momma, what's wrong? You look like you've seen a ghost, for cryin' out loud!"

We all try to think of what could be the cause of Donna's behavior, and Judy's the first to speak her fears. "Oh, no! It's not Bobby Ray or Travis, is it? I told them to hang out here, instead of going back to Travis's place."

Donna is catching her breath, waiting for Judy to finish. "No, Punkin, it's not Bobby Ray or Travis. I'm not sure I'm not over-reacting, but I need to talk to Kenneth."

We look at her, at Kenneth, back at her, waiting for additional information, but none is forthcoming.

Before we can even react, Donna has Kenneth by the arm and is leading him into her office. Judy and I look at each other, both of us wondering just what the fuck is going on.

Has Donna finally decided to tell Kenneth about the history between her and Kenneth's daddy, just in case something happens tonight?

Before either one of us can put our thoughts into words, we hear a low, moaning wail start up behind the door. It's followed up by Kenneth yelling, "No, dammit! Please don't tell me that!"

I reach for the doorknob, but Judy grabs me by the wrist.

"Momma must've had a reason for talking to him alone," she says, with a worried look on her face. She puts her hand in mine, giving it a hard squeeze. "Let's wait for a few minutes, see what's going on, okay?"

I squeeze back, give her a little nod. Our eyes meet, both of us feeling the pain expressed by our friend on the other side of the door.

We can hear voices, Kenneth's raised, Donna's subdued, but can't decipher what's being said. I'm about to bust, wanting to know what the fuck is going on, and Judy looks anxious, alternating between looking at the office door and me.

The door opens up, and Donna looks out. "He wants you guys in here," she says, and by the looks of her, it's not good news.

We go into the office, and Kenneth is sitting in front of the small television set, switching from one channel to the next, watching what appears to be live coverage of a major accident. He's also got the phone to his ear, impatiently looking at the handset every couple of seconds; he's clearly on hold.

"That bus," he starts out, pointing at the small screen, "is from Midsouth Convalescent Home—that place Janie's in. I'm trying to see if she was on the bus, but nobody knows anything, and I've been on hold just about long e-fucking-nuff!" He bangs the phone down and stares at the screen some more.

There's a banner scrolling across the top of the screen telling us that there has been a head-on collision involving a semi hauling a tanker trailer full of nitrogen and a bus from a Memphis nursing home. I reach over, take the remote out of Kenneth's hand, and turn up the volume. I set the remote down and rest my hand on his shoulder.

"Authorities haven't released any information about the number of casualties," says the local news bimbo, doing her best to look concerned for the victims.

She's standing in front of what's left of the bus. The entire left side and the front end back to about the third row of seats is pretty much gone. It appears the truck turned left in front of the bus and hit it in the left-front corner. The bus driver never had a chance. The tractor is pushed back into the tank on the trailer, but it doesn't look like there is anything leaking from it. That's good news; that stuff pouring out onto traffic would've been even more of a nightmare. If I remember right from my Navy days, the temperature of liquid nitrogen is around three hundred degrees below zero.

"The report we've received is that the bus was headed to Muscle Shoals for a conference on convalescent care for young adults, to be followed by a concert tonight. No victims' names are being released at this time."

At this, Kenneth just sits down, hard. He looks like someone has punched him in the gut.

"Kenneth," Donna says, "we don't know Janie was on that bus. I doubt if the people at the home in Memphis know anything, and I doubt they'd tell you anything, even if they do. I'll take you out there right now, and we can figure out what to do from there. Come on, let's get moving." Donna's back to being herself, and isn't going to take no for an answer.

Kenneth looks at Judy and me. "But—" he starts to say, and Judy overrides him.

"No buts, Kenneth. You go do what you need to do. If you want me to come with you, I will. The assholes in Huntsville can wait."

I hate to admit it, even to myself, but this momentarily pisses me off. I don't want to wait. But sanity returns in a flash; this is Kenneth Dutton we're talking about. If it means completely forgetting this whole deal, that's what will happen. I need to be with him to help him through whatever he finds out there on I-72 near Cherokee, Alabama.

"That's right," I tell both of them. "We can do this later, or not at all. We'll come with you and take care of whatever needs taken care of."

Judy's nodding her head vigorously, but Donna's shaking hers slowly back and forth.

Kenneth turns to me and growls, almost viciously, "Bullshit. I need to go find out if Janie's on that fuckin' bus, but you guys need to go get Shirley and put a kink in Smutly's dick. Dammit, Ricky . . . Jonnybob, this is important! If Janie's not on that bus, I'll figger out a way to git to Chubby's by midnight. If she is, I'll jest need to do whatever I need to do. But I don't want you to wait. Go kick their asses and git that little girl."

There are tears—whether of anger or grief I don't know—running down his cheeks, and he seems to have grown a couple inches taller. He's right, of course. We can do this without him, and we won't even have to change our plans. I can take care of the fire-starting and tail-twisting by myself, and that may be how it should be. This is my war, after all.

"Okay," says Judy, and I echo her. "You go with Momma, and we'll see you when this is over, if not before. If you need to, you can leave messages on my answering machine, or here with Sammy."

She hugs him, hard. He hugs her back, then turns and hugs me.

After a few seconds, I say, "Go."

He nods, takes a last look at the TV, and follows Donna out of the room. He's in good hands. I imagine that woman can handle anything that happens.

Judy and I are left in the office alone, staring at the small screen and wishing good thoughts for everyone on board the bus, but especially for Janie, Kenneth's delicate little sister, that sweet girl who means the world to him.

Dammit!

FORTY-ONE

Judy and I finally went ahead and got some supper, eating it in Donna's office and watching the tube for updates on the crash. We haven't talked about anything else since Kenneth and Donna left. I asked Judy how her momma had known that bus belonged to the place where Janie was living. She just shook her head and said Kenneth must have told her while they were talking about his family the other night. Maybe, or maybe she just saw the report on the television and figured, since the bus was from a convalescent home in Memphis, she'd better tell Kenneth, just in case.

However it came about, I'm glad she saw it and told him. I can't imagine how bad Kenneth would've felt if he hadn't heard anything about it until days later. None of his friends or neighbors knows where he is, other than Jimbob, and I don't think he knows how to contact us.

Christ! I need to call Jimbob and let him know about the wreck. Only thing is, I don't have his pager number. I should have thought of that earlier. It's just another example of my being in over my head . . . good thing I have these people to make up for my lapses. It's hard telling where Jimbob might be, and if I do happen to reach him, is he going to want to head out to the crash site, too? If so, then what? I hate to actually have to kidnap Shirley and hope we can convince her we're the good guys without having Melody to talk her into the van.

Judy senses some of what I'm thinking, and reaches over to give my hand a gentle squeeze. "We just have to do the best we can, hon. In a few hours, this will be over. Then we can do whatever needs to be done for Kenneth and his little sister. For now, we just need to get our game face on and give those assholes a butt-whippin' they'll never forget. Getting that little girl out of Chubby's is important, and we might not get as good a chance as we'll have tonight.

"We've got the club strung out all to hell and gone, and the fire next door will have the remaining members jumping through their assholes, trying to figure out what to do next. And, on top of that, the feds will be busting up their meth lab at the same time. We'll never have as good a chance to do this as we have tonight, JB."

She makes damned good sense, and she's passionate about what she's saying. She's right; we'll never get as good a chance of making this happen if we don't do it tonight. So okay, motherfuckers, it's on.

"You're right, as usual," I tell Judy, gripping her hand in mine. "Let's do this, then see what we can do to help the Duttons with whatever needs done. At least we've got plenty of cash."

At this, she smiles, and that makes me smile a little, too. No matter what happens, at least there will be money to do whatever needs to be done for Janie, providing she survived the crash. Providing she was even on the bus, which nobody knows, yet. No need to borrow trouble, as my old chief petty officer used to say.

As we're sitting there, each of us lost in our own thoughts, there's a rap on the door, and Bobby Ray sticks his head in. He has a worried look on his face, and says, "Sammy said he thought you were in here."

He and Travis come into the office, and Bobby Ray gives Judy a hug. "Sammy said your momma and Kenneth hauled ass outta here a while back, and you two have been holed up in here. He said whatever's going on must be pretty bad, because all of you looked like the world was coming to an end. What's going on, Cuz?"

Bobby Ray is holding onto Judy while he's talking to her, and Travis is looking at me quizzically.

"There was a wreck out on I-72, by Cherokee," says Judy, trying not to cry. "There was a bus involved, and it's from the place where Kenneth's little sister Janie lives. It was headed to Muscle Shoals, and got hit head-on by a semi hauling a tanker full of liquid nitrogen. We don't know if she's on the bus, and nobody at the center would tell Kenneth anything, so Momma took him out there to find out all they can."

She's trembling, and Bobby Ray leads her over to a chair and puts her in it.

"Oh, shit," says Travis, shaking his shaggy head.

His beard is waving back and forth, and his voice seems even higher than normal. "That sucks, man. So are we gonna put this deal off until Kenneth gets back?"

This gets Bobby Ray's attention and he looks at Judy. She shakes her head and motions for me to explain.

I tell them about our conversation about whether or not to carry on, and the decision we made to go for it. Both of them are nodding.

Bobby Ray says, "Hell yes, it's on! We can do this. I know we would never get a better night to pull this off, and we're ready. As long as you feel you can handle the fire and all by yourself, JB, nothing else has changed a lick." I just give him a solid thumbs-up in response.

Travis is heading for the door, and says over his shoulder, "Be right back."

Bobby Ray is talking quietly to Judy, and she's smiling and nodding. They continue on like this for a couple of minutes, and Travis comes back into the office. He's got a package in his hands, about two foot by two foot and probably a half-inch thick.

"Here are those plastic numbers for the Malibu," he says, handing the package to me. "They're sticky on one side; all you need to do is peel the paper backing off and line 'em up on the doors.

"It's easiest to start at one edge and just kinda lay 'em down against the surface a little at a time, smoothing the vinyl out with your hand as you go. A few wrinkles won't kill anybody, so don't worry too much about it."

Hell, I'd almost forgotten about them. I need to get my shit together before I get someone killed.

Bobby Ray jumps in and tells us, "Kevin said this color is something he never uses, so it's on the house." No way.

"I'll take care of it tomorrow," I tell him, shaking my head. Man, it's hard to get people to take money around this place. "What do you think they're worth?"

"Oh, hell, I don't know," says Bobby Ray, scratching his head. "Probably ten bucks or so, maybe fifteen, but he said never mind, so he'll probably get pissed if we bring it up."

"Actually," says Travis, "he's out front right now. I saw his truck out there when we drove in, and I know Kevin well enough to know that he'll be here for a good while. He always runs a tab, and pays up at the end of the night, so we can just get Merle to slip the money in with his change." I give Travis two tens, and he goes out the front door into the bar. He's back in a couple of minutes, and says it's all set up.

Bobby Ray gives Judy a hug, shakes my hand, and says, "We'll see you in the parkin' lot, Judy. JB, you be careful, and we'll see you back here in a few hours. Now Travis and I need to go drink some beer and watch the naked girls dance. It's a tough job, but somebody needs to do it." We all share a laugh, and I shake Travis's hand as they head out. Judy yells at their backs to be goddamned careful.

When they're gone, Judy turns to me and gives me a shy smile. "Well, it's just you and me, hon. What do you want to do for the next couple of hours?"

Several things come to mind . . . Whoa, there, dammit. This is Judy, my new friend, and my old friend Kenneth's very sweet on her. On top of that, I really need to keep my head in the game—my big head, as opposed to the little one.

"Well, I think we should probably make sure you're in the general vicinity of that carwash a little early, so you can watch for Jimbob and Melody. It'll probably be best if you can talk to her for a few minutes before you head over to Chubby's to mellow her out, calm her down. She won't do anyone any good if she gets hysterical. And, I should be parked out back by the fireworks place by twenty till or so, to make sure I'm ready. It shouldn't take more than, what, a half-hour or so from here, right?"

She looks at me with her head cocked to one side, probably trying to decide if I'm just dense, or purposely ignoring her veiled offer. "Yeah, a half-hour is probably about right, depending on the traffic. We might want to allow forty-five minutes, just in case there's a wreck, or something."

As she realizes what she just said, her eyes widen for a second, and she gently shakes her head as if she's trying to clear it. The word wreck has brought her back from wherever she was going. The moment's gone, and I don't know whether to be glad or sad.

"Good idea," I tell her, pretending to be oblivious to what just happened. I'd rather have her thinking I'm slow on the uptake, instead of taking the chance of alienating her if she thinks I've somehow rejected her. I'm not great at dealing with women on a good day, and this has turned into one I wouldn't characterize as anywhere near good.

As I'm looking around the room, trying to think of something neutral to say, I notice the flashing BREAKING NEWS banner on the tube. I grab the remote from the arm of the chair next to Donna's desk and adjust the volume so we can hear the latest on the bus wreck.

There's a different bimbo in front of the camera—brunette this time—and she's saying ". . . closed until the State Patrol finishes their investigation and the wrecked vehicles have been removed from the highway. Eastbound traffic is being diverted onto the Old Lee Highway at the west end of Cherokee and routed back to US 72 at Brown Street."

There's a glitzy map of the area on the screen, with lots of arrows and flashing lights. It appears the truck driver turned left at Mount Hester Road, for some reason turning directly in front of the bus heading east. Fucking idiot.

"Jesus, Jonnybob," says Judy, obviously shaken by what we're seeing, "I wonder if that was the same jackass who pulled out in front of us yesterday."

Could it be? I know it's far-fetched, but what if

there's some connection to the trucker who nearly hit us and the one who took out the bus with Kenneth's sister Janie on it?

Same stupid move, pulling across a road without looking, but that would be one hell of a coincidence. I doubt if we'll ever know. I tell her so, and she just shakes her head, frowning. We've got other fish to fry.

FORTY-TWO

Jimbob must've been waiting down the street, because he shows up almost as soon as we pull into the carwash. I park in the darkest spot in the place, one of the bays. Judy pulls around by the vacuums and shuts Vanna off. Jimbob and Melody are in a gunmetal-gray Buick Regal with turbo badges on the hood. Nice car, and it should haul ass when whipped on.

Jimbob steps out of the Regal and walks over to where I am, with his hand out. He looks just a little apprehensive. I wonder whether he's heard anything about the bus wreck. I grasp his hand in mine, and we shake. I don't have to wonder long, because he comes right to the point.

"You must be Jonnybob." I nod. "Kenneth called me," he says, including Judy in the conversation as she walks up. "He still hadn't been able to get any information as of about ten o'clock, but was trying to button-hole some doctor from the home that showed up at the hospital." Judy and I trade worried looks, but there's nothing we can do at this point.

"Melody's in the car, and she's worried about Shirley. Kenneth didn't tell me exactly what you've got planned, but I've got to tell you that I'm worried, too. . . about both of those girls."

I don't blame you.

"Jimbob," says Judy, stepping forward, "I'm Judy, Donna Miller's daughter, and Kenneth's friend. Our main focus tonight is getting Shirley out of that place safely, and you can be assured that we will treat Melody's safety just as importantly. Jonnybob came up with a good plan, and we should be able to pull this off without any violence, as long as something unforeseen doesn't happen."

"And," I jump in, before he can get started, "if something does happen that we haven't planned on, we think we're prepared to deal with it. There are four of us, five with you, and as soon as Judy gets the van out of Chubby's parking lot and heads toward Mooresville, she'll have three vehicles running interference for her on her back-trail. Since nobody will have any reason to suspect where she's heading, I honestly can't see anyone heading her off. Even if by chance they do, Judy is damned handy, a hell of a driver, and steady as a rock."

Judy smiles her thanks at me for the endorsement, and she reaches out and takes Jimbob's hand in hers. "I promise you we will do everything in our power to keep those girls safe. Now, I'd like to meet Melody and talk to her for a few minutes before we head down to Chubby's. Jonnybob needs to get down there and in position so he can create the diversion we'll use to spring Shirley. Two men are already there, scouting out the place, ready to take her down the back stairs and into the van as soon as the fireworks—" we both smile at the use of that word, "start."

I give Judy a big hug and tell her I'll be right behind her on the way back to Donna's. I turn to tell Jimbob I'll see him in Mooresville, and climb into the Malibu. I can tell he doesn't seem too confident in my choice of getaway car, so I roll down the window as I drive past him, and say, "We'll run 'em after this is over, and I think you'll lose."

He looks surprised, offended, then incredulous as I chuckle and drive away.

FORTY-THREE

I'm parked behind the fireworks warehouse, backed up to a stand of kudzu, and I should have a straight shot out of the lot on the north side of the building. I drove in that way, making sure there aren't any big pot-holes, curbs, or rocks in the way to cause me grief on my way to the Parkway.

I moved the flash-bangs into the foot well on the passenger's side of the front seat, and also got the flare gun and flares in the canvas tool bag along with a short pry-bar on the seat before we left Donna's Place. Without Kenneth along, I need to be able to reach everything and keep an eye out for trouble at the same time. This will be the time when I'm most vulnerable, trying to get the fire started without allowing someone to sneak up on me.

The lot between the fireworks place and Chubby's is about a third full, and there are about six or seven bikes parked right in front of the sidewalk leading to the bar. I wander over there nonchalantly and look for PnB member stickers on 'em, so I don't fuck up some poor guy's bike who isn't involved. Luckily, they're all members' bikes, so I don't have any regrets about what I plan to do.

I removed the bulb from the dome light before we left so I can open the doors without highlighting myself or the weaponry to anyone who might be looking. I ease back over to the Malibu and grab the bag with the flare gun and the flares. I take three of the flash-bangs and put them in the bag as well. I reach around and make sure my nine mil is secure in my waistband, and shut the car door.

So far, I'm doing just fine. Nobody is outside, and there's no traffic through the lot at all. I push the button on the side of my watch and check the time; 11:52 p.m. As I start walking over to the rear wall of the fireworks outlet, a couple guys come out of the club, walk over by an old Dodge truck, and light up a joint. I really don't need this! Everyone else is depending on me to cause the diversion at midnight, and I can't be dicking around.

Luckily, they don't show any sign of noticing me. I'm in the shadows, away from the main parking lot, and the Malibu definitely isn't an attention getter. I continue toward the back of the metal building, angling off to my left to decrease the amount of time they'll be able to see me. I make it to the point where the corner of the building is between me and them and hurry the remaining twenty feet to the roll-up door on the back of the building.

I didn't bring a drill because of the noise it would make. I really hope I can just use the pry bar to bend some tin far enough to allow me to stick the flare gun through the resulting gap. No way am I going to use a light, and it's pretty dark back here. I get right up next to the edge of the door and start looking for a likely place to start with the bar.

I notice something in the corner of my vision, a red dot intermittently blinking on and off. As I try to quietly lean against the door to steady myself, I see it again. What I'm seeing is the ready light on a smoke alarm—inside the warehouse! There's a gap of at least three-quarters of an inch where the trim around the door opening has been bent, probably by someone running into it with a vehicle on their way in or out. Thank you, assholes, for making this easy! My pulse is starting to race, and I realize I'm holding my breath. I force myself to take a few deep breaths, trying to control my rising anxiety.

I take a quick walk along the back of the building to where I can ease my head around the corner and check out the parking lot. The pot smokers are still there, but seem to be moving toward the club. I can't wait. I'm just gonna go for it. With any luck, they'll be inside before anything noticeable happens.

Back at the door, I kneel down and make sure I can find the gap without any trouble. I screw a flare onto the launcher, lay out three more in a row at my knees. I've got the flash-bangs in a line right next to my right foot, just in case I need them before I planned.

My pulse is probably up around three or four hundred, and the adrenaline is pouring into my bloodstream like it's coming from a fire hose. Okay, fuckers, it's Hammer time!

I ease the first flare through the gap, and aim it as far to my left as possible. I slip the little button to the side and—whoosh—it's gone. I repeat the operation with the three remaining flares, adjusting my aim a little to my right each time. I can hear something happening in there, and there seems to be a growing source of light that I can see through the gap in the trim. I grab the bag, shove the flash-bangs back into it, and start walking back to the Malibu.

I check over my shoulder, watching for anyone in the parking lot. As I turn my head to check for the third or fourth time, I notice a bright light at the edge of my peripheral vision. I stop, turn my head a little farther, and see the source of the light; flames are licking around the roll-up door. There's a hole in the wall about fifteen feet up that is probably some kind of vent, and flames are showing there, as well. Time to hurry.

I get to the car, still alone in the lot, and pull three flash-bangs from the bag before tossing it inside. I need someone to sound the alarm for our plan to work. Bobby Ray and Travis should be waiting upstairs for the shit to hit the fan, and we can't wait for someone to notice the fire. Time for plan B.

I quickly approach the front of the club, watching the door. When I'm about thirty feet from the row of bikes, I walk behind an old Ford pickup and set the grenades on top of the bed rail. One at a time, I grasp a grenade, pull the arming pin, and throw it at the line of scooters. As soon as the last one is out of my hand,

I'm ducked down and running to the Malibu with my hands over by my ears, trying to keep the truck between me and the bikes as much as possible.

Before I've even taken ten steps, the first grenade goes off, and the noise is amazing, even with my ears covered. The flash is ridiculously bright, and I'm really glad I'm facing away from it. The other two go off in quick succession, and I take a quick look back to see what the results are. Two of the bikes are on fire. The tires and upholstery on the seats were probably ignited by the incendiaries.

The bar door slams open, and the entire population of Chubby's seems to be trying to come through it at the same time. Everyone's hollering, and the whole effect is hilarious. People start running around, looking at the bikes and each other, trying to get a clue about what to do next.

The nearest fire station must not be too awfully far away, because by the time I'm at the car and have the driver's door open, I can faintly hear sirens. I guess it could be a cop. Hard to tell from here.

I start up the Malibu, make sure the shifter's in neutral, and set the parking brake. I don't have long to wait, as a Huntsville PD patrol car comes sliding into the lot and stops about fifty feet from the burning bikes. Before the occupants can even exit the car, a fuel tank on one of the bikes cooks off and blows flaming gasoline all over a couple idiots wearing PnB colors who were trying to save their bikes. Chaos.

The driver of the cop car backs it up another twenty feet or so, and exits the car with his hand on his gun. His partner is standing behind his door, aiming his riot scatter-gun over the door frame in the general direction of the burning bikes.

I hear more sirens, and I need to time this right so I don't run into a fire truck or something. A rescue truck comes boiling into the lot, followed by an honest-to-god fire truck. I'm not sure anyone has even noticed that the building next door is burning yet. This is starting to get good, and just for a moment, I'm sorry I have to miss the rest of it. I walk out in front of the Malibu and start waving my arms and hollering.

"Hey, you assholes! Yeah, you, you fuckin' morons!" I continue in this vein until I've got a fairly decent audience, then raise both hands over my head, flipping them off with both hands. The old double bird. "Fuck you guys! I hope the whole fuckin' place burns down!"

Time to go.

I jump in the Malibu, shove the shifter into first gear, and squeeze—not mash—the throttle. I drive on the north side of the burning building and pull out onto the Memorial Parkway sideways, narrowly missing a Fire Chief's car. I look in the mirror, and there's no sign of anyone following me. Hopefully, enough people saw and heard me to make them think their attacker is north of here.

At the intersection with Green Cove Road, I move to the right and pass a line of cars. I hang a right, accelerating like a fuckin' drag car. Before long, I'm already at the point where the road heads off to the left. I get on the brakes, start down-shifting, and make the right onto Ditto Marina Parkway. I ease off the gas, trying not to attract any undue attention. I'm watching the mirrors, and I have my window down. I don't hear or see any evidence of pursuit. So far, so good. Now, if only things are going as well for Judy and the boys at Chubby's.

I find the turnoff into the trailer parking lot easily, and turn into it with my eyes peeled, as they say. There are five or six boat trailers, a couple of them with boats on them. There's a pair of jacked-up pickup trucks over in the southwest corner of the lot, surrounded by a half-dozen teenagers drinking beer, judging by the pile of empties.

No roll-back. No car-hauler of any sort. No Bo. Shit! I really don't need this. I roll over into the opposite corner from the beer-drinkers and back up into the darkest spot I can find. I'll wait for awhile; maybe he got hung up in traffic or something.

I wait for nearly ten minutes, and decide Bo's not coming. Is he just flaky, or was my original assessment true? Is he somehow hooked up with the PnB, plotting against us? I'm glad I didn't go ahead and put the damned numbers on the doors while I was waiting. That would really look stupid, driving around in a car with numbers on the doors. Although it's not unheard of in the South, it still looks stupid.

I ease the Malibu out of my parking spot, hopefully watching the Ditto for a roll-back truck. No such luck. At the road, I hang a right and slowly cruise down to Hobbs Island Road, the road that goes past the Speedway. To my surprise and delight, there is a line of traffic coming from the track—trucks and trailers hauling racecars toward the Memorial Parkway.

I let the first couple of rigs go by before squeezing into a gap between two others. At the Parkway, the two in front of me split up, one heading north and one south. I follow the second rig south, and am met with an amazing sight.

The fireworks warehouse is burning merrily, and there are now three fire trucks in attendance. Guffey's crew must be busy, because there's only one cop car here. Cars and trucks are parked on both sides of the road for blocks, and the looky-loos are as close as the cops will let them get.

It's a fuckin' circus. That suits me just fine.

Traffic is moving at a crawl. I don't much like that, but there's nothing I can do. I follow a pickup hauling a beat-up old Camaro as closely as I can while allowing some room for maneuvering if necessary. I'm watching Chubby's parking lot and don't see anyone paying me the slightest bit of attention.

As I drive past the club, I look over into the south lot, and realize things have gone completely to shit.

FORTY-FOUR

All Hell Breakin' Loose at Chubby's, Huntsville, Alabama
May 19, 1990

Vanna is sitting in the lot, which isn't good. Judy should be haulin' ass toward Mooresville by now. To make things worse, I can see Travis wrestling with some big ol' dude, and Bobby Ray seems to be holding off a trio of assholes with the sawed-off.

I shove the shifter into first, aim for the middle of the action and mash—not squeeze—the throttle. I come into the lot sideways, scattering people like quail. I jump out of the car and run over to Vanna, pulling my nine mil from my belt as I go. I hear a couple screams, but don't need the distraction of looking around for the source.

When I get to Vanna, I see why she's still sitting here. Both driver's side tires are flat, and all the coolant has run out of a hole in the radiator onto the ground. I jerk open the side door, dreading what I'm going to find. Empty.

I spin around, looking for Judy and the girls. I don't see any of them, but I see something I didn't expect. Kenneth—what's he doing here?—has an old boy down on the ground and is in the process of de-nutting him. Smutly, I presume. That's why Bobby Ray has the rest of the crowd backed up with the twice-by and Travis is trading blows with Man Mountain Mullet.

I don't see any guns, other than the shotgun, and that's a welcome relief. I have no idea how Dutton got here, but it doesn't matter; he looks healthy, and seems to be enjoying himself.

The screams are emanating from the illustrious Smutly, sounding eerily like a pre-teen girl. I run over to where Bobby Ray is performing crowd control, glad the two cops out front have plenty to keep them busy.

"Where are the girls?" I'm watching for any more unfriendly crowd members, basically standing back-to-back with Judy's cousin, hoping the answer isn't bad.

"They're with my arm," he says, carefully avoiding using anyone's name. He's pretty damned cool, considering the circumstances. "It got pretty hairy. That asshole over there," he says, indicating Smutly, "cut the tires and stuck a piece of rebar through the radiator on the van because my cousin and that girl from up north wouldn't get out. Me and my uncle came down the stairs to find it like that, and when he saw who we had with us, he came charging around the van."

"Your buddy showed up right then, driving the Caddy. He jumped out and tackled that one, then proceeded to kick his ass. The little girl with us called him by name, and that really started the shit."

"All the women took off in the car, but he," indicating Kenneth, "wouldn't stop. By then a crowd was gatherin', so me 'n him," indicating Travis, "been holdin' all these people off until he gets done." He's grinning ear-to-ear.

I look around and find Travis sitting on top of the big ol' dude, both of them bloody and gasping for air. Travis is tying the other guy's hands behind his back with what looks like barbed wire, although I have no idea where he found it.

I cautiously approach Kenneth, watching for interlopers, but everyone seems to have accepted the fact that we're in control. Good for us. This doesn't need to escalate any further.

"You about done," I ask Dutton, "or do you need some more time?" He looks up and smiles a wicked smile—a look that would make me piss myself if it was aimed at me. He's got blood all over him, and Smutly has been reduced to whimpers.

"I reckon I'm done," says Kenneth, punching Smutly in the face once more, just for good measure. He stands up and kicks him a couple times, and leans over to tell him, "Remember what I tol' you, boy. I have to come back, and you'll lose it completely." Smutly's cryin' and snivellin', but I think he's in agreement with this deal.

"I reckon he believes you, brother, so can we go now? We're pushing our luck." He looks at me, gives me a punch in the chest, and starts running for the car.

"What are you clowns waitin' for?" He's laughing like a loon, and has his .45 in his big ol' paw, covering Bobby Ray's retreat toward his truck. Travis is on his feet, wiping blood and snot from his beard. His hair has come loose, and he is quite the sight to behold.

Man Mountain Mullet is struggling but not making any headway with the wire around his ankles and wrists. He looks like someone ran him through a meat grinder. Travis gives him a last once-over, then staggers over to Bobby Ray's truck and gets in the passenger side.

"Go ahead," I tell Bobby Ray. "We'll be right behind you. Get movin' before the cops find us."

He shoots me a sloppy salute, hops into his truck, and fires it up.

Kenneth and I are both keeping the small gaggle of onlookers at bay with our pieces as we back over to the Malibu. I can't believe I left it running, but it seems I did. I'm glad nobody jumped in and took off. As we get into the car, Kenneth is careful to keep his gun trained on them, even as they start to slide over toward Smutly.

"Y'all might wanna find a better class of friends," he hollers at them as he jumps in and pulls the door closed. They don't seem to be paying us much attention, now that they can see what condition their buddy is in.

Bobby Ray is already gone, and I back up into the spot where he had been parked. I turn toward the road and ease out into traffic the first chance I get. I can't get over it; not one soul wandered over to the south side of the club to see what was going on. Everyone out front is mesmerized by the fire and each other. Things aren't exactly happening as planned, but we just might pull this off.

FORTY-FIVE

Turning west onto Alabama Highway 36 at Laceys Spring, I look out Kenneth's window at someone coming like a bat out of hell from the north on 53, the road we just left. I've been watching headlights gaining on us quite rapidly for the last couple of miles, and they've got me pretty jumpy. Kenneth has been watching out the back window, his .45 in his big right hand.

As I feared, the lights follow us onto Highway 36, and are now only about a half-mile behind us. I'm watching the road for an escape route, in case they try to force us off the road. I'm still driving the speed limit, just in case it's a cop instead of some un-named bad guys.

Whoever it is, it's not a cop—a black Firebird blows past us like we're in reverse. They don't even give us a glance. I can only guess, but I'm afraid they're after Bobby Ray and Travis. If they got one of their dirty cop buddies to run the plate on Bobby Ray's truck, they'll know exactly where they're going.

Kenneth looks worried, and just says, "Do it."

Of course, these guys in the Firebird could just be out driving around without any knowledge of anything that happened at Chubby's, but it doesn't feel right to me. I want to quiz Kenneth about Janie and how he happened to be at the club, but we've been too busy watching that Firebird. It'll keep until we get a chance to relax a little. I'm sure it'll be a hell of a story, one way or another.

I ease into that small-block Chevy, and we start gradually closing the gap. They're far enough ahead that I don't think they know we're following them, yet.

I keep gaining, little by little, until we're only about half a mile behind when they reach Alabama 67 and head north toward I-65. Dammit. Not good for the coincidence scenario.

As we make the turn onto 67, Kenneth says, "If these clowns are after Travis and Bobby Ray, they'll head over across I-65 toward Old Moulton Road. Were they headed home, or to Donna's?"

Good question.

"I really think they'll go to Donna's to make sure everyone made it okay," I say, glancing at him briefly.

I sure hope so. I know that's where I'm going, and I'd hate to find out that these guys in the Firebird had caught Travis and Bobby Ray at home, thinking they were safe.

"I'll just keep 'em in sight, and see which way they go," I tell Kenneth.

We've just blown through Somerville at over eighty miles per hour, and I'm really glad the local cops are somewhere else. Priceville is next, and the Firebird doesn't show any sign of slowing.

I'm staying just close enough to keep it in sight, but not close enough to cause the driver any concern.

We both blast through Priceville in a blur, and I can see traffic on I-65 ahead. If the Firebird turns south on the interstate, we'll be home free. If it goes straight west, I'll figure they're headed to Travis's house. We'll head north to Donna's and check on the women. All four of them.

Kenneth disturbs my calculations with a disturbing thought. "What if they know Bobby Ray's sister lives next door to Travis?"

Oh, shit! If someone back there did recognize Travis or Bobby Ray, they just might know some personal information about them. Christ, I can't take a chance on Raeann getting hurt if these assholes don't find the men at home.

"Hang on, Kenny!" I shift down into fourth and squeeze—not mash—the throttle. The Malibu squats on the springs and takes off like a fuckin' rocket.

We're overtaking the Firebird at a pretty good clip, and I guess someone in there finally takes notice. The Firebird wiggles slightly, then speeds up.

As we fly under I-65, headed for Highway 31, I'm only about a hundred yards behind them and closing fast. Within a few seconds, I'm pulling up on the Firebird's left rear quarter-panel.

The rear window comes down, and someone in the back seat sticks a pistol out of it. I'm not inclined to give whoever it is a chance to hurt Kenneth or me, so I use a trick I learned watching NASCAR races over the last twenty years.

My front bumper is just behind the Firebird's left rear wheel when I turn sharply into it, mashing the gas at the same time. The result is spectacular, and strangely satisfying. Whoever is in that car pointed a gun at us, and I feel no compunction at all about wrecking their asses.

The Firebird turns left and starts sliding sideways at probably close to a hundred miles per hour. I give him one last nudge, just before landing on the brakes hard to avoid the spinning car. As I'm doing my best to get the Malibu sorted out and slowed down, the sleek black car leaves the roadway into the median.

Sliding sideways into soft ground is a recipe for disaster. The Firebird's passenger-side wheels dig into the grassy median and the car starts to roll—once, twice, a bunch of times. I lose track as I'm sliding past, trying to stay on the road, myself.

Kenneth is hollering. "Holy shit! They done rolled plumb across the other side of the road into that damned slough!"

He's jabbering and yelling, and I finally register what he's saying. I get the car stopped and hang a u-turn across the median. As we cruise back up on the crash site, there's dirt, grass, broken glass, and other automotive debris strewn across the road. Off to the south side of the east-bound lanes is a big slough, and there is no trace of the Firebird, except for some trash floating along on a series of waves heading away from the bank. Screw it. And them. They pointed a gun at us. They *might* have been headed for Travis's house, and they *might've* hurt Raeann, but they *did* point a gun at us. That's enough of a reason.

I notice traffic coming from behind us, so I dodge the worst of the glass and junk and slowly speed up to the speed limit. I'm pissed . . . at the clowns in the Firebird, the asshole in the nitrogen truck, Bo, and the PnB for causing, in my way of thinking, all this trouble. Roundly cursing all of them, I hit the entrance ramp onto I-65 and head north for Donna's.

As soon as we're headed north on the interstate, I look over at Kenneth, who is wiping at his eyes. Jesus, here I am acting like a raving lunatic while my buddy is dealing with the possibility that his little sister has been hurt or killed.

What the fuck is wrong with me? I take a couple deep breaths to calm down a little and ask him, "Was Janie on that bus, buddy?"

He just nods, not taking his palms away from his eyes. Oh, Christ! "Is she okay?" It's the thing to ask, but I'm pretty sure I'm not going to like the answer.

"She's gone, man." He starts sobbing, shuddering in his seat. I can't wrap my head around all of this. Why the fuck did he come back to Chubby's if his sister is lyin' dead in the morgue somewhere? The answer hits me almost before I can form the question.

It's because of me. He did it because he figured I

needed him. I'm damned glad he did, and I understand why he was so set on taking care of that asshole Smutly. He doesn't want to see any more females from Fayetteville hurt tonight.

"She was sittin' right behind the driver, and never had a chance." He's rubbing his eyes and trying to quit crying, but it's more than he's capable of right at this instant. "That fuckin' idiot in the tanker had his head up his ass and just killed her . . . them . . . Christ, man, they wouldn't even let me see her."

He's deflated and looks ten years older all of a sudden. Jamie was the only family he had left, as far as I know.

"The really shitty part of it," he continues, the sobbing stopped for now, "is that the trucker lived through it. He'd better hope I never get a chance at him, I guarantee you that."

I can definitely understand his feelings, and if he decides to follow up at some later time, I'll help him.

Trying to think of anything at all to say, I blurt out, "So, what did you do to Smutly? There was so much blood, I couldn't really tell how much damage you did to him."

By the fear I'd seen in his eyes, Smutly would probably do everything in his power to prevent a return visit from my portly pal.

Kenneth looks at me, wipes snot and tears off his face and smiles, just a little bit. "When I heard Shirley holler at him by name, I just went bugshit. I barreled into him and knocked him into a parked car. His head bounced off the front bumper, and he clicked off like someone threw a fuckin' switch. Travis was fightin' with that big sumbitch, and Bobby Ray was holdin' off that other bunch, so I figgered it was now or never. I unbuckled his belt and yanked his britches down far enough to get at his pecker."

He chuckles at the memory, but not in a cheerful way, no sir. He's got this look on his face like some of those preachers who hang snakes all over themselves; crazed, somehow illuminated from within, but scary as hell.

"I was just gonna cut it off, ya know?" He's looking at me, and I've slowed down to about fifty miles per hour in the right lane, glancing over at him, transfixed. "But I decided to let 'im keep it . . . 'cause every time he looks at it, he'll think of how it damned near got him killed." He's looking out his window now, and his voice has softened up a little.

We're on the north side of the river by now, coming up on the intersection with I-565, so I just stay in the right lane and prepare to make the right toward Donna's. We're so close that I think it'll be best to wait and let Kenneth tell everyone about Smutly's fate at the same time.

FORTY-SIX

We pull into the lot at Donna's Place, and I drive around back and park in the little carport where Vanna has been resting for the last few days. I back in and shut off the engine, letting the silence settle around us. The lot is empty except for Donna's Caddy, Jimbob's Regal, Bobby Ray's pickup (thank God), and a car I haven't seen before. It's a Dodge mini-van, and has Tennessee plates on it. All the outside lights are off, and the place looks pretty much deserted.

Kenneth and I get out of the car, and I realize he's soaked with blood. Hell, he looks like he's been slaughtering hogs. I don't think his appearance would do anything to make the people inside feel any better, so I stop and turn toward him, our shoes scuffing in the gravel.

"Kenny, I think you might want to go inside and clean up some before you come over to the bar. You look like a refugee from a George Romero movie."

He actually laughs at this then looks up at the moon, which is just a sliver in the clear night sky. "I guess it's a damned good thing it's not a full moon, huh?" He shakes his head slowly back and forth. "If it was, things would really have been crazy." He giggles, a strange noise out here in this quiet place.

Kenneth looks worn the hell out.

Fragile, even. I love this man! He's my best friend, the man who just left his dead sister in a morgue to help me with my quest to put a stop to evil people preying upon the weak and vulnerable. I wrap my arms around him in a hug, hoping to show him in this inadequate gesture how much he means to me. Wordlessly, he returns the embrace, then pats me on the back a couple times to signal he wants me to let him go.

He shuffles off toward his cabin, telling me over his shoulder, "Thanks, son. I'll clean up, change clothes, and see you in a little while."

I'm worried about him. Losing Janie has really hurt him, and I'm afraid he doesn't realize just how badly at this stage. I head over to the back door, the one we've pretty much adopted as our personal entrance, and find it unlocked. Before I can walk the few steps to Donna's office door, it opens and Judy steps out into the darkened hallway. I can tell by the light spilling through the doorway that she's also changed clothes. I can hear voices coming from the office, and what sounds like a TV is droning in the background.

Judy runs up to me and throws her arms around my neck, burying her face against my shoulder. She's crying and laughing at the same time. I hold her for a minute until she decides to speak.

"God, I'm so glad to see you! We've been so worried. Momma's been quizzing Bobby Ray, trying to decide whether or not we needed to come looking for you guys." She looks over my shoulder, then asks me, "Where's Kenneth? He's okay, isn't he? Bobby Ray said he was with you!" She's getting agitated and has taken a step back, her eyes wide.

"He's fine," I tell her, "and he'll be over here in a few minutes. He's gonna shower and put on some clean clothes first."

Her stance softens, she wipes at the tears with the back of her hand, and she steps forward again until she's right in front of me. I can smell the shampoo she used, and I'm once again reminded that she is a very desirable woman. Now is not the time for such thoughts, I remind myself, but she's not making it easy. She leans forward, takes my hand in both of hers.

"I've got a surprise for you," she says, with a big smile lighting up her tear-stained face.

I don't know what to expect. She's too close, too soft, too . . . Judy. But she just turns and heads back into the office, tugging me along behind her. I can see that the door into the bar is open, and most everyone is in there. The only person in the office is Donna, and she's on the phone. Whatever she's hearing, it doesn't look like it's good news. She tips me a quick smile then makes shooing motions at us, clearly wanting us to leave her alone with her phone conversation.

Closing the office door behind us, we head into the bar.

And there's Janie, Kenneth's sister.

She's sitting at a table next to the wall, and Jesus

is curled up at her feet. My surprise must be apparent, because everyone starts laughing. I run over to where she is and hug her until she protests. Just wait until Kenneth sees her! Oh, my God!

It takes me a couple minutes to realize that there is someone else sitting at the same table. He's probably in his mid-fifties, distinguished looking, and seems to be having a pretty good time. He waits for me to let go of Janie, and leans across the table to shake my hand.

"James Popovich," he says, giving my hand a firm squeeze. Sincere, not a test of strength. "I'm on the board of directors at Midsouth Convalescent Home. I'm also Janie's primary physician."

He doesn't stand, and I guess that's because of the fact that his crutches are leaned up against the wall, out of his reach. They're that metal kind, with the bands at the top to put your forearms into, instead of the kind that you put in your underarm. I can't see from here why he needs them, but he must not feel comfortable standing without them. I like him immediately.

"Jonnybob Clark, an old friend of Janie and her brother Kenneth," I say, wondering what the heck is going on. Where did these two come from, and how come the people at the crash site told Kenneth she was dead? Taking a page from my own book, I figure they'd rather tell the story once, instead of repeating it over and over. I'll wait for Kenneth before quizzing them.

Janie is looking over my shoulder, watching

Donna's office door, obviously wondering where Kenneth is. She doesn't seem to have noticed my name change, and that's okay for now. We'll explain it to her later, after her and Kenneth's reunion. I can't wait to see his face! After being told his little sister was dead, he'll be absolutely blown away when he sees her here, safe and sound.

I look over toward the door, and realize that Judy's not in the barroom any longer. She must've gone back out into the rear hall to wait for Kenneth. Travis is sprawled across one side of a booth, his shaggy ol' head resting on the rear cushion. There's a bar towel full of what I imagine is ice resting on his left cheek, and he's nursing something amber in a tall glass.

Melody and a slim, dark-haired girl I figure must be Shirley are sitting in the corner booth, and Jimbob is over at the end of the bar by the restrooms, talking on the phone. He seems amazed at what he's hearing.

Bobby Ray is behind the bar, and I head over there for something cold and wet. He asks me, "You ready for something strong, or are you still on the wagon?"

He brings up a good point. Things went reasonably well; we're all alive, aren't we? That's more than be said for the assholes in the Firebird. I just don't feel as if we should relax our guard, yet.

"RC, please," I tell him, leaning against the bar with my right hip. "You?" I figure he and Travis are into the alcohol, but who can blame them? Surely not me. When this is over, I'm liable to tie on one that'll go down in the record books.

"I'm drinkin' sweet tea," says Bobby Ray, "and Travis is having ginger ale. So far, the only one wantin' liquor is that purty li'l gal we drug out of Chubby's. I figger she deserves it, but Jimbob told her to hold on until they get her back to Fayetteville. I don't think he wants to turn her over to her daddy with liquor on her breath. That is liable to be a pretty stressful occasion, and it'll probably be best if she's sober. Where's Kenneth?

"He wanted to clean up before he came in," I say, looking toward the office door. "I think Judy went to get him."

Just then, the door to the office opens and Judy comes through, with Kenneth right behind her. She gives us a wink, and he's looking around, obviously wondering why Judy came after him. I don't know what she told him, but I'm pretty sure it didn't have anything to do with Janie.

He's washed all the blood off, and he's wearing clean jeans and an old t-shirt with a Whitt's logo on it. He walks over to the bar and crawls up on a stool with his back to the room and asks Bobby Ray for a shot of JD. Everyone's eyes are on him, and he finally realizes it. He turns slowly around, taking in everyone in turn. He gives my arm a squeeze then nods at Jimbob, who's still on the phone. He smiles at Travis's plight, then swivels his stool around to see who else is in the room. This is the moment we've all been waiting for!

"Janie! Jesus! Janie!"

He's up and across the floor before I can blink, and he's got Janie up out of her chair and in a bear hug. She's telling him to put her down, and everyone else is laughing. He can't believe it. He's sputtering and starting and stopping like and old John Deere Johnny-Popper tractor. Everyone in the room has tears in their eyes, other than the two teenage girls over in the corner booth. They just look confused.

Judy sidles up next to me at the bar and asks Bobby for a refill of her tea. After she thanks him for it, she turns to me and lifts it, as in a toast. "Here's to you, Jonnybob," she says. "We couldn't have done it without you. I'm proud you let me help."

She leans over and kisses me on the cheek, but it doesn't feel like a kiss on the cheek should feel. It's not chaste, like a sisterly peck. It's sensual, hinting of other things in store. I really wish she'd stop. There's nothing but trouble at the end of this road.

I move away from her, searching her eyes for a hint of what the hell she's thinking. She can tell I'm uncomfortable, and seems to be enjoying it immensely. Her eyes are twinkling, and there's a rotten little smirk starting at the corners of her mouth.

My God, that mouth. Crap. I've gotta get away from her. This is insane. Stress makes people act weird. A couple of days from now, things will be back to normal and we'll all try to put the crazy shit behind us.

The door to Donna's office opens and she comes out into the barroom, smiling at the spectacle of Kenneth and Janie catching up across the room. She looks tired and rumpled, something I haven't witnessed before. It's been a long day for all of us. She leans across the bar and fills a rocks glass with ice and soda water.

"Do you think we should get everyone together to talk about what all's going on, or should we wait until later?"

That's a good question, but I'm not sure what to tell her. Everyone looks worn out, but I know Jimbob is going to be headed back to Fayetteville with the girls pretty soon, so if we all want to be in one place to compare notes, now is probably the time and this is probably the place.

"It looks to me as if we all need some time to rest up," I tell Donna and Judy, who's standing between us. "I need to hear what happened in Fayetteville, but Kenneth and I can drive up there tomorrow—later today, I mean—and talk to Jimbob. We also need to talk to Shirley's dad, and I need to see what I can find out about the raid on the labs in Huntsville."

"Maybe," Judy cuts in, "we should let Jimbob and the girls head home. We can put Janie and her doctor up for the night, if they want to stay. Travis and Bobby Ray can crash at my house, and we can all meet in a few hours to hear all the different stories, unless you think we need to do something right away."

That's a good point. Do we need to do anything right now, other than rest and recuperate? Is there some danger we're not aware of, or at least not thinking about? What's the best way to proceed? I don't know the answer to any of these questions, and that makes me decide that, for me at least, rest is essential.

"I think you've got the right idea," I tell Judy, and Donna's nodding her head. "I don't see any way Kenneth is gonna let Janie out of his sight for awhile, so I'm almost positive she'll be here for the rest of the morning, at least. I'll talk to Doctor Popovich, see what he wants to do. What with the wreck and all, he may need to get right back. I know the rest of us need some time to decompress, and anything we say will make more sense when we're all fresh."

"Besides," says Kenneth, who has walked up behind me as we were talking, "I need food before I'll be any good for anything." He cranes his head up and checks out the clock above the bar. "It's a little after two o'clock, so how about if we all meet around nine o'clock and compare notes? I'll hit the dining room as soon as they open, and have some time to talk to Janie before we all get together. She says she and that doctor feller need to go over to Cherokee for a while, but I'm gonna figger out a way to spend some time with her pretty soon. She doesn't need to hear what all we've been up to, though, so there's no need to include them in our pow-wow."

That makes perfect sense. Janie and Doctor Popovich can visit with Kenneth and me, then head over to Cherokee to deal with the aftermath from the bus wreck. Jimbob can get the girls home, and Kenneth and I can talk to him later today or tomorrow to find out the results of the Eagle Snacks affair. The rest of us can get some sleep then meet to discuss the evening's results, as well as anything we forgot or neglected to do. At some point, I'll need to find out how the raid on the labs went, but I won't be able to get in touch with Guffey until he gets back to The Beach, and I'm not sure I want to, anyhow. The last time we spoke, I told him he wouldn't hear from me again, and maybe I should leave it at that.

"Okay," I say to the three of them, "let's tell everyone the plan, get Jimbob and the girls on the road, and find everyone else a place to crash for a few hours. I'll meet you," I tell Kenneth, "in the dining room at six, when they open, so we can have a little time to talk before you wake up Janie. While you're talking to her, I'll try to find out as much as I can from the good doctor about how we can best take care of her arrangements at Midsouth. He seems like a pretty good guy from what I can see, so what I tell him will depend on how suspicious or helpful he wants to be."

Judy has wandered off and is talking to Travis and Bobby Ray. They're nodding and picking up their glasses and stuff as they head up to where we're standing. They mumble something about how they'll see us in the morning, and go through Donna's office into the hall and out into the dark-ass night. Judy finishes cleaning up behind the bar.

Jimbob is off the phone and leaning over the table at the corner booth talking to Shirley. Melody is curled up against the booth back and looks like she may be asleep. Shirley doesn't look real happy with whatever Jimbob is saying, but her resistance seems to wear down as I watch. She finally nods and starts to slip out of the booth. Melody, who apparently wasn't quite asleep, sits up and follows Shirley.

Jimbob walks over and says, "We're headin' home I'll see what I can find out, and you guys can call me or come by later and tell me what happened at the strip club."

He looks at Kenneth without asking the question, but Kenneth just nods. Jimbob smiles a tired smile, gives Kenneth's shoulder a squeeze, and says, "What a fuckin' night! Damn, Kenneth, I'm sure glad Janie's all right. I need to tell her good night before we take off. Good job, you guys."

We start to pick up the glassware and trash, and Jimbob leans over and talks to Janie for a minute. Doctor James, as Janie calls him, is studiously avoiding listening to their conversation. The girls walk up to where Kenneth and I are putting trash into a plastic bag and Shirley gives him a big hug. He looks distinctly uncomfortable. He's probably never even talked to her before. She rises up on her tip-toes and gives him a kiss on the cheek. His face is turning a deep crimson as she whispers something in his ear then she turns to me.

"Thank you," is all she says.

She gives me a quick hug and a perfunctory peck on the cheek, turns and takes Melody's hand. They head out of the room with Jimbob right behind them. I hear the deep bass rumble of Bobby Ray's pickup idling as he waits for Judy.

Donna sticks her head through the office door and says, "I'm goin' home. I called Sammy and told him someone else needs to take care of the biscuits today. I'm too old for this shit."

Kenneth and I chuckle, but Judy looks concerned.

"I've never heard Momma admit she was too old for anything," she says, shaking her head slowly. "Hopefully, some sleep will help."

Janie has handed Doctor James his sticks, as he calls them, and the two of them are heading over to where Kenneth and I are sweeping up with a couple of those little roller-brooms. She looks whipped, and I don't imagine we look much better. It's been a very long day for all of us.

"Judy's going to show us her cabin before she goes home. She says there are two small bedrooms, so we can stay here until morning. I'll see you," she says to Kenneth brushing his stubbly cheek with the palm of her hand, "after you get your breakfast." She turns to me, and says, "I'm so glad whatever you two are up to seems to be over. Please don't get Kenneth hurt."

I feel like a heel for even taking the chance of getting this sweet girl's only living relative hurt or killed. No matter that it was his idea. No more.

FORTY-SEVEN

Donna's Place, Mooresville, Alabama
May 19, 1990

Kenneth and I were in the dining room at Donna's as soon as the doors were unlocked. Darla made sure we had drinks and menus as soon as we had a table picked out, and was her usual sweet self. She seems to be especially attentive to Kenneth, but, hey, he's almost a local. He didn't take his eyes off her until she returned to the kitchen. Damned letch.

While waiting for our food, I ask Kenneth for his version of the previous evening's events. Looking discreetly over his shoulder, he tells me, "I'll give you the high points after breakfast, then I'll tell the whole story when everyone is together, later."

Darla seems to understand our wish for privacy and seats the few others in the dining room at tables far removed from ours.

After polishing off our meal, I ask Kenneth for the highlights of his previous evening. He looks around, satisfying himself that nobody can hear our conversation, then leans forward and starts his tale.

"When Donna and I got to the crash scene, she drove down the frontage road and got as close as she could get. She sweet-talked the local cop into letting us park across the street from the roadblock, and told him I had a sister in the bus. It was fuckin' bedlam, man, with cops, relatives, reporters, and looky-loos everywhere."

It had taken quite a while to find anyone who would talk to him, and even longer to find someone associated with Midsouth Convalescent.

"The lady I finally found was a local nursing home administrator, sent to the scene of the wreck by Midsouth to deal with friends and family members of the passengers on the bus. She had a list of the passengers, and a seating chart, sent to her by the Midsouth staff that put the people on the bus in Memphis."

According to her, Janie had been on the bus, sitting directly behind the driver. Because of the horrendous destruction of that part of the bus, removing the bodies of victims was painstaking and slow. Kenneth wouldn't be able to see Janie's remains until the crews were finished at the scene and the bodies had been sent to the county morgue. It would probably not be possible until late afternoon on Saturday.

"That's why I asked Donna for a ride to Huntsvull. She tried to talk me out of it, but I told her there wasn't a damned thing I could do for Janie right then. I really wanted to get over to Chubby's and do what I could to make things easier for you guys. She finally gave up arguin' and gave me the keys. We made damned good time, and it looked like we got there just in time!"

Good thing they made the trip back, seeing as how Judy and the girls needed a ride. Fuckin' Smutly, believing any female should be receptive to his advances, had become enraged when Judy and Melody refused to get out of the van. He went berserk. I guess he thought disabling their vehicle would make him more attractive to them. Moron.

Donna and Kenneth arriving when they did was a real stroke of luck. It allowed Judy and the girls to get the fuck out of Dodge while the crowd was still small enough to be controlled by Bobby Ray and Travis. Kenneth burst on the scene in a big way. He took Smutly out of play and had a chance to do what he'd promised Shirley's dad he would do.

I decide to wait until we are all together for more details, and fill him in on how I had come to be there in the Malibu, sans roll-back. Kenneth has a few names for Bo, and suggests we find him later for a "discussion". Even though things worked out as they occurred, I would definitely like to find out what happened with Bo to make him miss our rendezvous. His not being there is damned suspicious. Maybe he's in cahoots with the PnB, after all. It makes me wonder how far I can trust Fat Bob.

We both agree that Donna had been preoccupied at the bar, and feel we should try to get an explanation without badgering her. I don't mention my conflicting thoughts about Judy's behavior. I probably never will, because I feel so strongly about this incredible friend of mine and never want to be the cause of pain for him.

While we're sitting here, Judy enters the room to appreciative stares and a few greetings from the regulars. She makes her way to our table and informs us that Donna, Bobby Ray, and Travis will meet us out at her house when we are through talking to Janie and Doctor Popovich. She refuses our offer of a chair, and says she is heading into Mooresville for some groceries. She promises to see us soon.

Kenneth has been visiting with Janie for almost two hours while I've been talking to Doctor James. The guy is cool, for sure. He is intrigued by the Malibu, which he had discovered as he took a walk around the lot while he waited for Kenneth and me. He seems to appreciate the work involved in making the car look rusty and inconspicuous, but is really interested in details about the mechanical stuff. He's a regular at dirt tracks around the Memphis area, and is very knowledgeable about the parts and skills needed to be successful.

Time flies, as they say, and soon Kenneth comes over with Janie to fetch the good doctor so they can go over to Cherokee. A small bus is waiting there for yesterday's passengers who are able to travel, and Janie will return to Memphis with them.

Kenneth and Doctor Popovich are talking, leaned up against the wall of the bar. Janie is inside Judy's cabin, making sure she hasn't forgotten anything.

"I want you to know just how much it means to me," Kenneth says, looking the older man in the eye, "that you brought Janie over here so's I'd know she was okay. If there's anything I can ever do for you, just ask."

"I'm glad I could help," says James, reaching out and putting his hand on Kenneth's shoulder. "Janie is a special young woman, and I think a great deal of her." He and Kenneth shake hands, and I see Janie step out of the cabin, shading her eyes against the sunlight. She looks better than I expected, given Kenneth's explanation of her condition.

"Kenneth, I want you to promise me you'll stay out of trouble," Janie says, making me wince and Kenneth laugh. "This horrible accident has made me think. Things can happen suddenly, costing people their family members. I surely don't want to lose you, so promise me you'll behave yourself."

Kenneth sobers up and takes her hands in his. "I promise I'll be as careful as I can," he tells her.

I don't say that I think this may be a prevarication on his part, but I think it. I guess he means he'll be as careful as he can, considering he's involved in a damned dangerous enterprise. It's not my place to interfere, so I don't. Janie seems to accept this as the best she'll get, and lets him slide.

After Janie and James leave for Cherokee, we have a short conversation that concludes with us cleaning and oiling our handguns and making sure there are a couple clean and loaded pistols hidden in the car. It won't do to be over-confident at this stage.

FORTY-EIGHT

As we pull into Judy's yard, Jesus pokes his head around the corner of the house and gives a couple pitiful little barks then runs back to wherever he came from. Kenneth and I just exchange disgusted looks and shake our heads. That's a sad little excuse for a dog. He's cute, but a serious chicken-shit.

We step out of the Malibu and just stand in of in the car for a few seconds, taking in the gorgeous day. The scent of honeysuckle is comforting, along with the fresh, clean air and abundant sunshine. In other circumstances, I might take a nap in the hammock hanging out back.

We hear Bobby Ray's voice raised for a few seconds, then a round of laughter from those present. We smile at each other and head to the rear of the house. I can't imagine anyone using the front door here; it may as well be nailed shut.

Donna and Judy are in the kitchen, judging by the sounds emanating from there. Bobby Ray is leaned up against the clothesline post, munching on a bowl of what looks like boiled peanuts. Travis is stretched out on the grass under one of the Sumac-looking shade trees along the western side of the yard. Jesus is snuggled up against him and tries to burrow under him as he spots us. Pitiful.

The screen door opens and Donna comes out with a pitcher of sweet tea and a tray of doughnuts. "Mornin', boys," she says as she sweeps past us on her way to the patio table. "How're you this mornin'?"

I'm glad to see she seems to be feeling much better than she did a few hours ago. "You get enough sleep?"

She laughs at my question.

"Hell, it's like vacation, being able to sleep until seven in the morning. Maybe I should retire and do this more often."

We all laugh along with her, but I wonder if she's serious. She's probably just worn out from all the worrying about Judy and the rest of us and will be fine as soon as she's had some time to wind down.

Travis is scratching the puppy's ears and looks much better than he did earlier in the bar. His face is still pretty swollen up and discolored, but he seems to be moving a little better. He's got his hair back in the pony tail, and has showered all the dirt and blood off.

"Mornin'," he says. His high-pitched voice is a little ragged from something, probably hollering at someone at the bar. "How's your sister, Kenneth?"

"She's good," says Dutton, settling into one of the lawn chairs at the table, "considering a bunch of her friends got killed or hurt bad last night in that wreck." I hadn't even considered that; she probably knew everyone on that bus. "The girl that they thought was her, the one sittin' behind the driver, was a gal named Jamey. Her last name was Durrance or somethin' like that. That's how that doctor feller thinks they got the idea Janie was on the bus. She was supposed to make the trip, but canceled so she could go to some car race there in Memphis with that doctor and some other patients from the home. Hell, I didn't even know she liked races."

"She may not," says Judy, and Donna's grinning and nodding her head in agreement. "I think it's Doctor James she likes, not necessarily the races."

"Well, of course she likes him," says Kenneth around a mouthful of doughnut. "Up near that place she lives and he's her doctor, to boot. Wait a damned second," he starts, noticing the looks on the faces of these two women, "you don't mean she's sweet on him, do you?"

I think that's exactly what Judy meant. Thinking back on their behavior this morning, I figure she's probably right. They were too damned comfortable with each other; if we hadn't been so busy with our own thoughts, we probably would have noticed it, too.

Donna says what the rest of us are thinking. "Kenneth, I'm pretty sure Janie and James are more than just doctor and patient. I've had a few years to hone my skills at observing human behavior, and I'm usually a pretty good judge of character. I think they're really close, maybe even more than friends."

"Well, I'll be damned," he says, shaking his melon back and forth a few times. "If that's true—

and I'm inclined to trust your judgment," he says, looking at Donna, who's smiling at him, "then Jimbob is shorely gonna be disappointed. I think he's been slowly gettin' up the nerve to ask Janie if they could be more than just buddies. Maybe he waited too long; I guess we'll see."

We spend the next few minutes discussing this development, then Kenneth fills the others in on how he and Donna happened to be in Chubby's back lot at just the right time. Judy tells us all about how Smutly had accosted her and Melody and, having been rebuffed, decided to beat up Vanna just for spite.

"He strutted up to my window and asked who I was waiting for," Judy says. "When I told him I was waiting for some friends, he said I should party with him instead." She's shaking her head, with a disgusted look on her face as she remembers his advances. "I tried to be nice, so he would leave us alone, but he got nasty. He said maybe I wasn't interested in a real man, asked me if I was a lesbian." Why is it that some men automatically assume a woman is lesbian because she doesn't want to have anything to do with them?

"Melody was getting scared, and I told him to fuck off and leave before my friends showed up," Judy continued. "I rolled up the window, and he backed up a little and started looking around the ground. I thought he was looking for a rock. He found a metal rod and started smacking the windows with it, hollering at us the whole time. I had my pistol in my hand, just in case he actually tried to get into the van. He seemed intent on beating the hell out of the van, and he finally stuck the rod into the radiator. Hot water squirted out, all over his hands. He was getting all worked up, and I was afraid I'd have to shoot him when Travis and Bobby Ray came out the back door with Shirley. Momma and Kenneth showed up right then, and you know the rest. I'm waiting to hear what Kenneth did to him as punishment for his treatment of Shirley."

I'm thinking that he may deserve even more punishment at some point, and vow to myself to be present when it's administered. Dickhead.

"So, Kenneth," I start, asking the question we've all been thinking about. "What—exactly—did you do to him?"

We're all raptly watching him, waiting for the details of his surgical procedure.

"Well," he says, leaning his elbows on the table, obviously enjoying his time in the limelight. "After I knocked him stupid, I got his belt undone and his britches down enough to grab hold of his pecker." Everyone giggles at the thought of this. "As I told Jonnybob," he continues, nodding at me, "my first inclination was to cut the damned thing off." Everyone is nodding, most of us smiling at the thought. "But I had the thought that mebbe it'd be better to leave it there, but make it a permanent reminder of what an asshole he is."

Confused looks from us.

"I took out my Ol' Timer and started carvin' on it," he says, grinning, "like it was a chunk of pork, or a chicken neck." Donna barks out a laugh, and the rest of us join in. The mental picture is definitely amusing. "I started just under the head and cut a spiral around it about two-thirds of the way down, like a fuckin' barber pole, before he came to. He was thrashin' around and squealin' like a stuck hog, so I bounced his melon off that car's bumper a few times until he shut up again. I hurried and finished that up, then took the small blade and carved NO on the end of it. I figger that'll serve as a warning, both to him, and any girl who sees it."

I have a feeling that Shirley's daddy may think that isn't enough, but I have to applaud Kenneth's imaginative punishment. That should indeed serve as a reminder to Smutly that he's bein' watched. It just may save some other teenage girl from the hell he put Shirley through, along with any number of other females.

After another hour of listening to Travis and Bobby Ray's versions of the events at Chubby's, as well as Donna's recollections of her rescuing the girls and Judy, we all take a short break for lunch. There is cold fried chicken, biscuits, a big pot of baked beans, and a tub of potato salad. Apparently, Donna told Sammy to fix us up a picnic lunch when she called him to have someone else make the biscuits.

Bobby Ray and Kenneth walk down the lane a

ways, pitching rocks at birds and fence-posts. Travis is back under his tree, which, Judy informs me, is a Chinese Pistache, a sort of cousin to the Sumac I thought it was. She says they're really pretty in the fall, and tells me I need to see them. She's got that smirk back on her face, and seems to take pleasure in making me move away from her when she gets a little too close. If Kenneth wasn't so taken with her, it would be different; I'd be trying everything I know to get her in bed, or under a tree, or . . . Dammit! He may have a rude awakening coming about her, but I'm not going to be the one responsible for telling him about it.

After everyone has taken their turn in the bathroom and given their lunch some time to settle a little, we all congregate back outside at the patio table. I figure it's my turn to give an accounting of the events, and I'm just about to start when the cordless phone, which Judy has sitting on the table, rings, making all of us jump.

Judy picks up the phone, says "Hello" to whoever is on the other end, then progressively turns paler and paler, moaning deep down in her throat before asking a barrage of questions and jumping to her feet. She clicks off the phone and turns to Donna.

"That was Sammy. A bunch of biker-looking guys came into the restaurant about ten minutes ago, looking for me. They said they were Jimmy's friends and just wanted to say hello.

"Darla told them I was on vacation, but they

kept asking if she knew where to find me. They went out into the lot and caught Jason on his way to the dumpster. Oh, Momma, they beat the shit out of him! Jason told Sammy to call us. Jason says he didn't tell them how to get here, but he thought he'd better warn us. Sammy wanted to call the cops, but Jason pleaded with him not to. He's had some problems with them, and doesn't want to get them involved. They also think the cops may have some questions for me about why the assholes are looking for me. I agree with them; getting the cops in the middle of our shit now is definitely a bad idea. But I will personally take care of the ones that hurt Jason. Those assholes will regret messing around with that sweet boy!"

Sonsabitches! Somehow, her involvement has made Judy a target. I don't know which bikers are looking for her, but I'd almost bet the farm that it's Chief's boys. If they beat the directions to this house out of poor Jason, the dishwasher, they could be here at any moment.

Travis is already around the house, watching the road. Bobby Ray runs over to his truck and returns with the double-barrel, his expression grim. Kenneth has his .45 in his paw, and I'm herding Judy and Donna, who seems to be in shock, into the house. Judy isn't putting up much resistance. In the house, I go to the window by the front door and look out toward the southeast.

There isn't any traffic I can see, but that doesn't

mean much. Travis hears me move the blinds and waves at me. I wave back and turn back toward the women, who are both on the sofa, clutching each other and crying. I can't blame them. The people at Donna's Place are like family to these women, and having one of them attacked in broad daylight is a huge shock.

As I'm thinking of what to do next, Judy jumps up off the sofa and strides into the rear of the house, returning with a pump-action Mossberg riot gun—twelve gauge if I'm not mistaken. She also has a couple bags in her other hand, and they look heavy.

"You know," she says grimly, "even with all the planning and talking we did, I never fully expected a fucking shooting war with these pricks, but they've asked for it and, by God, they're gonna get it."

She spills the contents of the bags onto the rag rug in the middle of the room. There are boxes of shotgun shells, probably twenty of them at a quick guess.

Judy squats down and picks one up. "HE rounds," she explains, to my amazement. She picks up another, this one with different colored markings on it. "CS gas," she says, and picks up another differently marked box. "Double-ought buckshot," she reads off the label.

Holy shit! The room is suddenly awash in heavy-duty ammunition and weapons. I think the security at Redstone Arsenal must be just a little lax, considering what I've seen in the last few days.

"HE?" asks Donna, leaning forward and looking at some of the boxes within her reach. "What does that mean?"

"High Explosive," I explain, and Judy nods. "CS is tear gas."

I wish I'd known she had all this before we went against Chubby's, but maybe it worked out best that I didn't. And, like she said, Judy never really thought things were going to get as ugly as they have. Now, with this new development, this stash of armament might come in very handy.

"You got anything else hidden around here that might help?" I look at Judy, who is looking out the front window.

She turns around and there are tears on her cheeks. If I'm any judge, they're tears of rage. She just gives me one of those hard, measuring stares like I used to use on prospects who got out of line.

"I have one more thing that you might be interested in," she says, returning to the rear of the house.

She comes back a couple of minutes later carrying a metal box, some kind of gun safe. It's too big for a handgun, and too small for a rifle or assault weapon.

As she opens the lid, I exhale explosively, and grin like fucking lunatic.

"Damn!" I say, laughing with delight.

It's an Ingram MAC-10, and the fitted suppressor, or silencer, is fitted into a foam notch in the case.

There are also at least four thirty-round magazines. I pick one up and turn it so I can see the rounds in it. Hot damn, it's a .45 ACP, same as the Tommy guns of gangster movies.

If I remember right, the MAC-10 fires about 1,100 rounds a minute in full auto, allowing the user to infect his target with a serious case of lead poisoning. I look at Judy, and she's got her head cocked, looking at me with a "so?" look on her face. I step over and give her a big hug—just for a second or two. I step back and look her square in the eye.

"We'll get those fuckers," I tell her, and I mean it.

We might've been "playing war" before, but now all bets are off. We just need a little time to get our shit together, plan a way to take care of business without all of us ending up in a federal prison.

"Okay," I say, "let's get everyone out front so we can keep an eye on the road, and see what we come up with."

Donna and Judy wordlessly head for the front door. I guess it's a good thing it's not nailed shut, after all.

I head out back and tell Bobby Ray and Kenneth to come around to the front of the house. I walk back through the house and into the small front yard, where Travis is still watching for traffic. Kenneth and Bobby Ray come around the west side of the house carrying all the lawn chairs folded up and stacked. We unfold them and set then in a loose semi-circle facing the road.

"Travis," I ask, "do you want me to spell you for awhile?"

I figure whoever is standing watch can see well enough from where we are, as long as they're on their feet, and they can hear what the others are saying.

The shaggy beard wags back and forth as Travis shakes his head, but he does step over to where he can more easily hear what's being said. "I'm good," he says, taking a look over his right shoulder.

Judy is assembling the Ingram, much to Kenneth's surprise—he looks just plain awestruck. Everyone else is looking at me, so I say what I've been thinking.

"Considering the way things happened at Donna's and seeing as how nobody has shown up here, yet, I figure there are a couple of different ways to play this. If Jason got the directions to Judy's beaten out of him, the people who did it should be here by now. They're not. Why not?

"I think Jason kept his mouth shut, or we would have heard from those assholes by now." Nobody has anything to add, so I continue.

"If Jason didn't give Judy up, it still won't be long before they get the info from someone else. Are you in the phone book, Judy?" I ask, wondering why they would go to the restaurant and cause such a ruckus if her name is in the phone book.

"No," she says confidently, shaking her head, causing her hair to shimmer in the sunlight. I can't believe I noticed that. Shit. I need to get my head back in the game.

"Jimmy always was really paranoid about anyone knowing where we lived. He always met people at his shop behind Momma's. Only a few of his lowlife buddies had the phone number, and I changed it about six months ago, so none of them knows the new number. On top of that, the new number is registered to Rellim Yduj, my name spelled backwards. The address just lists Belle Mina, no street address. Even if they could talk someone into searching the unlisted numbers, there's nothing in my or Jimmy's name."

Thank God for paranoia, I think. Jimmy's caution may just have saved all our asses. Whoever they are, the people who went to Donna's looking for Judy probably assumed she would be there, and weren't prepared for the alternative. When they found out she wasn't there, and nobody would tell them where to find her, they reverted to brute force. All that did is shine a spotlight on 'em, making their quest even harder.

"That's really good news," I say, looking around the arc at everyone before continuing. "Every minute they have to spend searching for you gives us time to prepare. Judy, would you please go call Darla and ask her if she or anyone there recognized any of the bikers?"

She looks perturbed for a second, but nods and hands the Ingram to Bobby Ray. She stands up and heads for the front door. I catch her before she gets there. "You might ask her if anyone saw what they were driving, too, so we know what to watch for."

She just nods without stopping and lets the screen door close behind her.

As soon as Judy enters the house, Donna stands and announces that she's heading to her place. "Don't even try to talk me out of it," she says with a determined look on her face. "That boy is like family to me, and I need to go see to him. I'll be in touch and if you think of anything I can do, call me."

There's no use trying to talk her out of leaving, so I don't. She shouldn't be in any danger there; the earlier incident will have everyone on guard and, between Sammy and Merle, she'll be in good hands. She may even be able to find out some more information about the people who that hurt Jason and what they were driving.

As Donna is backing out onto the road and driving away, Judy returns to the gathering carrying the cordless phone. "Why didn't you have Momma wait until I was off the phone?"

She looks aggravated, and I guess she has a right to be, although I'm not sure what we could have done, short of physically restraining her, to keep Donna from leaving.

"There's no damned way we were gonna stop her," says Bobby Ray, grinning at Judy, "short of hog-tyin' her. You know her well enough to know that.

She said she was goin' and that was that."

Travis just snorts. Kenneth even chuckles, although he's watching Judy pretty closely for her reaction. I'm trying real hard to keep a neutral look on my face.

She smiles a rueful smile, and acknowledges that Bobby Ray is right. "Yeah, I know how she is, believe me. I guess I'm surprised it took this long for her to leave. She loves Jason. Hell, she loves all of the folks that work for her. Messin' with one of them is a sure-fire way to get on her bad side. From what Darla told me, it'll be a good thing to have her there. I guess the place is in an uproar."

Judy sits down on a lawn chair and reaches down to scratch Jesus between the ears. I hadn't even noticed him lying there, without him cryin' and whinin'. "Darla said she's pretty sure the guys that beat up Jason are PnB, but they weren't wearing colors. She put one of our regulars, an old guy named Norman, on the phone. He said he recognized one of them as the son of a friend of his. He said the young guy's name is Marty but his nickname is Pickle. Norman says Pickle didn't see him. He didn't know what they were up to, or he would've got in their faces. He's a crusty old guy, used to hang out with my daddy back in the day. He doesn't like Pickle, says he's a punk. He rides with the PnB, who Norman also thinks are a bunch of punks." We're all grinning, picturing an old-timer spouting off about punks on bikes.

"Norman said Pickle and the others drove up in a Ford crew-cab pickup, probably a mid-eighties model. The really interesting thing is that he said there was another car there that drove in right behind the Ford and parked next to it."

That doesn't sound good. How many of these assholes are we going to need to deal with? And how in the hell did they find us? I guess it's *us* they're looking for, not just Judy.

As if she can read my mind, Judy continues. "There were four of them in the Ford, and Norman said there were at least three people in the Blazer. He's pretty sure one of the passengers in the Blazer was a woman, or a 'girl', as he put it."

Blazer? Oh, fuck.

"Did he say what color the Blazer was?" I'm pretty sure I know the answer, but I have to ask. "Is it one of the big ones, or one of the little S-10 Blazers?"

Everyone is looking at me, wondering what I'm getting at.

"That's weird . . . he did mention it was one of the big ones. Something about the fact that he had one like it a few years ago. He said it was a dark gray, like a primer or something, because it was really dull. He also said it was two-wheel drive, and sat pretty low. Why?"

"Chief has a Blazer that looks just like that." Groans, exclamations of disgust. "I saw Polly in it a couple times. It sounded like it oughtta run damned good. I imagine they use it when they don't want to stand out in a crowd."

I wonder if Chief got away from the Eagle Snacks ambush, or if Polly is orchestrating this search. The others are shaking their heads. The news just keeps getting worse. Time to get hold of Jimbob and find out what went down in Fayetteville so we can get an idea of who we might be dealing with.

FORTY-NINE

We're all sitting around the patio table. Kenneth and Bobby Ray brought it around front, so we can all sit out here while we eat lunch. Bobby Ray made a plate and is eating standing up, having spelled Travis at the roadside so he can watch for traffic headed this way. We're putting a really big dent in the food Judy and Donna brought out earlier, and the normal act of sharing a meal has settled everyone's nerves a little.

Kenneth is on his second plate and seems finally to be slowing down a little. Travis is done with his lunch and has Jesus in his lap, giving him a belly rub. Damned dog is going to be spoiled rotten. He's a cute little bastard, but pretty much worthless. Judy is toying with some potato salad and a chicken breast, but isn't actually eating much. As I was always told during flight ops at sea, you eat and sleep whenever you get a chance, because you don't know when you'll get another chance. Bearing that in mind, I've had a few pieces of chicken, a fair-sized pile of potato salad, some baked beans, and even a couple glazed doughnuts. Just doing my duty, you understand.

Kenneth stands up to carry his plate into the house, grabs the cordless handset, and says over his shoulder, "I'm gonna see if I can find Jimbob. If not, I'll page him and give him this number."

Good idea, I think. We need to find out all we can about what happened up there, as well as the DEA's success in Huntsville. It's hard to believe that all happened less than twelve hours ago. It's really hard to believe that someone is already on our trail . . . well, maybe not, considering the Firebird that may have been following Travis and Bobby Ray. I need to tell everyone about that, but I should wait until everyone is back in one place. I'll wait until Kenneth reaches Jimbob and talks to him. If he has to leave a number on the pager, I'll tell them about our trip back from Chubby's while we're waiting for the lawyer to call us back.

Bobby Ray gave the Ingram back to Judy when she returned from talking to Darla and Norman, and she has since returned it to its case, which is under her chair. The Mossberg is leaning against the porch railing about two feet from my right hand. We've all got handguns either on us or on the table near us. It doesn't even seem out of the ordinary.

I hear the phone ring, followed by Dutton's voice, progressively getting louder. He comes bustin' through the screen door with a drumstick in one hand and the phone in the other. "He's on his way here," he says, his face red and his eyes bright. "He says we need to stay out of sight. Actually, he said *you* need to stay out of sight," he says, looking right at me.

"I guess some really weird shit happened out at the Eagle Snacks place, and he thinks we should all get together instead of me and you headin' up there."

Kenneth is speaking fast, nearly breathless. "He's bringin' a couple of Bennett's men with him, for some added muscle. He says if we don't want 'em here, he'll have 'em check into a motel close, in case we need 'em later. He's purty spooked."

Holy shit! Now what? I'm slowly (too slowly) realizing that I'm not as good at this shit as I thought I'd be. I'm in way over my head, and am dragging a bunch of people down with me. Maybe I should just either turn myself in to Guffey or drive up to Chief's house and see if I can get things taken care of without anyone else getting hurt. This has gone completely sideways, and it's all my fault.

"Don't even think it," says Travis, his voice a little stronger than it was earlier.

I must look startled, because he laughs out loud. Kenneth and Bobby Ray are looking at him quizzically, wondering what he's talking about it.

"I can tell exactly what you're thinkin', Jonnybob," says Judy, joining in, "and I'm telling you not to think like that. We are all here because we want to be. Don't give up now. That would be the worst thing you could do to us. If someone gets hurt, we'll have to deal with it, but being abandoned at this stage by the guy we're following would hurt a whole lot worse."

"Did I miss something?" Kenneth looks sorely confused. He looks at me and says, "Jonnybob, what's goin' on?"

I look at him, digesting Travis and Judy's words. I

must be pretty damned transparent.

"Well, Kenneth," says Travis, grinning at me conspiratorially, "I think that, just for a minute, your pal was thinking about throwin' in the towel and givin' himself up so nobody else gets hurt. Am I close, bro?"

He's got me. He knows it, and so does Judy. The look on Kenneth's face slowly changes from confused to angry.

"Goddammit, we've been through this shit before! You," he says, leaning across the table toward me, "need to get it through that thick fuckin' skull o' yers that nobody's gonna let you do this alone. So jest fergit that stupid way of thinkin' and let's figger out who's fuckin' with us and how we're gonna take care of 'em in a way that'll convince them and anyone else thinkin' of fuckin' with us that it's a really bad idea."

Damn, that may be the most words I've ever heard him string together in one sentence. Telling him that is probably not a great idea right now, because he is seriously pissed off.

"Okay," I say, hands up, trying to look contrite. "I'm sorry if I pissed you off. I won't mention it again"

I'm not lying . . . I won't mention it again. But if the perfect opportunity arises for me to end this mess in a manner that ensures I'm the only one in danger, I'll jump on it.

"I'm serious this time, dammit." Dutton is not going to be mollified so easily. "You get any silly ideas from here on out, I'll kick yer ass up around yer ears, and if I can't get it done, I think these boys'll help me. That is, if Judy doesn't do it herself."

He looks at Bobby Ray, Judy, and Travis in turn, and they nod. Whatever happens I'll need to keep my cards close to my vest until the moment to act. That's liable to make things harder, but hey, maybe things will work out just dandy. Yeah, right.

"Jonnybob, will you help me carry these plates and stuff into the house?" Judy is standing, gathering up plates, silverware, and the like.

I stand up and help. I'm pretty sure we all know this is a ruse for Judy to get me off somewhere out the others' earshot. I figure she's going to read me the riot act, much the same as Kenneth has just finished doing. Hell, she probably doesn't want to embarrass me further by hollering at me in front of the boys.

We go through the screen door, me holding it open with my foot as Judy heads into the house. As I release the door and cross the threshold, she says, "Close it," pointing at the wooden door with a nod of her head.

Oh, crap. This is going to be even worse than I thought.

I push the door closed, and I can see Kenneth and the other two laughing. I guess we're all on the same wavelength. Jonnybob's going to get his ass chewed, but good. As I turn to cross the living room into the kitchen, I see Judy closing the back door. Jeez, she must be planning to really let me have it, if she thinks she needs to close all the doors so the others can't hear what she's got to say.

In the kitchen, I place all the stuff I'm carrying on the counter, except for the potato salad, which I shove into the fridge. I take a deep breath and turn around to take my medicine.

Judy looks stern, and is fiddling with a lock of her hair. She's staring as if she's trying to see through me. She takes a couple steps and stands right in front of me. I'm not sure what her deal is, but it looks serious. She is one of the main reasons I want to end this before it escalates any more. I'll never forgive myself if she gets hurt. Hell, a few days ago, the worst thing that might happen to her was a drunk customer at the bar to deal with. Now, because of me and my damned war with the PnB, she or any number of other people might get hurt or killed. Killed, dammit!

To make matters even worse, my best friend is also in danger, and he'll be devastated if this woman gets hurt. He's been enamored with her since the first time he met her.

I wish he'd see the sense of me turning myself over to the cops or the club, if for no other reason than protecting this extraordinary woman he's so fond of. This woman we're *all* so fond of.

"Jonnybob, I want you to listen to me," she says, "because it's something I've been wanting to tell you for a few days. I've been chicken, thinking it would be better to wait, but the time for waiting is over." At least she's not yelling. Yet.

"I respect you for worrying about all of us, but you seem to be missing the fact that we all have a reason for being involved. I lost a husband I used to love to meth. Travis and Bobby Ray have no use for it and are willing to do whatever it takes to slow its spread around here. And Kenneth wants to kick ass for the PnB taking a neighbor's teenage daughter and whoring her out. On top of that, he loves you."

She's making good points, but I still feel this is my fight, my war, my responsibility.

"I like you a lot, myself," she continues. Her face is right in front of mine, and her eyes are locked on mine. She looks as vulnerable as I've seen her.

What did she just say? My mind seems to be working in slow motion as she steps closer, until our toes are nearly touching. Her intentions are obvious. She reaches out and takes my head in both hands, leaning forward for a kiss.

"Wait," I say, backing up a step until I bang my hip into the counter. Shit! "Judy, this is a bad idea. You're right, Kenneth loves me, and I love that man like a brother. I won't do anything to jeopardize that relationship."

She's staring at me with her head slightly cocked to one side, with that infuriating smirk on her lips. Dammit. I try again.

"You know how he feels about you. He can't even breathe when you walk through the room. You told me

472

you think a lot of him. How can you do anything that would hurt him so bad?"

I don't understand women in general, but this one has me even more confused than normal. She seems to honestly care for Kenneth, and she doesn't seem evil or mean, so I don't have a clue what she's thinking.

"Jonnybob, for being so smart, you sure are an idiot." She backs off a step or two, and I remember to breathe. "I would never hurt Kenneth! He's one of the sweetest men I've ever met. I know he had a crush on me at first, but I knew that he and I didn't have any sort of future together, other than as friends."

Well, shit . . . I don't think *he'd* like to hear that.

"There's something you should know," she starts out, and I'm thinking I don't really need to hear this, whatever it is. "Kenneth and Darla have really hit it off."

Say what?

"What? He just met her a couple days ago, and he hasn't had any time to even talk to her." Maybe I misunderstood her; this makes no sense at all.

Judy's just smiling that maddening smile that makes me feel stupid, like I've missed something important.

"Darla was attracted to Kenneth the first time she saw him, kind of like he was to me, but a lot more seriously. She's been talking to him every chance she gets. They were in my cabin Wednesday night . . . Thursday morning, I guess it was, for three hours or so. She asked me to bring him over when we were through with our planning session, and she waited until after Bobby Ray and Travis took my car home to paint it."

"You mean after I went to bed he went over to your cabin to talk to Darla?" This sounds pretty weird to me.

"No, I just asked him to come over for awhile. He wanted to go get you, but I asked him not to. I wanted to give him and Darla some time to be around each other, see what happened. Darla asked me if I had any designs on him that first time she waited on you guys.

I told her how I feel, that I would try to get the two of them together and see what happened. So I didn't even tell him she was there . . . I just wanted to let whatever was going to happen develop without any interference on my part."

No interference? Sounds to me like she interfered plenty. Fuckin' matchmakers.

"So, what, you just had him come over and said, 'Here's Darla. Let's see how you two crazy kids get along?'"

I'm not sure why, but I'm getting angry. Maybe it's because I'm so totally lost about what the fuck is going on around here. Jesus, I'm clueless.

"I'm sure he thought you invited him over so you two could be alone. It seems kinda shitty to me that you sprung the whole Darla deal on him just to make it easier on yourself."

Uh oh, that may have been a little strong, because

she takes a deep breath and I honestly think she's going to slap me.

"Sorry," I say, honestly chastened, "that was a rotten thing to say. I'm just out of sorts. I don't seem to have any idea of what's goin' on around here, and I guess I'm just frustrated."

She doesn't actually hit me, but I can tell she's pissed. Really pissed.

"Dammit, Jonnybob, I'm trying to tell you what's going on, if you'd pull your head out of your ass and listen!"

She's pointing a finger at me like you do when you really want someone to pay attention. I'm not sure whether to be pissed off or amused, so I just keep my yap shut and wait for the rest.

"When Kenneth showed up at my door, he was nervous as hell, and was really flummoxed when he saw Darla on the sofa. He asked me to step outside for a minute, asking her to excuse us." Yeah, I think, he was probably going to tell you he wanted to spend some time with you alone. "As soon as we were outside, he said he wanted to get something off his chest before things got out of hand. He told me he's sweet on Darla. He also said he thought I was pretty and a real nice girl, but, to be honest, I'm too 'bony' for him, in his words."

I almost swallow my tongue, teeth, and tonsils trying not to laugh out loud. That wouldn't do. No sir, not at all. But what she's saying reminds me that Kenneth does, indeed, like his women with some meat on their bones. And I'm remembering the way he's been watching Darla in the dining room. That sneaky shit.

"He also said that you are the best man he's ever known, other than his father." God, if she says any more shit like that, I may tear up. "He told me that he's pretty sure you're sweet on me, and he'd sure appreciate it if I wouldn't hurt you any more than necessary, do anything mean to you." Hmm, that sounds familiar.

"In fact, he gave me almost the same speech you gave me while we were waiting for him at the dry cleaners. You two are lucky to have each other, that's for damned sure. Most people don't have even one friend that good."

The smirk is slowly coming back, and I'm glad to see it for once. I'd rather have her call me an idiot than be mad at me.

"Jimbob and his crew will be here before long, so I need to tell you this before we run out of time. God knows when we'll get another chance." She's right back in front of me, causing the counter to bang into my hip again. She's twisting on that lock of hair again. "As things worked out, Kenneth and Darla acted like they've known each other forever. I ended up going to bed, leaving them alone. The next morning, Kenneth told me he likes her a lot, and wants to see if anything happens after this mess is over. That's probably another reason he's so adamant about helping you see this through to the end, bloody or not."

Yeah, okay, that makes some twisted kind of sense, I guess, but now he has someone else to stay alive for. Christ! I start to say this to her, but she stops me with a gesture.

"Whenever you saw us out in the parking lot, that's what we were talking about. Darla, and you. Like I said, I like you a lot. A whole lot, dammit. Maybe too much, but I guess we'll figure that out at some point in the future. Every time I try to let you know, you run away. I think I know why, now, but I have to tell you, my self-confidence has been taking a beating."

Oh shit. This is interesting—damned interesting—but we've got a whole bunch of shit to worry about besides this, and as she said, Jimbob will be here pretty soon.

"Judy, I would never purposely do anything to make you feel bad about yourself. I've been avoiding you because of my mistaken idea that Kenneth was wanting something with you himself. You're gorgeous, smart, tougher than nails, and I've had some fairly unholy thoughts concerning you." She smiles, and even starts to blush, just a little. "I tried to stay out of situations that prompted those thoughts, because I'm basically weak. I'm not sure how long I could've avoided your advances before I did something about them, or just packed up and left before I did something that would hurt Kenneth."

"So," she says, taking a step toward me with that damned smirk back on her face, "when this deal is over, can I expect you to quit running away from me long enough to find out if we're any good together?"

Now that is something I have no doubt about. Unless she is actually a result of some deviant science project, I'm sure we will be just fine together.

"Honey, we'll be so good together you won't be able to uncross your eyes for a week."

She really blushes at this, and barks out a laugh. Then another. And here come the hiccups, right on cue. She wraps her arms around me and she kisses me—hard. I kiss her back, and if we didn't have people waiting for us outside, I seriously believe we wouldn't have even gotten out of the kitchen.

"Whoa," she says, backing off a couple steps, "we've gotta wait. But I don't want to. Shit!"

I feel your frustration.

"We need to get back outside and we can't be carryin' on like this until this is over." I look her in the eyes as I say this, and I'm lost. "Agreed?"

Please say no. Grab me. Kiss me. Those guys can wait.

"Agreed," she says, although I think she may be thinking thoughts similar to mine.

She jumps forward, kisses me hard on the mouth, and she's gone, headed for the front door. That's just not right.

FIFTY

As we come out of the house, Kenneth busts out laughing, and the other two join in. I must look confused, or mad, or kissed, or something, because he comes over to where I'm standing and puts his arm around my neck.

"I'm glad we got that out of the way," he says, giving me a shake. "You two have been plumb comical to watch."

He walks back over to his chair and sits down. Judy looks like I feel; embarrassed, but happy. Travis and Bobby Ray are still chuckling, amused at our discomfort.

I'm just about to respond in my normal sarcastic manner when Bobby Ray stiffens up and says, "Company comin'."

Chief? Polly? Jimbob?

"How many vehicles?" I've got my nine mil in my hand, and Kenneth is fishing his .45 out of his britches.

Travis is beside his nephew, and turns his head enough to say, "One car. Looks like Jimbob's Regal."

Bobby Ray is checking the Mossberg to make sure there's a round in the chamber, and Judy has taken the Ingram out of its case, threading the suppressor onto the end of the stubby barrel. She puts Jesus in the house and walks over behind the corner of the house, just in case. Kenneth and I squat down behind the Malibu and Travis heads through the front door into the house. Bobby Ray stands his ground until the car turns toward us on the lane, then joins Travis inside.

As the sounds of tires on gravel approach the driveway, I peek around the corner of the Malibu, right down against the ground in order to present as small a target as possible.

It is Jimbob, and he has three other men in the car with him.

I call out, "It's okay, everyone. It's Jimbob."

We all abandon our hiding spots as the four new-comers step out of the car. They look suitably impressed with our preparations. At least it looks that way to me. Jesus peeks out of the front window, and ducks out of sight when Kenneth notices him. What a dog.

The passenger in the front seat is a little older than the rest, and looks like he's been around the block a few dozen times. He's not real big, but he's solid, wearing jeans and a khaki western shirt with pearl snaps. Just the way he carries himself says he's not used to being fucked with. The other two are probably my age, beefy-looking fellas wearing windbreakers to hide their pistols in shoulder rigs.

Jimbob lets out a low whistle and says, "Y'all look like you're ready for just about anything." He's starting to relax a little, and grins at us.

"I brought some gentlemen who'd like to help out. We've all got a dog in this fight, as they say.

"This is Rafe Bennett, Shirley's daddy," he says, inclining his head toward the older guy. "The other two are Rafe's nephews, Ronnie," the taller of the two gives us a nod, "and Burt." The other one nods. "They're good boys to have on your side in a scuffle."

They definitely look as if they'd be useful, as long as they're not dumber than a couple bags of hammers. Rafe Bennett gives the impression of being damned competent and he surprises me by stepping forward to give Kenneth a big hug.

"Thank you so much for helping us get Shirley back," he says, pounding on Dutton like he's trying to dislodge a lung. He eases up and steps back a tad, refusing to let go completely.

"Jimbob said you would come through, and he was damned right about that. I want you to know that I'm sure as hell gonna fulfill my obligation as you two discussed."

I guess he doesn't want to say too much about his "obligation" in front of all these people. Little does he know that all of us are going to split up the laundered cash when this is over.

"I understand you took care of that lowlife asshole who took Shirley down to Huntsville," he says, his eyes boring into Kenneth's. "I'll want details, when we get some time to talk about it. For now, I just have one question: will he live to regret what he did?"

I wonder which answer would make him happiest. I can't imagine him being broken up over the thought of Smutly being dead, but I really hope he appreciates Kenneth's version of justice. I shift my gaze to Dutton, who's beaming.

"He'll live, and I guarantee you he'll regret his actions for the rest of his miserable life. I'll be plumb tickled to fill you in on the details when we get some time. I also made it crystal fuckin' clear to that waste of skin that if I ever hear of him doin' bad things to little girls again, I'll find him and make what I did last night look like Christmas."

Bennett is grinning a really nasty grin, nodding his head along as Kenneth continues. "All of us are damned glad to have helped. It wasn't just me—I just did the carvin'. I want you to meet the other people who made it happen."

He dislodges himself from Bennett's grip and walks over to where I'm standing.

"This is my best friend Jonnybob Clark, the feller who put this whole thing in motion. He found the stuff Jimbob talked to you about." I guess he's concerned about mentioning the money in front of the beefy boys. "He's the one who did the lion's share of the plannin' and schemin' to get Shirley sprung, and he set up that fracas up to home."

Bennett extends his hand, and I take it. "Everyone here helped make it possible to get your girl back to you," I say, trying not to flinch from his iron grip. "These two," I say, waving my free left arm toward Bobby Ray and Travis, "actually went into the club and brought her out, protecting her long enough for her to get in the getaway car."

Rafe walks over to them and shakes each of their hands in turn. They both wince. I feel better. They introduce themselves, and tell him how happy they are to have been of service. He pivots on his boot-heel and comes back to where Judy and I are standing.

"I understand you're the one who took Melody over to that damned place and waited for these fine gentlemen to bring my baby outside," he says, taking Judy's hands in his. It doesn't look like he's going to squash them. Either that, or she's tougher than we are. "Melody told us how scared she was when that idjit started tearing up your van, but you were calm and tried to keep her calm, too. Between you and your momma, you're her new heroes." Bennett gives us all another smile, and an abbreviated bow. "Well done, my friends. But now we need to tell you some stuff you don't know, and it isn't very good news."

Ronnie and Burt decide to watch the road for any unannounced visitors, while the rest of us retire to the back yard again. After walking through the house and picking up the puppy, Travis has once again taken the responsibility of providing Jesus with a lap to lie on. The rest of us are either on lawn chairs or, like Bobby Ray and Kenneth, sitting on the grass, leaned up against the house.

Jimbob waits until everyone has a glass of water or sweet tea before he starts his yarn about what he found out when he got home last night—this morning, I guess it was.

"When I left Rafe's, after dropping off Shirley and Melody, I called Randy Miller." He looks at Bobby Ray and Travis as he elaborates, "He's the chief deputy in the sheriff's office back home." He addresses the group as he continues. "He put together the group that was out behind Eagle Snacks waiting for the two different biker clubs to show up."

He looks at Kenneth and me in turn, then says, "I had to give him enough info to make sure he was prepared for what he might run into, but I didn't mention any names or where I got my information. So, he knew that someone had set up a meeting between the two clubs, and that there might be some trouble. He had his guys in the brush out there, waiting and keeping hid."

This all sounds about like I figured the sheriff's office would play it. I'm kinda surprised sheriff Billy himself didn't have a bigger part to play. Maybe he's just a chicken-shit.

"At about ten minutes before midnight, a white Chevy van pulled down that little dirt road with the lights off and drove past that empty lot to the end. It turned around, and a couple of guys got out and approached the empty lot on foot. Apparently, they didn't see anyone because they returned to the van and it just sat there, backed up in the shadows by some trees."

Chief and his boys, bein' careful.

"At about ten after midnight, a dark-colored

Dodge van turned off the highway onto that little road and stopped. It pulled up to just about where the fence ends, and whoever was driving cut the lights and parked it across the road, blocking it pretty good."

It just keeps getting more interesting. Why in the world would Slippy think he needed to block the road? And why was he so late?

"One guy got out of the Dodge, with a flashlight. A guy got out of the Chevy, also with a light. The blinked 'em at each other, and the guy from the Dodge started walking toward that little empty lot where you thought they'd go. The guy from the Chevy also walked to the lot."

What the fuck was going on? This makes no damned sense at all. Nothing was said to either club about flashlights, signals, blocking the road, any of this. I'm starting to get a really bad feeling.

"Randy had himself wedged in a culvert right there where the ditch runs along the east side of that lot, directly under the driveway into that lot. As luck would have it, that's where the two guys met. He heard everything they said."

Jimbob's staring right at me, and everyone else just follows his gaze until everyone is focused on my handsome mug. I'm liking this less and less.

"The two that met there were a guy named Chief and a guy named Slippy, if Randy heard right. Where do these guys get these names?"

I figure that's a rhetorical question and don't answer. Neither does anyone else, although a couple of them snicker.

Actually it's a good question. I could write a book about nicknames and their origin. Maybe I will, if I live through this mess.

"The one named Chief asked Slippy, 'Where is he?' and Slippy answered that he didn't have a clue. He thought 'he' would be here. They cursed for a while, pissed off that this unknown person hadn't shown up. Then Chief says something along the lines of 'Fuckin' Hammer!' and Slippy agrees."

Oh fuck! I've been played. I thought I was doing so well . . .

"Oh shit!" mutters Travis, and Bobby Ray nods. Judy shoots me a nervous grin.

Rafe and Jimbob are watching me closely, and Kenneth looks like he swallowed a dog turd. This changes everything.

Jimbob leans forward and says, "I assume you all know who this Hammer person is . . ." letting his sentence trail off while observing me like a hawk watches its prey. "Rafe and I have a pretty good idea who it is. Would you like to include us in whatever happens next? We are thoroughly prepared to do whatever is needed, but, from now on, no more secrets. We've got to know what's going on, who the players are, and anything else pertinent to the issue at hand; namely, two outlaw biker gangs wanting to string up our friend Hammer and anyone who is helping him."

How did things get to this point? All I wanted to do was shut down the Tidewater chapter's meth operation, make my conscience feel a little better, and ride off into the sunset. Now I'm wanted by the cops, the feds, two different bike clubs, and the families of whoever were in that fucking Firebird. I need a nap.

"You deserve to know anything we can tell you," I say, talking to Jimbob and Rafe.

I just met the guy, but I'm inclined to believe Rafe will be a very valuable asset in whatever happens next.

"You're right, I'm Hammer. I used that name while riding with the PnB in Virginia." Surprised faces. "I got sick of the meth and prostitution they were into, so I dropped a dime on 'em and made things seriously hot for them up there." I smile, thinking about the clubhouse burning merrily on the news.

"I came down here to lay low, but ran across the S&S boys that crashed into that tree on Molino Road. I'm pretty sure Jimbob knows most of what happened from there." Kenneth and the lawyer trade glances, and I'm pretty sure that confirms my suspicions. "I'll sit down and answer any questions you have when we have more time, but I think we need to decide right away what our next move is."

Everyone is crowded up close now, paying attention a little more closely than they had been.

"I'd like to hear the rest of what Randy told you," Judy says to Jimbob, no longer any trace of a smile on her pretty face. Nods and murmurs of assent from the rest of us.

"Okay, after the two of them cuss Hammer out for a few minutes, they get back to the reason they're looking for him. It seems Chief and Slippy set up some scam requiring Chief and his old lady to disappear. They apparently planned to dress up some vagrants in PnB club colors and pretty much mutilate them beyond recognition. This would allow Chief, his old lady, and a couple of her brothers to abscond with the money, leaving the territory around here open for the S&S to sweep in and take over. They were both really pissed that Hammer had somehow gotten his hands on the money and whatever other stuff was involved with the charade."

Fuckin' Chief! He sure didn't waste any time setting this scam up after the shit hit the fan up in Virginia. He must've been thinking about it for a while, and when the opportunity appeared, he jumped on it. I'll bet he had some big fuckin' disaster planned, planning to take out a bunch of his members along with the unfortunate people he dressed in the disguises I found. With everyone believing that he and Polly were dead, along with a good number of the local PnB chapter, and the chapter in Tidewater being no help at all due to its own problems, the S&S would have very little trouble taking over the PnB business down here.

They'd "patch over" what surviving members they thought they could trust, send some of the Nashville crew down to supervise, and take over the meth labs,

Chubby's, and whatever other PnB enterprises they wanted. *That* is what was worth five million bucks. It would have been a stunning coup, and nearly painless for the S&S.

But they never figured on a chance encounter with someone who would seize upon an accident and fuck up their entire world.

Jimbob looks around to see if everyone was paying attention, then continues, "It seems that when you called Chief with the wild tale about saving the cargo from some S&S members intent upon causing harm to his club, he went batshit. He called Slippy, and after a bunch of yelling and name-calling, was assured that nothing like that happened. Listening to them, Randy figured out that they were on to you pretty quickly, and were very upset when they couldn't lay their hands on you. They saw their time slowly slipping away to make this deal work. And, of course, there was the matter of the missing money."

We all share a chuckle at this. Judy reaches over and takes my hand, giving it a squeeze.

"So," says Kenneth, scratching his noggin, "they already knew Jonnybob was lyin' when we saw those assholes lookin' for him in Hazel Green. Man, I'm glad you were so damned careful, old buddy." He winks at me, and Judy moves her hand from my hand to my forearm.

"Okay," Jimbob goes on, "what I don't understand, and it may be nothing, but those two kept talking about Hammer's real name, how they'd had their crooked cops looking for him by that name in motels and the like. That name isn't Jonnybob Clark, or anything close."

He's looking at me, as is Rafe Bennett, waiting to see what other secret we've been keeping from them.

"Come to think of it, you told me and Momma that you two," Judy says, glancing at Kenneth then back at me, "had done some stuff to hide your identities, like that nonsense about calling Kenneth 'Junior,' even though we know his real name and nobody else around here does."

"My *real* name is Eric Thorssen," I say, "but I have the John Clark identity fully established, with papers, a bank account, and my van registered in that name, as well. Oh, shit! The cops are liable to have that name by now, if they ran my van through the DMV. Dammit!"

Bobby Ray pipes up, interrupting my worries with a small ray of sunshine. "Maybe not," he says. "The plate on it is registered to Raeann, and it belongs to a white Chevy van. I told her we were using it, so she won't be surprised if they contact her. I'll call her, see if she's heard anything." He picks up the phone and walks around the corner of the house.

"Okay, as I was saying," I say to those remaining at the table, "Chief doesn't know anything about the Clark identity, and neither does anyone outside this group. I've been damned careful about keeping myself hidden from them and everyone else who's looking for me. I thought the club in Virginia might've put some stuff together and called him to be watching for me, but it seems he's looking for me because of the S&S connection, not anything from up north."

Judy slips her arm through mine and asks, "So you're going to stay Jonnybob? Or will you go back to your original identity, if JB gets tied in with the fracas at Chubby's?"

Hell, I don't know.

"I guess it depends on a lot of different things that I can't control right now, so it will probably be a decision I need to make after things have played out."

Rafe and the others nod, and he looks me in the eye as he leans across the table. "If you need another ID package, I can set that up, and I can do the same for any of you that either needs or wants to have a spare identity for a rainy day."

The ridiculousness of the whole situation sinks in, and we all have a good laugh.

"I appreciate the offer, and may need to take you up on it," I say, "if things go completely to hell." Or if I give myself up, it won't matter. Of course, I don't voice this option. "Here comes Bobby Ray. Let's see what he found out, then we can figure out what to do next."

Bobby Ray leans up against the back of the house and hands the phone to Judy. "I think we'll be okay with the van," he says. "The cops called Raeann this morning, and asked her if she owns a white Chevy van. She told them she does, and they asked her if she knew where it was. She told them her brother had borrowed it and she hadn't spoken to him since. They told her it is at Chubby's, was vandalized last night, and needs to be moved or they'll have it towed. It doesn't sound like they have any interest in it other than that. I imagine the PnB crew played stupid, didn't admit to ever seeing it over there. The cops told her she should do something with it before long."

It sounds like we got a small break at last. We can use it.

"Judy," I say, "will you please call your momma and have her get in touch with Bob and see if he'll pick up the van and take it to his yard? If he will, that's one thing we won't have to worry about."

She nods, stands up, and heads into the house with the phone. Maybe we'll even find out what happened to Bo.

FIFTY-ONE

"Holy shit!" We all jump at Judy's exclamation, and turn toward the house. She appears at the back door with the cordless phone to her ear, and says, "Y'all have got to see this. Get in here and check out the TV!"

We all get up and troop into the house. Judy is still talking to someone on the phone, asking questions, and impatiently motioning for the rest of us to go into the front room of the house so we can see the television. Bobby Ray is the first one to appreciate what he's seeing.

"Damn," he says, "that is some serious shit right there."

He looks back at me as I enter the room and grins. On the screen is the ever-ubiquitous BREAKING NEWS banner as well as a box of text at the bottom of the screen proclaiming, "Meth lab crackdown nets fifteen arrests. More to come."

The scene on the screen is from earlier this morning, while it was still dark. The main focus of attention is a warehouse of some sort, with a motley assortment of vehicles parked just inside a fenced lot on the right end as we're seeing it. There are six or eight men lying face down on the sidewalk, cuffed and awaiting transportation. Between the light from multiple vehicles trained on the building's entrance and the lights from the news teams, the area is lit up quite well. Add in the red and blue strobes from the cop cars and fire trucks, and it's a circus of light.

There is, of course, a news bimbo in the foreground, telling everyone in an appropriately somber tone of voice, with just the right amount of outrage, how the DEA, as well as state and local law-enforcement personnel, raided this *alleged* meth lab at midnight in concert with raids at three other locations around the Rocket City.

In the background, some of the suspects are being helped to their feet and led toward a prisoner-transport truck. I don't recognize anyone, but that doesn't surprise me. The studio talking heads break in and are yammering with each other about the latest developments.

As we're all making remarks about what we are seeing, the studio news team is interrupted by someone in their headphones and the scene rapidly shifts to a shot of another nondescript concrete-block building surrounded by police cars. There are SWAT team members visible, and a reporter is hastily trying to get to a position where he can broadcast his on-the-scene segment without the cops shooing him away. The camera is shaky, and there is a sense of urgency in everyone's actions and body language.

"Turn it up!" hollers Dutton, and Bobby Ray cranks the volume up to full blast with the remote.

This male reporter is just as screwed up as his

female counterparts, trying to look and sound important, while, in actuality, he's just a source of background noise. The real attraction is at the front door of the warehouse, where a large, bald dude is holding a hostage tight up against him, an automatic handgun pointed at the hostage's head.

According to the reporter, the hostage was taken a few blocks from here during a shootout during the midnight raid at a suspected meth lab in south Huntsville. Police had been conducting a building-by-building search of the area, and as they entered this small industrial park, they were met by gunfire. According to the scrolling banner at the top of the screen, this standoff has been in effect since about nine a.m. The news-rookie looks like he might throw up he's so nervous. I'm guessing this isn't his regular gig. He appears to be listening to someone on his earpiece, and he blanches at what he hears.

"As Wilma and Reggie reported earlier, this group of suspects escaped capture during the raid on the suspected meth lab on South Triana Boulevard, shooting and killing three police officers in the process. They commandeered a car belonging to the DEA, killing the driver and taking the passenger hostage in the process. The driver, Agent Lenny Brewster of the New Orleans Field Division, was shot and killed in the car-jacking and the unidentified passenger was taken hostage in the ensuing escape."

Holy shit, things went seriously haywire. I thought

the feds would have very little trouble taking down the labs, seeing as how they had the element of surprise on their side.

The news-rookie continues, as he consults his hastily-scribbled notes while being very noticeably coached through his earpiece. "We have just learned that the hostage taken during the escape is a sergeant with the Virginia Beach, Virginia, Police Department, on loan to the hastily-formed task force responsible for the series of raids during the early morning hours in the Huntsville area."

Oh fuck!! I know what this guy's going to say next.

"The hostage is being identified as Sergeant Edwin Guffey, a narcotics officer with the Virginia Beach Police Department, who was largely responsible for the highly-successful campaign against the methamphetamine trade in the Tidewater area, especially the large-scale bust involving the Pist-N-Broke motorcycle gang."

Everyone is looking at me, and I have no idea what to say. This sucks. How in the fuck did Guffey end up as a hostage? He was supposed to stay back, just be an observer.

The scene on the screen is heating up. The person holding who we now know to be Guffey is shouting and gesturing at the nearest cops. He's digging the end of the pistol's barrel into Guffey's head, and I'm pretty sure I know what he's saying. He wants the cops to back off, or Guffey's toast. The cops aren't budging, and things are getting pretty tense.

Just then, the door opens behind the two of them and the guy holding the gun turns his head slightly to talk to someone inside. As he does, he presents just enough of a target for one of the SWAT snipers to take a shot. There's a sudden appearance of a red stain on the door behind the gunman and he stumbles back a step. He doesn't realize he's dead yet, and continues to hold Guffey around the throat. His weight keeps Guffey from getting a clean start, and he is slow to take advantage of his reprieve. Shit. Run, dammit!

The news-guy is babbling on, seemingly near hysterics, but I can't focus on what he's saying. I'm glued to the events unfolding on the screen.

The door opens a crack wider, and a stubby, evil-looking black machine pistol emerges from the opening. It bucks a few times, and I'm yelling, "Look out!" waiting for Guffey to stagger and fall. He falls forward onto his hands and knees but continues crawling, scrabbling toward the nearest cop car.

But there's no blood, no sign that he is hit. It looks like what I took for the gun in the doorway being fired was actually the gun moving as a result of the shooter being hit multiple times by rounds from the feds and police officers. He steps out into the small alcove surrounding the door, bloody and staggering, and starts spraying lead into the crowd.

The news-dope is now freaking out, squalling incoherently, but the cameraman is doggedly recording the action from behind what seems to be a stone planter.

Guffey is out of the view of the camera, so I don't know whether he's been hit or not by this latest barrage, but there's no doubt about the fate of the shooter in the doorway. He's riddled with bullets, and is only upright because he's up against the wall and can't fall down.

"Jesus!" Judy speaks eloquently for all of us.

This is something you don't see every day. There's a lull in the action, and I can hear the cameraman exhorting the news-chicken to show himself and get back to his job.

"We have just been notified that two of the suspects tried escaping out the back of this warehouse as the gunfight was raging here. They have both been shot, and the report is that they are both dead. It is currently unknown how many, if any, suspects are still inside the building. It is also unknown whether there are any other hostages inside."

The poor guy's voice is actually getting a little stronger as he goes, but he looks like hell. His hair is all jacked up from his time hiding under a car or somewhere. His shirt is dirty and has a good-sized tear on one sleeve.

The SWAT team appears to be massing for a frontal assault, just waiting for the go-ahead. Everyone seems to be holding their breath, including all of us in Judy's front room. Ronnie and Burt are right outside the screen door, listening to the events as they unfold. I can't blame them; I just hope at least one of them is watching the road.

While there is a lull in the action, we all start talking at once. Guffey is the topic of much of the discussion, and we're all trying to make sense of what we've just seen. I have more questions than answers, and it seems that is the case with the others, as well.

Clint What's-His-Name, the news-dope, is conversing with the crew in the News Suite (News Suite? Are you fucking serious?) about the events of the past few minutes, and rehashing the news from the early hours of this morning. They have a map superimposed on the screen, complete with flashing arrows and what look like little campfires. There are four arrows, and two of them are in pretty close proximity to each other in south Huntsville. The other two arrows, with some kind of whirligig action behind one of them, are west of Redstone, and are apparently in the neighborhood of the location of this latest shootout.

Wilma and Reggie are gushing on about this tragedy, while trying not to laugh at the killer ratings they're gonna get for this coverage. Reggie tilts his head, grabs his ear, and says, "We now return to Clint What's-His-Ass on the scene of this latest development, where it seems the SWAT team is preparing for an assault on the warehouse where the suspects have been holed-up."

We've all drifted to seated positions around the small room. We're all concerned, but content to watch the drama as it unfolds. Kenneth has even taken the time to wander into the kitchen for a plate of food during Wilma and Reggie's jabbering. Travis brings out glasses for everyone, and Bobby Ray fills them with tea and lemonade. It's almost like a weekend afternoon spent watching football with friends, except for the serious nature of the "entertainment".

As Clint the news-dope appears on the screen, it is apparent that things are ratcheting up in the action department. He has prudently backed off a few yards, and the scene behind him is one of controlled chaos. The cops have moved some vehicles into positions affording the personnel behind them more cover, and there are even more of the body-armored SWAT team members visible, obviously preparing for action.

"There are more officers and federal agents preparing to breach the rear of the building, aided by another dozen SWAT personnel," says Clint What's-His-Nuts, seeming to get more comfortable as he goes. "There haven't been any indications of other suspects inside the warehouse building, according to an unnamed source within the Huntsville PD," Clint informs us, in his best hush-hush, serious, news-guy voice, "and the DEA agent in charge is reportedly only moments away from ordering the assault on this building, known before this morning only as a storage facility for the local McGarrity's Greenhouse chain."

As we're all pondering this earth-shattering revelation, there is a tremendous noise and a huge dust/smoke cloud rises above the rear of the building. Clint the news-dope is holding onto his ear for all he's worth, trying to get his cameraman to follow him. The police, however, are telling him to stay put, in very forceful terms. There is general pandemonium, and the cameraman is doing his best to cover it all.

As he swings his camera back to the front of the building, the door opens and a man sprints into the alcove, carrying what looks like a machine gun. Actually, sprinting isn't quite correct. It appears that he was *propelled* from the door, not really in control of himself.

Dozens of gunshots ring out, and he is slammed against the wall where he slides down to almost the exact spot the former gunman came to rest. People are shouting, and the cameraman zooms in on the dead assailant. It appears that the gun has been taped into his hands.

Before anyone can react, another body, this one definitely in control of itself, barrels from the doorway. I'm struck speechless.

It's Slam, the former king of the meth labs in Tidewater, who I thought I'd seen incinerated on live television a few days ago. He's got a pistol in each hand, and is bellowing at the top of his lungs. He takes out a cop who is carelessly looking around a car fender and fires both guns at anything that moves until he is finally cut down. Amazingly, he makes it almost twenty feet from the door before he is stopped.

I don't know how he got away from that huge explosion in the swamps of Virginia, but he's not getting away this time. The sidewalk in front of the doorway, from the alcove to where Slam lies, is soaked with blood. There are what seems to be dozens of pock marks on the walls from bullets that missed their mark. There is smoke hanging in the air from all the gunfire, and I can imagine the smell of cordite.

Clint What-the-Fuck is babbling incoherently, and the cops all seem to be yelling at once. Nobody else comes through the door, and the SWAT team makes its charge. They file through the door, and everyone waits for a reaction from inside. There is now a plume of smoke visible from the loading area behind the building, billowing up over the rear of the warehouse.

The BREAKING NEWS banner is throbbing ecstatically, and Wilma is trying to get Clint's attention while Reggie is gesturing to someone off-camera.

After a few minutes, Reggie announces that the officer-in-charge has announced that the building is secure. No other suspects have been found, and the fire in the loading-dock area is under control.

Over the next few hours, the officials will put together the details of Slam's Last Stand, but we will be too busy to worry about them for quite a while. We can watch the TV later for details. I hope Guffey is going to be okay, but it's time to kick some ass while every cop in the whole damned area is busy, if we can figure out which ass to kick and where to find it.

FIFTY-TWO

The television is still murmuring in the background, and someone goes into the house every now and then to see if anything remarkable is happening. So far, the news seems to be the same as it was a couple of hours ago; five cops dead, Guffey shot in the ass and in fair condition at Huntsville Memorial, an unconfirmed number of SWAT team officers being treated for smoke inhalation and burns, sixteen suspects in custody, and seven dead suspects, all rumored to be PnB members. The man shot to death just before Slam charged out of his hiding spot has been identified as Phil Beegle, the manager of the McGarrity's operations. It seems he had stopped by the warehouse to pick up his motorcycle, which was stored inside. Still on the scene when Slam and his crew showed up with Guffey, he'd been made a second hostage. Four suspected meth labs were raided, one resulting in a three-alarm fire. No wonder the cops didn't give much of a shit about a van with a broken windshield and a couple of flat tires sitting behind a titty bar.

We've been discussing how best to proceed. There have been recommendations ranging from "just wait it out" to "let's go kick some serious ass." Kicking ass is currently enjoying a clear lead in the voting.

"We may never get another chance to act while all the cops are spread out and disorganized like they are right now," says Travis, leaning across the puppy to make a point. "We need to find whoever was at Donna's earlier and see who they are and what they know. If Chief and Polly are still around, they'll be looking for you," he says, looking at Judy and me, "and if they've hauled ass, we need to know that, too."

Bobby Ray is also on the ass-kicking side of the issue. "We've got the advantage," he says, "because they don't know who all they're looking for. They don't know that Hammer looks totally different from what they remember, and they sure as fuck don't know about any of the rest of us."

Not so fast, I think.

"Bobby Ray, they may be onto you and Travis." I look at Dutton, and he's slowly shaking his head back and forth.

I don't know whether he disagrees with my telling everyone about the Firebird, or is just sad about the circumstances.

Everyone looks at me quizzically, including Judy. I haven't told any of them about the Firebird, partly because we've been busy with other stuff. When I did think of it, I convinced myself it would keep until later. Well, it's later.

Starting with leaving Chubby's, I tell the others about Kenneth and me seeing the car bearing down on us, the subsequent trip across the countryside, my conclusion that they might be headed to Travis's or Raeann's house, the gun coming out of the rear window, and the spinning of the black 'bird into the slough.

There is complete silence when I'm done, and people are looking at me with varying emotions from admiration (Bobby Ray and Rafe) to something that could be disgust, or at least disappointment (Judy). It's hard to tell what the others think. Travis seems on the verge of saying something, but doesn't.

"I was going to wait until we heard who was in the car before I said anything," I tell them. "If it was some assholes connected to the PnB, I'll figger they were headed to Travis's or Raeann's and I won't lose any sleep over it. If it was someone just out haulin' ass across the countryside who wasn't in any way connected to our situation, I'll need to decide on a course of action at that point."

"Let me call Raeann and see if she can find out anything on the local news," Bobby Ray says, getting up from his seat on the ground. "She may have already heard about the wreck."

He picks up the cordless phone and heads into the house to call his sister. The rest of us don't have a lot to say, mostly waiting to see what, if any, news is out there about the Firebird running into the slough.

After about ten minutes, Bobby Ray is back, carrying a note pad. Consulting his notes, he relays what he found out from his sister. Raeann told him that the story has been big news on the local television and radio stations all morning. She tells Bobby Ray that, according to the latest reports, the driver of a late-model Pontiac Firebird headed westbound on Highway 67 at a high rate of speed lost control of his car and skidded into the median. At that point, the car began to roll, ejecting one of the passengers, who died at the scene. Damn, I didn't see anyone laying in the median, but I was concentrating on the slough, watching for evidence of the Firebird or its occupants.

The Pontiac continued to roll across the eastbound lanes of traffic, ending up in the slough, where it submerged. The other three occupants were trapped in the car and drowned.

The driver of the car was identified as Virgil Scott, 48, of Huntsville. The passengers were identified at the scene as Charles Stuart, 27, Keith Johnson, 29, and Beauregard Stults, 33, all of Huntsville. Stults was the victim who was ejected from the car as it rolled. Travis looks thoughtful at this news, nods his head a couple of times, but doesn't interrupt his nephew's recitation of the news.

There were no witnesses to the accident, but a driver coming up on the scene reported seeing a car stopped there as he approached from the west. The vehicle drove off before he could get close enough to get a good look at it. The newcomer saw the debris strewn across the roadway and stopped to see what had happened.

He had his window down and heard what sounded like someone moaning. He looked out the left side of his car and saw what he thought might be a person lying on the ground. He parked his car off the roadway and walked across to Stults and saw that he had apparently been crushed by the car after he was ejected from it. He was still alive. The motorist drove to the nearest convenience store and called the police, but Stults was dead before emergency medical personnel reached the scene.

The police searched the area with spotlights and discovered the Firebird in the slough. It was lying on its top on the bottom of the waterway. When it was winched out of the water, police found the other victims, as well as a large number of weapons and drug paraphernalia. The Police are still investigating, and asking for help from anyone with information relevant to the accident.

Thank God it wasn't a bunch of high school kids! I'm not sure I could live with the knowledge I killed a bunch of stupid kids. It's bad enough that four adults are dead at my hands.

Something is nagging at me. One of the dead guys was named Virgil. Chief told me Polly's brother Virgil was running Chubby's for the PnB. Could the dead guy be the same Virgil? If so, I'm not going to feel very bad. My original scenario about a PnB crew heading after Travis and Bobby Ray may have been right on the money.

"Do any of you know any of those names?" Judy is looking mostly at Travis and Bobby Ray, but also gives me and Kenneth a quizzical glance.

I'm about to mention my suspicion that Polly's brother might have been driving the 'bird when Travis pipes up.

"Three of those guys are PnB," he says, "Two of them have been to my place before, when I was painting a scooter for Pinto. His real name is—was—Keith Johnson. The other guy, the one who came out to the shop with him, was Charlie Stuart. I remember his last name because he swore he was related to Jeb Stuart, the Civil War hero. They were both a couple of dickheads, but Pinto's older brother Gayle is a buddy of mine, and asked me to do it for him." Travis looks across the table at Judy and continues.

"Virgil is the brother of that crazy bitch that Chief lives with. He's been running Chubby's for the club, and I've talked to him a few times. He's done some time, and he's a hard bastard." Travis stops for a drink of sweet tea before continuing. "I've heard stories about him doing some hits for the club. I've never seen any of them in a black Firebird, but that don't mean anything."

"Well, son," Kenneth starts in, scratching his melon, "I guess you don't have to feel real bad about runnin' those assholes off the road. You were right; they were headin' out to see if Travis was home. I wouldn't be at all surprised if that guy Pinto's brother hadn't mentioned that Bobby Ray's sister lived next door to where he got his bike painted. If this Virgil guy is as bad as he sounds, he might well have decided to ask her where to find Travis and Bobby Ray."

"For all of our planning and scheming, it doesn't seem like we were very far ahead of these guys," says Judy, reaching over and taking my hand in hers. "Somehow, someone recognized me, and they had a crew following Travis and Bobby Ray not long after they left."

"Lots of people came out to Donna's to see Jimmy before he went down, you told me." I'm talking to Judy, but I'm also thinking about what I'm saying, figuring it out as I go along.

"I guess it stands to reason that one of the crowd in the parking lot could have recognized either you or your mom when she showed up. That's how they knew to come out to Donna's this morning looking for you."

Travis chimes in, in that high-pitched voice of his. "That just means we need to finish this shit right away. We can't just hide out and wait for them not to be pissed off anymore.

"They don't know Hammer by sight, and they may not even know anything about Kenneth at all. Rafe and Jimbob are off their radar screen, and so are Ronnie and Burt. We have six people to do some snooping around and find those pricks."

"What about that other club, the one from Nashville?" asks Rafe, joining the discussion for the first time in awhile.

"If we take care of the PnB, will that be enough, or will we need to worry about those other assholes, too?"

That's a good question, but I think we are better off than we may know.

"If Slippy was running this deal with Chief pretty much on his own, we might be able to deflect any attention from the S&S by taking him out of the game."

I watch the others as I say this, looking for resistance to all of the violence we're proposing.

Rafe tips a look at Jimbob, who nods almost imperceptively. "Let me take care of this Slippy asshole. My treat. I have a number of associates in Nashville who would be happy to do me a favor. If we decide there are any more of his people who need dealt with, just let me know."

His grin is chilling. This guy is no lightweight, that's for sure. My estimation of Ronnie and Burt rises just a bit, thinking Rafe would most likely not put up with people who don't measure up, family or not.

I don't reply, but Rafe knows I'm in. He gives me a wink, and turns his attention to Judy. "I suppose I should tell you I posted a couple of my men at Donna's Place as we came by. They will stay in the background, be inconspicuous, but available if needed. They'll keep their eyes open, watching for anyone who seems to be paying too much attention. They'll page me or Jimbob if anything comes up."

Judy starts to say something, but Rafe cuts her off

with a wave. "I've known your momma for a long time, and I knew your daddy too." She looks surprised, but I'm not, really. "I'd hate to see her or any of her family or friends get hurt, so please let me help. They're good men, and won't let anything happen to your momma. I promise you that."

"I have to say, Rafe," I say, "that I'm really glad Jimbob brought you down here. Now that we know who was in the Firebird, I'm not gonna worry about that. It doesn't sound like anyone got a good enough look at us to cause us any trouble, and if we don't have to worry about Slippy, we can concentrate on Chief and his people."

"Jonnybob, you seem to be fergettin' somethin' old son." Kenneth is picking his teeth, leaning back in his chair. "There was one other old boy in that car, one that knew who you are, what you look like, and where you were gonna be last night."

What? Who, that guy that got killed? Who was he, and how did he know me? What was his name . . . Beauregard something . . . ? Oh, fuck!

"Bo," I say, wondering just where his uncle Bob stands in this affair.

God, I hate to think he was part of Bo's efforts to derail us. We need to warn Donna. Judy is already up and heading inside with the phone. The screen door slams behind her, drawing a yelp of surprise from Jesus, who was asleep on Travis's lap. Fuckin' dog.

FIFTY-THREE

While Judy's in another room talking to Donna on the phone, the rest of us move into the house and take up positions around the kitchen table. We've been talking about our next move. I keep kicking myself in the ass for not doing a better job of planning our efforts last night: I thought I'd covered all the bases, but it's apparent that I left some gaping holes. Luckily, none of our group got hurt or killed because of my fuckups.

With Rafe taking care of Slippy and the S&S, we can concentrate on making sure Chief and his crew don't pose a threat to Judy, Donna, or any of the other locals. Like Travis said, Kenneth, Jimbob, Rafe, his employees and nephews are all unknown quantities to the PnB. They haven't actually seen what I look like, so I can probably get close enough to factor into whatever we decide to do to them—as long as I'm careful.

We decide it will be best if Travis and Bobby Ray head home and change vehicles. The crowd at Chubby's saw Bobby Ray's truck this morning, so there's no need taking a chance on them recognizing it. They head out, saying they'll check in at Donna's on the way by and introduce themselves to Rafe's men so they'll know who all is on what team.

Rafe, Jimbob, Kenneth, and I are trying to figure out just how many people we may be dealing with, but without knowing Bob's loyalties or how many people Bo told my details to, we're mostly pissing in the wind.

Judy finally comes into the kitchen. She's turned the television off, and has made sure Ronnie and Burt have food and drinks. Rafe says they're used to waiting to be told what to do and they take directions really well. I tell her that Travis and Bobby Ray have gone for another vehicle, and she nods.

Judy grabs a clean glass and fills it with ice water. She scoots a chair up next to mine, and blows an errant lock of hair out of her eyes. She looks tired; hell, we all do. It's been a long day.

"Momma talked to Bob," Judy says, looking concerned, "early this morning, about the time you and Kenneth got back." She looks at me, to make sure I'm listening. "He called her, wondering where you were. Apparently, Bo called him about midnight and told him he was at the bar, all fucked up, and had forgotten that he was supposed to take the roll-back to that marina parking lot to meet you. Bob hurried out there in the roll-back and waited for a while, but never saw you. He saw the commotion at Chubby's and decided to drive by there. He saw Bo's car sitting at the end of the lot, next to the road, where he always parks." Judy's looking right at me, and I feel I'm missing something. "Bob got pissed and was going to go in and give Bo a piece of his mind, but a cop waved him off, so he turned into the parking lot across the street and went back to the marina lot. He waited another half-hour or so, then went home. He tried calling Momma at home and the bar until she answered."

So Bo didn't screw me up on purpose . . . maybe. I didn't tell him anything at all about where we were going to be or what we were going to do, so I'm pretty sure he couldn't have told anyone anything about our plans, other than my wanting to meet him. He didn't know my real name, where I'm from, what my plans were, any of that. He even thought the Malibu was still baby-shit yellow. None of us had told him anything that could cause us any trouble. I'm glad, seeing as how he hung out at Chubby's. But what was he doing with Virgil in the Firebird, if he wasn't onto us?

Judy takes a long drink of water and continues. "The car those guys were in, the Firebird, was Bo's. According to Bob, he almost never drove it because he always got in trouble in it. He figures Virgil needed a ride to chase down Travis after the fight in the parking lot, but Bo was too fucked up to drive, so Virgil was driving when you saw them. Virgil intimidated Bo, according to Bob. He would do anything Virgil told him to do."

Christ, what a mess! Bo may have gotten killed because he was too afraid to say no.

"Does Bob know how they got wrecked?" This is a good question, and I should have been the one asking it, not Kenneth. "Do we need to worry about his reaction along with all this other shit?"

I really hope we can get through this without destroying a bunch of life-long friendships. Where did things go so terribly wrong?

"Momma says," starts Judy, leaning back in her chair, "that Bob knows Bo was up to no good, and she thinks he has an idea that the wreck happened as a result of our plans, but it doesn't sound like he's blaming anyone other than Virgil, and Bo himself. He told Momma that Bo had been in and out of jail and trouble for years, that he couldn't seem to get his shit together for very long at a time."

He picked the wrong time to decide to hang out with Virgil and the boys this time. I've known a bunch of people who died or came to a bad end in much the same way. Hell, it's amazing it never happened to me, considering the life I've led for the last fifteen years or so.

"Okay," says Rafe, quietly asserting an air of authority over those of us sitting at the table. "We really need to hit these people as soon as we can. They think we're hiding from them, maybe even running away. They'll never expect an all-out attack against them. They probably think that the fire and all at Chubby's was totally unrelated to the lab busts. Why would they connect them? One was a federal operation and the other was caused by somebody setting their fireworks place on fire. A fight in the parking lot over a girl? Happens all the time, I expect."

The rest of us are nodding. He could be right, that I may not be connected in their minds to anything beyond fucking up their plans to get rich and haul ass.

"Not knowing just how involved Hammer is in any of this, they may even think the drug bust was a continuation of the trouble in Virginia." Rafe is on a roll, and I feel confident letting him go on. "They may just think they had a really bad night. It happens. There's nothing to tie the three events together, but the combination of the three events—four if you count four assholes dead in the Firebird—has got to have them shook up.

"Even if someone recognized Donna or Judy, I doubt they would tie them in with Hammer. There's no reason to. They probably think Donna and Judy are somehow related to the girl they took out of there, and their relatives and some unknown redneck helped them spring her. None of this is in any way related to the stuff Jonnybob found in the wrecked car or the scheme behind it. They've got to be reeling, and I feel now is the time to take advantage of that and hit them. Hit them hard."

I'm starting to feel a little better, hearing the facts from a different perspective. I've been thinking that everyone knows I'm involved in everything that has happened, when that's probably not the case at all. If I take myself out of the equation, there really isn't anything to tie all of the PnB's troubles together. As long as the PnB in Tidewater hasn't shown any undue suspicion about me, the only reason Chief would be looking for me is because I fucked up his retirement plans.

"With the PnB having its members identified in the

lab raids and the shootout this morning," says Jimbob, "I expect the remaining club members will be keeping a very low profile. The one place where we'll be able to find Chief and—what's her name—Polly?" Nods around the table. "Polly. They'll be having a wake somewhere for their fallen brothers. What remaining members they have will convene somewhere for a period of drinking, storytelling, and talk of revenge."

"You're right on," I say, looking around the table. "I've been involved in a few wakes like the one he's describing, and if we can find out where it is, we'll have them all in one spot. With them hiding from the law and the press, they won't be at their clubhouse or any of the normal places they would gather. Chubby's is out, the fireworks place is unusable, their labs are gone, Chief's house and the clubhouse are out of the question. We need to find someone who knows the club well enough to tell us where they'll go. There can't be that many other options they'd be comfortable with."

"Meanwhile," says Rafe, "I'll have my guys in Nashville making it hard for Slippy and his guys to pay attention to anything but their own safety." He gets up and takes the phone into the other part of the house.

I'm definitely glad Rafe is here to help, seeing as how the rest of us are amateurs at this sort of thing. After all of the planning and preparations that have gone badly, I'm doubting my abilities as a strategic thinker. But if Rafe's men can keep the S&S busy in Nashville, even I might be able to think of a way to deal with the remaining PnB crew—at least Chief, Polly, and whoever else was in on the plan to disappear with the cash and leave the rest of the club to deal with the S&S takeover.

Rafe comes back into the kitchen and sets the phone down on the table next to Judy's elbow. He's smiling, and seems relaxed, considering the stress the rest of us are feeling.

"I don't think we'll need to worry about Slippy or any of his people giving us any trouble," he says, turning his chair around and straddling the back of it as he scoots up to the table.

"The gentleman I called is checking to be sure, but there was a report on the news earlier about a bunch of assholes being arrested in Franklin after they refused to leave a bar when it closed. It seems the owner of the bar pulled a shotgun, and one of the assholes shot him in the back. Unluckily for the assholes, the owner's son was asleep upstairs. The son is also a deputy sheriff, and he called for backup before getting dressed."

Oh boy, if the assholes in question were Slippy and his boys, they're even dumber than I thought.

"A state patrolman saw the van leaving the bar and gave chase. The people in the van fired a few gunshots at him, but didn't hit anything. A couple of sheriff's office cars joined in, and they finally herded the van into a spot where they had some spike strips laid out. They gave up fairly easily after that, and nobody else got hurt. The bar owner should live, and his son got winged, but should be okay."

Holy shit! What a bunch of morons . . . all of that because of not wanting to leave when the bar closed.

"My informant says the news identified the assholes in the van as Spikes & Spokes Motorcycle Club members, including Albert 'Slippy' Green and other club officers. They're all in the county jail, being held without bail under attempted murder charges, for now. Even if they bail out later, they shouldn't be a problem for us."

Far out! If this proves to be true, it's just one less thing to worry about. Slippy may still come after me later, but he doesn't have any idea about the others helping me, so if I get out of the area, they should be safe.

"Anyone have any idea where to find someone who might know a place the PnB might be holing up, holding their wake?" Jimbob looks tired as he says this. He may not have gotten any sleep at all, by the way it sounds. "If we can find them while they're all in one place, while the S&S are occupied with their own problems, we may be able to take care of business all at once."

The phone rings, making most of us jump. Judy picks it up and answers tentatively. "Hello?"

I imagine its Donna, checking up on us, or Travis and Bobby Ray checking in from Donna's Place on their way back from Decatur.

"What? When? Stay put and we'll be right there."

Oh, fuck. What now? This can't be good news.

"That was Sammy. Jason got drunk and was talking shit about finding the people that kicked his ass. Everyone figured he was just talking shit, until he left with one of the local idiots about five minutes ago. Jason was talking about how he knew where to find them, and was going to go make them sorry they fucked with him."

Fuck! If Jason actually has an idea of where to find the PnB, we could use that info to do something about it. Jason and some drunk will just get hurt, more than likely—and make the PnB aware that people know where they are. Double fuck!

Rafe's pager goes off, and he looks at the number. "I need the phone," he says, moving toward the handset. "That was my guy at Donna's."

He dials the number, and whoever is on the other end answers immediately.

"What's going on?" Rafe listens for a minute or two, then says, "Hang on to them, and we'll head over there. Get some coffee into them, and keep them somewhere quiet until we get there." He listens again and smiles. "That'll work. See you in a few."

Looking at the rest of us, Rafe says, "That was Petey, one of my guys at Donna's. When the dishwasher drove off with his buddy, he and Lenny heard the bartender and the cook talking about what was going on. They were trying to decide what they should do when the dishwasher's buddy came back in, looking for his cigarettes."

Thank God for drunk smokers!

"My guys grabbed him up and went out and grabbed the dishwasher, too. The bartender and the cook knew my guys were there to help, so they showed them a place to keep the two drunks until we get there. They put them in a cage in the garage, some place where they keep tools locked up or something."

Judy laughs, and it's a great sound. "That's the cage where the mechanics lock up the tools that are too big to fit in their toolboxes. Big drills, air tools, that sort of thing. As long as Jason and his buddy don't tip something heavy over on themselves, they should be fine."

"Let's get down there and see what Jason's got to say." I'm up and trying to decide what I need to take with me. "If he actually knows where the PnB might be, we can take a look. If we find them, we can decide what to do next."

If I have my way, this will be the last time I deal with the PnB.

Once everyone has gathered up their gear and we're all outside, I get Judy and Kenneth headed to the Malibu, then turn to Jimbob, who's scratching Jesus between the ears.

"Race you to Donna's," I tell him, running for the ugly-ass old Chevy.

We're all laughing like loons as we slide out onto the lane, spraying gravel everywhere.

FIFTY-FOUR

Judy suggested that we let her and Donna talk to Jason before the rest of us scare the shit out of him, and I agreed that this was probably the way to go. The two of them, along with Sammy and Kenneth, have been in the shop for about twenty minutes, and the rest of us are killing time impatiently. Rafe, Jimbob, and I are in Donna's office, along with Travis and Bobby Ray, who drove into the lot at the same time we did. Ronnie and Burt are in the bar, munching on a couple chickens, while Rafe's other guys watch for trouble. We are also having some supper in the form of a huge pot of beef stew, corn on the cob, and mashed potatoes smothered in gravy. Kenneth's gonna be pissed when he finds out we all ate without him.

Conversation has been fairly sparse, as we all are waiting to see if Jason actually knows anything important or if he was just spouting shit. Travis and Bobby Ray showed up in an old Ford pickup, which they told us is used mainly for "chasing parts". It's a dirty, off-white color, and is about as inconspicuous as a vehicle can get. It's also the polar opposite of Bobby Ray's shiny loud Dodge.

Taking into account Jimbob's Regal and the supercharged Thunderbird Rafe's boys brought down, we have a pretty good supply of vehicles the PnB shouldn't be familiar with. Travis's job on the Malibu makes it a real sleeper, too, so we have at least four vehicles to use for reconnaissance and information-gathering purposes. Travis and Bobby Ray said they had thought of bringing their bikes, but decided against it for the simple reason that they were too recognizable.

As we're discussing our options, the back door of the office opens and Kenneth comes in, gnawing on a huge steak sandwich. He swallows and grins at me, making me remember just how much I like this goofy guy.

"Jason finally decided to listen to Donna and Judy after quite awhile of talkin' macho bullshit. It sounds like he actually might know something of value, so they're gonna get him a bite to eat and some more coffee, then bring him up here so we can talk to him. If it wasn't for those women, I'm not sure he would've told us anything. He's determined to kick some ass."

I can sympathize with him, but he's obviously not in any condition to attempt any retribution, not to mention that he's seriously out-manned.

Dutton makes short work of the sandwich and grabs a bowl of stew. The rest of us are pretty much through eating, and the plates and stuff have been stacked in a pile on the table against the wall. It seems as though this whole mess hasn't affected any of our appetites much.

After another twenty minutes or so of small talk, the back door opens and Judy comes in, followed by

Jason and Donna. Jason looks like hell. Those assholes worked him over pretty damned well. I can tell he's pretty hammered, but the food and coffee seem to have at least made him ambulatory. At least he's not stumbling around and pissing his pants.

Judy walks over and takes my hand in hers, leans up and kisses me on the cheek. She whispers, "Jason sounds like he knows where Chief's hiding, and wants to help us take him down. Let him tell it his way, and I'm sure we'll get whatever he knows out of him. Just don't lean on him too hard. He's feeling pretty stupid already."

I nod, reluctantly disengage my hand, and walk over to where Jason is standing, looking embarrassed.

"Jason, I want you to know we all appreciate your taking a beating without giving those PnB assholes any idea of where we were." He starts to say something, but I wave him off. "You have a right to be there when this thing happens. If you can tell us where to find Chief and the others, we'll make sure you're there to help."

I don't say it, but the most help he can provide would be staying out of the way. We'll figure out a way to include him without making him a liability, if possible. If not, he'll just have to get over it or get used to it. He won't be the first person I've lied to, after all.

Donna sits down at her desk, and she looks like hell, too. I guess she must be worried sick about Judy, Jason, and the rest of her people. Hopefully, things will get back to normal for her soon.

Jason looks up and says, "I'll do whatever I can to help. I *am* pretty fucked up, though."

Good. At least he recognizes the fact he's impaired. Too many drunks feel ten foot tall and bulletproof.

"I know where they are . . . at least I knew where they were a couple hours ago. There's an old ice plant out southwest of Arab, about a quarter of a mile from my Aunt Sally's place. The PnB bought it a while back from my uncle Donnie. He was kinda curious about who was buyin' it, seein' as how they tried so hard to stay anonymous. But Lester Greenwald, the realtor, told Uncle Donnie the PnB was behind it."

Well, well, well . . . could this be another lab the feds missed? Or is this another "storage facility" for the club?

Jason continues. "The price was right, so Donnie sold it to them. He says he almost never sees any sign of 'em, except for a couple guys who live in an old trailer beside the big building."

No traffic? That doesn't make any sense. What the hell are they up to out there?

Judy speaks up, looking like the light just went on. "Of course. Jimmy told me about a place the club bought to hold motorcycle shows, rallies, swap meets, that sort of thing. They bought the place, then the locals refused them a business license or some such deal. It was a few years back, and I'd forgotten about it completely. It would be a good out-of-the-way place to stay out of sight, especially if they moved out there a couple people at a time, and not on scooters. It would be the perfect place for their wake."

"Yeah, an old ice plant would have plenty of room to park cars and trucks," says Kenneth, perking up. "There might even be room to park inside, so nobody would pay any attention."

"Wait a second!" says Travis, scratching his beard. "So they own an old building out in the middle of no-where . . . what makes us think they're actually there?"

Good point. Here I go again, jumping ahead of myself. I really don't seem to be so good at this shit.

Jason stands up from the chair he'd sunk into. "I was going to tell you, but things got going and I forgot. I saw Chief's Blazer and that Ford crew-cab that Pickle and those other fuckers were in. They were parked out back, next to that trailer house."

"How the hell did you see them, Jason?" This is Bobby Ray, looking pissed off. "You just happen to be driving around Arab, looking for the PnB hidey hole?"

It *does* seem a bit of a stretch to think Jason just happened to see the people who beat him up parked out in the country behind an old abandoned building 40 miles away.

"I know it sounds like I'm making it up," says Jason, looking pleadingly at us, "but I tell you I saw them. I took Mom out to Aunt Sally's earlier, after I got my ass kicked, just wanting to get the hell away from here. I was out behind the barn toking on a joint, just trying to mellow out, when I looked across the field between Sally and Donnie's place and the old ice plant. I saw some vehicles over there, which is pretty rare. Donnie was in his shop, working on an old tractor so I just casually asked him if someone else had bought the old ice plant. He said he wasn't aware of it selling, that nobody would want it until the county got their heads out of their asses and let whoever had it get a business license."

Okay, it does sound far-fetched, but weirder shit has happened—this morning, to be precise.

Jason looks around the room, trying to tell if any of us believe him. "Donnie has an old .223 rifle he carries around for shootin' varmints—it has a little scope on it. I asked him if I could use it for a minute, and he said sure, as long as I didn't shoot anyone. He thought that was funny, but he didn't know why I wanted to look." Good thing nobody was outside, or Jason might've given them a big surprise. "I looked through the scope and recognized the Blazer and that Ford crew-cab from the descriptions that old guy gave Darla. Nobody was out there. I waited for a few minutes, until Donnie said he was going back inside and was going to take the rifle with him."

The more I hear, the more I'm inclined to believe Jason's tale. Talk about a coincidence! I'm really glad he didn't go poppin' shots at the place. Maybe we can sneak up on 'em.

"Did you tell your mom or anyone about what you

saw?" Rafe asks, taking it all in.

"Nossir, I didn't say anything to any of them. I just told Mom I didn't feel too good and wanted to go home and take a nap. We went home, and I started drinking some Jack out of a bottle in my room. The more I drank, the madder I got. I called Louie and had him come get me, and we came here. We kept drinkin', and I just got more and more pissed off. We were gonna go out there and do something, but we didn't even get out of the driveway before those Tennessee guys snatched us up and locked us in the tool crib in the garage."

It's a good thing, too. He and his buddy would've probably gotten killed, and the PnB would know they'd been spotted.

The rest of us take a few moments to think about what we've heard. No matter how improbable, I believe Jason's telling us the truth. Now we just need to hope our luck holds long enough to allow us to do something about this new information.

"You know, the more I think about it," says Jimbob, who's been quiet up until now, "I think the club came out here to find Judy because of the stuff that happened out behind Chubby's; the fight, Shirley getting away, and that asshole gettin' his private parts custom engraved. That's why they never showed up at Judy's house. They were in a hurry to head down to their hidey hole.

"They may have been going out to see the place

Virgil and those other guys drove into the slough, then over to Arab to lie low. This was on the way, and they probably thought they'd find Judy and try to find out what her part in the festivities had been. I don't see them tying all of the morning's events together. I know what happened, and I have a hard time believing that a small group of people caused all that damage in that short a period of time."

I hear you, I think to myself.

"I guess we need to decide what it is we want to accomplish," continues Jimbob, "if they're still there when we get there. It's been a long day, and they may be feeling pretty safe right about now. Are we gonna just go in there and kick ass on everyone we see? Or are we going to target this guy Chief and his old lady? I think we need to act right away, so let's get a plan together and do it."

It has been a long day, for us as well as the PnB, but I really have to agree with Jimbob's assessment. We need to do this right, do it once and for all. I take a few moments to look into myself for some direction; how far are we willing to go? I can't see picking and choosing targets, because that will just slow us down, and hesitation could get someone killed.

"Okay. You're absolutely right, as far as I'm concerned," I tell Jimbob, taking the time to look everyone at the table in the eye, looking for dissention. I don't see any, so I plunge ahead. "I think we should hit them hard, as hard as we can. I don't consider anyone there to be innocent. They've been planning to kill their own members, as well as some civilians, to make their escape, not to mention the meth they make and sell to people around here. Then there are the girls like Shirley, who they turn into hookers and addicts to line their pockets."

Rafe winces at my terminology, but looks as if he's more determined than before to inflict some serious damage. Good.

"We can't let the fact Polly is a female stop us or slow us down, either. She's a dangerous bitch, and heartless as anyone I've ever met."

This is something I think might bother some of our bunch; the violence against a woman, or women. But nobody voices any objections, so I continue. "This started out as me against the club, but now we have a pretty formidable team. I can't imagine they have any idea what they're up against. I honestly feel we can swoop in there and finish this. If we can take out Chief, Polly, and the others involved in the plan to take the S&S money and run, I really think we'll be home free.

"Rafe's men are watching the S&S, but it sounds like they'll be tied up for a pretty long period of time. By the time they get out of jail on bail, things here will be over. Slippy won't have anything to go on, as far as tracking Hammer and his money. He won't like it, but I can't see him coming down here, breaking his probation. So if he comes at all, it'll be later."

By then I hope to be long gone, along with any

memories of the people in this room being in any way involved with today's activities.

"The PnB lost some people today, and have a bunch in jail over the lab busts, so there can't be many of them in Arab. Their main problem is their attitude; they feel invincible. They will be feeling less so after the stuff that happened earlier today, but they will be thinking they're safe in their hidey hole. That will help us a lot." People are nodding at me, and Judy gives my hand a squeeze.

Rafe leans across the table and asks, "Does anyone have a good county map of that area? If we can get a good idea of what kind of terrain and how many houses there are, we can get a basic plan of attack that will minimize the chances of us getting caught or hurting any innocent locals asleep in their beds."

That's a *really* good idea. It reminds me of something I thought of earlier.

"Rafe, I'd like you to take charge of planning this deal." I hold up my hand to forestall his objections and keep right on talking. "My planning has shown itself to be pretty weak. I've had to abandon about half the plans I made. A lot of my big ideas turned out to be wastes of time and energy. I'm really not the strategic thinker I thought I was when this started. It's a lot more difficult than I imagined to plan and execute something like this without things going to hell."

Nobody says anything, but I'm sure at least a couple of them know I'm right; they've seen the results of my mistakes and bad decisions.

"I'll do it if you really want me to," says Rafe, "but I'd be more comfortable using my guys, mostly. They all work well together, and have proven to be good at this sort of thing. I don't for a second believe y'all will stay out of it, but I'll want my guys to be the first ones in the door. Once we're inside, the rest of you can come in and do whatever you think you need to do. Is it a deal?"

He holds his hand across the table and I grab it. I also wince a little, forgetting to steel myself against his formidable grip. I look around the room, and it seems we have everyone's approval. Good. So, back to his original question.

"Good. Donna, do you have a map around here that might help us? Something that has all the county roads and as much detail as possible?"

She looks perplexed, trying to think. Jason steps over to the table and holds up his hand, like he's asking permission to speak.

"If we can just find a road map, I can fill in as much detail as you want. I spent a lot of my days as a kid out there at Sally and Donnie's running around the fields and all. I know where the ditches are, where the houses and other buildings are, which ones to avoid and which ones are empty. I also know the layout of the ground around the ice plant, so I can show you the best way to sneak up on it."

I'd almost forgotten about Jason, but he just

proved his worth to this undertaking. If he can fill us in on details about the area around the target building, his contribution won't be able to be ignored. We can keep him out of the way and still allow him to feel like he helped.

"I have a good map in the glove box of the parts chaser," says Travis in that high-pitched voice of his, getting up and heading for the door. "I'll be right back."

While he's gone, people stand, stretch, and a few take turns heading to the restrooms in the dining area. Judy has her arm around my waist, and mine is around her shoulders. The embrace feels natural, comforting.

Everyone looks tired, but Donna really looks whipped. Judy disengages herself from me and walks over to Donna's desk and talks quietly to her for a couple of minutes. Donna nods, gives Judy a grateful smile, gathers up her purse, and comes over to where I'm standing.

"You watch out for yourself, Jonnybob—or whatever you call yourself whenever this is over. And take care of Judy . . . I'd be lost without her."

I promise to do all I can to keep all of us safe, and she heads out to her car.

Travis returns with a map. We pick up the dirty plates and silverware and take them to the kitchen. Dutton is munching on whatever he can find, and gives me a big grin. What a great friend he is, I'm thinking. I bring all this into his life, and he just deals with it, all because of me. I'll never measure up as a friend anywhere near as good as this guy.

Rafe has cleaned off the desk and has the map spread out across it. Jason is leaning over it, getting his bearings. I want to get a good idea of what's going to happen, but then I'll get out of the way and let Rafe show his guys the map and make their plans. This day may finally be coming to an end that we can all live with.

\

FIFTY-FIVE

Judy, Kenneth, and I are sitting in a booth at Jill's Cake and Steak in Arab, trying to stay calm while we wait for midnight. This little joint closes at midnight, and the waitress keeps glaring at us, clearly wishing we'd leave and let her get a start on getting out of here. Kenneth is still working on his second piece of pecan pie while Judy and I nurse sweet tea.

"That little gal," says Kenneth between bites, "is shorely wishin' we'd get the hell out of here."

You think? She's been just barely civil for the last twenty minutes or so, but we really don't want to leave and drive around this burg to kill time.

We're supposed to meet Travis and Bobby Ray at the junction of County Road 1815 and Barma Road, just south of where Jason's aunt and uncle live. Jimbob gave us his pager and we'll head to the old ice plant from there when we get the signal. We just need a few more minutes before we head that way, if the surly teenager doesn't throw us out before then.

The cook is on the phone—arguing with someone, from what I can tell. She calls the waitress into the kitchen and there are voices raised, a serious difference of opinion. The snotty girl starts banging around, cursing under her breath, making up a bunch of to-go boxes. So that's the problem. Somebody waited even later than us to call in an order. At least it takes us out of her crosshairs for awhile.

"Probably some of the bar crowd wanting some chow to take to a party," says Dutton, and Judy nods her agreement.

It's a bummer for the waitress, but she'll just have to wait another few minutes before hauling ass to meet her boyfriend.

"Or someone at a party realized it's almost midnight and called before this place closed. I didn't see any other options for food, other than a couple of convenience stores," says Judy, who seems to be somewhat sympathetic toward the girl's plight. I guess waitresses stick together.

The smell of burgers and fries is getting heavy and Kenneth looks like he's thinking about asking for some. I get his attention and shake my head forcefully in the negative.

"If you focus her attention back on us, I'll stick a fork in your eye," I tell him.

Not really kidding. It's pretty nice having her anger aimed elsewhere. He barks out a laugh, drawing a dirty look from the little snot.

I give him the stink-eye, and he at least has the good sense to not laugh out loud any more. Judy is giggling into her napkin.

We get our shit together and quietly spend the next fifteen minutes avoiding little miss snotty's glares. Judy says she's going to visit the restroom before we head out, and Kenneth volunteers to escort her.

As they're turning into their respective destinations, the front door opens with a tinkle from the bell over it. A big dude in jeans and a black t-shirt enters, followed by . . . Polly. Oh, fuck! I start to panic, but remember she has no idea what I look like. The short hair and beard, coupled with the nondescript clothes I'm wearing help me look like just another redneck out for a late meal with his friends.

The big guy looks me over pretty well, but doesn't seem to see anything that bothers him. Polly is being her normal self, acting as though the waitress and cook should bend over and kiss her ass. She's making the young girl add more plastic bags of sporks and knives to the bags, and is badgering her for more ketchup. She didn't even give me a second glance when they came in.

Polly pays the bill, and the big guy is standing by the door, ready to head outside, with both hands full of bags overflowing with food. Where are Kenneth and Judy? We might be able to get the jump on them if we catch them in the parking lot with their hands full.

Just as the snot gives Polly her change, Kenneth comes ambling back to the table. Polly and the gorilla are talking about something, and she's not very happy. She finally helps him set the bags on the table closest to the door and tells him to hurry the fuck up.

He takes off at a near run for the restroom, and Polly is just standing there fuming. She keeps looking out the window next to the door. Is she watching for someone? Or is she just nervous? I can't believe she's very concerned, or she wouldn't have gone out in public to make a burger run. Unless she needed to get out of the others' sight to do something. Who's the big dude? By his age, I'd guess he's a prospect, sent along to do whatever Polly tells him to do.

Making up my mind, I ease to my feet and head over to the pay phone by the restrooms. I stand there for a few seconds, until Polly looks back outside. I try the restroom door, and it's unlocked. Must be a two-holer. I enter the room, and find it empty—almost. The stall door is closed. The gorilla must've had a gastric disturbance. In a couple seconds, that will be the least of his worries.

I take a leak and turn on the water in the sink to wash my hands. The sound of the running water masks the sound of pulling my shirt tail up and easing my nine mil out of my waistband. I slide it behind my belt in front, where I can reach it easily. The sounds coming from the stall are disturbing. I don't know what this guy's been eating, but I don't want any.

The moans and cries slowly abate, and the toilet is flushed. I ease over by the side of the door without the hinges, so I'll have a good shot at him as he exits the stall. I hear the latch slide back, and the door starts to open. He's got his back to me, grabbing a handful of toilet paper from the roll. I bring the automatic out and stick the end of the barrel right behind his left ear.

"Don't," I tell him, jabbing the barrel forcefully

into his head. "Not a fuckin' word, asshole." I'm using Hammer's enforcer voice, and it works, as it usually does. The guy is off balance, with his knees up against the toilet bowl. I've got his weight pushed forward so his hands are against the walls of the stall and he can't regain his balance.

"Is anyone else out in the car?" I'm whispering, but still with enough force in my voice to get his attention. He shakes his head no, but keeps his mouth shut. "What's Polly up to? How come she came into town with you?"

He seems shaken that I know her name. I jab the auto into his head again and say, "Quietly, asshole. Answer my fucking question."

"She wanted to make a phone call," he says, barely above a whisper. "I don't know who to. She had me let her off at the Kwik Stop, and was on the phone for a couple minutes. Then we came here."

I'm running out of time, and I know it. Any second Jolly Polly will be beating on the door, wanting to know where her pet gorilla is.

"Sorry," I tell him, and crack him a good one right behind the ear with the barrel of the gun. He goes down like he's been hit by a truck. I manage to make him slump over the stool so I can get the door closed behind him.

As I leave the restroom and head back to the table, I can see Judy and Kenneth with their heads together. By the look on Judy's face, I assume she recognized

Polly. They're both looking at me as I head to our table, and I'm bound and determined to reach them without giving the petite bitch any reason to pay any attention to any of us.

"Hey, bud," she says to me, putting an end to that fantasy, "is my friend okay in there?"

She inclines her head toward the restroom, which I see as I glance her direction from the corner of my eye. If I ignore her, it will only make it worse.

"He's pretty sick," I say, reaching our table and reaching for my wallet. Kenneth takes the hint and gets up, pulling his wallet from his pocket. Judy senses something is up and puts a few bills on the table.

"I got it," she says, pointing to the bills on top of our dinner ticket. Dutton and I both reverse directions, sliding our wallets back into our pockets.

"Sick? Whattaya mean, sick? He just said he needed to shit." Good old delicate Polly. She's looking right at me, but doesn't seem suspicious, just pissed.

"It must be something he ate," I shrug, trying to keep her from getting too close a look at my face. "He's throwin' up his socks."

Kenneth laughs, and the snotty little waitress looks seriously disturbed. Cleaning the restrooms is probably her job.

We need to get moving, because it's hard telling how long the gorilla will be unconscious. I don't need him coming to, bellowin' at Polly while we're still here.

"He seemed to be taperin' off a little," I tell her as

we try to slide past her and out the door.

Polly looks pissed, but doesn't seem to know quite what to do next. What happens next boggles my mind.

Judy heads down the little hallway to the restrooms, calling over her shoulder, "We can't just leave him in there. What if he chokes on his own puke?"

What? Why do we care? That would be a good thing, for all I care. Polly takes off after her, not at all happy at this turn of events.

"Wait a second, dammit," she says, trying to catch up with Judy. "He's with me. Let me check on him. No need for you to go bargin' in on him if he's sick."

Maybe she's afraid someone will call the cops if they suspect an overdose. Maybe she just hates being upstaged. For whatever reason, she pushes past Judy into the men's room, hollering.

"Tiny!" Of course his name is Tiny. No surprise at all. "What the fuck is wrong with you, you big tub of lard?"

She's so tender, so warm and fuzzy. Tiny doesn't answer, and she walks right up to the stall door. I couldn't lock it from the outside, so all she needs to do is pull on it.

"Jonnybob," Judy says, looking at me with a piercing glance, "go get the car and bring it around to the back door."

What? What the fuck is going on? I walk to the end of the little hallway and try the knob on the door that leads outside. It's unlocked, so I open the door and head out into the parking lot. I hear female voices being raised behind me.

I don't know what Judy has in mind, but I need to trust her. She's pulled my ass out of the fire a couple of times, and has proven to be damned smart. I just hope whatever she's got planned works, for all of our sakes.

We had parked out back, so it isn't very long before I return to the back of the building and jump out of the car. I realize the place is dark; all of the lights seem to be off, except for a light over the back door. As I'm heading around the front of the Malibu, the back door opens, and Judy shoves Polly through it. Judy has Polly's braid in her left hand and her hand-cannon in her right. Polly's left eye is swollen damned near shut, and her nose is bleeding copiously. Kenneth brings up the rear, huffing and puffing, pushing the door closed behind him.

"Grab the door," Judy tells me, pointing at the passenger side of the Malibu. I open the door and Judy shoves Polly into the back seat, following her in. "Come on, let's go!"

Kenneth and I jump into the car, and we're out of the parking lot heading west on Cullman in a few seconds. Just when I think things might go as planned, stuff goes completely haywire. Judy has taken over, and I just need to go along until I can figure out what the fuck's going on.

I'm trying hard not to speed. We really don't need to be pulled over right now. I exit the town proper, and when we get to the intersection with Hulaco Road, I hang a left onto Barma Road. Now I can open it up a little, and I do, driving down the dark road at about sixty. We pass Jason's Uncle Donnie's house and continue south to the stop sign at County Road 1815, where I pull off into a little turn-out. Travis is parked there in the old Ford parts chaser, and he and Bobby Ray are outside, leaning against the grille.

They are both starting to speak when Judy drags Polly from the car and pushes her onto her hands and knees in the dirt. Polly starts to protest, but Judy bounces her head off the ground and tells her to shut the fuck up. I've never seen Judy like this, and it's a revelation. She's as tough as anyone I've ever known, and although she is normally a rational, even compassionate person, I see now that she has a capacity for violence. Hopefully, it won't ever be directed at me.

Kenneth comes over to where I'm standing, and he's all shook up. "She killed him," he says, watching the two women in the light spilling from the interior of the Malibu.

"Judy? Killed who?"

Hell, now I'm really starting to freak out. Has Judy finally snapped? Are we going to be forced to do something with her? Shit, shit, shit!

"Not Judy," says Dutton, his eyes wide and still short of breath, "Polly. That big boy started to tell us something, and Polly just pulled a fuckin' razor out of her pocket and cut his throat. Jesus, Ricky, that bitch just opened up his windpipe, quick as you please."

Holy shit! Now what have we gotten ourselves into?

"Judy," he continues, "acted right away, smacking that bitch in the face with her pistol, then swinging her by her braid into the sink. I figger she's got some broken ribs, the way she slammed into that thing. Christ, I was tryin' not to puke, and Judy's kickin' ass!"

"What about the cook and waitress?' I ask Kenneth this, fearing the worst. I can almost hear sirens heading west on Cullman looking for the crazy bastards that killed a man in the shitter of Jill's Cake and Steak.

He swings around to watch Judy yank Polly to her feet by her hair. If she lives through this, I wouldn't be surprised if she shaves her head. That fuckin' long hair makes a hell of a handle.

"They're fine," Kenneth says, "although they're gonna have one hell of a story to tell. That young'un came down there to the head, hollerin' at us about her needin' to get the place cleaned up. As she made the turn into the bathroom, she got a good look at that ol' boy bleedin' all over the floor, not to mention Judy pounding the shit out of that blonde bitch. That little girl just kinda sighed and her eyes rolled up in her head. I grabbed her before she hit the floor, but she was out like a light." At least that shut her up.

"Judy hollered at the cook, told her we had a medical emergency. As that gal came down the hall, Judy pointed her gun at her and told her to stop right there and not make a fuckin' noise. By then I was starting to get my shit back together, so I ran past the cook and locked the front door. Thank God there wasn't anyone out there. I turned off all the lights and turned the sign to CLOSED. I saw the walk-in cooler behind the kitchen and yelled at Judy. She told the cook lady to help me get the kid into it, and I shoved the two of 'em in there and shut the door. There's a hole in the latch where they put a bicycle lock to lock it up, so I locked 'em in. They'll get plumb cold, but at least they won't be callin' the cops for a while. I turned on the inside light, and turned the thermostat to the warmest setting."

Well, at least they won't freeze to death, hopefully. By the time someone thinks to come looking and finds Tiny, we just might be far enough away to stay out of it.

"Judy was hollerin' at me, so I ran down the hall and we went out the door. You know the rest."

His breathing is almost back to normal, and he gives us a sickly smile. Travis and Bobby Ray came over to listen in to his tale, and are trying to decide whether they should be smiling or not.

I hear Polly making some protesting sort of noise, and turn to look over to where Judy has her up against the tailgate of the Ford.

Judy has found some electrical wire, and is tying Polly's hands together with it. Polly obviously is badly hurt; she's having a hard time catching her breath, and her eye is now completely closed. Her nose is probably broken, and there is quite a bit of blood down the front of her clothes.

"Who . . . who are you people?" she stammers, talking through the blood and swollen tissue. "Why're you doin' this to me? What did I ever do to you anyhow?"

Judy backhands her across the face so hard, my head moves in sympathetic reaction.

"Shut up, you worthless bitch! You have one chance to keep your worthless life, and you'd better listen close." Judy is holding Polly by the neck, and has her face right up in front of Polly's. "I didn't know that man back there, but I do know he didn't deserve to be slaughtered like a pig. I also know the people you and Chief planned on dressing up in your clothes and killing didn't deserve whatever you have planned for them."

Polly is visibly shaken by this. She may have been scared before, but the look on her lumpy, bloody face is now one of pure terror.

"I . . . we . . . you . . . don't know what you're talking about," Polly says, looking wildly from face to face. There is no sympathy in view, and she's getting desperate. "Let me go . . . I'll . . . keep—keep my mouth shut, but you've got to . . . got to let me go."

Good luck with that, you goofy bitch.

Judy grabs a handful of Polly's hair and jerks her damned near off her feet. "Listen to me, Polly." Judy isn't yelling any longer. She's speaking in a measured, almost quiet way that is much more unnerving than the hollering was.

"It's over. Virgil's dead." Polly flinches as if struck. "The club's lost its labs, a bunch of members are dead or in jail. Chief is over in that old ice plant with a few guys, but we have it surrounded and they'll all be dead in a few minutes."

Polly is thrashing around, shaking her head, mouthing words that don't quite make it out into intelligible speech.

"You played your hand, challenged the odds, and you did pretty well for a while. But IT IS OVER!" Polly is now sobbing uncontrollably, hanging by her wrists from the chain that holds the tailgate closed. "You and your fucking friends have caused enough damage. It's going to stop right fucking now."

The rest of us are mesmerized, watching the interaction between these two women. There's something going on here that none of us quite understands, but I have a feeling we'll find out what it is before long.

"Don't you recognize me, Polly?" Judy gets right in Polly's face, grabbing her by the chin and making her look at her. Polly's trying to shake her head no, but Judy won't let go. I think things are going to get much clearer real soon.

"You fucked my husband, fed him meth until he was strung out so far there wasn't any way back. All because of that fucking club! You and those other whores kept him in pussy and dope until he got to the point you felt he was a liability. Then Chief set him up and got him arrested."

Judy's crying now, wiping angrily at the tears running down her cheeks. So that's it: Jimmy was doing stuff for the PnB, probably hoping to patch over from whatever little club he was riding with. They used women and dope to get him in too deep, then cut him loose in the most cruel way when he proved dispensable. Happens all the time . . . seems like there's never a shortage of wannabe's willing to give up everything to belong to the club. They give up their friends, family, self-respect, all in a bid to be one of the inner circle. Too bad more of them don't find out about the Chiefs and Slippys of the world before it's too late.

"The Huntsville chapter of the PnB is dead as of tonight. Get that through your hard head, bitch. You just killed a man for no reason other than some selfish desire to keep him from talking to us. It didn't have to happen! We already have it taken care of. He couldn't have done any more harm, don't you see that? You killed that kid for nothing!"

I'm not so sure he couldn't have told us something we could use, but I'm not about to correct Judy, and none of the other males present seem inclined to, either.

Travis jumps, causing the rest of us to jump along with him, as the pager in his shirt pocket goes off with a shrill beep. Time to join the party! I'd been so engrossed in the drama playing out in front of me that I'd forgotten we needed to be ready to move when the pager summoned us.

Judy looks over at me and asks, "What do we do with her?"

Polly's one good eye is jumping around like she's just snorted a couple tablespoons of speed. She's tugging at the wire, trying to get her hands free. Before I can say anything, the problem is taken care of.

Travis takes about three giant steps, grabs Polly's head in his hands, and gives it a savage twist, then another. Before he lets go of her, it's apparent she's dead. It was quick, and totally unexpected.

"Dammit! I didn't want to actually kill her!" says Judy, as surprised as the rest of us.

She's standing there, staring at Polly's body, seemingly at a loss as to what she wants to do next.

"Fuck her!" says Travis, in a tone of voice I haven't heard from him before. "She would've given us up, Judy. She knew too fuckin' much about you to let her go. We need to be moving, right now. Yell at me later, if you have to, but let's get the fuck moving!"

And get the fuck moving is what we do. Judy snaps out of her trance, apparently remembering that there are other fish to fry. Kenneth is already in the back seat, and Judy piles into the passenger side of the Malibu as I crawl behind the wheel.

I fire up that long-rod engine and shove the shifter into first. I head east on the county road, and Travis falls in behind me. As we turn north onto Mayapple road, I remind myself to go easy on the throttle, so as not to wake up the family living in either of the houses on the corner.

Rafe decided earlier to approach the building from across the fields surrounding it, leaving the vehicles parked at a couple of different turn-outs, one on Barma Road and another on a little lane north of the ice plant about a quarter mile or so. Jimbob is waiting in his Regal over on that little lane, and Jason is sitting in Rafe's Thunderbird over on Barma Road a couple hundred yards north of his uncle's house. It was agreed that Jason would have the best chance of explaining why he was in that neighborhood, and it gave him something to do. He could always say he was too drunk to drive home, and was sleeping off the beer he'd swilled at his Uncle Donnie's place.

As we approach the ice plant, I can't see any sign of movement. There is the Blazer we were expecting and a couple of other vehicles are parked nose-in to the rear of the building. One of them is a white van, probably the one they took to Fayetteville. The other car looks suspiciously like an unmarked police car. It's a dirty grey Ford Crown Victoria with three or four antennas sprouting from it. What now? This is not the time to worry about it, because Rafe and his people are already inside if things went as planned. He seemed to think they'd be able to take the occupants by surprise, overwhelming them with sheer firepower and balls.

Rafe had given the Mossberg riot gun to Burt, as well as all of the double-ought, HE, and CS gas shells he could stuff into his pockets.

Rafe himself had appropriated the Ingram, against Judy's initial protestations. "I'll give it back to you when you get inside," he'd told her with a wink.

She finally relented, shoving her pistol into her belt. We still have a bunch of handguns stashed around the Malibu, too.

Rafe's other men all have at least a couple handguns on them, as well as other weapons, including at least one carbide-coated wire garrote, in case anyone needs their head sawed off.

I park the Malibu at the corner of the building, facing the road. I take the keys out of the ignition and place them on top of the left front tire, making sure everyone sees where they are.

It wouldn't do to have everyone come out in a hurry, carrying or leaving behind the one person who knows where the car keys are. Travis is parked right beside me, leaving enough room for unobstructed access to either vehicle and plenty of room to maneuver if we need to haul ass out of here in a hurry. He also puts his keys on top of the driver's side front tire, providing a little continuity. In full flight, we'll need all the help we can get.

It's damned quiet out here. The only thing I can hear are the engines ticking as they cool. There's no sign of anyone, not even a sign of any kind of a struggle. Just as I start to walk over to the small door on the back wall of the plant, a voice speaks up from the dark, next to the trailer house.

"Don't shoot," the voice says, making every one of us jump about a foot in the air. I guess whoever this is hasn't heard what happens when you scare the shit out of me in the dark. We all point our guns at the place we think the voice came from, but nobody actually fires off a round.

"It's me, Ronnie," the voice declares, but it's impossible to see anyone and I wouldn't recognize Rafe's nephew's voice if I had to. "Rafe told me to wait out here and make sure nobody followed you. We saw a car taking off with a couple of people in it as we were coming across the field, and he wanted me to watch for them in case they returned."

We're all still wound up as tight as guitar strings, trying to see the speaker. None of us is ready to relax just yet. Kenneth speaks up. "Where can you get the best barbecue in Fehvull?"

What? What the fuck is he talking about?

"Whitt's, no contest. Although, I liked the sauce better when Big Al was cookin'," says the voice, and Kenneth laughs.

Apparently, the speaker in the dark has passed the test, proving he's a Fayetteville local.

"Ronnie, come on out, son. We won't shoot, but be careful, all the same." Kenneth is still chuckling to himself. A shadow emerges from behind the planter someone built to hide the trailer house's tongue and hitch assembly. As he stands up and steps forward, we're all still pointing our weapons at him, except for Kenneth.

As he gets to within ten feet or so of us, we see that it is, indeed, Ronnie, Rafe's nephew. "Everyone else is inside," he says, shaking Kenneth's hand as he speaks. "That was a good thing to ask. Only a local from up to home would be able to sound like he knew what he was talkin' about." He and Kenneth are both chuckling.

"I'll stay out here, just in case. Uncle Rafe and I have a signal figured out if I see anything suspicious. I still haven't seen that other car that left, so I don't know if they're coming back or not."

I'm sure Ronnie would just as soon be inside for the action, but he's doing what he was told, and he's doing it well.

"They won't be back." Kenneth gives Ronnie a hard stare as he says this, getting the message across without any further explanation necessary.

Ronnie nods, pats Kenneth on the back, and says, "See you guys in a little while."

He steps over and knocks on the steel door with the butt of his pistol. Once, a pause, once, a pause, then three quick raps. He walks back over to his observation post and disappears into the darkness.

FIFTY-SIX

One of Rafe's guys who had been at Donna's throughout the day—I don't remember his name—opens the door and leads us down a warren of dark rooms and into the large room where the ice-making operations used to take place. There are stacks of boxes and miscellaneous crap on the raised portion of the plant floor, on what I assume was the former loading dock. There is a sunken area in the center of the huge room, being used as a rough living area, from the looks of things.

There's a big, rough wood bench with a couple microwave ovens and one of those big coffee makers like you see at government offices on it. At a right-angle to this bench are a couple folding tables, one covered by all manner of junk food containers, the other holding three big coolers, probably full of beer and whatever else they've been drinking.

There's a pair of old sectional sofas arranged into a horseshoe. They look like they came from the dump, or maybe an alley somewhere. Seated on these are a total of seven individuals, all wearing a scowl and a pair of hand-cuffs. I'm not sure where all the cuffs came from, but I'll wait until later to ask. Rafe is beaming, and almost runs over to us as we make our way down a short set of steps into the sunken living room.

"It couldn't have been easier!" he says, laughing out loud. "These dumb-asses left the door unlocked. After we took out the pair in the trailer, we just waltzed in and made 'em our bitches." He's obviously having fun.

"Who the fuck *are* you guys?" asks Chief, looking absolutely defiant, despite a big ugly bruise on his forehead.

He glares at Travis and Bobby Ray, then checks out the rest of the newcomers. He doesn't recognize me, and skips right past Kenneth to Judy, whom he shoots a malevolent glare.

"I know you," he says to Judy, pretty much sealing his fate in my book. "You're that chick that was married to that weasel-dick Jimmy the Wrench. We kept trying to get him to bring you around, let us have a shot at you, but he wouldn't go for it. He fucked our women, did our dope, but wouldn't let us have a shot at your fine ass. But then, he got his, didn't he?" He rears his head back and laughs a mean, ugly laugh.

Before she can react, I've crossed the space between us and hit Chief right in the eye socket with the butt of my nine mil. He roars in pain and outrage, but before he can say anything, I grab him by the hair and look him right in the eyes . . . eye.

"Hello, Mikey," I say, and wait for him to put it all together. Just as I'm about to give up, he jerks upright and starts tugging at his restraints.

"Hammer! What the fuck are you doing? I don't

know what the fuck you're up to, but you need to get your shit together and let me go."

"I'll tell you what I'm up to, you piece of shit," I tell him, shoving the barrel of my pistol into the soft tissue under his chin. "I'm making damned sure you don't hurt anyone else . . . ever."

I whack him again, this time right on his left temple. I feel bone give way, and his body slumps. His silence is sudden, and terrible to behold for his compatriots.

Rafe and his people, along with my crew, have them covered, and nobody is dumb enough to stand up. They're not happy, no sir, but they're not totally stupid, either. I take a deep breath and back up a few steps, shaking my head and trying to combat the adrenaline high I've got going.

Rafe looks at me and winks. He motions with his eyes for me to join him as he moves twenty feet away, toward the rear entrance, where we're out of sight of those sitting on the sofas.

"Ronnie tell you about the car that left as we came across the fields?" He's grinning—he's actually enjoying himself.

I never want this guy pissed at me. I nod, looking back to see if Chief has moved. Nope.

"We ran into them," I tell Rafe, "in town. Chief's old lady, Polly, was in the car with a big dude named Tiny." He's watching me keenly, making sure he doesn't miss anything. "They came in the place we were in, and things just went crazy. I took Tiny out of play in the restroom, and Judy lured Polly back there saying he was sick. When Polly saw Tiny in the shitter, blubbering about something, she killed him."

Even Rafe can be surprised! His eyes grow wide, and he doesn't say a word.

"Polly always carries a straight razor, and she pulled it out and cut Tiny's throat with it before anyone could move. Judy clobbered her with her pistol, then swung her into the sink by her braid. I'm pretty sure she broke some ribs, because from then on Polly was no problem to control."

Rafe's nodding along as I tell the story, and he looks back at Judy with an admiring glance more than once.

"Kenneth locked the employees in the cooler, locked the front door, and turned off all the lights. We took Polly with us and hauled ass out to meet Travis and Bobby Ray. That's where we were when you paged us."

I look over at Chief, but he's still not moving. The others on the sofas are being pretty still, showing that they have at least a little good sense.

"Where's this Polly now?" Rafe is watching me, waiting for an answer.

"She didn't make it," I tell him, figuring that will be enough for now. He just nods and tips me a wink.

He reaches out, grabs me by the forearm, and turns me back toward the center of the room, propelling me ahead of him.

Judy, Kenneth, and the rest of our crew are standing at various stages of the horseshoe, watching the disconsolate people on the sectionals. Rafe and I walk out into the middle of the open space and he says, "Which one of you wants to live?"

This gets their attention!

"The first one to convince me he should be allowed to live will get a free pass," says Rafe, watching the prisoners' body language, looking for a weak link.

A young guy, probably twenty-one or so, is fidgeting, drawing stares from those around him. I figure he's a prospect, judging by the disdain with which he's regarded by his neighbors. He appears to be fighting an internal struggle, trying to decide which move to make.

"Okay," says Rafe, walking over to a tough-looking old bastard sitting on the end of the dirtier of the two sectionals, pulling his Glock from his belt as he goes.

The old guy is looking pretty apprehensive, but nobody's actually been killed yet, right? He takes a quick look at Chief, trying to see whether or not this thought is accurate, just as Rafe shoots him in the left knee.

"Jesus Christ!" the old guy bellows, grabbing his knee the best he can, seeing as how his hands are cuffed. Everyone else on the sofas suddenly look a whole lot less convinced that they're going to get out of this.

"Motherfucker . . ." the old guy is really hurting,

yet he still has the sense to be pissed off.

One of the guys on the other side of the horseshoe forgets himself and says, "You chicken-shit bastard! Let me loose and I'll kick your sorry ass all the way back to wherever you come from."

I have a feeling he's going to regret that outburst. Burt uses the butt of the Mossberg to attempt separation of the loudmouth's head from his spinal column. The dude shuts up right away—probably attributable to the fact that, at the very least, he's unconscious.

That's all the young guy needs in the way of incentive, and he bolts up from his place on the sofa, "I'll tell you whatever you wanna know," he says, his eyes wild, watching for an attack from his companions. "I just got here, and I don't have any reason to protect these people."

This doesn't make him very popular with the others, judging by their muttered threats and malevolent stares.

"Got here from where?" I ask him, prodding him away from the others with the barrel of my nine mil. He's shaking, nearly shuddering from witnessing the sudden violence.

"Arkansas . . . up by Mountain Home. My daddy was retired PnB, used to ride with this chapter back in the 60s and 70s. He got cancer, knew he wasn't going to be around long. He made me promise to bring his colors back here and give 'em back to the club for their clubhouse."

"That sounds plausible, but how did you get involved in this shit? And why did they bring you out here to their secret hideaway?"

"I got in here late yesterday afternoon, and these guys took me out to their bar to party. Around midnight, all hell broke loose. Somebody set fire to the building next door and blew up a couple scooters in front of the bar. While we were all out front, somebody beat the fuck out of a guy named Big Willy out back, and cut up another guy pretty bad."

Well, his version meshes pretty well with what I know. Still, how did he get from there to here?

"What's your name?" I ask him, leading him over to the table with the food piled on it.

I've noticed a few of the guys on the sofas trying to surreptitiously look toward the back door, probably hoping Polly and Tiny will bring back reinforcements. Sorry, guys. No such luck.

"My name's Gary, Gary Lawlor," he says, seeming to relax a little, although he keeps looking over to where the crusty old dude is clutching his knee and moaning.

"Okay, Gary, why are you here? I mean here, right here. You came into Huntsville to give your old man's colors back to the club and ended up at Chubby's when the shit hit the fan. What happened then?"

"It was almost daylight before we got out of there. These guys took me to the clubhouse. We hadn't been there very long when Chief and a couple other guys I hadn't met came in and started rounding everyone up, telling them to get moving. There was something else going on, and Chief kept blaming someone named Slippy for double-crossing him. They'd all been shootin' meth all day, and they were wired up like Christmas."

So, Chief, in his meth-induced paranoia, got it in his head that Slippy had somehow caused all of his problems, including the attacks on the club labs. That's just beautiful! I may get away unscathed, after all. Other than the ones in this room, any other PnB members will think the S&S caused all their problems.

"They wouldn't let me leave, made me go with them. They were all packin', and like I said, everyone was wired up to the max."

Aha! Now I'm starting to see how he happened to be here at this particular time and place.

"Somebody called and told Chief some stuff, and he went absolutely bugshit. Something about his old lady's brother gettin' killed. There were a lot of hush-hush meetings, and everyone was rushin' around grabbin' guns and food and stuff. We all piled in a couple cars and headed over to pick up that bitch Polly." The kid's a good judge of character, at least.

"After we had her in the car, we drove to a little town out to the west where a couple of the guys went inside looking for some woman they wanted to talk to about one of the dancers from the bar. She wasn't there, and I guess they roughed up somebody that worked there, but didn't find out anything useful."

That could have been the biggest mistake Chief ever made. If they hadn't messed with Jason, he wouldn't have had any reason to know what they were driving or cared what they were doing at the old ice plant in Arab. Payback is a bitch.

"Where did you go then?" I ask the kid, thinking we probably had it figured pretty close. Finding him here is a stroke of luck.

With a little prodding from the ever-resourceful Rafe, we're getting some good information. Good news, so far.

"Chief was getting more and more crazy, and he was snortin' crank almost constantly. Polly said something to him about it, and he punched her in the gut. I thought he'd hurt her bad, but she seemed to come around later."

I wonder what that was all about. Could it have something to do with Polly wanting to get away from the rest of them and make a phone call earlier?

"We went over to Decatur to see where Virgil and those other ol' boys got killed in a car wreck. We drove by there, turned around and drove back by. Polly wanted to stop, but Chief wouldn't hear about it. He was afraid the cops were watching, and he wanted to get out of there. He wasn't making any sense, and I could tell Polly and a couple of the others were worried."

Paranoia is an insidious thing, and meth breeds paranoia better than almost anything else humans in-gest. I've seen people wrecked on crank threaten to shoot their family members, feeling that they were plotting against them. A big violent guy like Chief in the throes of meth-induced hysteria would definitely be a frightening prospect.

"We drove here on back roads, and met a few other guys that were here when we arrived. Everyone had loosened up, and I got the impression they thought this place was safe. More than once I heard someone say nobody would find us here. I really wanted to get out of here, but I was really afraid to mention it to Chief. He was just plain nuts."

I can sympathize; if he'd tried to talk Chief into letting him leave, he probably wouldn't have lived through it. With all the shit that had happened since midnight, Chief would have leaped on a chance to blame someone for his troubles. I'm actually surprised he didn't decide, in his delirium, that this kid was the cause of all his problems.

The people on the sofas are getting restless, watching me quiz Gary. His endless unloading of information has them worried, for sure. They can't hear us, but I'm sure they know it's not good news for them. The tough old bastard on the end is unconscious, having finally succumbed to shock. Chief hasn't moved. Either I killed him—or not. I really don't much care one way or the other. He wasn't going to walk out of here alive, one way or another.

The rest of our crew is getting antsy, or restless, or

something. They keep looking over to where Gary and I are, not really having anything to do. The ones on the couch who haven't been clubbed or shot aren't giving anyone a reason to do anything to them. They've even stopped mumbling obscenities, perhaps thinking they'll be spared if they're nice. Not much hope of that, you miserable assholes.

I need to wrap this up and confer with the others. We need to make a decision about what to do with Gary, then take care of these other assholes.

FIFTY-SEVEN

Abandoned Cullman Ice Plant, Arab, Alabama
May 20, 1990

So far, it looks like eliminating the human trash in this room will keep us in the clear. Yeah, it's a harsh decision, but none of us wants to be worrying about these people or their cronies coming after us in the future. I worry about the after-effects on Judy, Kenneth, and the others. If they choose not to participate, I won't hold it against them. I'm prepared to do whatever is needed to protect all of us.

Slippy and his crew are going to be really busy, and they don't have any information about any of us. None of them ever knew me as Hammer, and wouldn't recognize me if they had. Bo's gone, killed on a fool's errand with Virgil. I honestly don't think Bob will say anything for fear of getting Donna tied up in it. Same goes for the people at Donna's Place. They'll keep what little they know to themselves so Donna and Judy stay out of trouble.

After a short conversation, Rafe tells me he's good with whatever we decide, as long as we don't let anyone other than Gary out of here alive. I'm glad he's okay with letting Gary go. The kid just got stuck in the wrong place with the wrong people while trying to honor his dad's last wishes. We just need to do it in a way that protects us as much as possible.

I gather up Judy, Kenneth, Travis, and Bobby Ray for a huddle over in the corner farthest from where the sectionals are arranged. I tell them what Gary has told me and what Rafe and I discussed. Kenneth is visibly torn between the need to take care of business and showing some compassion for people he doesn't even know.

"Damn, Jonnybob," he says, scratching behind his ear with the barrel of the .45 he's got in his big ol' paw. "I tol' you from the get-go that somebody was liable to end up dead, D-E-D, DEAD, if they fucked with us. I've known there was a chance that would happen, but it just doesn't seem right somehow to snuff all these clowns just because they're with that asshole Chief." He looks back over his shoulder toward the gathering in the middle of the room.

"Speakin' of which, I think you turned his lights out for good. Too bad in a way, 'cause I'd really have liked to hear him beg fer mercy."

We all reflexively look over there, looking for some sign Chief and the loudmouth are still alive. Nothing.

"I guess what I'm tryin' to say," Kenneth continues, "is I agree we need to do whatever needs done to protect the five of us, Darla, Donna, Sammy, Jason, Rafe and his boys, Jimbob, and anyone else that could get hurt if any of these jerk-offs talk."

I notice Darla is right near the top of the list. I'm sure he's also thinking about Janie, not wanting to consider what she would think of her big brother if she found out he killed a bunch of people.

Judy speaks up, taking Kenneth's hand in hers. "I know it's hard to think about, Kenneth, but we need to finish this. We can't take any chance of Momma, Darla, or anyone else getting hurt. This is our chance to bring this whole damned deal to a conclusion and get on with our lives without looking over our shoulders the rest of our lives." Damn, she's one tough woman!

"You know," says Travis, looking haggard, "I'll take care of what needs done, and I'm pretty sure Rafe will help. You guys get out of here. Take that kid with you and send him the fuck home. Put the fear of God in him, and tell him if he ever talks, we'll find him and skin him alive. I think he'll believe you, after what he's seen this morning."

"Bullshit!" I'm not going along with this, although I think leaving Judy, Bobby Ray, and Kenneth out of the last act of this play is a good idea. "I'm in this until it's over. If anyone is going to stay back and take care of these pricks while everyone else hauls ass, it's gonna be me. I started this whole fuckin' thing, and I'm not leavin' until it's over, one way or another."

Bobby Ray speaks up with a concerned, almost sheepish look on his young face, "I really think someone needs to take Gary out of here before he sees anything else that can cause any of us trouble. I've got to admit that the excitement and the conviction that we're the good guys has kept me going, but I'm not sure if I can be here when this next shit happens. If you won't think I'm a chicken-shit, I'd like to haul Gary to the bus or however he got here and get him started home.

"I want to help . . . really."

He looks miserable. I can't blame him. This has gotten pretty heavy for some good ol' boy just hangin' out with his uncle and cousin. This may actually be a blessing, because now we won't have to convince someone against their wishes to haul Gary out of here.

"Nobody's gonna call you a chicken-shit," says Kenneth, his eyes wide in outrage. "At least, not around any of us. You've proven yourself a warrior, and now you're takin' action none of us want to, for the good of us all. You go, take that kid all the way to Arkansas if you need to, and we'll see ya later. I'll buy you all the beer you can drink."

He steps over to the younger man and takes him in a bear-hug. Bobby Ray returns the gesture and we all heave a sigh of relief. At least that's taken care of.

"Anyone goin' with him?" Travis asks us in that high-pitched voice that's so incongruous with his appearance.

We all look at Judy, and she's offended. Her eyes blaze in indignation as she puts her hands on her hips. Her hips . . . later, dammit.

"I am *not* going anywhere until the rest of you do. Bobby Ray, I'm so glad you volunteered to take care of Gary, but I need to see this through. I need to put an end to the part of my life these assholes ruined and get a new start."

She looks at me with such conviction and promise that I forget to breathe for a moment.

"Okay," says Kenneth, "Let's quit yammerin' about it and do this."

We all smile. I love this guy! We all step forward without a word and take each other's hands much like a sports team breaking out of a huddle. Nobody says anything, but our bond is strengthened and cemented: We'll all be friends for the remainder of our days.

FIFTY-EIGHT

Abandoned Cullman Ice Plant, Arab, Alabama
May 20, 1990

Rafe sends one of the men who had been at Donna's with Bobby Ray and Gary. "Just in case," he tells us with a wink. He seems to wink any time he's trying to make a point without being bossy.

The remaining prisoners who are still conscious seem to sense that things are heading to a conclusion. A couple of them have tried to get Rafe's attention, hoping to buy themselves a reprieve. No such luck, boys. The one-time offer has been accepted by the man who just left the building.

Rafe leaves Burt to watch the prisoners. "You have an idea of how you want to do this?" He looks from face to face as he asks us, waiting for a response. It's the perfect time of day, when most people are in their deepest sleep of the night, so we need to act now and get the hell out of here.

It's a good question; do we just shoot 'em all in the head? That seems like the quickest, most sure-fire method, but it's a drastic step. What about knockin' 'em all unconscious and stackin' 'em up in the house trailer? We could set it on fire and take care of all of them at once. Those who woke up while they were being burned would die a horrific death. Maybe that's a little extreme. I've never had to think about this before. This isn't a split-second reaction to a situation that results in someone's death. It's cold-blooded murder, pure and simple. Can we do this? Can *I* do this?

"If you'd rather," Rafe says, looking more like a farmer than an organized-crime figure, "my boys and I will take care of it. This isn't our first rodeo, as they say. This is a line you may not want to cross. If so, I completely understand."

He's staring at Judy, obviously thinking she'll be the first to flinch. She surprises all of us.

"Actually," she says, matching him stare for stare, "I was thinking maybe you and your men might like to be somewhere else when we finish this. When the alarm goes out about the dead guy at Jill's and Polly's body is found, the local cops are going to go apeshit."

At least. There will be a shit-storm like they've probably never seen before in Arab, Alabama. Rafe starts to object, but Judy waves him quiet.

"I'm serious. The four of us have planned from the beginning to finish this. We all appreciate your help. Without it, we might very well never have gotten to this point this quickly." She waves her index finger under Rafe's nose, looking as fierce as I've seen her. "But you need to think about an exit strategy. A Tennessee license plate will attract more attention than a local one. Why take the chance? If you're out of here before the shit hits the fan, your chances are much better for getting home to Shirley."

Oh, now she's pulled out the big guns.

"Judy," Rafe begins, not matching her intensity,

"if it weren't for you people, my daughter would still be dancing in that filthy place. I appreciate your concern, but I have no intention of not making it home to my recently-returned baby girl. Let's do this and get the fuck out of here before anyone finds Polly or the guy she killed. Let the locals try to figure out what happened after we're all safely away from here."

We keep saying it, but we're still standing here talking about it.

Travis pivots on his heel and walks over to where the prisoners are seated. They're watching him pretty closely, and look as if they know something bad is about to happen. He walks up to Burt, whispers something into his ear. Burt looks over to Rafe with a question on his face, and Rafe nods.

Burt hands the Mossberg to Travis, and they have a short whispered conversation before Travis heads back toward us.

Before anyone can react, Travis turns, takes a few steps, and puts the barrels of the shotgun about a foot from the head of the old guy with the shattered knee. He pulls the trigger, resulting in a spray of blood and brain matter that covers the next couple of guys on the couch and causing a major uproar.

Judy is yelling. Kenneth is yelling. I'm yelling. But Rafe is grinning. Travis can't hear anything we're saying, because he is marching along the line of cuffed prisoners, working the Mossberg's trigger in a methodical rhythm, just mowing them down one after another.

He skips Chief and the one Burt nearly decapitated, and before any of us can react, it's over.

He turns to us and with one eyebrow cocked, as if he's saying, "Well?"

Rafe steps over to the one who called him a chicken-shit before he got his head dislocated and takes aim. He fires the Glock twice, the reports nearly indistinguishable from each other. A ridiculously small wound appears on the biker's forehead, right above the bridge of his nose, but the resulting mess sprayed onto the couch cushion behind him is an awful thing to behold.

Before I can change my mind, I walk over to Chief and aim my Smith at his forehead. Before I can fire, Judy is at my side, holding onto my sleeve. I look at her and our eyes meet. Both of us aim our pistols at Chief's head and fire, nearly simultaneously. The result is something I never want to see again. His head is reduced to pulp. I have a really strong urge to vomit, but somehow avoid actually puking all over my shoes.

It's over.

The smell of cordite is heavy, and gunpowder smoke hangs in the air like low-lying clouds. The silence is deafening after all the gunfire, and those of us still breathing are motionless, almost as if someone has hit the pause button.

Rafe breaks the spell first, motioning for Burt to join him. They start picking up all the shell casings, as well as the spent shotgun shells. The rest of us break out of our trance and start looking around to decide what we need to do next. The back door bangs open and Ronnie bursts into the room, handgun up and ready. He takes in the scene in an instant. He nods, nods again, and heads back outside to keep watch.

Travis has his t-shirt off, wiping down every surface he thinks one of us may have touched. Burt has the Mossberg back, and is conferring with Rafe at the open end of the bloody horseshoe. As they talk, Burt methodically unloads the shotgun, removing the rest of the double-ought rounds. These he slips into a jacket pocket before he reaches into another one for a handful of different, black-colored shells. The HE—high-explosive—rounds.

Judy has joined in with Travis, wiping down every surface one of us may have left prints on. Travis has even been to the restrooms, apparently figuring Rafe or his guys may have been in there before we showed up. Judy runs up the hallway to the back door. She wipes down the doorknobs, both inside and out.

It's eerie; nobody is talking. We all seem to be dealing internally with the aftermath of the violence. Kenneth is helping Rafe pile all the bodies together on the floor in the open area of the horseshoe. Travis and Judy seem to be through with their chore, and I've got all of the trash and garbage bags full of refuse piled up next to the bodies. I've been collecting everything that might give any clue as to who these dead people are, and if what I think Rafe has planned works, we just might make the cops' job a lot harder.

We all seem to wind down in our efforts, gravitating to the end of the hallway headed outside. Burt is up on the catwalk that runs around the big room, probably for access by the maintenance people who used to work here. He's stuffing wads of toilet tissue into his ears, preparing for the final act of destruction.

Rafe leads us all outside, where Ronnie joins us. "I haven't seen any traffic at all," he reports, "and nobody turned on any lights that I saw after all the gunfire. It really wasn't very loud out here at all."

Good. My ears are still ringing from all the gunfire inside and I imagine the others are in the same boat.

"Good," says Rafe.

He's taking a careful look around, assuring himself that nobody is up and wondering what's going on at the old ice plant. I keep expecting to hear explosions from inside. That will do it, I think to myself. At that point, we will all need to be moving, and quickly.

"I told Burt to wait for me to signal him when we're ready to go," he says.

So that's why nothing has happened. Rafe is always at least a step ahead of me. "Ronnie, go over to where that dishwasher is waiting and get the hell out of here. I'll go get Jimbob and we'll wait for Burt. You guys," he says, looking at my friends and me, "just as soon as Burt blows up that mess inside, get in that ugly-ass Chevy and get the fuck outta here. Ronnie and Jason will he headed back to Mooresville, and Jimbob,

Burt, and I are going to find our way back to Fayetteville. I need to take my family to church in a couple of hours."

This dude is one very cool customer. After all that he's been involved in, he's headed back home to take his family to church!

Ronnie takes off at a lope, disappearing into the darkness as he heads across the field to where Jason is waiting. The rest of us back up by the trailer house as Rafe walks over to the door and walks inside. He's back out in a couple of minutes, nearly running as he slams the door shut behind him. He runs over to where the rest of us are standing, breathing hard.

Before anyone can say anything, we hear four sharp reports from inside the building, one right after another. The noise is considerable even out here. The sound inside had to be incredible! The flash from the explosions is visible through the cracks around the doors and looks like something out of a science-fiction movie.

Before the five of us have time to process what we just heard and saw, Burt comes barreling out of the small door, slamming it shut behind him. He's grinning a terrible grin, and even in this light, his eyes are gleaming.

"Go!' says Rafe, pushing me toward the Malibu.

Burt shoves the Mossberg into Kenneth's hands, along with a plastic bag full of shells as he and Rafe race off into the black night, headed for Jimbob and home.

We all pile into the Chevy, Travis holding the passenger door so Kenneth and Judy can slide into the back before joining me in the front seat. I've got the Malibu running and rolling quietly along the north side of the building toward the road almost before his door is closed.

As we head south on Mayapple Road, we see a few lights on, but no sign of anyone outside, trying to figure out what the commotion was. Even if someone is out listening, there won't be any further loud noises to help them pinpoint the source.

I don't really want to drive past Dolly, but also don't want to drive all over the unfamiliar countryside, either, so I hang a right and head west on County Road 1815. Nobody says anything as we drive past the Barma Road intersection, and we're all pretty quiet for the first mile or two as we head west through the black Alabama night.

FIFTY-NINE

Sitting in the bar at Donna's, Kenneth, Travis, and I are having cold ham and cheese sandwiches, along with a pitcher of RC and a tray of cold biscuits smeared with butter and strawberry jam. We considered a pitcher of beer, but collectively decided it would be weird with the jam. Also, I think we're all afraid we'd fall asleep where we sit if we drink any liquor. After all, the sun just came up a few minutes ago, and we've all been awake for a long time.

Judy took her car out to her house so she could get a shower and change clothes. I guess women just aren't as willing to wear clothes for days at a time as men are. Now, I'm just as fond of a shower and clean clothes as anyone, but that's not my first priority after a day like yesterday/today.

Bobby Ray is curled up in the corner booth, fast asleep. He said he took Gary to where his car was parked and sent him on his way. He handed the kid a couple of the hundred dollar bills we had given him and Travis earlier for fuel expenses and such, telling him to make some miles before he stopped. He also suggested that Gary not pay any attention to any news from northern Alabama and a case of selective amnesia would be a really good idea for the young man. It seems Gary was all for that, and eternally grateful for the chance to go back home.

The three of us at the bar are comparing recollections of the last few days, some of them funny and some of them not so much. We're all glad Shirley is home, but none of us is sure she'll stay there. Kenneth is damned sure Smutly won't ever take a piss without thinking of him. Not in an amorous way, I hope. I don't share that thought with him, but my buddy knows me pretty well; he flips me off and goes back to his sandwich.

None of us bring up the gritty stuff. Nothing is said about Polly's demise or Travis's taking matters into his own hands and slaughtering the PnB members at the ice plant. The man was willing to do what was needed without prompting or being asked. He'll always be special to me, whatever happens to all of us in the aftermath of our shared adventure.

As we eat and wait for Judy to show up, Kenneth and I talk for a few minutes about Janie. After the scare of thinking he'd lost her, she's been on my portly pal's mind quite a bit, it seems. He wants to make sure she gets the best treatment, but more importantly wants her to be happy. Life is tenuous, we've all been reminded.

We discuss her and Doctor Popovich, agreeing that there is something there beyond the doctor-patient relationship. Jimbob won't be happy, but he just flat waited too long to make his move. According to Kenneth, he didn't want to take the chance she'd reject his advances. It seems the dirty lawyer is basically clueless around women—has been since he was a kid. Maybe that's why he's so ruthless: he's getting back at everyone for his not being more successful with the ladies.

Judy shows up and lets herself in the back door, coming into the bar from Donna's office. I get up and walk over to her, taking her in my arms. She smells like apple blossoms, and appears to be refreshed from her time in the shower at home. She gives me a short but fierce kiss, then backs up a tad to look me in the eyes.

"Are we done yet?"

I know what she means. We said we'd wait until our quest was over to take our relationship another step; lovers instead of friends. No, that's not right. Lovers *as well as* best friends. I honestly believe we're very close, but it may be too early to let our guards down.

"Almost," I tell her, pulling her back against me.

What an incredible woman! In a few days she has captured me completely, heart and soul. I've never felt like this about anyone else, and I'm not quite sure how to act.

"Travis," Kenneth says with a rotten grin on his face, "mebbe we should go somewhere and leave these two alone."

Travis snickers, Judy giggles, and I flip him off. As soon as he catches up with Darla, I'll be able to return the favor.

"I don't know about the rest of you," says Dutton, smearing jam on a biscuit, "but I need a nap."

Bed sounds good, and I might even get some sleep. Later.

"That sounds like a plan," I tell my companions. "Travis, if you and Bobby Ray want to head back over to your place, we'll all get some rest and take some time to mellow out."

"I was thinking that," says Travis, sounding tired. "We'll go get some sleep and take it easy until we hear from you. Today's Sunday, right?"

I'm not sure. I look at Judy, and she's nodding.

"Okay, we'll wait for you guys to call us. Let us know by tonight, because Bobby Ray is supposed to be heading to Arizona for a job and needs to know what to tell them."

I really can't imagine Bobby Ray going back to work as a pipe-fitter after we split the money and put this whole deal behind us. But, who knows how long it's going to take for Rafe to get the money laundered and to us?

Travis hauls himself to his feet and walks over to where Bobby Ray is crashed. He smacks the younger man on the bottom of a foot and tells him to rise and shine. Rise, maybe. Shine . . . I don't think so. He looks worn out, and I think the violence really shook him up.

As they leave the room, Kenneth gets up from the table and stretches, groaning loudly. "I'm gonna catch a few hours shut-eye, and I suggest you do the same," he says, looking from Judy to me. "Although I don't imagine you'll listen. You two gonna be at Judy's?"

Good question, buddy. I look at Judy, and for an answer she takes my hand and hauls me to my feet.

"Yeah, we'll be at my house. I think you should give Darla a call after you take your nap. You do have her number, don't you?"

Kenneth actually blushes a little, and mumbles something about having Darla's number written down somewhere, if he can remember where he put it. Yeah, right. Like he doesn't know exactly where it is. More likely he's got it memorized.

Kenneth heads out through Donna's office, on his way to the cabins out back. Judy and I clean up the mess and she locks up as we leave the building through that door I've become so used to. We get into the Malibu, with Judy driving.

"Well, Jonnybob, or whatever your name is going to be," Judy says, as she starts the car and lets the engine idle for a minute. "Are you ready to finally let me love you?"

Let her? Hell, I think I should vigorously encourage her.

I smile at her, afraid to say something sappy and ruin the moment. She reaches over and puts her hand softly against my face. The smile on her face melts my reserves, and I reach up and put my hand over hers.

"Yeah," I say, "I'm ready. Love me."

She takes her hand from my face and puts it on the shifter. With a mischievous smirk, she gives that long-rod engine a little gas and starts toward the road. I may be in for quite a ride.

As she turns onto the pavement and gets the Malibu pointed north, she mashes the throttle and gleefully exclaims, "Hang on! It's going to be a wild ride!"

EPILOGUE

It's been quite an eventful spring and summer. After the smoke cleared, the Mooresville Gang, as I now think of us, spent some anxious times watching the news and our backs. We finally came to the conclusion that we are in the clear—a monumental feat considering the amount of mistakes and blunders I made.

Rafe came through much more quickly than I imagined; within three weeks we had a little over five million dollars divided up between us, each of us picking a bank to deposit our "stock dividends" into. Rafe's knowledge of such matters, combined with the expertise of our personal crooked lawyer, Jimbob, made things happen seamlessly. Springing Shirley from Chubby's was definitely the best thing we ever did, both as the right thing to do and as a way to get professional help with our illegal gains. Rafe is a man of his word, as well as someone I never want to piss off.

Travis and Bobby Ray promptly bought one of those "toy-hauler" RVs, loaded their scooters into the back, and headed west for a ride along the coast before hitting Sturgis in August. They didn't come right out and say so, but I suspect Raeann got something for her help, out of a sense of guilt for nearly putting her in harm's way.

Donna continued to feel worse until Judy loaded

her up and took her to a doctor. Luckily, it's nothing too serious, just a thyroid problem that was easily treated with medication and some rest. She's back to her old self, raising hell with Hogbody and coddling her employees. She is one employee short. Darla left for Fayetteville.

Kenneth spent a couple of weeks making sure Janie is taken care of, and spent a lot of time with her and Doctor Jim, as he calls her physician and fiancée. She's moved from the Midsouth Convalescent Home into Doctor Popovich's house, and her health is steadily improving.

After he returned from Memphis, Kenneth spent some time with Darla, who by then had served her two-week notice and was ready to head north. They loaded up a small U-Haul trailer behind Kenneth's old GMC and left Donna's, causing lots of tears—both of joy and sorrow.

Rafe had a surprise for Kenneth, which he presented to him at Whitt's, which it turns out he owned. He had Kenneth and Darla join him and his family there for a celebratory dinner. Shirley, against all of our predictions, was still at home, planning to enroll at Tennessee State in Nashville. After dinner, Rafe handed Kenneth a bulky manila envelope. As the others watched, my old buddy opened the envelope to find he was now the proud owner of the property he was currently on, as well as the Whitt's business and assets, effective as of noon that day.

Kenneth had the good sense to leave things pretty much as they were, except that Darla took over as the manager. Big Al returned for sauce-making duties. I hear it's as popular as always, maybe more so. Although nobody talks about the details, it appears most of the locals know Kenneth was somehow instrumental in getting Shirley back to her parents.

Randy Miller is now the acting sheriff, having taken over when it was discovered that Billy Neece was a closet cross-dresser. Last I heard, the word is that he's somewhere down here in the Keys serving drinks in a grass skirt.

From what news I could gather, Guffey seems to have fared pretty well, other than acquiring a bullet scar in his ass cheek. The Huntsville newspapers reported that he was named to a federal task force formed to deal with the methamphetamine problem in the southern US. Good for him. Someday I might call him up and say hello. Then again, I might not.

Judy and I had a couple weeks of bliss, spending nearly every free moment together, waiting for the other shoe to drop. We couldn't get enough of each other. Her eyes were crossed repeatedly, and she had hiccups on a great many occasions. I've never been as happy—or as restless.

One morning we drove down to Donna's to open up Jimmy's old shop. Judy helped me sort and stack parts, making room for a sturdy table I found, big enough to build a scooter on. I gathered up the parts of my beautiful black chopper, laying them out in order, getting a plan together.

Jimmy had a really nice custom frame stashed in one corner, a hard-tail with a stretched backbone and a moderate rake. The forks from my bike were the perfect length, so things went fairly quickly from there. I got the engine and transmission in the frame, found a belt-drive setup that fit, and had the basic scooter together in a couple of days. Using stuff from my bike, as well as some of Jimmy's stash, I got it wired, found the small stuff to complete the rolling chassis. Travis had told us where he kept a spare key hidden, so I painted a different rear fender and some miscellaneous brackets and such out at his place. When it was done, I took the title Judy had signed over to me down to the DMV and got it titled in my name: John Robert Clark.

After some anxious moments, we finally got it running right and spent a few days going for rides out through the countryside. We rode out past where the bus accident happened, remembering how things had progressed from that wild night.

Judy and I talked about our dreams, our vision of the future. It became apparent that she didn't want to leave, and I didn't want to stay. Many tears were shed, and nothing was resolved as the days turned into weeks.

The sex was incredible, Judy revealing a side of her I hadn't dared imagine. Wantonness is too tame a name for her unbridled celebration of carnal delights. I was constantly challenged to match her enthusiasm and inventiveness. I like to think I did a pretty good job of holding up my end of the bargain.

As summer neared its mid-point, I needed a change, incredible sex and conflicted feelings of love notwithstanding. Maybe I'm incapable of being the man Judy needs. She wants stability. I need motion. She wants to stay home to help her mother. I want to put that part of Alabama in my rear-view mirror.

After a couple days of making sure Vanna, the bike, and I were ready and trying my best not to start any fights with Judy, I pushed the scooter into the back of Vanna, using a two-by-twelve plank as a ramp. After making sure everything was tied down and ready, I got in and fired up that sweet-sounding Ford small block, letting it warm up a little before heading out.

Before I could put it into gear, Judy drove into the lot and parked right next to where I was sitting. She got out of the Malibu, which is now a gorgeous pearl blue—about the color of those cobalt blue electrical insulators you see in antique stores. As she approached me, I was wondering whether I could actually leave with her present.

She was smiling and carrying a small package. I got out of the van, and we embraced, standing there without speaking for a few moments. As we broke the embrace, she handed me the package, still smiling. Thank God she wasn't crying . . . I don't know what I would have done.

"I have something for you," she said, brushing an

errant strand of hair from her eyes.

I came close to changing my mind in that moment. She was standing there, mine for the asking, as beautiful a woman as I've ever seen, stronger than most of the men I've ever known.

I took the package from her, which turned out to be a small blue velvet bag with a draw-string holding it closed. As I pulled the top open, I could see something coiled up inside. I drew it out and I realized it was a braided leather cord, beautifully made, with a small heart-shaped pendant on it, made from filigreed silver.

"Read the back," Judy said, leaning against me and putting her arm around my waist.

I turned the pendant over. "You'll always have my heart" was engraved into it. We both had tears in our eyes, and I was at a loss for words—one of the few times I can remember.

"I know you need to go," she said, holding me tightly. "Just please, don't forget me."

Like that could happen. She spared us both the agony of a long farewell by grabbing my head in both hands and kissing me, hard. Before either of us was ready, she broke away, ran over to the Malibu and drove off, spraying gravel in twin rooster tails all the way to the pavement.

I'm an idiot.

So here I am, sitting in one of the bars that is still as I remember it from the time I spent here a dozen or so years ago. Key West has changed a lot since the crazy days of the late Seventies. Gone is most of the gritty atmosphere, replaced by a more tourist-friendly vibe. Gays run most of the shops, rotating between here and Provincetown, where they have sister stores.

I rode my scooter down here from Islamorada, where I parked Vanna in a little mangrove-surrounded campground, taking my time and enjoying the ride. I go by JR now, mostly, having grown tired of the Jonnybob moniker. It served its purpose, but isn't something I wanted to be saddled with.

I'm now JR Clark, successful businessman on an extended vacation. Anyone asking more is politely told that I don't want to talk business.

I have no idea where I'll end up, but I never start a day without slipping that leather cord with the heart pendant over my head.

Leaving a ten dollar bill on the table, I stand up and grab my helmet (God, I hate wearing these stupid things!). I step over the short railing onto the Duval Street sidewalk and I'm startled by a car that nearly sideswipes my bike then squeals to a stop. It's a black Eldorado with black-tinted windows, gleaming in the sun like some sinister apparition. The passenger window starts to slide open, and I'm overcome with the thought that I'm a sitting duck. Before I can get my new Glock out from under my shirt tail, the window is down and someone is leaning across the seat toward me.

"Hey sailor, looking for some action?" It's Judy.

I don't know how she found me, or why she's in Donna's Cadillac, or why I was so slow getting my gun out, but I'm happy she's here, glad she found me, and ecstatic that I didn't shoot her.

Leaving the car parked in the middle of the road, she bails out and runs to me. Traffic is already heavy, and horns start blaring. We hold each other so tightly it's a surprise either of us can breathe. After the longest, most incredible kiss I've ever experienced, we come up for air, and realize that the bar's patrons—as well as passersby—are applauding.

We hop into the Caddy, leaving the scooter at the meter. I can afford the fine, I think, laughing out loud.

Judy looks over at me with a glint in her eye and asks, "You ready?"

I nod, pulling the seat belt tight. She stands on the gas, holding the brakes with her left foot. Smoke starts to roll out from around the front tires, and she steps off the brake pedal, leaving twin black stripes of rubber on the pavement as we head west to A1A . . . and the rest of our lives.

Yeah, I'm ready.

D-U-N, DONE

ABOUT THE AUTHOR

Larry Garner is a Colorado native, but has traveled the United States extensively, both as a civilian and as a member of the US Navy.

During his six years in the Navy, he earned the nickname Animal, which has stuck to this day.

He has been riding motorcycles since 1968, and has raced cars, built and painted custom bikes and cars, and earned his living as a welder, fabricator, mechanic, and general Mr. Fixit.

D-E-D, DEAD is Animal's first novel. He lives in the beautiful San Luis Valley of Colorado with his wife Marcia.